The Education of Mrs. Bemis

ALSO BY JOHN SEDGWICK

FICTION
The Dark House

NONFICTION
Night Vision: Confessions of Gil Lewis, Private Eye

*Rich Kids: America's Young Heirs and Heiresses,
How They Love and Hate Their Money*

The Peaceable Kingdom: A Year in the Life of America's Oldest Zoo

The Education
of
Mrs. Bemis

A NOVEL

John Sedgwick

HarperCollins*Publishers*

HarperCollins books may be purchased for educational, business, or sales promotional use. For information, please write: Special Markets Department, HarperCollins Publishers Inc., 10 East 53rd Street, New York, NY 10022.

Epigraph is from *The Collected Poems of Wallace Stevens,* by Wallace Stevens, copyright 1954 by Wallace Stevens. Used by permission of Alfred A. Knopf, a division of Random House.

A small portion of this novel originally appeared, in different form, in the *Boston Globe Magazine.*

FIRST EDITION

Designed by Christine Weathersbee

Printed on acid-free paper

Library of Congress Cataloging-in-Publication Data
Sedgwick, John
   The education of Mrs. Bemis : a novel / John Sedgwick.—1st ed.
    p. cm.
  ISBN 0-06-019565-7
   1. Psychotherapist and patient—Fiction. 2. Women psycholoists—Fiction. 3. Female friendship—Fiction. 4. Boston (Mass.)—Fiction. Aged women—Fiction. I. Title.
PS3569.E3164 E38 2002
813'.54—dc21   2001051815

02 03 04 05 06 RRD 10 9 8 7 6 5 4 3 2 1

For Megan, as always

. . . Only we two are one, not you and night,

Nor night and I, but you and I, alone,
So much alone, so deeply by ourselves,
So far beyond the casual solitudes,

That night is only the background of our selves,
Supremely true each to its separate self,
In the pale light that each upon the other throws.

—WALLACE STEVENS
"Re-statement of Romance"

Prologue

"W ant to?" The college boy from the party set his beer bottle down on the deck of the boathouse, and undid the buttons of his shirt. "There's nobody around."

A gentle breeze was blowing in from the bay, and Jackie swept back some hair that had flopped down over her glasses. She glanced back at the fancy houses behind, the lights spilling across the front lawns that sloped down toward the water. It was another Saturday night blowout in Duxbury, maybe the last one of the summer, and she could hear snatches of dance music from the party they'd left. She took a last hit off the joint he'd passed her, then stubbed it out on the railing.

A few stars were out overhead, and a skinny moon. Around them, the sea slapped gently against the sides of the dock. Beyond the harbor, where a few sailboats tipped this way and that on their moorings, the wide, dark waters opened out into Massachusetts Bay, glimmering in the moonlight.

The college boy, Tim, stripped off his shirt and draped it over a wooden post.

Jackie stepped out closer to the water. She felt a little unsteady as she looked down. "Are you sure there isn't anything gross down there?"

"I've swum here millions of times. It's fine."

She slipped off one of her platform slides and stuck in a toe. The water was warmer than she'd expected.

"See?" Tim turned her toward him and slipped his arms over her shoulders. He kissed her lightly on the lips, rubbed his nose against her cheek—a move that seemed practiced—then reached around her back to ease down the zipper on her spandex dress. She could smell the beer on his breath.

"Come on." Tim stepped back and dropped his pants. His skin was fishlike in the near darkness. He wasn't wearing underwear.

She backed away from him, thought for a second. "Okay—but don't look." She waited till he'd turned his back, then unzipped the rest of the way, and wriggled her dress up over her head. She draped it over the railing, then crouched down shyly, sure that she would be visible from the houses up on the shore. She wasn't wearing a bra.

Tim stepped down onto the stairs. The float rocked for a moment. There was a splash, and then a voice boomed out of the darkness, "It's fucking great."

Jackie folded up her glasses, unhooked her earrings and tucked them in a shoe. She slid off her underpants, and stuffed them in the other shoe. Everything was a blur, but she found the ladder, swiveled, and lowered herself down. The water rose up to her ankles, to her knees, then she let herself fall back. Her nipples tightened, and her breath came faster as she worked her arms to stay afloat. She called for the boy again, but got no answer. Just the sound of halyards clanging against metal masts, off in the distance. Where was he?

Finally, a rippling off to her right.

"That you, Tim?"

No answer. She swam toward the rippling sound, then realized she shouldn't go out this far. The water lapped at her chin. She turned back toward the streaks of light on the shore. She kicked once to propel herself forward—and then felt something tug her ankle and slide up the inside of her leg. Startled, she shoved her feet down, tried to stand, but the water was too deep and she nearly went under. Then an explosion to her right, and laughter. "Got you!" It was Tim, joyous. His voice echoed off the water.

"Don't!" she shouted. "Okay? Just don't."

She pushed on toward the blurry lights, sure they'd lead her back to the pier. More strokes, more quickly. She wanted out. Now.

Finally, the dock by the boathouse loomed up in front of her. She grabbed the edge, then maneuvered along the side, feeling for the ladder.

But something soft and wet brushed against her side, just grazing her right breast.

"*Quit* it, okay?" Fed up, she pushed out an arm to fend off the boy, sure he'd been groping her.

But it wasn't Tim she touched.

Alice

She was in Filene's downtown, trying to decide about bath towels. The ones she'd had since college—like the silly, "Welcome to Disneyland" beach towel sent to her by her older sister the travel agent and the plush one an ex-boyfriend had lifted from the Four Seasons—didn't seem quite right anymore. But which did? She stood before a long wall of towels in every possible color and texture, each variation fraught, no doubt, with psychosocial significance. Should she go for midsize or full? Burgundy? Chartreuse? Mist gray? And would four be enough? Her new love, Ethan, slept over fairly often these days, and her new living room sofa pulled out to accommodate other visitors. All these decisions.

Alice looked considerably younger than twenty-eight. Girlish, from most angles, with a shy smile, blue eyes that people were always commenting on, and an endearing softness to her cheeks; she wore her hair down to her shoulders in a simple cut. Alice was a first-year psychiatric resident at Montrose Psychiatric Hospital, the distinguished, Harvard-affiliated institution to the west of Boston, in Concord, but, to her distress, people still sometimes took her for a teenage candy striper. Nevertheless, she was *Doctor* Matthews now, so she had to think more about appearances.

Dr. Matthews. In truth, that still seemed to her like somebody else, somebody more substantial. But, having finally secured a legitimate, paying job after four years of medical school, and another for an internship, she'd upgraded her apartment, moving out of her med-student studio in a litter-strewn section of the Fenway and into a reasonably nice single-bedroom along a tree-lined street in North Cambridge, by the Somerville line. Not that big, but it was just her and Fido, the mouse she'd saved after a psychology experiment at BU. Now she needed towels.

"We have the Chantelles, ourselves," the saleswoman, Frankie, was saying. She'd let Alice know she was due in September. "They're very popular."

Alice ran a finger through the deep plush of the chartreuse Chantelle. She wasn't sure that she wanted "popular." And what did towels . . . mean? Alice caught herself pondering the emotional implications of comfort, warmth, dryness.

In the end, she settled on the Arbor House ones, simply because she loved the luxurious feel of them against her cheek, in a "serenity blue" that she hoped would go with the bathroom tiles. A set of four, with washcloths and hand towels to match. She was toting her purchase past the sleepware section, toward the exit, when she sensed a sudden shift in the mood of some of the shoppers around her. They were staring back toward the bedding department. Alice slowed. Had someone been caught shoplifting?

Behind her, a woman's voice rose over the general bustle of the floor: "She all right?"

Finally, Alice got a clear view of the four-poster bed around which a few onlookers were frozen in orbit. It seemed at first that there was only a heap of blue fabric in the middle, nothing more. But then she realized that the "heap" was in fact a person. An older, gray-haired woman in a blue skirt, curled up on her side—looking for a moment like the Grand, Alice's grandmother at the nursing home back in Latrobe. She lay like that sometimes on Alice's visits, her mind floating off somewhere while Alice read to her from *Peter Pan* and *The Wizard of Oz*—the stories that the Grand had read Alice as a child. Was this woman's mind gone, too? Her stillness was disturbing, especially in a place like Filene's, which was normally nothing but movement, as shoppers surged about, bent on their purchases. The woman was alive—Alice could see that much. A street person, sleeping one off? A possibility, but this woman seemed too well dressed for that. A bit of jewelry glittered on one ear.

"Call security, would you?" someone said. "Tell 'em we've got a medical situation here."

Alice approached, steeled herself. "I'm a doctor," she said quietly. "Can I help in some way?"

It was Frankie, her saleswoman, her enormous abdomen protruding. "Wait, a doctor?" She gave a relieved smile. "That's great. Oh, *thank* you."

"A psychiatrist, actually. But I'm an M.D."

"Well, maybe you should take a look," Frankie said. "She's kinda . . ." She beckoned Alice over to the bed where the woman lay on her side. The few shoppers who had gathered around stepped back. Alice stepped around to face the woman, aware of the mild buzzing of some wall clocks behind her. The woman wasn't quite as old as the Grand. Seventy, maybe seventy-five. Her gray hair was streaked with white; she wore it in a tight bun. Besides her blue suit, she had on a frilly white shirt, dark stockings, and old-fashioned, black shoes. She might have come from church. Was she praying? Her knees were drawn up nearly to her chest, her hands curled lightly around her shins, just below her knees, to pull her body into a protective egg. She seemed to have been overcome by something, but what? Her eyes were wide open, and she was whimpering faintly.

Alice crouched down next to the woman, who stared out blankly. "Ma'am?" Alice asked. "I'm Dr. Matthews. Are you all right?"

The woman didn't answer, but continued to stare.

"A customer noticed her like that a few minutes ago," someone told Alice. "Hasn't budged, so far as I know."

"Ever see her before?" Alice asked.

"Nope. Haven't a clue where she came from, either. Just boom, there she was."

The woman wasn't prostrate and quivering like the stroke victims Alice had seen. Also, there seemed to be some strength in the arms curled about the woman's legs, and there was no evidence of the asymmetry Alice had been taught to expect after a stroke, either.

"She dead?" a young boy asked from somewhere behind Alice. His mother shushed him.

Alice turned back to the people gathered around. "Give us a little room here, would you please?" The onlookers retreated a few more steps.

"Ma'am?" Alice asked the woman again.

No response.

"Okay now, I'm just going to feel for a pulse here." Alice put her knee down on the bed, leaned down, and reached toward the woman's neck, feeling for her carotid artery. The skin was thin, almost filmy, and it slid easily over the tendons underneath. The woman's pulse was a steady blip. The skin wasn't clammy, either. So that ruled out shock.

"Can you hear me?" Alice asked.

No response.

"Are you in any pain?"

Her lips moved, but no coherent sound came out. Then her eyes roved to Alice's, her lips quivering. "Moth." The word was little more than a breath.

"Moth?" Alice replied, unsure she'd heard right.

"*Moth,*" the woman repeated, emphasizing the last *th* this time. "Moth."

"I'm afraid I don't understand," Alice told her. "Like a butterfly? That kind of moth?"

"Moth," the woman said again, more faintly.

The security personnel arrived. They looked down at the old woman on the bed. "We'll get an ambulance," the taller one said.

"Where are you taking her?" Alice asked. She was beginning to feel protective of the old woman, defenseless there on the bed.

"And you are?" the taller security person demanded.

"I'm a psychiatric resident at Montrose Psychiatric Hospital."

The security man seemed unimpressed. "Where she goes, that's up to the medics. But I'd guess the emergency room," he said. "Boston City. That's pretty much standard."

The bed rustled as the woman shifted position.

Alice knelt down to her once again. "Excuse me, ma'am. Are you all right?"

This time, the woman's eyes moved toward Alice's, but she still didn't answer. The look was pained, confused. And when her gaze slid past Alice to take in the store around her, the old woman seemed to recoil, as if bewildered by the profusion of too-bright colors, the jumble of shapes, the range of products for sale.

"Do you know where you are?" Alice asked.

"Where I—?"

"You're in Filene's, ma'am," the taller security guard said. "Sixth floor. This is the bedding department."

The old woman looked astonished. "The what?"

"Bedding, ma'am," the shorter security guard said. "Sixth floor."

"You don't remember coming here?" Alice asked.

She shook her head.

"Any dizziness there? Are you feeling at all faint?"

The woman slowly brought a hand to her face, and lightly rubbed her forehead with her fingertips, as if she were trying to remember what it—what she—felt like.

"I feel lost." The woman eased her head back onto the pillow.

• • •

Her name was Madeline Bemis, and she lived at 12 Deaver Way in Milton, one of the wealthier suburbs to the south of Boston. Mrs. Bemis herself did not immediately acknowledge that this was her name, but her face matched the photo on the driver's license that Alice found in the wallet inside a small black handbag that lay beside her on the bed. A gold wedding band on her ring finger established that she was—or had been—married. She did not respond to any further questions from Alice, or from anyone else. Instead, she stayed on the bed. On her back this time, with her hands folded over her middle, her eyes shut tight. Like a willful child, Alice thought, pretending to take a nap.

After a few minutes, Mrs. Bemis was able to answer some basic questions, albeit foggily. She recognized her home address, although she expressed no desire to go there. When asked where she did want to go, she said, "I have no home." By now, it appeared to Alice that Mrs. Bemis did not seem to be suffering from a purely medical problem, but, when the medics arrived, they agreed with security that it would be best to take her to the emergency room at Boston City Hospital all the same. That was, they said, their "protocol." The lead medic tried to lay out the situation to Mrs. Bemis, but she paid no attention. Alice felt sorry for her, having to deal with a crew of insistent strangers. Still, Mrs. Bemis did not resist when the medics lifted her onto a gurney to take her down in the elevator to the ambulance.

Alice stayed with the woman, holding her hand, until she was in the ambulance. Even after the vehicle drove off to the hospital, lights flashing, Alice couldn't let the situation go, and, from a pay phone on Washington Street, she called the emergency room at Boston City herself. She couldn't get through to Dr. Faulkes, the attending physician she'd flirted with during her own rotation there a year and a half previously, but she left a message with a nurse to expect an elderly patient, Madeline Bemis, within the hour. Alice strongly recommended that, once Dr. Faulkes ruled out all the various medical explanations for her behavior (as she was sure he would), he transfer Mrs. Bemis to Montrose for a full psychiatric work-up. "It's the best place for her," Alice said. To make sure that the nurse understood the message, Alice had her read it back. "I'm at Montrose, you see," Alice added, as if that explained everything.

"Got it," the nurse replied. "And your name again?"

"Alice Matthews," she replied, then corrected herself. "Dr. Alice Matthews. He'll remember."

two

The first time she saw it, Montrose Psychiatric Hospital reminded Alice of a small New England college, a Bennington or an Amherst or any number of small, elite schools that her college advisor back at Latrobe High had never mentioned to her. When she was growing up, New England had seemed a universe away from western Pennsylvania, and it still did, with its jagged coastline, baffling rotary intersections, and overfondness for brick. But it had been nearly six years since she had migrated north to BU Medical School, and she was starting to feel she might someday pass for a native.

The Montrose "campus," as it was called, spread across a gently sloping hillside that included a former pear orchard, a topiary garden (although only the metal frames remained), and, on the far side of a narrow road that cut through the property, a meadow where sheep had since grazed. Most of the Montrose buildings, like the gabled Danzinger and the vaguely Georgian Hargrove House, were stout, redbrick buildings that dated back a century or more. Their grandeur evoked a more generous time, when mental patients (those of a certain class, anyway) were treated with warm baths and string quartets. The nervous cousin, the fragile aunt, the sad sister who needed a break from the world—these populated the original Montrose. In the evenings when the light was right, Alice sometimes imagined these displaced relations flitting about the shadows. There'd been some old photographs up in the executive building—still grandly confident, with pillars out front—when she'd come in for her interview last winter, and Alice had lingered by them, charmed, and a little puzzled, by the sight of these troubled souls in their fine clothes, taking tea and playing croquet.

In the managed-care era, of course, Montrose had had to cut back on the amenities. Like the psychiatric eminences for whom they were named, the once noble buildings were showing their age. The bricks needed repointing here and there, and many of the shutters thirsted for paint. The stunning Victorian gardens were long gone, the orchard was left untended, and some of the larger buildings— like the vast Holmes and high-Victorian Wharton—that could no longer be filled with long-term patients had been boarded up with plywood. Their once lavish interiors held only unwanted furniture, empty file cabinets, moth-eaten carpets—and the ghosts that haunted such places. Vines now overran them like something out of a bad dream, blinding all the windows. On certain days, the sight of these old buildings slowly being engulfed made Alice frightened of the wind that blew up from the valley below Montrose. Even the billowing clouds in the summer sky occasionally seemed portentous as they cast cool shadows across the grounds.

But on this particular morning, Alice was feeling cheerful as she turned in the gate and ascended the winding drive to Montrose. It was a warm day, the car windows were down, and the breeze jingled her earrings. The radio was playing a fast song by Creed, a favorite.

After she pulled into her spot in the B lot, she warbled along in her reedy soprano for a few bars while beating a tattoo on the steering wheel. Finally she switched off the engine and yanked the hand brake. She was still a few minutes early, which was impressive considering the jam-up on the Alewife Parkway, and the dry cleaner's misplacing her dress, the hot-red number that she was going to wear to Ethan's gig upstairs at the Middle East later in the month. They'd had to turn the place upside down looking for it.

Her light jacket billowed and her jade necklace skidded across her Lycra top as, still humming, she made her way past the rows of sunbaked cars toward Nichols House. At parties, when Alice told people where she worked, they sometimes looked at her askance, as if she might be a trifle off herself. Actually, Alice liked the idea of facing up to the harsher aspects of life that scared others away. It made her feel on top of things. Montrose might be a "fucking freak show," as her older sister, Carla, once described it, but it was becoming a home to her.

At least Nichols was. Just down the ridge, it had been the old arts building, and it still had some spirited stained glass and jaunty brickwork. In the palmy days, Nichols had housed painting studios, a music conservatory, even a stage for amateur theatricals, but now, only the stage remained, used mostly for sparsely attended lectures by psychiatric luminaries like the neo-Freudian Dr. Michael Scheinhorn, whom Alice considered a snob, or his major debunker, the hunchbacked Dr. Hildegard Blythe, a silver-tongued firebrand whose appearances Alice never missed. All the rest had been stripped out in the early eighties when Freudian psychiatry had finally given way to faster-acting pharmaceuticals, and spelled the end to the old, leisurely way of handling madness.

These days, Nichols was a way station for incoming patients while the staff sorted them out. They usually passed through in a matter of days, but some remained a few weeks or even more. It was a mixed bag—the psychotics, borderlines, and antisocials all together. A bit like New York, as Alice once cheerfully told her mother when she'd called yet again to vent her anxieties about the chosen profession of her youngest child. As the least experienced of the first-year residents, Alice was being eased into the job. She led several group-therapy sessions and, in consultation with her superiors, provided short-term psychiatry for a handful of patients on the ward. In keeping with current Montrose practice, this meant providing drugs, mostly. Valium, Prozac, thioridazine, the tricyclics, the MAO inhibitors . . . the full range of modern psychopharmacology. But despite the fun of hearing Dr. Blythe sound off, Alice still believed in the talking cure. To her, it was as natural as opening the windows to let in fresh air to a stuffy room. So she tried to build in the time with her patients to discuss their troubles. The conversations were not always easy. Still new to the field, without the thick skin of her more experienced colleagues, Alice sometimes feared she was too sensitive for the job. Screaming fits above a certain decibel level, blood, even bad language, if it was spat at her with a certain degree of venom—they all still threw her, but she was getting better. Just last week, an elderly woman had called her a "shitty cunt" and she had been nearly unfazed.

Now, as Alice approached Nichols, she wondered if Madeline Bemis was up behind one of the darkened windows on the second floor. Alice had been worrying about her. When she'd gotten home the night before, she'd had a message from Dr. Faulkes concurring with her analysis (and cheekily asking if she was seeing anyone), but he'd left no word on whether he was transferring her to Montrose. When she'd called back for more information, he'd left for the day, and no one else could find any record of a Madeline Bemis ever having been there. The poor woman was lost, Alice thought, just as she'd said.

Alice stopped by the front door to slip out of her cross trainers and into tan pumps. A couple of EMTs lounged with cigarettes on the little patio there, taking in the morning sun by a couple of the marble swans from the old sculpture gallery. She could smell just enough of the burning tobacco to imagine that she was sucking a

Camel unfiltered from the sinful days when she still smoked. It made her fingers twitch.

She took a cleansing breath. She needed to let go of Ethan's arrival last night—finally!—at two A.M., tossing pebbles at her bedroom window like some fifties Romeo, then vaulting up the stairs after she'd buzzed him in. He'd come with a bottle of cheap Rioja (his apology for being so late), and, after a nightcap, they'd slid into bed together for well over an hour of what he called "just playing around" before she fell asleep, spent and happy.

Enough. She pulled open the glass door that led into the dimly lit foyer.

The Nichols architects had apparently been under instructions to avoid the heavy asylum look when they'd rehabbed the interior. But they'd ended up with something closer to barebones HMO. A few overly cheerful prints hung by the entrance, but that was it for amenities, if you didn't count the Coke machine. Nothing anybody could pick up and throw, that seemed to be the design principle.

With a wave, Alice glided by the sullen receptionist behind glass, inside the door, then made for the waiting elevator. With each step down the dim hall, she sensed she was getting in deeper. It was a little like the rare bits of genuine therapy she was able to practice: there was always a bit of fear inside the excitement as she ventured deeper into the psyche of her patients. She stepped into the elevator and reached into her handbag for her key to activate the button for the locked ward on the third floor. Her fingers tickled her change purse, a few loose Tampax for emergencies, her dark glasses, Kleenex pack . . . She peered in, a bad feeling spreading through her chest. No keys. Not in the handbag, nor in any of her jacket pockets, nor in the tight pockets of her slacks. Shit. She closed her eyes, trying to find a spot of calm.

"Tired?"

With a sharp breath, Alice jerked open her eyes, afraid she'd find her boss, Dr. Maris, the ward's psychiatrist in charge, who took a dim view of such forgetfulness. But it was only Victor Burns, the senior psychiatric resident from Harvard Medical School. He was tubby and morose, but harmless.

"I seem to have misplaced my keys," she told him.

"Ah." A standard psychiatric response. He drew his own key off a retractable cord that attached to his belt, and inserted it into the slot for the third floor. "You should get one of these," he told her, holding up the cord.

"I don't really like the idea of things being attached to me."

"Oh?" Victor replied with a raised eyebrow.

"Victor, please. Don't go Freudian on me, okay? It's way too early."

They rode up in silence, except for the elevator's grinding hum. Beside her, Victor pursed his lips repeatedly. *Another* nervous tic. Alice couldn't help noticing all the twitchy mannerisms of the staff. Dr. Bowersock over in Danzinger had that sudden lurching of his head down toward his left shoulder, as if he were trying to fling something out of his hair.

"Did a Madeline Bemis come in yesterday?" Alice asked him. "Elderly, kind of old-line?"

"Oh yeah, last night." He turned to her. "That's right. There was something about you in the report. You saw her at Filene's."

"So Dr. Faulkes did send her on."

"Yeah. EMTs brought her. I did the intake." Victor pursed his lips. "Strange case. Real heavy depression, looks like. She's taking a break in her room. Napping, I think. She seemed pretty spent."

Finally, a click, and the doors opened onto the waiting room, where several wasted-looking newcomers sat watching Jerry Springer on the communal TV.

"The one on the left there thinks he's Jesus," Victor said, sotto voce, referring to a large, dark-skinned man in a Celtics jersey who was gazing at the show openmouthed. "He came in this morning."

He pointed out a scraggly-haired teenage girl in a Phish T-shirt. "And Rose there tried to kill herself on Saturday."

Alice noticed the sallow skin, the drawn expression, the fingernails bitten to the quick.

"Slashed her ankles in the bathtub," Victor added.

"Oh, God." Alice couldn't help grimacing.

"Yeah." Victor nodded. "Her little sister found her. We put her on Valium. She's still pretty closed down. Parents are hysterical. We're going to be talking to them later today, see if we can figure out what's going on."

A couple of the other patients looked back at Alice. Alice smiled a greeting. "Morning," she said cheerfully, trying to radiate a little warmth. No one said anything back, but the older one, a dour, unshaven executive named Jim, nodded at her.

The big black nurse, Rita, rose into view in front of them, producing a breeze in the ward's stale air. "Oh, Alice. Fi-nally." She grabbed her by the elbow, gave her a tug. "I been looking all over for you, honey. That boy, Chris B?" She meant the curly-haired student from MIT who'd come for a return visit after a suicide attempt. He was not to be confused with the joyless Greek immigrant, Chris Z, with whom Chris B had briefly overlapped the first time. "He says he won't take his meds unless you're there." Rita cocked an eye at her, then whispered conspiratorially, "I was afraid we were gonna have to take him into the quiet room, but Dr. Maris said, 'What the hell, why don't you go find Alice.'" She resumed her booming voice again. "Where you been, girl? I been looking all over for you."

Right here, Alice was going to say. But she could see that any reply would be wasted on Rita, already leading her past the nurses' station to Chris B's room at the end of the hall. A mountain on the move. Alice could feel the eyes of some of the other patients lift up as she trailed past down the wide hallway. The anorexic, the cutter, a couple of the more out-of-it bipolars, the girl with the purple hair who'd tried to set herself on fire. Their eyes rolled toward her dreamily. As if she were one of their own, Alice thought with a shudder as she hurried by.

three

Chris B's room was down to the left. Like all patients' quarters, it had a sink, and a hospital bed, but no curtain to be pulled all the way around for privacy. And like all the others, it had been carefully stripped of anything sharp, and the hand cranks had been removed from the casement windows that offered a blurry view of the meadow across the road. Still dressed in his paisley pajamas, Chris B sat silently on his bed, watched by a pair of beefy mental health workers, his slippered feet tapping the floor. A battered radio transmitting a perky A.M. voice sat next to a sketchpad on the table by his bed.

Chris B smiled at Alice, but just a flicker. His eyes were serene. Twin orbs of swimming-pool blue. A mystery, that was Chris. At moments, his mind seemed to be locked away in a safety-deposit box someplace. Other times, he was so completely there, he seemed magnified. He'd just finished his sophomore year at MIT, majoring in high-energy physics. He'd come in the first time after the police had found him clad only in a pair of boxers at three A.M., raving about satellites while hugging a streetlight on Massachusetts Avenue a good ten feet off the ground. He'd returned last week after he'd thrown himself in front of an MBTA train. Two miracles: the engineer had been able to stop in time, and Chris B had avoided the third rail.

"It's okay, Donnie," Alice told the nearer worker, the one with the shaved head. "He'll take his meds." She turned to Chris. "Won't you?"

"Yeah, sure," Chris said, as if there'd never been any fuss. "Sure, sure, sure."

"Well, watch yourself," Donnie whispered to Alice now as he moved to the doorway. "He can get weird."

Alice and Chris had had a breakthrough of sorts that first time. He'd been all riled up, and Alice had figured she'd have a nurse quiet him down with some Atavan. But then she sensed that he was *trying* to put people off with all his yelling. So she'd leveled with him. Did he want an injection, or to chill out on his own? He'd smiled his loopy smile, said he'd be good, and they were soon chatting amiably about a ski trip to Vermont he'd been planning.

"So here she is," Rita told Chris B. "Your new best friend. You gonna help us out now?" She said it loud, as if she were trying to get through to some sound-insulated space inside him. Without waiting for an answer, Rita handed Chris the pills—a pale blue Chlozaril for the schizophrenia, and two small white ones to fight the side effects—on a plastic tray. Chris picked up the pills, his fingertips like the beak of a tiny bird. He placed them on his tongue, then washed them down with water from a paper cup. He set the cup back down and rubbed the palms of his hands on his pajama bottoms.

"Thanks," Alice said.

"No problem," Chris said.

Rita picked up the empty pill tray and headed for the door, and Alice started to go, too, but Chris snagged her elbow. "I got something for you." He pulled open a drawer by his bed and drew out a sheet of paper from his notebook. It bore a charcoal sketch of a woman's face, Alice could see. Quickly drawn, but a lot of energy. Her face. The image had her eyebrows all jagged, and her hair like straw, but there was something piercing about the eyes that caught her.

"Hey, thanks." Alice took the picture from him and started again for the door.

"Your boyfriend sleep over last night?" This time, Chris's head was tilted at an odd angle, with one ear tipped up toward the ceiling.

Alice could feel herself color. Had Ethan left a mark somewhere? She thought of his hands on her, exploring.

"That's enough of that," she told him. Boundaries.

"The satellites don't just watch *me,* you know." Chris craned his head toward the ceiling. "See 'em?" He pointed toward a far corner of the ceiling where there was a blurry triangle of reflected light.

"I don't want to hear about it." Alice let her eyes tell him that he'd gone too far. "There aren't any satellites. We've talked about this."

"You shouldn't have let him touch you."

It was probably true: things with Ethan were going fast. It wasn't just the sex, it was the kind of sex. Ethan pushing almost dangerously deep into her, making her gasp with an edgy sort of pleasure that was more than she'd ever felt, ever allowed herself to feel. No, this was certainly not something to venture into with a patient. God no. No, no, no. Just withdraw quietly and let the medication take effect.

She started to step away, but, lightning quick, Chris reached out and grabbed her hand. "I've been touched, you know."

"Let go of me, please," Alice told him, alarmed. This was way over the line. She tried to free herself, but Chris did not let go.

"Not by Joni," he said loudly. He'd mentioned his girlfriend to her more than once. "By a body." He tightened his grip on her wrist. "I wanted it away from me. But it was just floating there." Chris stared hard at Alice. "Its face all ripped off."

A low, rumbling sound filled the room. Like a foghorn. It evoked the spreading gloom that, to Alice, was the sea. Chris's mouth was shut. Was he . . . humming? In that bare space, with its harsh surfaces and bare walls, the sound might have been coming from anywhere.

Alice glared at him, but Chris B stared right back; the sound grew louder and rose higher in pitch until it became a squeaky, girlish hum. His lips were vibrating. It was him.

"Stop that, would you?" Alice had to regain control. "And let go of me."

Chris B released her, clapped his hands over his ears. But the hum grew louder than ever, his face turning blood red.

Alice ducked out into the hall, called for Rita, but she was already on her way. "We've got a problem in here," Alice told her.

There was a shout in the hallway, and Donnie and Al pushed past some residents to charge back into the room. They closed in on Chris, who wheeled around at them.

"Get away from me!" Chris screamed, his arms flailing. "Get *away!*"

Donnie grabbed one arm and, although Chris swung the other one viciously, Al grabbed it and hung on. Together they pinned him on his bed.

"Okay, Chris, how about we try to relax a little?" Al asked through gritted teeth.

"No! No!" Chris B shouted, kicking furiously into the air. "Fuck you! Okay? Fuck you!"

"Get the stuff, wouldja?" Donnie yelled at Rita.

Rita reached for the kit at her belt. But another nurse, a man named Sidney Irons, was already there, his necktie swinging, a hypodermic at the ready. "Okay, hold him."

"Don't gimme that shit!" Chris screamed, kicking furiously. "I don't want that shit!"

"Just a moment now," Sid said.

Donnie bent over Chris and forced him down while Sid yanked up his pajama sleeve, swabbed the tricep with alcohol, and shoved the needle in. Chris howled and tried to wriggle loose, but the orderlies were locked on tight. Time was on their side now.

Sid turned to Alice, who was watching from the corner of the room. "You okay there?" he asked gently.

"Yeah," Alice said, her pulse still pounding in her ears. "Sure. Fine."

Chris moaned and thrashed about, but gradually the fight went out of him and he lay limply on his back diagonally across the bed, his outstretched arms held down by the orderlies.

"I think he's done," Donnie said.

"Fucking finally," Al said, relaxing his grip and straightening up. Sweat dripped off his chin.

"What was that all about?" Donnie wiped his forehead with his sleeve.

"A corpse in the water," Alice said. "He said the satellites had told him about it."

"Oh, Jesus. That corpse thing again?" Donnie said. "He's been going on about that all morning. I told him, you don't need satellites to find out about it. It was on the news." He gestured to the radio, which was still on. "You didn't hear? There was a thing about it on TV last night. Couple of kids swimming, bumped into a corpse. Can you believe that? A corpse, just floating there. Face ripped up something ugly." He ran his hands down his chest to his belly, as if to reassure himself that he was still all there. "It'd freak me out, that's for sure."

"Who was it?" Alice asked, suddenly curious. "Anybody know?"

"Brendan somebody," Donnie said. "I forget. They had it on the news."

"Hurley," Sid said.

"Yeah, that's it. Brendan Hurley," Donnie said. "Face was pretty much gone from what they said. So how the fuck they identify something like that?"

"DNA probably," Al said. "They use DNA for everything."

"He's lucky he didn't lose his pecker," Donnie said, not listening. He laughed uneasily. "No wallet, no papers, nothing. Zip. No face, either. Weird, huh?"

Alice nodded. "It's all relative, I guess."

A smile spread across Donnie's thick features. "Oh. Yeah. All relative. In a place like this," he said. "Hah! I get what you're saying."

Alice turned back to Chris B, who was leaning back on his bed, dazed. His head was tipped, one ear angled up toward the ceiling, as if he were trying to hear something even now. His legs were still stretched out over the edge of the bed, and Alice had Donnie help her lift them back up and ease them down onto the bed once more. Her exasperation turned to pity, Alice pulled a blanket up over Chris's shoulders to keep him warm as he slept.

four

*C*offee helped, after something like that, and Alice was sitting quietly, Styrofoam cup in hand, at the nurses' station when Marnie came in. Gruff and bulgy, despite her Slim-Fast diet, she'd been on the ward forever, twenty years anyway. Childless herself, Marnie instinctively regarded Alice as somewhere between daughter and sister, which was okay with her. As a transplanted Pennsylvanian, her three sibs scattered about the country, she was open to the concept of surrogate family.

"Don't let it get to you," Marnie told her as she reached for the coffeepot. "It's just yelling and screaming."

"And kicking." Alice should never have agreed to let Chris dictate how he would take his meds.

She swirled the last of her coffee around in her cup, then looked up. "Can you tell that Ethan came by last night?"

"Why, did Chris hit you with one of his 'observations'?" She landed on the last word skeptically.

Alice nodded, and Marnie checked her over for a second. "You look a little tired maybe." Marnie looked at Alice differently. "You really went at it, huh?" She was a shameless snoop, always digging.

"*Marnie.*"

In fact, Alice had kept Marnie up on most of the Ethan developments over the last three months. Alice suspected Marnie feasted on the details because her own marriage was drying up, but Alice tended to be open about such things. Besides, this one had started so unusually—at the magazine stand of an all-night drugstore—that she needed to check her bearings. Blown out after the late shift, Alice had been flipping through the tabloids, amusing herself with the latest on Tom Cruise, when she'd noticed a striking young man—slim, angular, in black jeans—checking out the heavy-metal magazines at the far end of the rack. He looked cool, but she feared that he might be full of himself in the way that the few cool boys she'd known tended to be. Of late, she'd tended to stick to "nice guys"—clean-cut, hardworking—like that Dr. Faulkes, but she'd found herself wondering about the muscles under this young man's T-shirt, the curve of his forearm. She must have been staring—she did that sometimes when she was tired—because he glanced back at her. "Do I know you?" the man in the black jeans asked.

She blushed, as she often did in situations like that. "No," Alice said hastily. "I mean, I don't think so." She smiled, trying to retrieve the situation. "Sorry. I'm just spacing out here. Long day."

"No problem," the man said, and he took his magazine to the checkout counter.

Leaving the store, she saw him unlocking his bicycle, on the sidewalk. It was a mountain bike, with fat tires, but it was endearing; she'd expected a Harley, or some obnoxious Italian sportscar at least. Still, she hadn't planned on speaking to him, and walked on by, but he pedaled up to her at the corner. "Hey," he called to her. "You interested in this?" He handed her a postcard from his back pocket; it advertised a group called the She-men that was playing at a club in Somerville in a few days. "Check us out, okay? Want to?"

"This is your group?" Alice didn't know any musicians.

"Not mine, but I'm in it. I play guitar, and I sing." He looked at her again. "So come, okay? Maybe we can talk afterward or something." He swung his leg onto his bicycle. "Oh, I'm Ethan," he said, turning back to her.

"My name's Alice," Alice told him, and put out a hand to shake, feeling a little silly about such propriety.

"Cool," Ethan said.

Alice talked it over with her friend Kristen, an internist she'd met at BU Medical School. Alice was dubious; it seemed risky to pursue a relationship that had started at a magazine rack, but Kristen said that Ethan could have been "a whole lot pushier" and advised her to go ahead with it. What did she have to lose? She said she'd go with her to hear him play, then added the kicker: "Or maybe I'll just go by myself."

So they went together. The music was loud and not particularly to the taste of either of them, but Alice was stirred by Ethan's intensity. At the drugstore, he'd seemed slightly standoffish, but up on stage, all in black, standing out in front of a serious-looking five-man band, he threw himself into the music. The veins on the side of his neck bulged and his fingers ripped at the guitar strings as he wailed about lost love, mostly, although there was one song about taxi drivers that got a hand and a few shouts when he started in. The place was dark, and they were sitting toward the back, so Alice wasn't sure he'd noticed her, but he came straight to their table after the break.

"Well?" he asked Alice.

"It's pretty loud," Alice said.

"I think that means she likes it," Kristen told him.

Ethan smiled at that. "Oh yeah?"

As the second set was ending, Ethan said he wanted to dedicate the last song to a "pretty lady who took a chance and came here for the first time tonight." It was a slow, soulful tune called "The First Girl I Never Knew," and Alice found it to be almost unbearably sweet. It made her think differently about him. When he was done, Ethan hopped down off the stage and sauntered back to her table. "I hope I didn't embarrass you."

"Not at all," Alice assured him.

Unsure of what to do, or say, next, she stood up to go, but Ethan caught her hand. "Can I call you sometime? Maybe we can have coffee?"

"Sure," Alice told him, and she wrote out her number for him on a napkin.

Kristen thought it was fine. In fact, she seemed a little jealous. Still, the whole business would have greatly surprised her own psychotherapist from her med school days, the very grave Dr. Horowitz, if Alice had still been seeing him. He was convinced that she was too repressed to act on her "most authentic impulses," as he said in his ridiculously heavy German accent. And Marnie was surprised by Alice's daring when she told her about seeing Ethan the next morning. For the next few days, Alice's heart raced every time she checked her answering machine, sure that any blinking light indicated a call from him. But it didn't, not for the longest time. He finally called a week and a half later, said that her number had gone through the laundry. (Marnie thought that a good sign. It meant he did wash.) They'd gone out for ice cream that night, and then ended the evening dancing until well past midnight at a place Ethan knew of in Charlestown.

"Look, I bet Chris was just projecting," Marnie said now, returning to the question at hand. "His relationship with his own girlfriend is a big thing in his life. You're young, pretty. So he projects his relationship onto yours. It's all pretty standard stuff."

"Yeah, but you didn't see him."

Marnie tossed the last of her coffee into the sink and washed out the mug. "They don't know you. They don't know you from a hole in the wall. Schizophrenics especially. People in here, they're here because something's missing, and we're supposed to find it and put it back. I'll bet that's why Chris B is so focused on that faceless corpse. He's lost his own identity. The point is, none of this is about you. It's all about them. You're hardly even there."

"I'm supposed to find that reassuring?" Alice replied tartly.

"This isn't a classroom here, Alice. It's not always pretty."

Alice would have pursued it, but Rita popped her head in the door. "Dr. Maris wants to see you."

Alice's stomach tightened; she was sure that Dr. Maris was going to light into her for what had happened with Chris B.

"Next time, we'll discuss *your* sex life," she told Marnie. "Okay?"

Rita stared at Marnie, then at Alice. "Did I miss something?"

Alice put her cup in the sink, and went around to Dr. Maris's corner office with its sweeping views to the far green hills, faded now in late summer. His many diplomas and certificates hung on the wall; his desk was clear except for a pen stand; a pile of journals and reports rose up on the table beside it. Dr. Maris was staring into his computer, his back hunched uncomfortably. "Oh yes, Alice." He had a learned, owlish face, and he looked out at her over his half-moon glasses. "I heard we had some trouble this morning."

"I should've seen it coming. I'm sorry."

He peeled off his glasses. "Oh now, we're not seers. Human behavior can be unpredictable, even for professionals. We're all guessing here, and lots of times we're wrong." He wheeled his chair away from his computer and reached for a file on the side table. "That patient of yours, Madeline Bemis. I gather you found her in Filene's."

"Right. Curled up on a bed there on the sixth floor."

"Curious." He flipped through the folder in his hand. "A hard case. Withdrawn, almost antisocial. Widowed, set in her ways. Very difficult." He closed the file, handed it to her. "But you might be able to work with her."

"I'd certainly like to try."

"Take a moment and read that, why don't you? So we're all on the same page."

Alice opened the file. It was the intake summary that Victor had compiled. Alice flipped past the opening pages, detailing Mrs. Bemis's height, weight, date of birth, and other basic statistics, and went straight to the text:

ID/CHIEF COMPLAINT: The patient is a 76-year-old widowed white woman with a history of depression who presents for her first Montrose admission, referred by Gerald Faulkes, M.D., of the Boston City Hospital (BCH) emergency room where she was taken after being found completely disoriented in a Boston department store. Emergency personnel had taken her to BCH. Patient agreed to be brought to Montrose for diagnosis and treatment. "I have failed everyone, and now I'm failing myself."

HISTORY OF PRESENT ILLNESS: The patient had been seen intermittently since the fifties by a Boston psychiatrist, K. Paul de Frieze, M.D., who died last fall. Because of Dr. de Frieze's death, it is difficult at present to determine the exact nature, purpose, and scope of the therapy. When asked about it, patient says: "Different things." In the months following, her doctor's death seems to have triggered increasing distress. Patient reports decreased concentration and memory, bouts of high anxiety, decreased motivation, general aimlessness, and severe guilt around being "a terrible burden to my few friends." She also has decreased appetite with resulting unquantified weight loss. She seems to be prone to episodes of disorientation of the sort that occurred at the department store, Filene's. She has occasionally lost her way driving her car about Milton, although she has lived there for almost fifty years. Of late, she has rarely ventured farther. It is unclear what compelled her to go to Filene's, or how she got there. She was found lying in the fetal position on a four-poster bed, refusing, or unable, to move. When asked by sales personnel where she lived, patient reported: "I have no home." This according to the sales manager named Henry Mayer who was quoted in the medics' report. Patient is sensitive to Seasonal Affective Disorder (SAD), and says that she sometimes feels "overwhelmed" by the prospect of the coming fall. Her husband died on September 13 or 15, 1979. (Patient was uncertain.) She has begun to have passive suicidal ideation. She has contemplated burying herself alive, but says she hasn't the strength anymore to hold a shovel. The patient also has increased physical complaints, such as arthritic pain in her right shoulder, and blurred vision.

PAST PSYCHIATRIC HISTORY: Since her longtime psychiatrist, Dr. de Frieze, is deceased, no records are immediately available. But, according to her physician's records, she has been prescribed Lithium, Effexor, Prozac, Serzone, and Zoloft.

MEDICATIONS ON ADMISSION: Wellbutrin, 150 mg. b.i.d.; Vitamin C, 500 mg. b.i.d.; Vitamin E, 400 international units b.i.d.

SUBSTANCE ABUSE HISTORY: The patient reports having had a long-standing history of one ounce of bourbon per day. She also has a history of tobacco use. "It killed my father and my doctor. I am hoping it will kill me."

FAMILY HISTORY: Patient became confused when asked about her family. Asked about her father, she began to describe her psychiatrist, the aforementioned Dr. de Frieze, who seems to have been a central figure in her life. When informed of her mistake, patient rapped the side of her head with her knuckles. "It's my head. It's not working."

SOCIAL HISTORY: The patient was born and raised outside Boston, in Dover. She attended what she termed the "better" schools, naming Miss Southwick's Academy for Girls. She offered little information about either her father or her mother, but did acknowledge that she was an only child. She has never held a paying job, but has worked for many years as a volunteer for the New England Horticultural Society, and served for a decade as its president

(1964–1974). She married at nineteen. No children. Her marriage seems to have been remote and unsatisfactory. Her husband, Ronald Bemis, died of a brain tumor. She continues to live in the same house in Milton that she moved into after her honeymoon, in 1946. She admits to some considerable difficulty keeping it up, but has made no plans to move into an assisted-living arrangement.

Alice read quickly through the portion on Mrs. Bemis's medical history. It gave no hint of any cardiovascular or neurological issue that might have accounted for Mrs. Bemis's episode at Filene's. Madeline Bemis seemed perfectly healthy for a seventy-six-year-old. Alice's eyes dropped down to the final paragraph.

MENTAL STATUS EXAM: On admission, the patient is alert and oriented times two, but only intermittently cooperative. She is well groomed, with normal psychomotor activity, but tends to avoid eye contact. Her speech is normal in tone and volume, but slightly slow in rate. Her mood is "depressed," affect is dysphoric. She endorses decreased sleep, interest, energy, concentration, appetite, and activity. She has marked guilt, with passive suicidal ideation. There is no homicidal ideation, auditory or visual hallucinations, or paranoid ideation. Her thought process is linear, but easily disrupted. Her insight is dubious, judgment fair. On formal cognitive testing, she had accumulated a mini-mental status exam score of 15 for 15 before refusing to continue.

VICTOR BURNS, M.D.
Resident in Adult Psychiatry

Alice looked up when she was done reading. Dr. Maris had resumed his work on his computer, the keys clacking steadily. She closed the file noisily to get his attention. When that failed to work, she coughed into her hand.

"So," Dr. Maris said, glancing over to her. "As you see there, she's rather prone to disorientation." He paused, touching his fingertips together. "A most curious episode in Filene's. I'm sure there's more to it."

"At least she agreed to come here." A voluntary admission always helped.

"With some prompting from Dr. Faulkes, apparently."

"Actually, I put him up to it."

"Oh, did you? That's very good." He gave her a radiant smile, which faded quickly. "Fortunately, there seems to be no Alzheimer's, either. So we're lucky there as well." He shifted in his seat. "Depression in the elderly is such a scourge. My father had it, did I ever tell you? Terrible. Sat for hours in his rocking chair. Rocking, rocking. Try to help, and he'd bite your head off. Awful! But the drugs are always hard to calibrate. There's intolerance. The patient can grow set in his ways. Needing change, resisting it. In fact, hating you for it. Sometimes, I'd rather take on a schizophrenic. But this could be an interesting one."

"Because of all the drama, you mean?"

"Well, there is that." He took off the glasses, fiddled with them. "But—I'm sorry. I keep forgetting you're not from around here." He paused. "The Bemises are socially very prominent. Madeline especially. I used to read about her in the newspaper." Dr. Maris's eyes brightened. "She gave remarkable parties. Masked balls, musical extravaganzas, receptions for visiting dignitaries. Quite impressive, especially for around here. I seem to recall the young Prince Charles coming to one. Always got quite a write-up."

"That's why she was willing to come here, do you suppose?" Montrose was still known as one of the "better" psychiatric institutes, as Mrs. Bemis might put it.

"It may have figured in her thinking, sure."

"Why not give her to Victor? He did the intake. He seems to have made some progress with her." Personally, Alice imagined that someone like Victor would only make depression worse. But he had graduated third in his class at Harvard Medical School, and he had three years' seniority on her besides.

"No, definitely not Victor. Not for this."

Alice nodded. "Fine."

"I thought you might take an hour out of your day to meet with her, offer counseling. See where it goes."

"I'd love to. Really."

"All right then." He turned his head back to his computer screen; the keys starting clacking again. "I'll supervise, if you don't mind. So check in with me later," he said without looking up. "Let me know how you're doing."

Alice waited, sure that there would be more.

"That's all, Alice." He waved his hand again, as if to dispel her.

Alice's anger-management group ran late, leaving her only a few minutes to review the report again over a tuna sandwich in the cafeteria before the staff meeting at one. It was quite a remarkable history. Besides finding herself lost in Filene's, Madeline Bemis had brooded about burying herself *alive?* For someone so depressed, she did have a flair for drama. To Alice, it seemed almost unimaginable to have reached seventy-six, to have been widowed for—what?—twenty years? She looked down at her hands, which were slim and, she sometimes thought, her best feature. She had difficulty imagining them wrinkled, with age spots and blue veins. And the money. When her rent check cleared, she'd have scarcely a thousand dollars in her checking account. That plus the $3,500 or so she had in savings represented her entire net worth, plus whatever she could get for her car, her furniture, and the clothes off her back. And that didn't even take her horrendous med school loans into account.

She'd never known anyone who was really rich. At BU Medical School, there was a daughter of some Arab oil sheik; she owned a gold Mercedes and threw racy parties, but was completely obnoxious and ultimately flamed out after her second year. And, back in Latrobe, she'd known a few kids who'd gone off to private school. One of them, Bradley, had tried to feel her up at her friend Debbie's sweet-sixteen party. What a jerk. She'd told him to keep his hands to himself.

Alice tucked the report under her arm after she dumped her tray and raced off to the staff meeting. Yet more boring organizational stuff. Then rounds, to discuss some of the new cases. Chris B's case commanded a fair amount of airtime. Fortunately, no one seemed to blame her for what happened, although Alice suspected they were simply going easy on her. And the corpse story hadn't been all over the air, which was a relief. Most of the other staffers hadn't heard anything about it either.

It wasn't until the end of the meeting that Dr. Maris told the staff that Alice would be providing psychotherapy for Madeline Bemis. The three other psychiatric residents, all of them several years older than Alice, turned her way, as if checking out the new girl for the first time. There was a moment's silence before one of them, Georgine, commented that Madeline seemed to get on well with Chris B. She'd seen them eating lunch together the previous day, quite absorbed.

"You might want to keep an eye on that," Dr. Maris said. "Okay, Alice?"

Alice noticed that Victor looked a little down, which gave Alice a jolt of guilty pleasure. One that became more acute when Dr. Maris then asked Victor if he'd mind covering for Alice so that she could squeeze in a first meeting with Mrs. Bemis that afternoon. Victor professed to be fine with that, but when he huddled with Alice to make the arrangements, he didn't sound so happy. "I'm sure I can juggle some things around," he said with his usual sigh. "I'll just stay a little later. But that's okay." Classic Victor—so passive-aggressive.

Alice met Madeline Bemis in the small conference room off the end of the ward. When Alice arrived, Mrs. Bemis was looking out to the trees from the room's smudged window, the immense Rita at her side. Lost in thought, Mrs. Bemis didn't turn when Alice entered the room, so Alice's first view of her was in profile, with the light on her cheeks. She was somewhat taller than Alice had expected after seeing her curled up on the bed at Filene's. But, even when sitting in a metal fold-out chair, she had the refined, almost regal, bearing that Alice had noticed on some of the fine ladies she sometimes saw strolling in the Back Bay. Upright, she looked both sturdy and delicate, like fine porcelain, with her whitening hair and papery skin, flowered with red veins on her cheeks. She remembered how the Grand had carried on so forcefully, her very presence lifting people up, before the Alzheimer's had hollowed her out. Older women have such dignity, Alice thought. As at Filene's, Mrs. Bemis had on a blouse and a skirt, but a plaid one this time, and heavy shoes that she must have owned for decades. A sensible outfit, although a warm one for August.

Rita stood up with a groan as Alice came in. "All right then, Madeline," Rita said. "I'll come back for you in an hour."

The elderly woman said nothing, continued to stare out the window.

"Good luck," Rita whispered to Alice before she left, shutting the door behind her.

The room's silence had a hard edge.

On the ward, all the patients were first-named. Perhaps it was Alice's upbringing, but that didn't feel right with this elegant woman nearly her grandmother's age. "Mrs. Bemis?" Alice asked tentatively.

No answer. No movement, either. Nothing to indicate that this woman was even aware of Alice's presence.

"Mrs. Bemis?" Alice asked again. More gently this time. She thought of going closer. With anyone else, she might have put a hand on her shoulder, tried to soothe her with her touch. But the way the old woman was perched there on her seat, her face turned away, seemed to discourage contact. It was like the subway—some people you could sit down next to, some you couldn't.

Again, the silence filled the room. It made Alice aware of the drab carpeting, the blank walls, their pale pink broken only by an ill-framed watercolor that hung off-kilter by the door. No wonder her elderly patient was looking out the window. Alice went over for a look herself, thinking she might spot some unusual activity—a brushfire, perhaps, or a dogfight. But, coming closer, Alice could tell that, from Mrs. Bemis's angle, she could see only the sky, which was milk white with low clouds this afternoon, and the roof of Holmes, where thick vines had started climbing toward the chimneys, as if the building were burning with a green flame.

"My mother was there," Mrs. Bemis said finally.

"Where—in Holmes?"

She nodded. "I visited her once with my father."

"When was this?"

"Sometime in the forties, I expect." She sat for a moment, staring at Holmes. "Odd, isn't it."

"How do you mean?"

"That she was here, and now I am. It seems like fate."

"I'm not sure I believe in that," Alice said.

The old woman turned to Alice, looked at her as if she were seeing her for the first time. "And you are?" The words were clipped, intimidating.

"I'm sorry, I should have introduced myself." Alice smiled, instinctively trying to pump some warmth into a relationship that had gotten off to a bumpy start. "I'm Dr. Matthews. I'm the psychiatric resident who's been assigned to your care. I'm here to talk to you about how you're feeling."

"I'm not feeling very talkative at the moment, thank you." Mrs. Bemis turned back to the window.

Alice took a seat in a stiff wooden chair across from her patient. The chairs were all mismatched, and they were arranged in a loose circle, left over from the impulse-control group earlier that afternoon.

"Your mother, was she depressed?"

"That's a reasonable interpretation. Scarcely said a word my whole visit so, yes, I'd say so. Simply sat there. Knitting, as I recall.

The click of those needles. Insidious! I don't think she'd ever knitted before. Probably never knitted again." A slight smile teased the corners of her mouth. But then Mrs. Bemis turned away from her, and Alice imagined somehow that her patient was shutting a door between them.

"I saw you in Filene's, you know," Alice reminded her.

"Did you."

Alice recounted how she had been shopping for towels when she'd discovered Mrs. Bemis on the bed. "I'm glad you decided to come here. I think we'll be able to help you."

"Total folly," Mrs. Bemis said. "*Total.*"

"What is?"

"Being here. It's absurd. Why, my dear, look around. Have you ever seen such a place?"

"Then why'd you agree to come?" Alice asked sharply.

"Yes, why indeed?"

There was a pause in the conversation as the two women considered each other. Alice was struck by the force of Mrs. Bemis's anger. No, more than anger, imperiousness. Was it a vestige of her social position, a sign of her class? Or was it a bitterness over the way things had turned out for her—landing her here at Montrose, despite all her advantages? Or was it, in some way, directed at Alice herself, as if, for all her good intentions, Alice had succeeded only in antagonizing her? There was a lot to piece out here, clearly. Still, despite its sting, Mrs. Bemis's rage was a good sign, therapeutically speaking. It showed that the ego was still intact, still battling. It meant there was something for Alice to work with. Whatever else it signified, Mrs. Bemis's odd behavior at Filene's did not signal defeat. The woman had not given up.

The patient fixed her eyes upon the psychiatrist. "Now, what did you say your name was?"

"Dr. Matthews." Alice let that sit there for a moment. The title was starting to mean something.

"Yes." Mrs. Bemis sounded noncommittal. "Dr. Matthews. Well, perhaps you may call me Mrs. Bemis."

"All right," Alice said, grateful for the new tone of respect she heard.

Alice was determined to remain cheerful, to present an image of positive-mindedness, and smiled again. "We'll get to know each other as we go along."

Mrs. Bemis looked at her dubiously. "You think so?"

Alice saw Mrs. Bemis a couple of times on the ward, just in passing, before their next session. Each time, Mrs. Bemis was sitting at the card table, playing a game of solitaire. As Alice passed by, Mrs. Bemis rarely looked up, which was unusual. Most of the patients welcomed distraction; their eyes were alert to the slightest novelty on the ward. Struck by her power of concentration, Alice couldn't tell if she was focusing so intensely on the cards, or whether she was willing the world around her into oblivion so that she could find relief from this loud, inelegant place. Alice did not say hello, lest she intrude on her patient's seclusion.

Toward the end of the week, they met once again in the end room with the mismatched chairs. Alice took a seat, pulled out the Bemis file and a pen to take notes.

"Tell me what happened at Filene's. Perhaps we should begin there."

"I'm not sure I can tell you."

"And why's that?"

"My dear, I simply don't recall a thing about it." There was a note of triumph in her voice.

"You were on a bed, Mrs. Bemis. All curled up."

"Yes, I suppose I was." Deflated now.

"Suppose?"

"People tell me I was. That man—"

"Dr. Burns?"

"Yes. He told me."

"You don't remember it?"

"No." A new force to her voice.

"Do you remember going there?"

"No." Very firm. Oh, she was a feisty one. Alice had to admire that.

"Do you remember coming here?"

"Yes."

That was a start. "What do you remember about that?"

"The drivers, the ones in the van. They smoked." Mrs. Bemis looked up combatively. "Disgusting habit."

"I thought you smoked." There was a reference in the intake report. A thin smile. "That's how I know." Her eyes flickered with delight.

"At Filene's, Mrs. Bemis, were you shopping?"

"I guess I must have been."

"What for, do you remember?"

She shrugged. "I haven't any idea."

"You were in the bedding department."

"I must have been shopping for bedding, then."

Defiance was beginning to seem like Mrs. Bemis's primary characteristic. Depression manifested itself so widely. Not just as sorrow. That was, if anything, fairly rare. More often, there was a terrible jumpiness, as patients practically leapt about in their anxiety. Or giddiness, even. But, at depression's heart, it seemed to Alice that there was always a vacancy—a gap where something vital should be. And that's what impressed her now. Mrs. Bemis was definitely snappish, but defensively so. It was as if she wanted to keep Alice away from some primal wound that was still too raw to touch.

"But you were curled up on a bed," Alice said gently.

A look of suspicion. "Are you sure?"

"Mrs. Bemis, I saw you there. You seemed to have lost track of where you were."

Finally, she weakened, and a softer Mrs. Bemis emerged, one who seemed to have been hiding behind the gruff one. "Yes, that happens to me sometimes. My mind just . . . goes."

"But you did a mental test with Dr. Burns this weekend when you came in. Your score was perfect—until you stopped."

"Oh, who cares about a stupid thing like that."

"Mrs. Bemis, I'm afraid you'll have to help us if we're going to help you."

"Will I."

There was something submerged about the old woman's intelligence that made Alice think of an alligator in a swamp. "You're sharper than you know, Mrs. Bemis."

Mrs. Bemis looked back at her skeptically. "Then I should know why I was in a place like Filene's, now shouldn't I?"

"Did you sleep all right last night?"

The old woman reared back. "Here? My child, I never heard such a racket. And then, as soon as I fell asleep, somebody came around to give me a sleeping pill. Now, I ask you."

She must have been imposing once, Alice thought. She could see her hosting immense parties, chatting with Prince Charles. She waited a moment to let the anger dissipate. "What are you feeling right now?"

A stupid question, Alice realized, since the answer was evident.

Mrs. Bemis folded her arms across her chest, as if to fend off further idiocy, and she set her mouth tightly. Alice suddenly feared that she had been dismissed like a maid who'd dropped a tray once too often.

"Mrs. Bemis?"

Something flashed in the old woman's eyes. A jolt of recognition? The chilliness of her manner gave way to a softer, almost maternal way of being. It was as if a switch had been thrown, although Alice had no idea how or why. "Come closer, would you?" Mrs. Bemis asked her. Uncertain, Alice rose from her chair, afraid she was being drawn to the front of the class, to be made a display of. But she did as she was asked, and warily moved to a seat beside her patient.

"Tip your head down for a moment."

"Mrs. Bemis, I—"

"Indulge an old woman, would you? I'd like to see your hair better. To feel it, if I could."

Alice blushed. "My hair?"

"Would you mind? The way it caught in the light just now, it—"

"What?"

"It reminded me of something." She dropped her hands in her lap. "Oh, heavens, never mind."

"It's all right." Alice angled her head slightly toward Mrs. Bemis, her thoughts flying in a thousand directions.

"You can touch it, if you want," she told her patient. "It's fairly clean."

Alice felt a tickling as Mrs. Bemis's fingertips touched the tips of her hair, bringing prickles to her scalp. It was the lightest sensation, as if an insect were flitting about her ears, and she nearly flicked Mrs. Bemis's hand away. But she remained still, letting the old lady feel the ends of her hair.

Finally, Mrs. Bemis released her, and Alice straightened up once more.

"You say I remind you of something—or of someone?" Alice prodded. "A person? Someone you used to know?"

"No, no. Nothing like that."

"So . . . you just like my hair?"

"Yes. That's all." An artificial smile.

It bothered Alice all weekend. She even asked Ethan what he thought, a rarity, since he'd been put off when he'd first discovered where Alice worked and almost never ventured into psychological realms. "Maybe she just wants to know what it feels like to be young," he finally said with a shrug. It was as good an explanation as any.

On Monday, as Alice sat across from Mrs. Bemis late in the afternoon, she asked about some of the details that Victor had gleaned for his intake report. Mrs. Bemis's marriage, her interests. But the topic evoked little beyond a date or two, and some horticultural details that meant nothing to Alice. They discussed her medication, and Alice asked about previous bouts with depression. Mrs. Bemis's eyes were glassy, and her face bore a weary expression.

"I'm curious as to why you took such an interest in my hair the other day," Alice said.

Mrs. Bemis looked up, momentarily startled. "When I what?"

"You looked at my hair. You wanted to touch it, don't you remember?"

"Oh, yes." Her face soon settled back into its previous stonelike visage. "I suppose I did. I thought I'd dreamed it." She looked at Alice sorrowfully. "Some days I honestly can't tell if I'm asleep or awake."

"It seemed to fascinate you," Alice persisted. "I'm wondering why."

"Oh, I'm just too tired to think anymore," Mrs. Bemis replied wearily.

Alice took pity on her patient. "Well, why don't we call it a day then," Alice told her. "You do look tired, and I don't like to push it." Alice glanced toward the door. "I'll walk you back to your room."

Alice reached for the old woman to help her up, but she ignored Alice and rose out of her chair on her own. Together, they went outside and down the corridor, Mrs. Bemis striding slightly ahead, as if to make a point.

"My room's down there." Mrs. Bemis pointed down the wide hall to their right, although Alice knew perfectly well. "Horrid little place."

The door was open, and Mrs. Bemis went in directly, without waiting for Alice. But she slowed once she was inside the room, with its nearly bare walls and linoleum floor, as if the very thought of being there was exhausting. She sat down on the bed, then swung her legs up to lie back. Alice helped her remove her shoes, a bit of assistance that went unacknowledged. There was a light blanket at the foot of the bed, and Mrs. Bemis drew it up over herself. "You must excuse me," she said.

"I'll check in on you later," Alice assured her.

As Alice left the room, she saw Mrs. Bemis lift her eyes slowly to the window. She saw them fill with light.

Maddy

~

five

"Would you mind if I took a bit of your hair?" That's what he'd asked, wasn't it, that long ago afternoon in that high, boyish voice of his? And so solemnly, too. She should have laughed and been done with it. Saved herself no end of trouble. Taking a bit of her hair. Honestly! If only she'd giggled, or given him a poke, or done *something* to let him know he was being ridiculous, then everything might have turned out differently. Ronnie would have seen that she wasn't at all the quiet, endlessly appreciative girl he took her to be, and that would have been the end of it. But, instead—well, instead . . .

These were the war years, of course—no time to be young. She was Maddy then, not yet eighteen, Ronnie scarcely a year more. He was quite skinny besides, with absolutely none of the heft he would have later. His hair was blond—much lighter than hers—and, unlike himself, unruly. It never lay down smooth no matter how often he brushed it. It was as if some scamp had come and ruffled it on purpose—but, of course, no scamp would ever have dared do such a thing to Ronald Bemis. In Maddy's world, he was a god, even at nineteen. Everyone knew his exploits on the football field at Exeter, where he'd been captain in his junior *and* senior years. Everyone knew, too, how many houses his family owned—four, including the ranch in Wyoming and the big summer place in Nahant. Ronnie had hardly any beard except around his chin, and sky-blue eyes, so pure and clear, as if they'd never been touched by any unpleasant sight. Once or twice Maddy had been tempted to slide her underpants off right in front of him and swat him with them just to shock him, to see those eyes cloud over. Oh, she could be awful! She'd done that to her cousin Freddy once when he was eleven and she was thirteen, and it was *fun.* But Freddy, of course, was not Ronnie.

Ronnie's question had startled her, that's what it was. She hadn't expected him to be anywhere near so forward, and the tremors went clear down to the small of her back. But wartime confused everything. So, instead of laughing, Maddy had merely raised her hand to her hair protectively. She was pleased with her pageboy cut; Ernestine, on Newbury Street, had finally gotten it just right. And all Maddy could think was that Ronnie would ruin her hair.

"It's so pretty in the light, Mads. Would you mind terribly?" And the way he asked, the urgency of it—that stopped her, too. It wasn't at all like him. Without waiting for an answer, he brought out a small pair of scissors from the outside jacket pocket of his uniform. They gleamed as he brought them toward her.

It astounded her that he'd planned all this ahead of time, actually thought to bring scissors. "What—whatever for?" she asked, like a goose.

"To have, silly. To remember you by."

"When you're flying?"

He nodded. Perhaps it was romantic, somehow. "Well, I suppose it will grow back."

"Of course it will." Ronnie moved to her, brought the scissors to her hair, and, moments later, Maddy heard a snip and then another.

He drew his hands back, and perhaps fifty hairs of hers were in his palm. They were nearly half an inch, much longer than she'd expected, and she worried that he'd left a gap in the line of her hair that Ernestine had slaved over. But she didn't dare go to the mirror, or bring her hand up to feel.

Ronnie smiled broadly, wickedly almost, as if he'd gotten away with something, and pulled out an envelope from his pants pocket. He opened it and, scraping his palm with his forefinger, slid her hairs inside, then closed the envelope to seal them up. "Wonderful," he said.

The deed was done.

They were in the living room of the Dover house, with its great big windows opened out to the garden, and the light was streaming in, but not much breeze. It was late spring, a day with a lot of summer in it, and the tulips were up around the birch trees. As she stood there beside him, she could feel the warmth on her back and all down her legs as if it, too, were trying to prod her into something with him she wasn't quite ready for. She'd heard what other boys had been expecting before they went off to war. Her friend Ellen Baxter had told her that the night before her boyfriend George Loomis left, he'd come to her house for a last walk. They'd strolled down to the park and stopped under some trees by a pond. That's when he'd reached into his shirt pocket and pulled out a rubber. "Look what I have," he'd said, dangling it before her eyes. Ellen had nearly jumped. She'd feigned illness and taken a taxi straight home, while George had cried out after her—"You'll write me, won't you? Won't you?" She told Maddy everything, breathlessly, the next morning. Maddy agreed with her that it was a terrifying story. Still, she wished that Ellen hadn't fled. She'd have loved to hear what happened next.

The very next day, Monday, Ronnie would be taking the train from South Station down to Pensacola Air Force Base, and from there he would fly to England in a transport plane to join the Eighth Air Force, outside London. He'd just been commissioned as a second lieutenant, courtesy of Major Dorris, a friend of his father's from

Bowdoin. After nearly a year of training, he was going to be a copilot on one of the B-17 bombers flying over Germany. Ronnie had telephoned to tell her the previous afternoon; he'd sounded very keyed-up. "My papers just came in, Mads," he'd told her. "I'm going off to the war."

The words gave her a thump, but little more. They weren't going together, not really. They had kissed only once. And anything more with Ronnie was out of the question. The whole conversation there on the phone by the fireplace in the living room seemed like something out of a movie, not a thing that was actually happening to her. She wasn't even entirely sure it was really him on the other end of the line. They'd rarely spoken on the phone before, and then only about trifles. Once, he'd called asking for directions to the Woodland Country Club. As if she knew. She'd golfed there only once herself, and didn't belong, and couldn't find her way to Newton if she tried, which she wouldn't. The significant part of the conversation came before it began, with the newly respectful look on her mother's face when she cupped her hand over the receiver and whispered that it was *Ronald Bemis* calling for her.

So Maddy felt somewhat numb as she passed Ronnie's news on to her parents. Their faces marked the gravity of the occasion, making Maddy feel rebuked, and declared that by all means he should come for lunch after the service on Sunday. They invited the minister, too, along with their old friends, the Scotts, and one of Mother's unmarried cousins. Four of the most boring people on earth. They brought out the good silver, and had a roast, and Maddy was astonished by how easily Ronnie fit in. It was as if he'd always had a place at the table, but had only now, finally, shown up.

The talk was entirely of war: the Luftwaffe, the Messerschmitt versus the B-17, German Air Marshall Goering, Churchill . . . Maddy didn't say a word the whole lunch, except to ask her drab cousin Irene to pass the salt, and then to thank her for doing so. She would have much preferred to see Ronnie that last time more privately, so they could talk about more interesting things, like Sally

McPherson's coming-out party last weekend, where her little brother Stuart had somehow managed to add half a bottle of gin to the punch bowl. Or the rumors she'd picked up from Ellen (God only knew where *she'd* acquired them) that Ronnie's aunt Jane and uncle Phil were considering a divorce. Or, whether Ronnie was— how to put this?—frightened to go off to war. She assumed so. But he didn't *seem* so. That was the puzzling part. He had the same confident smile as always.

When lunch was over, Father led the group into the library for coffee, and Mother whispered to Maddy that perhaps she'd like to take Ronnie into the living room for a few minutes. Maddy gave her mother's cool hand a squeeze of gratitude, yet as she stepped into the living room with Ronnie, she felt queer. Was it his uniform? He'd worn his airman's cap to the door, which had startled her before he'd slipped it off his head and stuffed it in his pocket.

No, it was because she'd always known him, but she'd *never* known him. He was like the wallpaper in her bedroom, an endless series of shiny apples. He was gorgeous, at least everyone else thought so. Ellen kept calling him "dreamy," which was annoying, since Ellen said that about a lot of boys. And he was, as her father would say, clearly the "right sort," meaning his family had plenty of money but weren't "showy" about it, meaning they spent it only on real estate. But what lay behind that, inside? She had no idea. He might have been her brother, a younger brother who's always pestering you, messing up your things, not that she knew anything about brothers, really. They'd played together as toddlers in Nahant; her mother had kept embarrassing photographs of them splashing about together in the wading pool at the yacht club. As twelve- and thirteen-year-olds, they'd learned to fox-trot together at Miss Eliot's. There must have been other boys there, but she couldn't recall dancing with anyone else.

At fourteen, she'd received a letter from Ronnie at the Whistling Pines summer camp, an extremely forthright letter asking if he could "go" with her. He'd signed it, "Sincerely, Ronald

Bemis." It sparked little except curiosity about why he'd put such a question that way. But then she'd shown it to Ellen, and she was jealous. So Maddy had written back: "If you like," and enclosed a sprig of pine needles for him to remember her by.

Things didn't seem much different when she saw him again later that summer, and it had taken another full year before Ronnie tried anything with her. That was at a matinee performance of *How Green Was My Valley,* and, as they sat together in the theater, she could feel him slide a hand over her knee. It sent tingles up and down the inside of her leg, and left her quivering for hours afterward, even though it was *only Ronnie.* It took another six months before the first, fumbling kiss. They were at his Sargent cousins' garden party, and he'd taken her inside to show her where the bathroom was. As they went down the hall together, he suddenly stopped and, without a word, turned her to him and pushed his lips up against hers. She'd broken away, saying that she was suddenly very . . . thirsty.

Afterward, he'd acted as if nothing had happened, and that had bothered her, too.

So, now, in the living room, she wondered who he was, this imposing fellow slipping the scissors back into his jacket pocket. His shoes, brightly polished and stiff-looking, seemed so big. And his hands, too, seemed enormous, as if they might knock her over, just by accident. Were they really bigger now, or had she never noticed?

As usual, Ronnie seemed unaware of her reservations. "You're really something, you know," he declared with a smile. "C'mere." And then, without waiting for a response, he'd reached out for her, cupped a hand around the back of her head and drawn her to him in a gesture that surprised her with its power, its need. She thought he might kiss her for real this time, finally. She was ready, almost eager. She'd been wondering what a real kiss would be like. She closed her eyes, softened her mouth in preparation as she'd seen Olivia de Havilland do in *Princess O'Rourke.* But instead, he brought her head to his chest, and cradled it against him. "You'll wait for me, won't you, Maddy?" he'd whispered into her hair. "I'll go crazy if you don't say you will."

She wasn't quite sure what he meant. Wait for him? Wait for *what?*

Still, it was a thrill to hear such words spoken to her. The room swam a little as Maddy leaned against him, inhaling the dusty scent of his gabardine jacket. "Of course I will," she told him. In her confusion, her eyes misted up a little, and she must have sniffled.

"Oh, Mads, I'll be all right," he told her. "You don't have to worry." Then he reached for her shoulders. He cleared away some of the hair that dangled down over her face, then inspected her eyes. They must have looked wet, although it irked her to think so. She didn't like the idea that Ronnie could think he could see into her.

He smiled at her reassuringly. "No Jerry's going to get me."

There was a gentle knock at the door. Ronnie dropped his hands from Maddy's shoulders and they turned away from each other. Maddy straightened her dress. "Yes?" she called out.

Her mother stepped into the room. "We should probably be leaving soon, darling."

Maddy looked at her blankly.

"To see Aunt Dot?" her mother prompted.

"Oh yes, of course." In all the excitement surrounding Ronnie's visit, she had forgotten that she had promised to visit her godmother, who was recovering from a fall.

"I should be going," Ronnie told Maddy's mother and headed out into the hall where the Scotts and Maddy's parents' other luncheon guests were just putting on their coats. As Maddy followed Ronnie out, she could feel everyone turning to her with a sense of expectation, not that Maddy knew quite why. She smiled at them. They smiled back at her, and they all shook hands with Ronnie.

"Good luck over there, son," Mr. Scott told him, patting his arm.

"Thank you, sir," Ronnie replied.

"I'll follow you out to your car," Maddy told him, eager to put some distance between herself and her parents and their stuffy friends. Ronnie pulled open the front door, and politely let Maddy pass outside before him.

Her arms were bare and she felt a chill on her skin as she stepped out into the open air. The two of them made splashing sounds with each step on the pebble driveway as they crossed over to Ronnie's Ford, which was parked on the far side. Maddy could hear the other guests gathering by the door behind them, so she knew that this wasn't a time for any particular show of affection, nor was she sure what show she wanted to give. Ronnie seemed bent only on getting to his car. But he did turn back to her after he pulled open the front door, and gave her shoulder a squeeze. "So you'll come tomorrow?" They'd made a plan for her to see him off at the train station.

"Certainly."

"We'll have some more time then."

"Yes."

He was about to climb into the car when he turned back to her once more. "What about tonight? You busy tonight?"

"I'm sorry, Ronnie. There are . . . things I'm supposed to do." It wasn't a complete lie. She'd told Ellen they'd go to the movies. Still, she could easily have put Ellen off, under the circumstances. Why didn't she want to?

"Yes, of course," Ronnie said. Was his face always so rigid? "Tomorrow then."

"Yes."

He took his seat behind the wheel and pulled the door shut with a thud that sounded like finality itself. She stepped back to let the car go, and watched as he turned right out of the driveway and disappeared behind the hedge.

As she returned to the house, Maddy's mother took her aside for a moment. "Well," she whispered eagerly. "Did he propose?"

Maddy whipped about, shocked. "Propose what?"

"Why, marriage, of course. Honestly, dear."

"Mother, please."

• • •

A wind on her from the car window, and her hair fluttering against her ear. She was sitting in the back of the Bemises' royal-blue Chrysler. Ronnie's father was driving, with his mother beside him. She was wearing an elegant hat with a wide brim, and white gloves that were periodically visible as she reached up to rearrange her hair. Ronnie was in the backseat; his legs were splayed in front of him, taking up space the way men do. Maddy would have liked to ride beside him, possibly even to feel the outside of his leg against hers. Hold hands, perhaps. Down low, where his parents wouldn't see. They'd never done that.

But—she'd come too late. She'd gotten distracted washing her hair with a new shampoo Ellen had raved about last night after the show, and, on this of all days, she'd gotten behind. The Bemises were all gathered around their car waiting for her when Maddy's family's aging chauffeur, Charles, drove her up in the Studebaker. Then, to Maddy's annoyance, Ronnie's little brother Jonny—skinny little thing, with a cowlick—had jumped in to the middle seat, leaving her on the outside. Jonny was only eleven, and very excited that his brother was going off to war. "Save some Krauts for me, okay, Ronnie? Okay?" he kept saying as they drove along Beacon Street, headed into town, and banging his brother's arm. Mrs. Bemis tried to hush him, he was being so inane. He brought his hands out of his pockets to make gun barrels of his index fingers as he noisily demonstrated what he would do if he could ever ride shotgun in a B-17 himself.

Maddy sneaked an occasional glance over at Ronnie, trying to sense his mood. She'd worn a light, almost filmy dress, an important concession on a hot afternoon when she'd much rather have been in shorts. It showed the outline of her legs, but Ronnie scarcely noticed. He kept smoothing out his pants with his hands and glancing at his watch and telling his father to hurry. She might as well not have been there. All she'd done was make him late for his train.

She kept wondering about what her mother had said about marriage. It had bothered her all the previous day, not that she'd said anything further to Mother. The idea—a proposal of marriage from Ronnie. Before she'd even finished Miss Southwick's! She wished she could discuss such a thing with him, candidly, expressing her uncertainties. But there was obviously no time or place for that now. War rushed everything! She'd thought that she might write Ronnie a letter about it, once he was in England. *Safely in England,* she thought, before she stopped herself. She hoped it would reassure him to know that she pondered such things, and that she was contemplating a future with him. Surely, that was what he'd want to hear, what any man would want to hear. Or why else would he want to take her hair? (Such a wonderful gesture, everyone had agreed when she canvased her friends by telephone. That had made Maddy feel like a heel.)

There was a mob of soldiers and sailors and airmen and who-knew-what at South Station. Mr. Bemis couldn't see any place to park. Even the curbside was jammed, so he pulled up in the middle of the street, got out, and helped his son get his bags out of the back.

Maddy saw Ronnie's father clap his son on the shoulder, but she couldn't hear what they said. The two were the same height, a little over six feet, but Ronnie's head was bowed slightly before his father as he listened to his father's words. Of farewell? Of love? Maddy couldn't imagine. Finally, Ronnie looked up, and Maddy expected the two of them to embrace, kiss even. She'd seen other men do that with their sons. But Ronnie gave his father only a nod, then hoisted the straps of his two duffel bags onto his shoulders and stepped between the parked cars to the curb in front of the station. He turned back to Maddy almost as an afterthought. "You coming in?"

"Be right there," Maddy shouted, and came around to the front of the car to follow him in. "Give my regards to Major Dorris," Mr. Bemis called out.

"Absolutely," Ronnie said over his shoulder.

Was he tearing up? Maddy wondered. Is that why he didn't turn his head? She was troubled that she didn't know him well enough to know. But it was also possible that Ronnie was the sort of person who, once he'd started going in a certain direction, just kept going, regardless of everything. Maddy watched his back as he kept on and plunged into the crowd gathered by the door. With the large duffel bags on either side, he made a wide swath as he pushed through the crowd to the main door.

"You going in?" Maddy asked Ronnie's mother.

"You go on with him, dear," Mrs. Bemis told Maddy, giving her a gentle push. "You'll want a few moments together. I'll catch up."

"I'm going in with her, too!" Jonny cried out.

"No, you stay with me," his mother commanded.

"But I want to see him!" Jonny cried and bolted into the crowd himself, drawing an anxious cry from his mother, which didn't slow him in the least. Maddy stole a glance at Mr. Bemis, who looked on resolutely, his jaw clenched. "You go on ahead," Mr. Bemis told her. "You'll want to see the boy off."

"Don't you?" Maddy was astonished. That whole day was a mystery to her.

"I've said my good-byes. I don't think I can do it again. Just tell him to take care of himself."

"Certainly." Maddy turned back toward Ronnie, but she could barely make out his head, with its airman's cap, as he pushed toward the two big doors at the entrance to the station.

She plunged ahead and managed to squeeze through the crowd to the doors. It was very noisy inside, with a great rush of sound that swirled around the high ceiling. She spotted Ronnie gazing up at the big board where all the tracks were listed. She shouted to him and waved. He looked back at her. Maddy was wearing high heels for the occasion, along with that scandalously thin dress. She wanted to give Ronnie a vision of herself, something to remember. But he'd scarcely noticed.

"Track ten!" he shouted to her. "Quickly. We've only got a couple minutes." He charged down the platform, a bag over each shoulder, and she hurried after, moving awkwardly in her heels. Track ten was on a separate level way at the end, and the train was belching great clouds of steam when, flustered and breathless, she finally reached it. A conductor had come around by the locomotive to wave for latecomers to hurry. Ronnie had already reached the stairs to his car, the third one down, when she rounded the train. He'd set his bags down, and was fishing for the ticket in his pocket to show the conductor. She rushed up to Ronnie, and from behind grabbed him around the waist, where his belt dug in. It was the first time she'd ever reached for him. But it seemed required, just then.

"Oh, Mads," he said, wheeling around to her. "Look, I'm sorry it's such a rush."

"It's my fault, Ronnie. If I hadn't been so late—"

"It's okay. Don't worry." He bent down and brought his lips to hers. Maddy's heart surged, and she felt flushed on her cheeks and chest. She closed her eyes, the better to feel the full, sweet touch of his lips. She craved it, suddenly. She wanted to clutch him with both hands, pull him to her, squeeze his chest tight against hers. But somehow his mouth landed off to one side, and theirs wasn't at all the long, passionate kiss Maddy had been dreaming of. Instead, it was more a quick smooch that her parents might have given her when she was little.

Still, he took her hands and looked into her eyes solemnly, as if they'd experienced a deep communion. "Don't forget me now, will you, Mads?"

"Of course I won't." She would have said more, but her mind was filled with disappointment, and her thoughts didn't congeal into words that she might say right then. Then a whistle sounded, a bell clanged, and the conductor yelled for everyone to climb aboard. Ronnie released her hands and drew back from her. She could feel him retreat: it was like the sun going behind a cloud. As he turned to climb the stairs into the train, she saw that the corner of his mouth was smeared with her lipstick, and she realized that this whole, possibly final encounter had gone wrong, and now her Ronnie—for he was hers now, wasn't he?—might go off and die and all she would remember was this vision of him with a red splotch.

"You have my——?" she called to him in as loud a voice as she dared. She didn't think she should actually say the word "hair," it seemed so suggestive.

"Your what?"

"You know."

"Oh that." He smiled. "Of course I do."

"Well, okay then."

"Write to me, Mads?" He'd promised to send an address as soon as he had one.

"Of course!" She said it gaily, to cover the heaviness she felt.

"I'll come back for you."

"Please do." That sounded all wrong! "Take care of yourself. Your father wanted me to tell you that." Wrong again! Would nothing ever go right between them? She squeezed her hands into fists, her fingernails cutting into her palms.

"You too, Mads."

Then a whistle blew again, more insistently, and the conductor put his hand on Ronnie's shoulder and told him to get on board. Maddy patted his back as he climbed the rest of the stairs into the train, but he kept on without looking back.

The train started to move, first with a jolt, and then more smoothly. As Maddy watched it go back up the track, she thought for a second that her whole life was somehow playing in reverse. But then she got a sense of progress, of motion forward, and she took a breath to calm herself. *It will be all right,* she assured herself. *He will be fine, and I will be fine. Everything will be fine.*

The train was almost out of sight when Mrs. Bemis reached her, with little Jonny by the arm. "He isn't gone, is he?" she declared, huffing.

Maddy pointed down the tracks.

Mrs. Bemis looked like she might cry. "We had the worst time finding it." She turned away to compose herself.

"Yes, it's confusing," Maddy said, trying to reassure her.

"We were looking and looking!" Jonny said.

Mrs. Bemis hushed the little boy. "That's enough now."

It wasn't until they'd left the train station and were approaching the car that Mrs. Bemis spoke again. "Tell me something, would you?" The words were quiet but urgent. "Are you in love with my son?"

"Who wouldn't be?" Maddy replied evasively.

Mrs. Bemis's gaze pressed down on her. "Yes, but are *you?*"

"Why, of course."

"You'll miss him then." It was not a question. Mrs. Bemis gave her arm a pat, as if this were their secret.

Is that when it was settled, right there?

Maddy ate little that evening at dinner, and she went to bed early. It was a warm night, and she threw open her windows and let the night air flutter the curtains as it drifted into her room. A thought stirred as she felt the air on her. An indecent thought. She went to the door and turned the key. Then she lay down on her bed on top of the covers, and slid the skirts of her nightgown up her thighs to her waist. She opened her legs a little, then a little more. It felt so good to have the warm air on her there, as if the lightest imaginable fingers were exploring her. She lay like that for a few minutes, then she remembered a book Ellen had once showed her with a lot of nervous giggles, and she took her pillow and pressed it up between her thighs, then gently squeezed her legs together, forcing the pillow up against her. She lay back again, and tried to imagine it was Ronnie there, pushing into her. She thought hard, tried to summon the image of Ronnie, long and pale and slim, with hardly any body hair, based on what she'd seen of him in his bathing suit at the club in Nahant. But, try as she might, the image kept dissolving into nothing. She kept waiting for a wave of feeling to rise up inside her, the way the book had said it would. But no wave formed; there was scarcely a swelling. Her bare skin was cool to her touch. She lowered a hand to press the pillow down harder against her pelvis, and allowed the other to fall lightly across her small breasts, through the fabric of her nightgown. She played with the tip of one tender nipple with her finger, felt it swell and stiffen. *It's Ronnie, kissing me there,* she thought. She closed her eyes, tipped her head back toward the ceiling, opened her mouth so that the air would enter her more deeply, and she tried desperately to think that it was indeed Ronnie on her, kissing her, sliding up inside. But she could not bring the image to life. She felt little beyond shame to be touching herself this way. Eventually, she removed the pillow and lowered her nightgown once more, then drew a sheet up over her. She lay still, waiting for sleep to come, until another thought nagged her—her fear of fire, one that she'd always had, ever since she was a girl. She went to the door and unlocked it once more. Otherwise, she was sure she would burn to a crisp, unable to escape the flames in her bedroom.

six

And the letters! It seemed they began to arrive the very next morning, but they couldn't have. Flimsy, blue aerograms filled with Ronnie's fear, his longing, his desire, sketched out in all caps from his balky ballpoint. He was outside London. The exact location was razored out by the military censors. But she knew it was a town called Great Ashfield in East Anglia. Her father had passed through there in the thirties on a bicycle tour of the English countryside. "Charming little place," her father had told her. It didn't sound like it in the letters. Maddy pictured a wide expanse of brown and gray, under the rainy skies she associated with England, just an endless patch of mud dotted with puffy Quonset huts on one side and a row of pewter-colored airplanes, the proud Flying Fortresses, as they called them in newsreels, on the other. She could tell Ronnie was trying to be brave, but the fear came through. There was a terseness to the letters, a tightness to the handwriting. He kept mentioning how cold it was way up in the sky where his plane flew, so much colder than he'd ever imagined when he trained in his little P-47, at five thousand feet, in Florida. Ice formed on the bomber's windows, blurring the view from the cockpit, and his feet went numb. Sometimes the whole plane shivered, as if it were breaking apart, even when it wasn't catching flak from the antiaircraft gunners in Germany below. And nothing ever worked right— at least, that seemed to be the point Ronnie was working toward when the censors sliced out the words. The other flyboys teased him for his Boston accent—not that she'd ever noticed it—and his please-and-thank-you manners.

"But I kept your hair, Mads. I fly with it, just as I said I would. And (don't tell anyone please) I put it under my pillow when I sleep." Then his closing words: "Wait for me, Mads. Please?"

Wispy clouds, dark against the night sky, and the throbbing drone of the engines as the planes drove hard into the buffeting air. So many nights that spring, Maddy would close her eyes and think of Ronnie, a copilot up in the cockpit, while she lay in bed under clean, light sheets, hearing the crickets chirp. The moon out her window, she imagined it shone down on him, too, glinting off his wings, slanting in through his windshield as he checked off coordinates, studied maps, his teeth chattering from cold and, surely, from fear, as the great airborne ship blasted ahead into the night, laden with bombs. Was it only dread she'd felt then? No love at all? So terrible to think so. He had his crewmates—Smitty the bombadier and that funny Harold someone who was the pilot. But still, Ronnie seemed so alone up there.

Many nights that spring she'd rise up from her bed. She'd take off her nightgown, drift about the room, feeling the spring air on her. The wind on her, all over, as she looked out to the trees from her bedroom. The wind burned the way ice burns, setting her nerves on fire. The moon was pale, the light silver. Maddy could see the last of the tulips, opened up so wide, so achingly wide, at the foot of the lawn in the moonlight. She could hear the wind moving quietly through the trees as it came toward her. It was roving, searching for something, she could tell.

There were too many letters, Maddy couldn't keep up with them. One every day, it seemed, sometimes more than one. All about the unrelenting gray skies, the mud, the fear. The other day, some flak had ripped through the underside of the plane a few inches from his feet. It had opened a great gash in the bottom of the plane. The plane had lost altitude, and Harold had fought hard to keep from going into a fatal spin. Through the hole, Ronnie had actually seen the ground below rise up toward him before Harold managed to get the big ship leveled out.

That one angered Maddy, it gave her such a fright. Why hadn't that bit of news been censored, she wondered, razored out like so much else? She wished it had been, so she didn't have to keep worrying about him. The thought of him up there, so high, with nothing underneath—

Maddy herself had never flown in a plane. Aside from Ronnie, she didn't know anyone who had. On this topic, at least, she agreed with her mother. She wasn't in such a hurry to get anywhere that she needed to fly there. It scared her, the thought of being up so high. And the Luftwaffe diving out of the sky right at Ronnie, and the chance of mechanical problems, or some stupid mistake, that Harold pulling up on the stick when he should have pushed.

It was all more than Maddy could take. She kept trying to push the worry back. She didn't mind Ronnie being a small, quiet worry. She almost liked that; it was a comfort, to have a mild concern to occupy her. But this was getting to be a big, loud one. It was taking over, grabbing great chunks of her attention. And she kept wanting to yell back, "But I don't even know you! I've *never* known you!" It was crazy, maddening. It nearly brought tears. She kept wanting to push at Ronnie to get him away from her, to give her some peace. But there was nothing to push at, just these letters that kept coming and coming.

Alice

Alice was in the bathtub with her knees up, the Bemis file propped up on her kneecaps. Her Sony was going on the windowsill. Classical music this time, since it was evening and she wanted to ease herself down after a trying day. She brought Fido, in the "mouse house" she normally left on the kitchen counter, into the bathroom with her for company, and he was rustling around in his shavings as she went through the Bemis file one more time, trying to find the one piece of information that would make sense of everything.

It was a deep, old-fashioned white tub, one of the special attractions of her apartment. At her feet, the bathroom window framed a gorgeous orange sunset over the Somerville skyline, a few brick steeples poking up above the surrounding rooftops. The sash was open a few inches, and a light breeze blew in, its coolness a luxurious contrast to the warm water of her bath.

Alice wondered what Mrs. Bemis would think if she could see

her like this, her cheeks flushed, her breasts reddened by the bathwater as she perused her file. Mrs. Bemis was so upright, so proper. Alice doubted that she'd ever allowed herself any such sybaritic pleasures. She was no sensualist; the elderly rarely are. Wasn't that so? Joints aching, senses dulled, their bodies don't seem alive to pleasure. Mrs. Bemis had seemed to recoil from Alice's touch the few times she'd reached for her. Or had her depression simply engulfed her the way the schizophrenia had overwhelmed poor Chris B?

When Alice was very young, her father had told her a story about a girl he'd gone skating with on the Monongahela when he was a boy. She'd plunged through a weak spot in the ice and then been swept past the hole by the current. Her father could see the poor girl clawing at the ice from underneath, her hair billowing, her face white and puffy, as she was dragged downstream. Alice sometimes wondered if she'd been a girlfriend, but her father had never said; withdrawn, uncommunicative, he wasn't the type for such intimacies. He'd tried to hack through the ice with his skate blades to get to her, but it was no use. They were just inches apart—he above the ice, the girl below. But gradually her arms slowed and she sank away. Her body was never found.

To Alice's father, gloomy and skeptical, it was a story about how quickly things can change, and change forever. How you can never be sure. She remembered how he'd slowly shaken his head when he'd finished telling the story. But, to Alice now, in her bathwater, perhaps it was a story about the ice that came between her father and the girl. Mrs. Bemis was like that girl, freezing, drowning, pulled by currents that only she could feel, and sealed away under thick, black ice. Would Alice—would anyone—ever break through?

The bathroom door opened, startling Alice, and a rush of cool air blew past her. It was Ethan. He was in a T-shirt and tight pants, his hair slicked back. "You're coming tonight, right?" Her mind elsewhere, it took Alice a moment to focus on him.

"To the Middle East. My gig, remember?"

"Oh, God. Sorry." She started to scramble out of the water. "What time is it?"

"A little before eight," he assured her. "It's still early. We don't need to be there for, like, another hour." He wiped the fog from the mirror, took a look at his face, and checked his teeth. "But you're still going to give me a ride, right?" Ethan didn't own a car, which is why he'd been on that bicycle the night they'd met. He had been borrowing his roommate's car, but now that Ethan was with Alice, he'd started depending on hers.

"That's fine," Alice told him, although, in truth, she'd been hoping to catch up on some of her paperwork tonight.

Ethan turned to her. "You sure?" He was sensitive to nuance, at least where favors were concerned.

"No problem," she said, and returned her eyes to the file.

She'd noticed that Ethan was touchy about possessions—having them, borrowing them, needing them. At twenty-six, he was two years younger than Alice, and he made almost nothing as a bagger at a health-food store in Cambridge, devoting the rest of his time to his music, which didn't pay a cent. Alice had quickly learned to tread carefully around financial issues. When he first showed her the tiny, cramped basement apartment he shared in working-class Medford, she couldn't help noting that it was smaller than her old place in the Fenway, and she'd had that all to herself. She thought she'd been delicate about it, but Ethan still zinged her for being "bourgeois."

That one exchange nearly derailed their affair before it began, but they talked it out: he was the youngest child of a couple of teachers at an alternative school outside Boston, and he acknowledged that he'd soaked up a lot of their countercultural politics. Alice told him that her father ran an electronics repair shop that never did very well—and was certainly not helped by his periodic, gin-soaked depressions, which forced her mother, to make ends meet, to work nights as a hospital receptionist when the children were young. This conversation was an important step for Alice; she'd never mentioned her financial anxieties to a boyfriend before, and Ethan had listened sympathetically. He'd said he was sorry; he hadn't meant to sound mad. They'd made love for the first time right afterward, standing up in the bedroom doorway, her legs hooked around him. She'd cried afterward, though, unsure as to just why.

Now, Ethan padded closer, toward her, across the bathroom tiles. He was in socks, as usual, since he always kicked off his shoes as soon as he could. "So, who've you got this time?"

"New patient." Alice hoped her clipped tone would spare her further questions.

"Not that one who touched your hair?"

Alice was impressed that he remembered. "Yeah, actually."

Ethan came closer, bent down. Alice shut the file protectively. "Ethan, I—"

"Just going to give you a kiss," he told her. "I've been thinking about you all day today."

Alice was always open to that kind of sweetness, and she lifted herself up a little to receive his kiss. He brushed his lips lightly against hers, then leaned down to kiss her nipples through the water. That tickled, especially once he started blowing bubbles.

"You silly," she said, playfully pushing his head away.

But he kept at it, blowing a great mound of bubbles that rose up, popping, over her chest.

Alice squirmed, trying to keep the file dry, but Ethan plucked his head out, grinning as the water trickled down his face to his chin. "Shouldn't you be going wild around now?" he teased.

"I'm a little preoccupied here, Eth, sorry."

"Yeah?" He reached over, plucked the file out of her hands, and started flipping through it before she could stop him. "Oh, Madeline Bemis," he read.

"You shouldn't be reading that." Alice lurched out of the tub and reached for the file. But Ethan just lifted it up toward the ceiling, well out of her reach. Naked, dripping, all she could do was grab his elbow, which was infuriating.

"Come on. Work's over." He wrapped his other arm around her, swinging her toward him. He slid a hand down her back, then pushed his thigh, in its rough jeans, up between her bare legs. "Let's dance, okay?"

Irritated, she pulled away, grabbed a towel, and cinched it around her. "The file, Ethan."

"You're so serious all the time. Lighten up, would you? Gimme a little something." He tugged impishly at the corner of her towel; his fingers grazed her bare thigh, fairly high up. "You know how I get before I go on."

She slapped his hand away. "Not now, Ethan. Jesus."

He waved the file at her. "Don't you want this?" he taunted.

She was not going to beg. She gave him a cold stare and crossed her arms in front of her.

"*Okay.* There—take it," Ethan told her and flipped the file toward her, but it flew past her into the bathtub, where it splashed down into the water.

"Ethan!" Frantic and furious, Alice bent over the tub to fish out the papers, which were already starting to darken with wetness around the edges. Fortunately, the file had stayed mostly on the surface, and she was able to grab it before it got totally soaked. "I can't believe you did that," Alice shouted at him, drying the file folder with the edge of her bath towel.

"I didn't mean to, all right?"

"This file's important, Ethan. This patient's important."

"I *know.* I'm *sorry.*"

"Well, be more careful."

"*Okay.*"

An uneasy silence while Alice finished drying off the file.

"She's the one who's rich, right?" Ethan asked.

"I wouldn't use that word." She straightened up and set the Bemis file on a high shelf above the spare towels.

"Well, maybe you said 'socially prominent,'" Ethan said. "But it's the same thing."

It pained her to think she had. It was a fair statement, but it wasn't the first thing she'd say about her patient. She hadn't spent much time on Mrs. Bemis's wealth in therapy, and, honestly, she hadn't thought about it much. It irritated her to think that Ethan found Mrs. Bemis unworthy of her sympathy. Was that what his outburst was all about?

"She's depressed, Ethan. She's old, lonely."

"My grandparents were rich, you know." Ethan jammed the towel back onto the rack. "Not zillionaires. But they had a big house and all this art. I ever tell you?"

Alice shook her head. It did fit, now that he mentioned it. Even though he never had much spending money, never seemed to worry about finances—at least, not the way she did. It was like the money was there, even if it wasn't.

"On my mom's side," he went on. "They moved to the Bahamas a few years ago, which was fine with my mom. She thought they were assholes, pretty much, completely into themselves and their art collection and their social position and all that."

"That bother you?" Alice dried the ends of her hair, only half-listening.

"Oh, a little therapy now?" Ethan said it gently, but it stung all the same. "It wasn't anything heavy," he went on. "She didn't refuse to see them or anything like that."

"So why'd you mention it?" Alice was still furious with him.

Ethan turned to face her, as if this was the important part. "Just that I know how people glom on to the rich, that's all. My mom was the only one who kept her distance. Everybody else just *loved* them— sucked up to them like you wouldn't believe. She saw that whole world. It's, like, anything the rich feel or do, it's soooo interesting, or soooooo tragic or sooooo something. It's sick, really."

Alice tightened the towel around her. "Oh, so you're saying that I only care about my patient because she's rich? Nice, Ethan. Really nice."

"It might be part of it, sure."

"Well, isn't that good to know." Alice turned her back to Ethan, pulled on her bathrobe, and headed into the bedroom to change.

Ethan followed her through the doorway. "Listen, I'm just saying it happens. You come from this little town in Pennsylvania. No money. I can see why you'd get all caught up in all the high-society bullshit." He wiggled his fingers when he said the last words, as if he didn't believe in such a thing.

Alice gave him an impatient look.

"I mean, like, why Montrose?" he demanded. "Why not some regular mental health clinic? Why's it have to be the fanciest one around?"

Alice clipped on her bra and stepped into a pair of fresh underpants, then wheeled on him. "Ethan, what are you *talking* about? Montrose isn't fancy. You should see it. Christ, half the buildings are boarded up."

"What about all the movie stars?" He mentioned a couple of them.

"Okay, Ethan, fine." She hated this conversation, hated *him*. "Yes, there are occasionally movie stars. But only because Montrose has a highly-regarded detox program." Alice pulled herself up, irritated to sound like a PR flak, but annoyed that she'd been forced into it. She crossed her arms in front of her chest, glared at Ethan. It shocked her how ugly a handsome man could become when he started behaving like a complete jerk. She didn't want to argue with him. She always hated arguments, especially stupid, pointless, boneheaded ones like this one. She simply wanted him to stop—stop questioning her motives, her sympathies. Maybe there was a kernel of truth in what he was saying. Maybe Mrs. Bemis did interest her in some small part because of her privileged background. Maybe she did wish that her father hadn't been a depressive drunk, and that her mother hadn't had to rush off to her job at the hospital in the evening when every other family in Latrobe was sitting down to dinner. Was that so awful? Was Alice supposed to apologize for wishing that it was another way? If Ethan had approached the topic more gently, at a better time, she might have discussed this with him. It was a subject she'd delved into frequently enough with Dr. Horowitz, God knew. But right now all she wanted was silence—peace—in her nice, new apartment that she'd worked hard for.

"I'm just saying—"

"I *know* what you're saying, Ethan. It's not that she's rich, or socially prominent, or important, or anything. Jesus. It's just that she needs help."

"Oh, you're the *helper.* Oh, in *that* case. Alice Matthews to the rescue. *Toot! Toot!*"

"*Stop* this, would you?" Alice's voice was quavering now, and she was afraid she might burst into tears or even hit him if he didn't shut up.

But he didn't. "I notice you haven't gotten so involved with your other patients. God, it's like she's suddenly become your new family or something."

"That's what this is all about? You're feeling excluded?"

"Maybe."

Normally, that sort of admission would have eased the two of them back onto a better footing. But Ethan had wounded her too deeply.

"I'm not going to apologize for caring about one of my patients." She crossed from the bureau to the closet, started flicking through the few clothes that hung from the pole, hardly seeing them she was so irritated.

"Maybe you should just think about why."

Alice whipped back around toward where he was standing by the bathroom door, staring at her. He sometimes got full of himself before his performances. It seemed like his way of preparing. But—was he on something? Would that explain his outburst?

"How about if we just concentrate on getting ready for your performance tonight?"

"Don't treat me like I've got some problem, okay?"

"Just get ready, all right?" She pulled some jeans off a hanger, stepped into them, and threw on a shirt, too. As she fumbled with the tiny buttons up the front, the phone rang and Alice picked it up, grateful for the break.

It was her mother. She usually called on Thursday evenings at nine, after *Who Wants to Be a Millionaire.* "Oh, hi, Mom." She tried to sound cheerful, as if everything was fine.

"You busy?"

Alice didn't say anything, and the voice darkened. "He's there, isn't he?"

Alice's mother had been dubious about Ethan since she'd first heard about him. She didn't like the idea of her daughter going out with a grocery bagger who performed with a group called the She-men. For this Alice had gone to medical school?

"Want to talk to him?" Alice asked drily.

She glanced back at Ethan, who'd sat down on the foot of her bed. He was in a rumpled T-shirt that seemed to have come out of a laundry hamper, if he actually had such a thing; his black Converse sneakers were on the floor, his crumpled backpack beside them. All of it suddenly looked historic now, as if this would soon be an image that was all she had to remember him by. The thought caused something within her—a major support, it felt like, holding up a big part of her life—to give way. But she steeled herself to say nothing about this to her mother, who went on about her arthritis, which had been acting up in the muggy heat they'd been having, and about her two brothers, who'd both called that week. Alice provided a few generalities about Montrose, going easy on the Chris B incident, and saying nothing about Mrs. Bemis. Finally, she told her she was just going out. "Can I call you back later?"

"Try to remember, okay, honey?" her mother said. "There are some things we need to talk about."

"Like?"

"Just call me sometime when you have a chance to talk."

Alice put the phone down uneasily, worried about what her mother had meant to say, annoyed that she didn't have the time to hear. She went to the mirror, gave her hair a few brisk, angry strokes.

"So you are coming," Ethan said.

Alice looked at him blankly. "To?"

"My gig, Alice. Jesus. At the Middle East. *Remember?*"

"I don't think so, Ethan." She needed to get out, calm down. Perhaps she'd take a walk instead. It was a nice evening. Maybe that would help her regain some perspective, some calm.

"Well, can I borrow your car?"

"If you want." Alice gave her hair another couple of strokes, forgetting that she'd already brushed it. "I'm sorry, I just need to get out. This is all too much, I'm sorry." She realized that her mother did that, sometimes, just bolted when things got difficult. But she needed air all the same. She turned back to Ethan before heading for the door. "It'll be okay," she assured him. "We just need to figure a few things out." She hoped for a kiss, a touch, a bit of softness in his voice, something reassuring, but Ethan only reached for his guitar case, which he'd left propped in the corner of the bedroom.

That's when it hit her that maybe she wasn't the one who needed to leave. Ethan was not the man for her. He could be charming and playful, sure, but he was too immature, too angry, for her to deal with, to love. How could he ever think of her as just some groupie for the rich? Obviously, there was more to it, but she couldn't think it through right then. She knew this much: her apartment felt cold and empty right now with him in it.

She turned to face him. "Look, Ethan," she began.

Ethan did not face her.

"Maybe it would be a good idea if your things were gone when I got back," she went on.

"*What?*" He glanced up, astonishment on his face.

"I'm saying, maybe we should take a break from each other for a while."

He hunched back down over his guitar. "Oh, like, fuck other people?"

Alice just stared. Ethan continued mapping out chords.

"Ethan, I'm serious," she told him, her voice rising. "I think you should leave now."

"Wait— *Now?*" Incredulous.

"Yeah, now. Call one of your friends in the band. Maybe he'll give you a ride. Or take a cab. I'm not going with you tonight, and I don't want you to take my car."

"Oh, man." Ethan stood up. "This is so fucked up! You tell me this now?"

"Yes. Now." She set her hairbrush back down on the bureau. "I can't do this, Ethan. I've got a job to do, people who need me."

"Oh, it's that lady again."

She nearly struck him. "Fuck you, Ethan."

Ethan stood up, came closer, so close that his face was monstrous, just inches from hers. "I don't need this," he said, his eyes burning into her. "Or you." He turned back to the bed, reached for the quilt folded neatly at its foot. It had been sewed by the Grand, years back, when she was a young bride, all gorgeous (at least in the pictures) and as sharp as anything. It was the only thing her mother had given her when she'd left home for college. Her proudest possession. Ethan had watched, fascinated, as she'd mended several of the patches just the previous weekend.

Horrified, Alice charged toward him, hands outstretched. But it was too late. With a quick, angry movement, he ripped the patchwork covering, with its tiny squares of gingham and calico, right down the middle.

She dug her hands into his waist, tried to shove him away, but he was too big for her. "Don't, Ethan! Goddamnit!" She reached for the quilt, fought to free it from his grasp. He hurled it back at her, pushing her back.

"You get away from me, Ethan," Alice told him. She was determined not to be afraid of him, and to keep control. "You get out of here. Now!" Her heart was beating wildly. The blood pounded in her temples, the tips of her fingers. This was worse than dealing with Chris B; this was worse than anything. "Get out! I am absolutely fucking serious. Get out! Right now!"

But his eyes were on the bureau. Alice had left the sewing scissors out after the weekend's repair work. He picked them up, opened them wide, and turned to her, a blade out toward her like a knife. "Now you're really pissing me off." He brought the scissors closer to her. They were small but extremely sharp, with needlelike tips.

"Ethan, put those down."

He was slowly backing her toward the wall across from her bureau. She'd hung some photos of her family along there, off long black wires from the picture rail by the ceiling. She brushed up against the middle one, a color print of her sister, Carla, as a teenager playing with their dog. She'd ever loved this man?

He moved closer, grabbed her wrist, wrenched her palm open, brought the blade down slowly, its point toward her palm.

She tried to squirm free. "Ethan, do not do this. This is *sick!*"

"You think so?"

"Stop it! Just stop it—or I'll call the police!" She tried to jerk her hand away from him, but he'd pinned her arm tight against his body. He started to force her wrist back at a sharp angle, sending a spasm of pain all up her arm. He forced her fingers open with the outside of his fist, then lowered the blade onto the soft hollow of her palm, where it burned.

"Ethan—don't—God—"

But the blade was already starting to cut. A searing pain as it pierced the flesh of her open palm. "Stop it!" she screamed and, thrashing and kicking, tried to yank her hand free.

Then a knock at the door.

"Everything all right in there?" It was Josh, the computer geek from downstairs. "Alice?"

The door was locked.

A look from Ethan made it clear that Alice had better remain silent, and not move.

Another knock, more insistent. "Alice?" Josh called again. "You okay?"

The knob rattled as he tried it. Ethan turned to look.

This was her chance. Alice rammed her body against his to knock him off balance. She jerked her arm free and ran for the door.

"Josh!" She turned the bolt and yanked the door open. Josh stood there, stunned. He was skinny, with a wispy beard and eyeglasses, but he was there. Alice pulled him to her. "Help me!"

"What is it?" Josh asked. "What's going on?"

"It's nothing," Ethan said calmly from the bedroom doorway.

"He cut me," Alice said. She showed Josh the cut on her palm, where some blood was smeared.

"*Shit,*" Josh said.

"We were just screwing around." Ethan retreated inside the bedroom and flipped the scissors onto the bed.

"Get out of here, would you?" Alice demanded, following him to the doorway. "Or I'll call the cops. I swear, Ethan. This is no joke."

"I think you'd better leave," Josh added from beside her.

"Sure. No problem." Ethan grabbed his guitar case and stuffed some clothes into the backpack he always carried with him.

"And leave my goddamn key!" Alice commanded.

Ethan pulled the spare key she'd given him out of his jeans pocket, held it up for her, and tossed it onto the bed beside the scissors.

Guitar case in hand, he pushed Josh out of his way as he stepped back through to the living room. "See ya." He shut the apartment door behind him.

"Wow," Josh said. "What was that all about?" He turned to Alice. "You okay?" He gave her arm a squeeze.

She slumped against him. "Oh, God," she said, grinding her cheek against his shoulder. "Just hold me for a second, would you?"

"Sure." Josh brought his left arm around her, then stroked the back of her head.

"Don't—don't do that," Alice said. "Just hold me, okay? Just hold me."

eight

Josh got her some juice from the refrigerator and helped her clean and bandage the cut. Then he sat with her in the living room watching a sitcom rerun on late-night TV. She was grateful for the jokes, the levity they suggested, even though she couldn't bring herself to laugh. Finally, around eleven, Josh left for the computer lab. "My life's not usually like this," Alice told him as she walked him to her door.

She locked the door behind him and returned to her bedroom. The torn quilt was in the corner where Ethan had thrown it. She picked it up to survey the damage, and some of the patches, pale from a thousand sunny afternoons, fluttered free like tiny flags, each one representing a memory. The Grand had pieced it when she'd first moved to Latrobe in 1953 with Alice's grandfather, who'd taken a job as an accountant in the brewery there. This was her lineage, her history, what was left of it. Over time, her mother had replaced the worn patches with scraps from her own old dresses, and, later, added a patch from Alice's first-grade gingham dress, and another from the black miniskirt she'd worn to the junior prom with her very first boyfriend, Lars Cooper.

How could she have fallen for Ethan? How could she have missed the anger, the suspicion? There'd been other boys who'd mattered more, starting with that sweet, innocent Lars. She'd been crushed when he'd gone out west to art school and fallen in love with a model. But Ethan had gotten to her, all the same. Just walking beside him or having breakfast with him could give her a charge. Little things: him in a heavy morning beard, wearing only a T-shirt while he slurped up his Cheerios. He could be self-centered, no question. But she thought she'd gotten inside that, become the one thing besides his music that he *did* care about. Become the exception. But now— How could he have been so horrible?

She groped for the pillow, drew it to the side of her face. She tried to believe what the Grand had always assured her was true, that everything always looked better in the morning. But right now, with the darkness pressing against the windows, and everything so quiet and still, it seemed as if every move she made, every thought she had, was fateful. Did anybody care about her? Sure, she'd had friends. Everybody had friends. From Latrobe, from Penn State, from BU. But they *weren't* friends, not really. They were just people she knew, like that nice Josh downstairs, or her internist friend Kristen. She was closer to her siblings—her brother Jeff, the cardiac surgeon in Detroit, and her sister, Carla, the Miami travel agent, especially. But they were both older, both married (Jeff for the second time), both with children. They were busy. Even Carla, whom she used to be able to talk to about anything (it was Carla she ran to the day she first got her period), seemed rushed with her on the phone. Barbed, too, interrupting her with remarks like "And in English?" whenever Alice tried to discuss something psychiatric. The Grand had always been, unfailingly, the one to cheer her up. The Grand with her stories, her handmade cards for her birthday, her songs for any occasion. But she was lost to Alice now, an Alzheimer's casualty in her special-care facility.

The tears started to flow, soaking into the pillow pressed tight against her face. What was wrong with her? How could she have not seen Ethan for what he was? She wiped her face with a tissue from the box beside the bed. She stood up, steadied herself, stepped out to the living room, tried to free herself from the memory of Ethan coming toward her, pressing the scissors down. But she still felt the sting. It was no use: the whole place felt so different now. It had been such a thrill to move in that first day, such a big step up from the Fenway. To feel the smooth walls, to have a proper molding up by the ceiling, to have a refrigerator that didn't rumble when it came on. She'd been so happy to hang her photographs on the walls, to make it hers. But now—

She wanted to leave, pack up her things, grab Fido, walk down the stairs, and never come back. Get in her little car and drive. But where could she go?

She spent the rest of the night in front of the TV. Not watching. Staring, the flickering image going to her eyeballs, then reflecting straight back.

nine

It was hard to concentrate at work the next day. She kept
fingering the wide Band-Aid on her palm. After rounds, she tried
to steer clear of Dr. Maris, who she knew would be disappointed if
he were to learn how little progress she'd made with Mrs. Bemis.
And she avoided Marnie, too, knowing that she was sure to ask
something about Ethan, and Alice was afraid she'd cry.

When she checked in on Chris B, he was sitting on his bed,
sketching. His parents were there. The mother had big hair and an
anxious expression. The father was by the foot of the bed, talking on
a cell phone, gesturing wildly with his free hand.

Alice kept expecting Chris to ask about the bandage, to make
some pronouncement about her breakup with Ethan, but instead he
said he was "real ticked" that she hadn't taken the portrait he'd done
of her. "I found it on the floor, Alice," he told her sternly. She tried to
apologize, said that a lot was happening that day, but he turned to
his sketchpad and tuned her out. She made for the door, leaving him

to his parents, but he called out to her before she left, "Glad you're taking good care of Maddy."

"Maddy?" Alice asked.

"The old lady," he said. "Madeline Bemis. Used to be called Maddy. Thought you'd know that by now." He tipped his head to the ceiling, smiled his loopy smile. "We've been talking."

Alice saw Mrs. Bemis that afternoon at three. Once again, she was playing solitaire at the card table. But this time, Chris B was sitting by her side, watching attentively. When Alice approached, Chris angled one ear upward. "We were just talking about you," he added.

"*He* was," Mrs. Bemis corrected drily. "I was doing my best not to listen."

Rather formally, Mrs. Bemis asked Chris if he would carry on with her game now that she'd taught him the rules, which seemed to be fairly complicated. Then, to Alice's surprise, she hooked an arm through Alice's to stroll with her down the corridor for their appointment. Their usual meeting room was occupied, and so this time, Alice directed her down to an unusual, rounded space inside the turret off the far corner of Nichols.

The room had a full view of Holmes, where Mrs. Bemis's mother had been treated years before, and, as the two of them gazed out at it silently, Alice again noticed the vines stealing over the building. There was a wildness on the edge of everything she knew, and it was forcing its way in. A psych professor, Dr. Randlinger, had once told Alice to concentrate on the nothing that surrounds everyone, giving them—as he said—their shape. The remark had stayed with Alice, and she thought that now, seeing Mrs. Bemis, she might finally know what he meant.

Mrs. Bemis took a seat in one of the folding chairs by the door and glanced over at Alice, who was still by the window, absent-mindedly picking at her Band-Aid.

"What happened?" Mrs. Bemis asked.

Alice didn't know what she meant.

"The bandage," Mrs. Bemis said.

"Oh, it's nothing." Alice smiled dismissively, then buried her hand in the crook of her other arm.

"Let me see, would you? Indulge an old lady's maternal instincts."

Frowning, uneasy, Alice reached her hand out toward her patient, palm up. The bandage had flopped open—it hadn't stuck on very well—and Mrs. Bemis pursed her lips as she surveyed the damage. "Well, I hope you used a disinfectant."

"It's not that bad," Alice assured her.

"What happened?"

"I slipped, that's all."

Mrs. Bemis eyed her. "You should be more careful." While she held Alice's hand, she turned it over to examine the back, too. "Beautiful," she said idly before finally releasing it. Alice sat back in her chair.

"I was young once, too, you know," Mrs. Bemis said.

Alice returned her gaze. The brittle hair, lined face, sunken eyes. "Of course you were," she said.

"Of course you *weren't,* you mean," Mrs. B snapped. "You young people, so caught up in yourselves. It's as if nothing ever happened before you came into the world! You see me here, hardly able to move, but I did things." She paused a moment. "Yes. I did."

"What things?"

The old woman turned away from her.

"Are you there?" Alice asked.

"Yes, of course I'm here." Mrs. B was looking about the room, taking in the dreary art, the meager furnishings. "Where else would I be?" She smoothed out her plaid skirt.

"You say you did things when you were young. Could we start there? What sorts of things?"

Her face had a faraway look. "Romantic things. Girl things. Mistaken things."

Alice tightened her fist around her bandaged palm as she leaned toward her patient. "Perhaps you should tell me about them?"

"Just the usual trifles." Mrs. Bemis shrugged. "He loves me, he loves me not."

"I'm not sure I follow. Is this a love affair you're speaking of? A first boyfriend?"

"Oh, what could it possibly matter now? It's nothing." Her voice was bitter.

"It's on your mind."

"Mind," she scoffed. "It's hardly a mind. A vacancy, more like. A nothingness." She looked up at Alice. "It's just wind inside me now."

The session continued for another half hour, but Alice made no further progress, encountering only Mrs. Bemis's usual evasions and half answers.

When their time was up, and they stood to go, a beam of afternoon light illuminated the red blouse she had on today and brought out the color in her cheeks.

"You are looking better, you know," Alice assured her patient as the two of them made for the door.

"Am I?" The thought seemed to cheer the old woman.

"A little brighter."

"Not my usual ghostly pallor?" she said wryly.

Afterward, Alice found herself returning to the advice of her long-ago professor: look for what's not there.

ten

Alice was finally drifting off to sleep that night when the phone rang, shattering the fragile peace of her apartment. She glanced over at the clock. Two-fifteen. Her first thought was that it had to be her mother calling back. Something was wrong at home. Then she was afraid it was Ethan.

But it was Victor. His tone was crisp, businesslike. "I think you'd better come in."

She pulled herself up onto one elbow. "Why, what's happened?"

"There's been an accident."

"*What?*"

"There's been an accident," he repeated. "That's all I should say right now."

"Mrs. Bemis? Is she—"

"She's . . . okay, Alice. She's fine."

"Then—?"

"Dr. Maris and I think you should come in. Please hurry."

• • •

The lamps along the walkways were on at Montrose when Alice pulled into the B lot, which was nearly vacant at a quarter of three. A slender moon shone dully through the overcast night sky, blurring the shadows from the lamplight that ran across the grass. A pair of police cruisers were idling by the door, their radios squawking.

Alice hurried through the front door, rode the elevator—she had her key this time—and stepped onto the ward. A policeman was interviewing Dr. Maris, a notebook in his hand. Dr. Maris was speaking slowly, quietly, his face pained. Alice met his eyes briefly, and he gave only the barest flicker of recognition as he ran his hand through his hair. She stepped through onto the ward. She was rarely here this late after dark, and she was surprised to see the blackness out the windows, the glare of the fluorescent light on the hallway floor. Groggy patients in pajamas and bathrobes were clumped in twos and threes in the hall, talking among themselves, their bodies slumped, their eyes anguished but watchful.

Alice searched among them for Mrs. Bemis, but didn't see her anywhere.

Instead, she found Victor in the hall by the nurses' station. "Oh, Alice," he said.

"Victor, what's going on?"

Victor sucked in some air through his nose. He beckoned her toward him. "It's Chris," he said quietly.

That was not the name she'd been expecting.

"He's hanged himself." He pursed his lips nervously.

The words weren't penetrating, but a bad feeling seeped into her chest all the same. "But—but that's not possible," Alice stammered. The hospital staff were careful to protect the residents from anything they might use to harm themselves.

"He used his bedsheets," Victor explained. "Twisted them into a rope, then hung himself from the top of the door. An ambulance just took the body away a few minutes ago. I didn't want to tell you over the phone because, well—I didn't think you'd want me to."

"Oh, God." Alice slumped against the wall. She thought of Chris B, the way he'd always looked for her, the portrait of her he'd drawn.

"It's bedlam in here. The new girl, Rose? She started wailing, just wailing, then everybody started flying. We're practically running out of sedatives." Victor looked like he could use one himself. His skin was pasty, and his temples were wet with sweat just below the edges of his frizzy hair. And his eyes had none of their usual clarity.

Victor noticed Alice glance toward Chris B's room. "Yeah, go ahead," he said. "Maybe it'll give you some . . . you know." He followed her down the hall.

The room was cordoned off with police tape, a chilling sight on the ward. But the door itself was still open. A lone inspector was inside, making notes. "He stood on that chair there," Victor said, pointing to a chair with metal legs just inside the room. "He hooked the sheet over the door here, tied the other end to the outside door handle, then kicked the chair away. Marnie found him."

"God," Alice said. "She okay?"

"Dr. Maris talked to her. She'll be all right."

She glanced inside the room once more; there was another picture on the floor by the bed. Chris's last? Alice recognized the strawlike hair and electric eyes as her own, but this time Chris had included her bare torso, with sharply pointed breasts and, instead of arms, a pair of huge black wings that nearly covered the page, making her look like a dark angel.

"Those damn satellites," she said.

"Yeah," Victor said. "I know."

He took Alice by the arm, turned her back toward the hall. "But look, Dr. Maris wanted me to have you check in on Madeline. He's worried about her. She's terribly withdrawn. Nearly catatonic. We gave her some Equanil, but she's still pretty wasted. She'd gotten close to Chris, you know."

Alice nodded. "I know. I've seen them together."

"She's in real bad shape. Keeps saying she wants you." He softened. "That's about the only thing she says."

Alice hesitated, looked back at Chris's room.

"Go on," Victor said. "There's nothing we can do about Chris now."

Mrs. Bemis lay in her nightgown on her bed, her hands folded on her stomach. There was a small framed photograph of an Alpine scene on the wall and a radio on the nightstand. Rita was sitting by the bed when Alice entered the room.

Alice glanced toward Rita to see how she thought their patient was doing, and Rita made a so-so gesture with her hand.

Alice turned to the old woman. "Mrs. Bemis?"

There was no answer. Alice stepped closer, bent over her on the bed. She could see that the old woman's eyes were open, but they were filmy, unseeing, as she stared at the ceiling. Alice called out her name again, and this time Mrs. Bemis slowly turned toward her and pulled her head back slightly on the pillow, as if she was having trouble focusing on something so close up.

"It's Dr. Matthews, Mrs. Bemis. How are you? You doing okay?"

Mrs. Bemis didn't answer right away. It seemed hard for her to get a word out.

Alice stepped closer, pulled a chair next to her bed, and sat down beside her.

"I'll leave you now, Doctor," Rita told Alice.

"It's awful," Mrs. Bemis said. "That poor boy."

"Yes, I know. I only found out myself. It's terrible."

"I should have—I should have done something."

Alice took Mrs. Bemis's hand, which was alarmingly cool to the touch. "There was nothing you could have done. There was nothing anyone could have done."

Mrs. Bemis turned away, toward the far wall.

"Mrs. Bemis, please." Alice reached for her again. Her nightshirt was sleeveless, and Alice touched the bare flesh under her arm. There was hardly any muscle; Alice could nearly feel the bone inside. She might have been one of the spotted puppies that, one winter when she was young, Alice's cranky Dalmatian had surprised her with—the fragile bones, the tiny, quivering heart. She could reach right into her.

Mrs. Bemis turned back toward Alice; her face was drawn with sorrow. "They all leave, don't they?"

"Who's left you, Mrs. Bemis? Do you mean Chris?"

"*Everyone.* I can't seem to hang on to anyone."

"Are you speaking of your husband?"

Mrs. Bemis ignored the question. She took a breath that made a rough sound in her chest. "I should have been the one to go. It should have been me."

Alice squeezed her knoblike shoulder. "You should try not to think that way."

"I'm no use to anyone. Do you know?" Mrs. Bemis's eyes found Alice's. "I have failed everyone I have ever known. I have no talent for living. None." She paused, took a breath. "Why, if I had an ounce of courage—" She stopped short.

"What?"

Mrs. Bemis rolled away from her again, but once more Alice reached for her.

"Are you thinking of harming yourself, Mrs. Bemis? I need to know." The hospital was very strict about this. Especially now. "Have you been thinking about suicide? Have you thought about what you might do?"

Mrs. Bemis fell silent.

"This is important, Mrs. Bemis. I can't leave you until you say."

Still nothing. Alice could sense her drifting away from her.

"Where are you?" She nearly whispered the words, so as not to jolt her. "Where have you gone?"

Silence. Alice eased back onto the chair again. She was getting nowhere. The two of them were wheeling about in a wide orbit. She pushed the chair back, to make some more space for herself so she could think.

There was a rustling of sheets, and Mrs. Bemis surprised her by swinging out an arm and clutching Alice's forearm. "Don't leave me. Not just yet. Would you mind? I'm an old grump, I know. A useless old grump. But stay, would you, for a moment?"

Her grasp was not tight, but Alice could feel the wanting in it.

"Of course I can. I'll sit beside you. Would that be all right?"

Mrs. Bemis shifted a bit to make room, and Alice settled herself on the edge of the bed. She was turned toward her patient. The way Alice was sitting, her hip touched Mrs. Bemis's ever so lightly through the covers. She bent down to her, close, like a mother with a frightened child. "What is it? What's wrong?"

"I have no one."

"You have friends. I hear you used to give remarkable parties."

"That was a long time ago." She clung to Alice's arm with her bony hand. "I scarcely see anyone now."

"No relatives, even? A cousin, perhaps?"

Mrs. Bemis shook her head. "No, no, no. Nothing." She released Alice's arm and clutched the blanket instead, worrying its frayed end. "I'm so tired. I have never been so tired."

Alice smiled at her. If Mrs. Bemis had been the Grand at her nursing home, she'd have stroked her hair. "Maybe you should try to get some sleep, then. I can get you a sleeping pill if you like. Would that be helpful to you? We can talk in the morning."

Mrs. Bemis lay back. "Yes. A pill," she said. "I need to rest now."

Rita came with the sleeping pill a few minutes later. But by then Mrs. B had closed her eyes and her chest was rising and falling with each slow breath. Lying there, her mouth in an inverted U, Mrs. Bemis looked so ancient, so serene. Alice returned to her seat by the bed. After the trauma of Ethan, and now the horror of Chris B, it was nice, a comfort, just the two of them, making some gentle progress together.

They might have been out in a boat on a lake on a calm evening, a full moon rising. Alice rowing, Mrs. Bemis riding behind, and only the sound of the oars dipping into the cool water as the boat glided ahead.

Alice thought of curling up on the couch in the day room. She didn't want to leave Mrs. Bemis. But it was nearly four, and she was exhausted. She'd be no good to anyone if she didn't sleep. So she made her way back outside to the parking lot, climbed into her little car, and headed home. The roads were nearly deserted, and she made good time and parked on a side street. She trudged up the front steps of her triple-decker, then passed through the front door and climbed to her apartment on the third floor.

A light burned in the kitchen. For a moment, she was afraid that Ethan had come back. She called out to him, tentatively, afraid she'd hear an answer, but none came. She poked her head in the kitchen, saw a juice glass still out on the kitchen table where she'd left it earlier in the evening. Fido was curled up sleepily in his mouse house on the counter. The living room was the same mess as before, with psychiatric journals piled up on the TV. "Ethan?" she called again, just to be sure. But no one answered.

The next morning, they were in the small conference room overlooking what had once been the topiary garden, off the old art studio. The garden must have been lovely at one time, but all that remained were a variety of rusting metal rods showing the outlines of different oversize birds.

"I'd like to get closer to you, Mrs. Bemis," Alice was saying. "I sense a certain protectiveness. A shell."

"You think I'm a crab," Mrs. Bemis replied. "Everyone does, eventually."

"That's not what I meant. I just think that it might help break the loneliness you spoke of last night."

"Last night was last night."

"And this morning?"

"Is this morning."

Mrs. Bemis eyed Alice for a moment, then gave the barest flicker of a smile. "That was a joke, incidentally," the old woman said. "It's a rarity, I know."

Alice smiled, and was grateful. It was an overture, a slight weakening of the force field that Mrs. Bemis had arrayed around her. "So——" Alice prompted, then stopped to let the silence gather.

Mrs. Bemis took a breath, and slowly released the air. Her face tipped down, and her shoulders fell. Finally, she slapped one hand over the other, in her lap. "All right, I'm feeling badly about that poor boy," she said.

It was startling how quickly the old woman's mood could switch. Like New England weather—storms one moment, sun the next.

"You two had become friendly."

She smiled weakly. "He was such a dear boy." She balled up her fist. "I hate using that word, 'was.'"

Mrs. Bemis brought a hand up to the side of her face, moved the loose flesh as though she wanted to remold herself. "Oh, it's so *awful!*" she said at last.

Alice thought Mrs. Bemis might cry. She hoped she would. "Take a moment, Mrs. Bemis. You're allowed to feel what you're feeling. It's okay."

Mrs. Bemis brought her hands together before her as if in prayer, and she inhaled another long, slow breath. Her frail body swelled with the air, but dwindled again as she exhaled.

"Go ahead," Alice reassured her. "Breathe a little. Let the feeling settle in. I can wait."

Mrs. Bemis looked at her therapist aslant. "You know sorrow, don't you, Alice?"

The observation pierced her. "Why do you say that?"

"A sufferer can always tell. You seem open to pain."

Alice felt again the sting of the cut on her palm, and something welled up inside her. She had to fight the urge to reach out and pull the fragile woman close. She knew it wasn't right. Not therapeutic, certainly not professional. "I try to be," she answered, trying to disguise the emotion in her voice. "Is that important to you?"

"I live with pain all day long. Sadness—the deepest kind of pain. The kind that lingers. Sometimes I think it's my only friend."

"I can be your friend, Mrs. Bemis."

Mrs. Bemis raised her eyes to Alice's.

"If you'll talk to me."

The two of them sat together quietly for what felt like a very long time while Alice waited for Mrs. Bemis to continue. Gradually, she grew more agitated, as if she were struggling with something. Finally, she spoke very quietly. "I shouldn't mislead you. It's not him. Not the boy. I mean—that's terrible. I do feel so *awful* for him. To die like that, to— But it's not the boy." She paused. "It's what he said to me."

Alice waited.

"I think he had a power. I do. The way he looked at me. It was as if he could see way down deep inside."

Alice remembered that feeling, how Chris B seemed to know her, what she'd done.

Mrs. Bemis continued. "Because of what he said to me. About that—that body."

"What body? The one in the water?"

Her patient nodded.

"*That's* been bothering you?"

Mrs. Bemis nodded again, more decisively this time.

Alice said nothing, waiting. But her patient simply looked away.

"Mrs. Bemis?"

"Tell me. Why? What does that mean to you?"

"No!" The word burst out of her. Her rough hands were at her face again, as if she were at war with herself. "You wouldn't understand."

"Then perhaps you could *help* me," Alice replied, with a calmness that she hoped would cover the frustration she felt. "Explain it to me, would you?"

Mrs. Bemis paused, then began again tentatively, her eyes everywhere but on Alice. "We talked about it, Chris and I. About the body."

Another pause. Alice let the silence linger, hoping it would push the conversation to a deeper place than any words could. It was a test of wills, hers and her patient's. In the end, Alice herself was the one to weaken. "Please, Mrs. Bemis, you must know, Chris was suffering a severe schizophrenic breakdown. He was—"

"Oh, I know all that," Mrs. Bemis interrupted. "He was bent on killing himself long before I came along."

"Well, then, you see?"

Mrs. Bemis fixed Alice with her gaze.

"He said that when he looked at me, he saw death," Mrs. Bemis said.

Alice was sure that she must have misunderstood.

"Yes, death. 'Death in the water.' Those were the words he used. He looked into my eyes, and that's what he said. I'm telling you, it was as if he could see inside me, as if he could see something right in my eyes."

"Had you seen it? The body?"

Mrs. Bemis was silent for a moment. "No." Alice expected an exclamation, a protest. But the word came out almost as a sigh.

"'Death in the water,'" she repeated.

"What do you suppose he meant by it? That could mean almost anything."

"I knew exactly what he meant. I knew. Please, don't ask me how I knew. But I knew."

"Mrs. Bemis, what are you trying to tell me?"

A long pause. Alice could hear steps down the hall, the wind outside.

Her words were nearly all breath. "I knew about the body. I knew who it was, what it was." She turned away.

"Speak to me, Mrs. Bemis. Please be clear. What do you mean? You knew that man?" Alice flashed back to what Donnie had said. "Brendan?" Wasn't that his name?

"Excuse me. No. I can't do this." She looked away, twisted her fingers, agony on her face. "I'm sorry. This was a terrible idea. I should never have come here."

A frightening thought surfaced in Alice's mind and grew. "Who is he, Mrs. Bemis? How do you know him? Please, speak to me."

The old woman brought her arms around herself as if she suddenly felt a chill.

"What's happening, Mrs. Bemis? What's wrong?"

Maddy

eleven

*H*e came into her life so suddenly. For years and years, he hadn't been there, and then he was—

Or was he? Was he ever there? It was so brief, so achingly brief, she couldn't say for sure. It all might have been a dream—a vivid, beautiful dream that left her touching her fingertips to her cheeks in the morning, trying to recall his hands on her.

It was a gray, windy day that promised a rainstorm. The hemlocks were thrashing about in front of the house, throwing shadows across the cobalt-blue Persian rug in the living room, where Maddy was flipping through the latest *Collier's*. She was on vacation, bored silly. A whole week and only one party, at the insufferable Molly Linden's, with talk solely of the war. If Maddy heard one more word about the war, she was going to scream.

She was terribly behind on her letters to Ronnie, and it was nagging at her. She kept seeing his plane up there, laden with bombs, pushing through the clouds in the moonlight. No one could possibly respond to all of his letters. Besides, she had nothing to tell him! He had his bombing runs, his close calls, his crewmates, and all the funny, sad things they said. What did she have to write about except a stupid party at Molly Linden's? There were her doubts and worries, of course. But she certainly wasn't going to bother him with those, not when he had so many more important things to worry about. She had nothing she could tell *anyone*. That was the problem, wasn't it: there was the her that everyone thought she was and the her that she was. And they were so completely different. That was her big secret, one she kept to herself, making herself miserable. She, Maddy Adams, who tried so hard always to be the cheery one!

He arrived with a sound, too. A chimes. Yes, those tinkling chimes that her mother had installed on the front door the previous fall in a rare burst of high spirits.

In those years, an unexpected visitor could give people a fright: the heavy tread on the step, the quiet words, the grave expression . . . But when the chimes sounded that afternoon, Maddy's heart pulsed with excitement, with the prospect of release. She might have been a caged bird. She heard Bridget go rustling by the living room door in her uniform—gray, with white ruffles—as she crossed the hall to the door.

Maddy shifted on the couch there in the living room to get a better angle. A gust of wind lifted Bridget's skirts when she opened the door, but Maddy couldn't see who it was who'd come to call. Bridget spoke a few words that Maddy couldn't hear, then closed the door and went into the library where Maddy's mother was talking on the telephone.

Maddy worked herself into a state from not knowing. Finally she called out, "Who is it?"

"No one important," said Bridget, who could be difficult sometimes.

"Bridget," Maddy wailed.

"A young fella," she said dismissively. "Wanted work."

"Here?"

"Yes." Bridget eyed her, and Maddy detected a flicker of suspicion in her gaze. "He seemed a bit common, but your mother's been needing someone. I told him to come 'round to the back." She turned away, toward the kitchen, throwing these last words over her shoulder. "When your mother's off the phone, she'll go have a talk with him."

Normally, Maddy would have let it go. Workmen came by the house seeking employment from time to time. But this was her vacation, and she hadn't had any fun in months. Besides, there was that word "young."

How young? she wondered.

Maddy waited until her mother had passed through the hall, then slipped off her shoes and stole across to the dining room. There was a view of the back door from there, out the bay window. She pulled back the velvet drapes, and there he was, the young workman, standing by the coal chute. He couldn't have been much older than herself. Twenty at the absolute most. He didn't look like any of the boys she knew, and not at all like Ronnie. He seemed rougher somehow, darker. Obviously someone who spent a lot of time in the out-of-doors. His chin was darkened by a bit of a beard; he had a funny way of squinting against the light. His shirtsleeves were rolled up to expose slender forearms that were not at all the bulky, hairy things she'd come to expect from workmen, and he wore snug and well-worn dungarees that were quite revealing in their way. She imagined him to be some kind of artist—a sculptor perhaps—and that he was doing this just for the money. (But then, Maddy scarcely knew anyone who absolutely *had* to work.)

When she pulled herself back from the windowpane, her breath had fogged the glass.

The young man started to speak, bashfully at first, although Maddy couldn't hear what he was saying, his head angled down. The conversation lasted only a minute or so, and then Mother stepped into view and led him back toward the big, shingled barn behind the house. They made an unlikely couple: Mother in that gaily patterned dress she liked to wear at the first hint of summer, and the young man in his work clothes. It was a gusty day, with occasional rays of bright sunshine bursting through the heavy clouds, and the wind whipped at them as they made their way across the drive, Mother holding fast to her hairdo.

Maddy returned to the living room and tried to lose herself in her magazine, but it was no use. Everything seemed so close—the infernal gold clock ticking there on the mantel, and the big mirror above throwing her own image back at her whenever she looked at it. She needed air, space. She considered telephoning Ellen, just to talk to someone, to catch up on what little gossip there was. And she had some Chopin mazurkas to work on; she'd been planning to play them at Mr. Bernheim's end-of-the-year concert in June.

"I set him to work in the asparagus bed," she heard her mother say to Bridget. "Douglas hasn't been able to attend to it." Douglas was their gardener, but for the last few months he'd been slowed by arthritis that acted up in cold weather.

"Very good, mum."

Maddy heard the door to the kitchen swing shut, then the click of her mother's heels as she returned to the library. To the telephone again, where even through the door Maddy could hear her address her bridge partner, Doris, in an enthusiastic voice she rarely used in person.

Outside, the wind continued to swirl. The thick rhododendron bushes off the patio were rustling, and the hemlock branches were twisting all about.

Maddy stood up and went to the Steinway. There was a big window by it, and she could see the young man's head and shoulders above the picket fence that bounded the asparagus bed. He must have been digging: she saw him bob and strain to a jerky rhythm, although no shovel was evident from her angle. Maddy took in the movement of his upper arms and shoulders as he worked, his head dipping, rising.

• • •

Is that when it began? Or had it already started, even before he'd arrived? Or was it later? Or did it never really begin at all? All in her imagination, nothing to it in the least?

She went to the front hall. "I'm just going outside for a little," she called out to her mother.

"Fine, dear," her mother shouted back. She was still on her call.

Maddy grabbed a light coat, the pale-blue one that set off her eyes, and stepped out the front door. The sun had broken through. It was suddenly quite bright for a cool day, and she wished that her parents let her wear dark glasses. It was ridiculous to be so restrictive of a teenager, especially one they were so obviously trying to marry off. She thought she might look like Ingrid Bergman if she had a pair.

The house was set back from the street, with that row of heavy hemlocks out the front, the branches tossing wildly. A storm was coming, surely. She passed through the side gate into the small yard where her father had once tried to interest her in playing catch. The daffodils were there, a whole flock of them, their yellow heads tipped down demurely.

What was that young man up to?

The barn door was open, and it knocked against the side of the building in the wind. Maddy wondered when the young man would go shut it. Wasn't that part of his job, to be helpful like that? But she watched him continue with his shoveling, as though nothing else existed. She'd have to shut the door herself.

She dabbed at her hair again. It was awful the way the wind sent it skittering about. She must be a sight! She should have worn a hat, but she looked terrible in hats. Oh! Her mind was in such a flutter. This thing, that thing, the other . . . She had to get hold of herself before she turned into a flibbertygibbet like that Molly Linden, whom nobody would pay any attention to at all if it weren't for the luscious pink champagne she served on the sly at her parties.

She continued on down the driveway, in a slow, sauntering, not-doing-anything-in-particular kind of way, her hands behind her, scarcely noticing the small, formal garden to her right with roses set about an Italian fountain that hadn't yet been turned on for the season. She was concentrating on the young man. As she neared the asparagus bed, she got her first good look at him. Maddy could see the sweat starting to glisten on the side of his face, and to darken his shirt in the middle of his back up around his shoulders. He was wielding a shovel, she could see now, but he must not have heard her coming. He continued to fling the dirt off the shovel to a pile on the far side of the asparagus garden, where it landed with a *woomp.*

She should not be the one to speak first, she knew that much.

She continued along to the barn, but more slowly, her mind weighed down by questions: Would it be *so* awful to speak to him? To say hello? Ask his name?

War or no, she was not used to addressing the men who helped out around the house. When Charles drove her, she politely answered any question he might put to her, but she never asked him any questions of her own. The idea! As for their gardener, Douglas, well, she didn't believe she'd ever said a word to Douglas. But this man was so much younger, practically her age, and attractive in a foreign, rough-and-tumble sort of way. Was he Irish? She suspected so, based on the way that Bridget was so curt with him. She could be hard on her own.

She passed a little closer by the asparagus bed than absolutely necessary. She longed to speak to this workman, if only for practice. She'd have to speak to all sorts someday. When she ran her own house, perhaps. Or Ronnie's.

Coming closer, she could see a few rows of the asparagus shoots poking up out of the dark earth on the far side of the garden. Despite the wind, she could hear him breathe. But she couldn't think what to say. Excuse me?

She stopped by the fence, staring at the young man quite openly, her heart knocking against her ribs. His back was turned to her as he continued to work.

She coughed into her hand.

He stopped, turned. His eyes took her in, but he gave her only a nod and returned to his shoveling.

"Hello," Maddy said.

He kept at his work. Deliberately?

"I was going to shut the barn door," Maddy called out to him, above the wind. "It was banging in the wind."

He stopped and looked over toward the barn. "Okay then." He had a deep voice, much deeper than Ronnie's, with a trace of an Irish lilt. Was he dismissing her? That possibility hadn't occurred to her.

"I'm Maddy Adams," she persisted. "I think you spoke to my mother."

"So you live here?"

Suddenly, she didn't think she should be proud of that fact. "Yes, I was born here. Well, not here. In a hospital. In Boston." He had her so twisted about! "I've lived here all my life since, is what I mean."

The young man looked past Maddy to the house behind her. Maddy, too, glanced back.

"It's a big house," he said.

"Yes, I suppose." She'd never thought about it. All her friends lived in large houses, many of them larger than hers. "You didn't tell me your name."

"No, I didn't."

"Well?" Was he toying with her?

"It's Gerald." A smile, finally.

"I'm pleased to meet you, Gerald," Maddy said, using her best manners. She extended a hand, and, when he shook it, she was struck by the leathery roughness of his skin. "I don't see too many boys my age anymore."

"Why, how old are you?" he asked, a bit forwardly. Unlike Bridget's harsh brogue, his accent, with its rumbled *r*s, sounded musical to her.

"Almost eighteen."

"I'll be twenty come December." Gerald was leaning on his

shovel now, eyeing her. She couldn't imagine how she appeared to him, especially with her hair all mussed.

"Well, we're close enough." Something about him made her want to laugh, and she felt the beginnings of a smile tug at the corners of her mouth. "You'll have to excuse me. You must think I've been drinking." She raised her hand to her face, stuck a knuckle in her mouth—*what was she saying?* If Ellen heard about this conversation, she'd howl! "I'm not usually like this."

"Oh, yeah? What are you like?"

That was *definitely* forward.

"I'm not sure I should tell you. You'll have to guess."

He didn't pursue the question. "I doubt you've ever been drunk anyway." He started digging again. A long trench, Maddy could see now. She should move on, but she couldn't bring herself to take that first step away from him.

"So why aren't you off at war?" she asked.

"Bum foot."

Maddy didn't understand at first, and nearly asked him to repeat that. But then she looked down and saw that his right foot was encased in a special shoe that had a buckle on it instead of laces. That foot was also a good two inches shorter than the other. The deformity was a shock. Why hadn't she noticed any limp? "Oh, goodness, I'm sorry."

"Had it my whole life. I'm used to it by now. It's saved me from getting my head blown off anyway."

"You didn't *want* to go to war?" Maddy had never heard anyone voice that opinion, although, frankly, it seemed quite sensible.

"The Germans never did anything to me."

"What do your parents say about that?"

He looked at her as if she was daft. "Nothing."

"Surely they must have said *something,*" Maddy persisted. Her parents had opinions on everything she did. Negative opinions, usually.

"My dad's not around, and my mother died when I was little."

He eyed her, some suspicion in his face. "My aunt raised me, but the man she was living with threw me out of the house when I turned fourteen. He said it was time I was on my own. He was right about that. I hated it there."

"So where do you live?"

"Here and there." He looked at her again, his head tipped slightly so that his eyes weren't level. "Why d'you ask?"

"I've never known anyone who didn't have parents before."

"Believe me, lots of people don't have parents."

There was a curtness to those words that she took as her cue to push on, although, as far as she was concerned, their business was not finished. She still had questions for this Gerald, hundreds of them. But she continued on to the barn door, secured it, then passed by the asparagus bed again on her way back to the house. He'd returned to his digging, but this time, he stopped a moment to watch her pass. She could feel his gaze warming the side of her body that was nearest to him. "Well, 'bye now," she said, in a whispery voice that she hardly recognized, and then, on inspiration, wiggled her fingers in a manner she'd seen Ingrid Bergman do in *June Night.*

He said nothing back, just watched her go.

As it happened, Bridget served asparagus that night at dinner. It was tender and flavorful and it reminded Maddy of Gerald, each bite. That night, after she went up to her room and closed and then locked the door, she pulled back the bedsheets again. But this time, instead of Ronnie, it was Gerald she thought of as she pressed her pillow up between her knees. She was astonished by how easy it was to summon him, beautiful, sly Gerald, his slim body bathed in the moonlight that streamed in the window, bending to her, breathing soft words to her with rolling *r*s. She felt him easing down between her legs, felt him inside. Her own breath turned husky, and her inside part started to burn like it never had before, and she could feel the sweat in her armpits and in the hollow between her breasts as she grabbed onto the edge of the mattress and squeezed her thighs together until, for the first time ever, she burst inward with a gasp. All the while thinking of beautiful, sly Gerald, whom she hardly knew.

twelve

For days she could not stop thinking about that Gerald, even though there was nothing to think about him. Nothing sensible or decent anyway. It was all idle frivolity. Absurd! And so utterly wrong—and unfair to Ronnie, whose letters continued to pile up on the little table by her bed. Her thoughts about Gerald, they were like that wonderful sticky stuff she'd had as a child when Ellen's family had taken her to the circus at Boston Garden. What was it? Cotton candy. Yes. Sweet, and delightful in its pastel colors, and yet, nothing. Nothing at all. Just an airy sweetness that, as her mother told her more than once, rotted the teeth and who knew what else. That was Gerald, and her wild ideas about him. Still—

Gerald came every day that week. It took him two days to dig out all the creepers that had sneaked into the asparagus bed, and to make room for two more rows next spring. Then Mother had him repaint the shutters by the laundry and, finally, fill in a pothole at the mouth of the driveway. With Father off at work, and Mother so busy organizing her bridge tournament at the club, Maddy spent a good deal of time by herself mooning about the house—all the while trying to dodge suspicious looks from Bridget. She tried to work on her mazurkas, but she couldn't get the rhythm right, and each time she ended up banging down the piano lid. Just for something to do, Maddy found herself checking various windows for the best view of Gerald as he worked. On Wednesday, from the sewing room upstairs, she got a good look at his shoulders and the back of his neck. But on Thursday, from the third-floor guest room, she could see nearly down to his waist.

It wasn't until Friday, however, that Maddy ventured outside again to see him close up. Gerald was working on the pothole that day. It was blazing hot, nearly eighty, and, gazing at him from one window or another, Maddy could see that Gerald had rolled his sleeves up clear to his shoulders, and he'd undone several of the buttons down the front. Still, the sweat darkened the shirt under his arms and in a patch across his chest. It was about three, and it looked as if he might be finished soon, and Maddy wasn't sure if Mother had any more jobs for him that might bring him back again the next week. In a panic, Maddy realized that this might be her very last chance to speak to him.

She decided her best plan was to go have a root-beer float at Mr. Beebe's, the town drugstore, since it would make perfect sense for her to walk right by Gerald both going and coming. Feeling daring on a vigorous spring afternoon, she changed out of her tan slacks and into her loose red shorts, the ones she sometimes exercised in. They ended well above the knee, and they'd held Ronnie's gaze, at least. And, instead of the starchy white shirt that drained all the color from her face, she pulled on a tight blue sleeveless blouse that she'd had to beg her mother to buy for her when they'd gone shopping last month at Mrs. Wexell's darling little shop off Newbury Street. And she put on some lipstick, and gave her cheeks a squeeze to bring some extra color to them. When that didn't quite work, she rubbed in a tiny dab of lipstick, as she'd once seen Ellen do.

She grabbed her pocketbook, the one with the long, thin strap that dangled down to her hip, and, with a shout of explanation to her mother (on the phone as usual), she set out the front door. As she watched Gerald struggle with a wheelbarrow, Maddy wished she'd thought to use, to command his attention, some of that new perfume she'd received for Christmas from Aunt Meredith in New York. Gerald didn't stop, although he must have noticed her, and Maddy charged right on past him.

In her frustration, she was in no mood for a root-beer float when she reached the drugstore. Rather, she took a quick turn about town, pausing only by the Community Theater to examine the poster for the new movie, *Thirty Seconds Over Tokyo,* with that dreamboat Clark Gable. Then she headed back.

She slowed on the sidewalk under the hemlocks by her driveway, to sweep a few stray hairs back off her forehead, tuck in her shirt, and pinch her cheeks again, all the while assuring herself that whatever happened would be for the best. If he said nothing to her, and she had to keep right on back to the big, lonely house, well, that was the way it was.

She turned in the drive. To her frustration, Gerald's back was to her as he poured some pebbles from the heavy sack into the gap in the driveway. And, despite the loud noise her shoes made on the driveway, he didn't notice her.

But she *couldn't* just go past him, not after all the effort she'd made.

"Hello," she said.

He stopped pouring, turned. She could feel his eyes travel down her body as he took in her clingy blue top, her red shorts. "Well, hello to you, too." He set the bag back down and straightened up. "Maddy, is it?"

She nodded. It was exciting that he remembered. She loved hearing him say her name.

"Pain in the ass job, this." He firmed up the bag to keep it from toppling, then straightened up again and reached into his shirt pocket for a pack of cigarettes. He tipped a Lucky toward her. It was provocative, the way the end of it poked out.

"I better not," Maddy said. "My parents." She bit her lip.

"What, they don't let you smoke?"

Maddy nodded.

"What else don't they let you do?"

"Lots of things." She frowned. "You'd be surprised."

He waited, obviously curious.

"Like talk to boys like you, for one."

"Boys like me," he repeated. "Oh, I see." He smiled and brought the package to his mouth and drew a cigarette out with his lips, a move that also commanded her attention, especially the way his bicep bulged as he raised his arm. He fished a pack of matches out of his pocket and lit up his cigarette between his cupped hands, then tipped his head back, hollowed his cheeks, and took a long, satisfied drag. Maddy's mouth felt dry, watching him.

He looked back at her. "Might I put a question to you, Maddy?"

She touched her hair, afraid that it had slipped down over her forehead again, making her look younger than she really was. "Why no, I don't suppose so."

"Now, I don't mean to frighten you. It's something that just occurred to me."

"All right."

Gerald took another puff off his cigarette and released a potent stream of smoke into the warm air. "I was just going to ask— Do you like music?"

She hesitated a moment, unsure of what she might be committing herself to. "Of course." Then she caught herself, afraid she'd misunderstood. "Why, what kind of music do you mean?"

"Irish music."

"*Irish* music." The term ran around and around in Maddy's head, but it found no home.

"With fiddles and pennywhistles. Dance music. You know."

Maddy surely didn't. "Oh, that."

"D'you suppose you'd like to hear some? Some of the fellas are playing in Jamaica Plain. Maybe we could go together, if you'd like."

Gerald might have lunged for her, the invitation was that brazen.

"You mean, just the two of us?" Maddy asked, trying to keep her voice calm. She'd never gone anywhere alone with a boy before. Not even with Ronnie. That sort of thing wasn't done, not at her age. At least, that was her parents' opinion, one quite strongly expressed on a number of occasions. And it appeared to be one that Ronnie's parents shared. How else to explain the fact that not once had Ronnie asked to take her to the Chanticleer Club downtown, which any number of her girlfriends had been to with beaux of one sort or another. Even Ellen had been there with that George Loomis, and she couldn't stop talking about the piano player there, the baby-faced one who sang show tunes in falsetto.

"I've got a car," Gerald added, "if that's what you're wondering about."

"No, it's just—"

"What?" Gerald looked down at his shirt, which was dark and fragrant with sweat. "Listen, I've got other clothes, if that's what you're wondering." He laughed, as if she had to know that.

"Oh, I'm sure—"

A shadow crossed his features. "Listen, I understand. Never mind then." He tossed his cigarette down onto the driveway and stamped it out, although it was hardly smoked. He reached for the sack of pebbles again.

She wanted to tell him about Ronnie, and about her parents, and what they expected of her—or at least what she imagined they expected of her. That was never specified, but it surely did not include her involvement with anyone like Gerald, with his lovely rolled *r*s and his bum foot and the tight muscles of his shoulders and back and quite possibly elsewhere, too. Muscles that she might like to feel, to explore— No, Gerald was all wrong for her. That was the point. He was everything that she was not, and that her future was not. And she realized with a terrible thud of her heart how much she hated what she was, and what she would be, and how she wished she could be some-body—anybody—else. And in her desperation, Maddy nearly cried out—but instead she did something far more drastic. She reached for him. Her palm skidded across a rough cheek before her fingers sunk into his thick black hair just up from his neck. "Oh, Gerald, God," she said. The words came out part sigh, part laugh. And she regretted them the moment they had left her, because they were all wrong, just as he was. But she couldn't stop now. She pushed herself closer to him, reaching for him, pulling her face up to his, opening up to him. His features blurred as she drew close. He went soft, almost vaporous, like a mirage. But she could feel his thick chest pressing against hers, and even though he might be ruining her beautiful shirt, she was so glad to feel him there. But then—

His hands were on her bare arms, and he was freeing himself from her grasp.

"Maddy," he was saying, the strangest look on his face. "Don't embarrass me now."

Embarrass *him?* What was he saying?

"Don't you want to kiss me?" she asked. Boys like him always wanted to kiss girls like her, didn't they? The caddies at the country club, the boys who pumped gas, she'd seen them look at her in her nice clothes with her hair all brushed.

"I don't know if I do."

Maddy stepped away from him, back onto the lawn beside the driveway, and she drew her arm up to hide her face. She could feel her cheeks burn. She saw her whole life float away up into the clouds. "I just thought you'd—"

"What?"

"I just thought you'd want to, that's all."

She was the most pathetic creature that ever there was. She was the worst sort of tramp, throwing herself at an Irish workman, and her Ronnie, as fine a boy as there was, up in the sky getting shot at.

"I'm sorry, terribly sorry." She heard a buzzing in her ears, and her knees buckled, and she nearly tumbled onto the grass, but his hands were on her, strong hands, just under her ribs, pressing in, holding her close. His smell, a man's smell, held her, too.

"Easy there."

She felt him against her. "I shouldn't—"

"Now, now," he told her. "Don't you worry about it any. You were just trying to flatter me."

He ran his hand over her head. She couldn't think how such a rough hand could be so soft. And then he spoke, quietly, in her ear. "How about the music, then?"

And that's how it had begun, if, indeed, it ever had begun.

Gerald was finishing up the last of his work at the house that afternoon, but he would come back for her the next evening, and they'd go out for some of his Irish music. He'd wait for her in a green Pontiac a short ways down her street. "It might be better if your parents didn't know," he'd told her quietly. She'd nodded, her heart pounding.

She scarcely slept that night, and, the whole next day, it was hopeless to work on her mazurkas, to read, to eat, or to think of anything else but Gerald. Her mind was like a hurricane, every thought swirling about. The wild, fiery ideas she had at night, when she lay naked in bed with her pillow between her legs—those were the only ideas she had. She could scarcely sit in a chair, she was so keyed up. And there was absolutely no one she could talk to about it, either. Her friend Ellen sensed that something was up when she called to chat that afternoon. Maddy must have tried to get her off the phone a little too quickly, because Ellen immediately asked, "Nothing's happened to Ronnie, has it?"

At that moment, Ronnie was the last person Maddy wanted to think about. "No, he's fine," she quickly replied.

"You must be worried sick about him," Ellen said.

The notion plagued her. Of course she *should* be worried.

"Yes," Maddy assured her friend, even as her mind drifted away. "All the time."

At dinner that night, Maddy's father and mother sat at opposite ends of the table, with Maddy on one side, her back to the window, which was open to the evening breeze. Maddy ate little and said almost nothing. When Bridget brought in some orange tarts for dessert, along with the demitasses, Maddy told her parents that she would be retiring early. Her father didn't reply. He'd often seemed preoccupied at meals lately, between business and the war, his face like granite. She wasn't even sure he'd heard. But her mother looked at her for a moment as if she had guessed her secret. "Yes, you do seem tired."

Upstairs, Maddy locked the door behind her just to be safe, then changed into a loose silk skirt and a darling pale-blue cashmere sweater that she'd bought with Aunt Meredith in New York last fall. Then she raised the window to its full height, lifted the screen, and climbed out onto the trellis Douglas had installed for some climbing roses that, in fact, had never succeeded there. She gingerly stepped out onto the top rail, then eased her full weight down. It held, thank goodness, and she climbed down like a fireman on a ladder, feeling adventurous and ridiculous, both, finally flinging herself over the rhododendrons onto the grass.

She was panting when she reached the street.

A large, rusty car was parked by the far curb. A Pontiac. That made her heart race. She approached it, peered into the shadows inside. A figure was scrunched down on the driver's side, a cap pulled down over his face. Gerald. It frightened her, seeing him there. He seemed like a complete stranger! Still, she tapped on the glass with her fingernail, and he turned to her, his eyes up under the brim of his cap, a grin on his face, and he leaned over and swung open the passenger door for her. The dome light flashed a moment, lighting up his tan cap and plaid shirt. "Just having a rest," he told her. "I wasn't sure you'd come."

"Of course I would."

Why hadn't he thought so? Shouldn't she have come?

Maddy climbed in beside him and pulled the door shut after her. The car smelled oily, not at all like the Studebaker, and there was a gash in the upholstery of the front seat, which was lumpy and uncomfortable as well.

"Any trouble with your folks?" Gerald asked.

The seat was so wide; it made her feel small.

"They think I'm in bed."

A smile spread across his face, and that cheered her.

"Oh, very good, Maddy. Very good indeed." He switched on the ignition, and the car started up with a roar that seemed to shatter the quiet of the street and gave her nerves a spasm. The car lurched forward as he released the clutch, sending her backward, but once he was out on the street, the engine calmed, and Maddy did, too, somewhat. Still, the Pontiac didn't seem nearly as secure as her parents' Studebaker, which always seemed to have a tight grip on the asphalt. The car seemed to glide a bit over the road. Gerald drove with just one hand, low, on the steering wheel. His other arm was up over the seat back, the hand near her shoulder, almost touching her.

When they came to a light, Gerald rolled on his seat and took out a small flask from his hip pocket. "Here," he said, pushing the flask toward her. "You might be wantin' some of this."

Maddy instinctively shook her head. "Oh, no. I'm fine, thanks."

He handed her the flask again. "Go on, just a little."

In the glare of the streetlight, Maddy could see her bare knees clenched together below the hem of her light skirt, and her joints did feel tight. Perhaps she could use some, after all. "Maybe a sip," she told him.

She took the bottle from him, tipped it to her lips. The liquor was as thick as cough syrup, but it had a definite bite. Nothing like the frothy champagne she was used to at Molly Linden's. This burned her lips and throat as it went down. "Strong." She wiped her lips with her index finger.

"You think so, do you?" He seemed amused again, although she couldn't quite guess why. There was a lightness to his voice, and a sparkle in his eyes when he looked over at her. Ronnie had never seemed to be amused by her, even when she was trying to be funny.

"You don't have a fella or anything like that," Gerald said. "I wouldn't want to—"

"Gosh, no," she said. "There's no one." Out the window, the houses flew away behind.

"You hear about girls whose boys have gone off to war, how they like to play around with whoever's around."

"I wouldn't!" Maybe it was the liquor, but the word came out with an Irish accent. It sounded funny coming out of her, and she giggled before she bit down.

"What, you're laughing at me now?" Gerald asked. They were stopped at a light, other cars gathered around them.

"I'm just amusing myself," Maddy teased. "Since you're not amusing me."

"Oh, that's what I'm supposed to do?"

She was definitely feeling the whiskey now. "Girls like to be amused when 'fellas' take them out for a drive in their cars." That brought out another giggle. Maddy was starting to take real pleasure in this rundown car with its lumpy front seat and the funny man at the wheel taking her God knew where.

"Do they," Gerald said.

Maddy had expected the music to be played in a hall of some kind, or possibly a club, so she was surprised when Gerald turned off a main avenue that sliced through Jamaica Plain. At least, she supposed it was Jamaica Plain. She wouldn't have been able to find Jamaica Plain on a map. After two or three more turns, Gerald pulled up by a white frame house. Some lights were on inside, revealing some small, sad rooms with almost nothing on the walls. Several cars and a few small trucks were parked along the street; a couple of them had pulled up right onto the lawn in front of the house. But Gerald turned into the slender driveway and drove past the house and then turned onto the rough grass behind and parked under a clothesline, laden with towels and trousers and even some under things, that ran between some trees.

"You sure this is all right?" Maddy asked.

"Why wouldn't it be? I live here."

"*Here?*"

"It's not much, but it's enough for me." He climbed out of the car and came around to open the door for her. He reached for her hand, which Maddy found gallant, although Gerald acted as if it were nothing special. She'd had several more sips of the liquor by now, was feeling looser than ever. She figured she could fly if she merely flapped her arms.

She looked at the house, a lean maple beside it.

"All by yourself in that big house?" Maddy asked. "Isn't that expensive?"

"It's a boardinghouse, Maddy. An Irish family runs it. There are six of us now. I'm up there on the very top." He pointed up to a small, dark window on the third floor. "That one there's mine."

Maddy could hear the music, now that they were outside the car. It wasn't coming from inside the house, but from farther up the drive. There was a garage of some kind up there; some other people were walking in that direction. A few of them were older, in their thirties at least, but several were plainly teenagers like herself. In their dark clothes, none of them was the sort of person that Maddy was used to, and, despite the liquor, they made her grateful that Gerald held her hand as he strode ahead, pulling her on toward the music. It was fast and high, accompanied by occasional *whoops* of enthusiasm from the listeners, who spilled out onto the grass from in front of the open doors. Maddy was conscious of his tugging her closer and closer to the light, with this spirited music, and these strange people who weren't dressed as she was. Her skirt felt thin, all of a sudden, and a chill ran up her legs, and she braced herself and drew Gerald back toward her.

"What?" Gerald asked.

"I'm not sure I want to just now," Maddy said. More people went by just then, and she saw a cold look in their eyes as they looked at her. "Can't we walk a little instead?"

Gerald paused a moment, looked up ahead, then turned back to her once more. "If you want."

The moon had come up, coating everything with its sugary light. Maddy had never been in a neighborhood where the houses were so tight together. She wasn't sure she could walk, she'd gotten so light-headed from the whiskey, but gradually her mind settled back down into her body and she started to feel good again, happy. As she strolled about with Gerald close beside her—so close that she could hear his clothes rustle with each step—picking up laughter from front porches, passing couples necking on benches in tiny parks, even spotting a few kids swimming in Jamaica Pond, she decided that Jamaica Plain was better than Dover, friendlier and more open. Gerald held her hand as they walked, and they walked slowly, savoring the gusts of mild air. She was aware of the hitch to his gait; she could feel it in his hand, the way it halted slightly when he stepped down on his shorter foot, but it didn't matter. Nothing mattered.

And she talked. A blue streak about everything and nothing, and, with Gerald there listening so attentively to it all, it was hard to tell which was which. Maddy confided about how Ellen bothered her sometimes, and that led her to admit that she'd always found Ellen's family snooty. "As if they're so important," she said. She'd never really thought along these lines before, but being with Gerald changed her. She held his hand tighter, and made him promise not to repeat any of this, ever, and then told him that she'd lately found her mother to be so irritating, too, the way she seemed to care more about her standing in the bridge club than she did about Maddy, and how frustrating it was to have a father like hers, so remote, always preoccupied with his business. "As if it matters," she told Gerald. "Sometimes I wish I could just run away," she told him, holding his hand, delighting in the sensation of each of his fingers closed around hers. "Don't you?"

"Maybe it's just as well I don't have parents," Gerald joked.

"I'm serious! I *hate* them!"

"I'm sure you do."

They walked along in silence a little longer, watching their shadows angle off ahead of them in the moonlight. "So what happened to yours?" Maddy asked. "Your parents, I mean."

He'd never known his mother, who died of "breathing trouble" when he was three, shortly after they'd come over from Dublin, and then his father left him with his mother's sister while he went to Chicago to find a job.

"And then?" Maddy asked.

Gerald shrugged. "Never heard from him again. I think he wanted to be rid of me, if you want to know."

"But that's awful!" Maddy gave his hand a squeeze.

"It's not so bad. I barely knew him," Gerald said bravely. "He's nothing to me."

They were standing together now under the street lamp, and he was holding her left hand in both of his, stroking it. "It's kind of you to come out with me like this, you know."

That was when she'd told him about Ronnie. She felt she had to. She spoke quietly, solemnly, her eyes down. She told him that what she'd said earlier, in the car, wasn't quite true. She did have a boy, a flyer . . . Gerald did not let go of her hand.

"Do you love him, Maddy?" he asked, finally.

"Oh, I don't know! I know I'm supposed to! Everybody makes it sound like I should. But I think of him and—oh, Gerald, I just don't know! Sometimes I think I absolutely hate him! Just hate him!" She felt the warm touch of his hand. "Hate *everyone!*"

"But why?"

Maddy fell toward him just then, pushed her face into his chest. "Oh, I don't know!"

"Easy now," he told her. "It's all right. You're not supposed to know."

"You think?" Tears were trickling down her face now, which was stupid.

"Oh yes, I think."

"Oh, Gerald. I just want to be with *you*."

"With me?"

"Is that so awful?"

"Of course not." He waited a moment. "But, I'm wondering, d'you think you'd ever love me?"

She just looked at him then, saw that dark face with its wonderful darting eyes and said, "Oh, Gerald, God!" And she pulled him toward her and threw her arms around his neck.

Finally, Gerald whispered that it was getting late, and he should probably be getting her home. They passed the garage on the way back to his car. The lights were still on, but the band had broken up, and most of the people had gone. One of the musicians was just putting away his fiddle. He couldn't have been much more than thirteen, but he was a friend of Gerald, and Gerald asked him to play one last song for his "fancy girl here"—he said that with a grin—who'd never heard Irish music. "Like that one about the lake," Gerald suggested. "The slow one."

"It'll cost you, Gerry," the boy shouted over in a high-pitched voice.

"Aw, come on now, little Mikey."

Mikey wiped a bit of rosin onto his bow, then tucked the violin under his chin and played: it was a sad song that seemed to bear the weight of the world upon it. Gerald reached for Maddy; he took her in his arms and they moved to the music. Maddy didn't know where to put her feet, but she let Gerald move her about the floor. Despite his foot, he moved lightly, smoothly, pressing his warm chest against hers.

Couldn't time have stopped there?

Gerald drove her home after that. They said little to each other along the way. But when he pulled up by her driveway, Gerald played with the hair behind her ears, before he went around and opened the door for her. He kissed her lightly on the cheek, and then, when she reached for him, full on the mouth. After that, Maddy could not get him out of her mind.

They went out for three more nights after that, even though Maddy had to go back to school the following Monday. They took more walks, longer, slower ones, once through the Dover graveyard, past the mottled gravestones of her ancestors on her mother's side, and twice in the park behind the town hall. They held hands, and sometimes stopped to kiss. He had plans, he whispered to Maddy, holding her hand tight, he wasn't going to be just another "fuckin' mick." The language scared her, and the passion behind it, too. He was going to start his own business, a landscaping firm to take care of the grounds of wealthy people like the folks around Dover. And he'd go nights to a business college for an MBA and really make something of himself. "You'd help me with this, wouldn't you, Maddy?" he asked.

"Of course I would," Maddy assured him. She was already scheming, thinking of people in the neighborhood she could ask. "Of course."

Each night, when they drove back to the house, it was harder to part with him. She'd sit in his car, breathe in the strange, wonderful smell of him, and stroke the side of his arm, and, once, lay her head against his shoulder, saying nothing as the starlight came through the windshield. On that last night, the moon was full, so high and bright it was almost like daylight, with deep shadows running away from the trees. It was a warm, lovely night, and she had on that nice cashmere sweater of hers, and her tightest skirt, and, as they sat together on the front seat, listening to the radio, he did something that surprised her. He slid his hand up the inside of her leg. Just partway, but enough for her to know what he meant by it. "Isn't there somewhere we can go?" he asked her.

And then they were on the driveway together, and she was leading him to the barn.

thirteen

The dry, dusty scent of hay. Marsh hay. There was a pile of it in the corner of the barn, up in the hay loft. Not for horses, though, for the gardens. Her mother, who wasted nothing, had poor Douglas store the hay up in the barn after he raked it off the flower beds.

Up they'd gone, up the narrow staircase to the dusty loft with its cobwebs and its walls of knotty pine. The moonlight streamed in the windows. "Here, darlin'," Gerald had said as he'd scooped out a kind of hollow in the hay for the two of them to lie in, and then he'd eased her down. He'd said nothing to her, and she said nothing back, as he raised her sweater up over her head, as he slid off her brassiere and cupped his rough hands on her pale white breasts, which had never before been touched by anyone. "You're so beautiful," he told her. He looked at her with such tenderness. And he went so slow. She never imagined that a man would go so slow.

Once his hands started to rove about her body, once she was his, no words passed between them. Did he need to tell her he loved her, that he would always love her—or was that somehow assumed? The silence made that night seem so fateful. All she could hear was the wind moving through the still bare trees. That and Gerald's breathing, which was slow, and her own breathing, which was faster.

The hay was crinkly under her, but soft, infinitely softer than the hard wooden floor at their feet. She lay there watching Gerald's keen eyes as he touched her, playing gently with her nipples, stroking the smooth skin around them, kissing them, even, to send a torrent of sensation down her body and between her legs. She made no effort to touch him back. She had no idea how to touch him back, or where, or whether she dared to. And he seemed glad enough. She simply watched him, taking such delight in her, and waited for whatever would come.

She took in a sip of air as he finally slid a hand down and undid the button on the waistband of her skirt. She lifted herself up, let him slide it off her, hoping she would seem experienced. She herself lowered her underwear—a pink cotton pair that she thought no man would ever see. Her eyes did not leave his as he took in the sight of her lying beside him with nothing on except her white socks. In the moonlight, his eyes were warm and eager; she hoped he couldn't see the fear in hers. Nothing seemed real, not the crinkly hay underneath her, certainly not the hand that moved about her body as if it were his own. Her heart beat madly in her chest. Surely he could hear it. And then he loosened his own trousers, and slid them down his thighs and he rolled over onto her. He gently opened her knees, and she felt her whole self opening as he did so. And then he was on her, and she gasped as he pushed inside.

She hadn't expected it to hurt, but it did. But she knew she deserved it, the pain. It was wrong what she was doing. She knew that even as it thrilled her. His smell surrounded her—the sweaty dampness of him, the sooty tobacco smell—as he moved over her, rocking. Each thrust stabbed her; she was sure he'd draw blood. Something within her did not want him in, not completely. Still, without a word, he kept shoving and shoving and finally the pain left her, replaced by a soft, warm, liquid pleasure that was like nothing she'd ever felt. Her breath came faster, as if to draw the bliss deeper inside. She laid her hands along the curve of his tensing buttocks. She wanted to feel the muscles that were driving him into her— pushing her out of herself. And then finally, it was too much, too beautiful, more than she ever could have imagined, alone with her pillow in her bedroom, and tears trickled down from the corners of her eyes, and she gave out a gasping sort of cry, one so loud and desperate that he cupped a hand over her mouth to quiet her. She could taste him as she sucked the air through his fingers.

But Gerald pushed into her, harder and harder, until, straining, he rose right up above her, groaned once, and then he slumped down onto her, and lay there, his lips by her cheek as she stared up, breathless, at the dark, angled ceiling.

Finally, he slid off her, and, lying beside her, he idly ran his fingertips through her pubic hair. Gradually her mind returned to her body. No man should ever touch her there. With a distress that was edged with terror, she shoved his hand away and lurched up. She saw his plump, spent penis glistening between his thighs, saw her beautiful sweater crumpled in the straw beneath him, and she realized the full, irrevocable evil of what she had done.

Alice

fourteen

The topic of Alice's anger-management class was keeping control, which got everyone talking. After Chris B's suicide, mournfulness had quickly given way to irritability, and it was with unusual prickliness that participants went on now about the ways that other people kept trying to control *them*. Charles, a CPA who'd tried to set his office on fire, was obviously steamed as he went on about "all the Mickey Mouse bureaucratic bullshit" he'd had to put up with at his accounting firm, and the seriously overweight Millie railed against her mother's having put her on a diet at age six.

Normally, Alice loved to get into the material of her patients' lives. But this time, she felt almost completely preoccupied. Not only with Chris, but with Ethan's terrifying move against her. And, on top of everything else, Mrs. Bemis's revelations of the other night kept drawing her attention down the hall to the conference room where Mrs. Bemis had told her about the body. The body in the water. Pale, bloated, sea-slickened, it seemed to float on the edge of her own subconscious, washing up out of the mist. Brendan. An Irish name. A foreign name. What possible connection could he have to Mrs. Bemis?

Alice scarcely even noticed when Charles accused Millie of getting fat just to keep people at bay. "It's a turnoff," he sneered. "And that's what you want."

"You're one to talk," Millie shot back. "You're a—you're a whatchamacallit."

"Oh, that's good. You don't even know."

"A pyromaniac, that's what you are," Millie said triumphantly. "There. See? I'm not dumb."

"I never said you were dumb," Charles said. "I never even said you were fat. Although you are."

"Dr. Matthews!" Millie cried out.

That brought Alice to. She managed to get Charles to apologize, and Millie to accept his apology, and for everyone else who'd been drawn into the argument to take a breath. When the class was over, Alice led everyone back out into the hall for a few minutes' break before the special grieving session that they'd brought in a specialist for, while she scurried to the nurses' station for black coffee.

But she couldn't stop wondering about Brendan. What was his last name? Despite the coffee, she couldn't remember. But the nurse Sidney Irons was there on the floor, and he was able to dredge it up. "Hurley," he said finally. "Brendan Hurley. Pretty good, huh?"

"Thank you, Sid," Alice told him, perfunctorily, to let him know that he hadn't gained anything from her.

Hurley . . . of course! Might that be Mrs. Bemis's maiden name—making Brendan a relative of some sort? A cousin? Or—who knew?—a half brother? She flipped through the documents she'd collected in the Bemis file. She searched through twice, but Madeline's maiden name wasn't listed. No middle initial, even. Alice thought of asking Dr. Maris, but decided it was better not to get him involved. The document did list the name of Mrs. B's personal physician, Webster Hawkins. Surely he would know.

She reached for the wall phone. Dr. Hawkins himself was not available, but the receptionist put her through to a nurse practitioner, who placed Alice on hold for an eternity while she went to check.

"Adams," the nurse said when she finally returned to the phone.

"Not Hurley?" Alice asked, stupidly. She'd convinced herself that it had to be Hurley.

"Nope." The nurse sounded annoyed. "It says here Adams. Anything else you need?"

That was her cue to hang up, but Alice pressed ahead. "Do you know her at all?"

"A little."

"What's your impression of her?" Alice was inclined to rely on her own ability to size up patients. But Mrs. Bemis had volunteered so little, and seemed to hold back so much.

"Well, I've noticed that she's always very well dressed when she comes in. Hair done up nicely. And she sometimes brings in flowers from her garden for Dr. Hawkins."

"That's unusual."

"Yes, very," the nurse replied. "Never says much, though. You can't thank her, either. Always makes it sound like the flowers are nothing. But they're big, lovely bouquets of I-don't-know-what. Fresh cut. Year 'round, too. She came in with some lovely ones this past winter. She said they were from her greenhouse. Dr. Hawkins was so pleased."

"Her health has been okay?" Victor had reported no significant medical issues, but it never hurt to check.

"A little arthritis, but nothing serious. Mental problems, though. But I guess you know all about that."

Alice read her the list of antidepressants from her file.

"Yeah, there's been a lot of depression. I believe that runs in the family. Her mother, especially in her later years. Madeline tends to cloud over when you ask about the past, though."

"Any idea why?"

The nurse laughed. "That's your department." She turned serious. "Like I say, I don't really know her. I don't think Dr. Hawkins does too well, either. She doesn't come in too regularly. Nothing like an annual physical. I'm looking at her chart here. I'm not sure she's ever been to a gynecologist."

"Is there anyone who knows her better?"

"Family, you mean?"

"Yes. Like family."

"She doesn't have any children, as you probably know. And she's been widowed for a long time now—"

"No cousins, nephews?"

"None listed here. But then, I don't suppose they would be. There was someone else, though."

Alice waited.

"A driver. A chauffeur, I suppose you'd say, but she always said 'driver.' Seemed like a nice guy. Very patient with her. Always waited for her in the waiting room, then walked her to the car afterward."

"He still work for her?"

"As far as I know. He lives at her place in Milton. Out in the servants' quarters or somewhere. On the property, anyway. He takes care of the place. He's done that forever. A very nice man, I suppose you could call him. I mean, I don't know why not."

"His name isn't Hurley, is it?" Alice asked.

The nurse thought for a moment. "No. Needham. I remember because I used to live there." She paused, evidently waiting for Alice to pick up on that, which she didn't. "That's a town outside Boston. I guess you're not from around here. Pete Needham. As I say, a nice guy. I'm sure you could call him if you had other questions."

Later, after the ward's grieving session for Chris B, which brought tears even from some of the staff, Alice went on rounds with Dr. Maris, Marnie, Victor, and several of the other residents. Her mind drifted while Gretchen, the sometime flight attendant, went on in a whisper about her paralyzing fear of water—bathtubs, lakes, pools, but especially the ocean, which had caused no end of trouble for her in her line of work. Maybe it was the sleeplessness, but, as Gretchen spoke, Alice imagined the body again, its bloated flesh pressed against her.

Alice's mind didn't fully clear until afterward, when she was back out in the hall, and Dr. Maris beckoned to her, asking if she'd come by his office.

Of course, she said, trying to mask her trepidation.

"Thunderstorm's coming," Dr. Maris said as they approached his door.

She glanced back out the hall window, saw the darkening skies and some swaying trees.

The blinds were pulled in Dr. Maris's office to protect his computer screen from any glare from the windows. The room was suffused with a warm, yellow light from the standing lamps—a relief from the blinding fluorescence of the ward. Alice might have been settling into a cocoon as she took a seat across from Dr. Maris's mahogany desk.

Dr. Maris eased himself into his executive chair. "So, how are you and Madeline coming?"

"Oh, that," Alice said, only somewhat relieved. "Well, I've only seen her a few times."

"Oh, I know, I know," Dr. Maris told her, leaning forward in his chair so that his face loomed over his desk like a full moon. "But first impressions can be important." He drew his fingertips together before his face. "What's going on with her, do you think?"

Alice felt light-headed from fatigue, and slightly nauseous, which was odd since she couldn't remember having eaten anything. Most of all, though, she felt protective of Mrs. Bemis, and reluctant to share with her eminent boss, or anyone, the secret that her patient had so recently entrusted her with. Psychiatry *was* secrets, after all. Secrets bound the patient to her past, but, once revealed in therapy, they also bound the psychiatrist to the patient. In Mrs. Bemis's world, news of her possible involvement with a floating corpse could be explosive; seeing Dr. Maris lean toward her, so curious, Alice could see exactly how explosive. It made her recoil slightly, both for her own protection, and for her patient's.

"I'm not sure I can say, just yet," Alice told him. "I'm still trying to establish her trust in me."

"Of course," said Dr. Maris with a slight trace of disappointment. "That's very important."

But she had to say something. Dr. Maris would not be easily put off—and Alice didn't want to give the impression that she was in over her head. "But I do feel her reaching out for me. She seems so sad, so lonely. And I keep thinking—" She paused, uncertain as to exactly how to continue.

"Yes?"

"Well, that there's another Mrs. Bemis, one nobody sees. You know how, well, how she seems to sag, how she seems so worn down by everything." Alice shifted in her seat. "There's a great deal of repression there, an unusual sort of blocked energy way down underneath. It's odd. It's almost as if—" She hesitated, unsure as to how this would sound.

"Go on."

"Well, as if there's a younger self hiding inside her someplace. Someone spirited and cheerful, not at all like the somber, depressed version of herself that she presents. At moments, you know, she strikes me as surprisingly girlish. But it's just the briefest impression. A flash, and then it's gone."

"Back into hiding."

"And doesn't or can't or won't come out. The other day, she told me that she was young once, too. Just said that, straight out. Hinted about some romantic trouble, but she didn't go on about it. She never goes on about anything. If I can get two words out of her, I feel I've done extremely well."

"Why this repression, this 'hiding,' as you call it?" Dr. Maris asked, tapping his fingertips together. "Do you suppose there's some dissociation there?"

"Possibly. I just sense that she's scared."

"Don't underestimate the power of social control to inhibit the upper classes," Dr. Maris added. "Especially her generation."

"I don't doubt that it could be fierce," Alice said, elevating her own language slightly to match her boss's. "Every time we start to talk about anything personal, she gets very withdrawn, starts looking out the window. It's as if she's running away from me to the outdoors, trying to escape. Did you ever have a secret hiding place when you were a kid?" Alice remembered the tree house in the backyard of her friend Debbie's house next door, in Latrobe. It was in a pine tree, only eight feet up. She and Debbie had built it with Alice's brother Jeff and sister Carla. It was meant as a refuge from their parents—especially the Matthewses—but it soon became Alice and Debbie's private clubhouse. Very rickety, with yawning gaps between the floorboards, but it held them. Such powerful secrets they kept there—news of the progress on their latest desperate crushes, the original charter of their Mutual Admiration Society, the romance magazines they both loved.

"I can hardly remember. I was a fairly conventional child."

"Oh, I doubt that, Dr. Maris."

The doctor shifted uncomfortably in his seat. "Well, perhaps not entirely conventional." He reached into a drawer and pulled out a case of mints. He offered one to Alice, who declined, then picked one out himself and noisily unwrapped it. "It sounds to me almost like some kind of adolescent regression."

"That's what I mean."

"The link between the elderly and the young has been widely noted in the literature, you know."

"Yes, of course." Alice restrained an impulse to roll her eyes. It had been a feature of her gerontology course at BU.

"Herb Wasserstein wrote about it brilliantly a few months back in *JAPA*." *The Journal of the American Psychiatric Association*. Dr. Maris popped the mint into his mouth, where it clicked against his teeth. "But now, from the way you're talking, I almost get the sense that you suspect that she is fleeing some trauma." He sucked on his mint. "That might explain a few things—the disorientation, for instance, the lingering depression. This sense you have of her being somehow blocked. Post-traumatic stress disorder may be overdramatized nowadays, especially in women experiencing major depression." He paused, deliberating. "But that alone is no reason to discount it. I assume you've inquired about the possibility of . . . abuse?"

Despite her training, Alice hadn't imagined that Mrs. Bemis could have been victimized in that way. She seemed too solid, too gruff. Or had she simply overlooked it? A film of sweat brought a prickle from the cut on her palm. Did she not notice *anything?* Was she in some idiotic denial?

"Not yet, no," she admitted. "I haven't asked her."

"And why is that?" Dr. Maris was newly stern.

Alice met his gaze. "I told you, I'm still developing her trust."

"I see," Dr. Bemis said, softening. "I keep thinking of Madeline there in the bedding department curled up in the fetal position. Seems so self-protective."

"I suppose." A chill went through her.

"So think more about that, hmmm?" Dr. Maris said. "But now, I'm interested in this observation of yours about the outdoors. She is an eminent horticulturalist, you know. Or was."

"With the horticultural society, you mean?"

"The New England Horticultural Society, yes. It was just an honorific, more administrative than anything. Actually, I was thinking of her orchids. She used to grow some spectacular orchids." He smiled. "My mother was an enthusiast, raved about them. But Madeline was reputed to be extremely knowledgeable about flowers of all sorts." He adjusted his glasses. "Sublimation, I suppose, if you believe Freud." He shifted the mint around in his mouth.

"You don't?" Alice prodded, glad to shift the spotlight back to her inquisitor.

"Well, let me say I definitely think there's a subconscious." He smiled wickedly as he added, "Especially among our beloved

Brahmins. So much repression—at least in my clinical experience. But I'd argue that now, with the general eroticization of daily life, Freud has, shall we say, lost some of the pertinence that he had in fin-de-siècle Vienna." Dr. Maris halted; he must have detected a slight glazing in Alice's eyes. "Well, no need to go on about that. I'll save it for the annual Forsythe Lecture this winter." He winked.

"Did you know her father, by any chance?"

"Heavens no. Before my time. He was heavily into real estate, I believe. A number of properties downtown. Quite a prominent fellow. All the right clubs and such. I seem to recall that her mother was extremely avid at bridge."

"The mother spent some time here."

"Did she? Really?"

"Depression. Madeline visited her once."

"Perhaps that's the trauma right there."

"It seems to have been disturbing, certainly."

"Something like that can go down very deep, you know." He stood up, walked to the window, and adjusted the blinds so he could see out. Alice could see darkening skies, trees twisting in the wind. "Definitely a storm coming. Too bad. Our friend Madeline must be longing to get outside."

"I was thinking that I might go for a walk with her."

"Splendid idea! Yes, take a stroll about the grounds—depending on the weather, of course. And if you think she's up to it. Plantings certainly aren't what they once were, but she might find some, what, some emotional sustenance out there? Sure—smell the flowers. Could get her juices flowing again. Might also firm up the bond between you two. Let her tell you about the local flora. No telling where that might lead." Then his tone turned solemn. "Keep at it, though, Alice. The meter is running, don't forget. Our friends over in the administration building won't let us keep her forever, you know. Tick-tick-tick, my dear. It's the way of the world."

"I'm doing my best," Alice said defensively.

He spoke for a few minutes more, reviewing the dose of the

Wellbutrin that Alice had been working out with Victor, debating the merits of adding ten milligrams of Prozac or possibly some Xanax. Finally he removed his glasses and wearily pinched the bridge of his nose with his fingertips. "A terrible thing the other night," he said.

"Chris's death, you mean?"

He nodded grimly. "And so distressing for everyone. Something like that—" He caught himself. "Well, it couldn't be helped." Then, with a mournful sigh, he settled himself back down at his word processor, where he let Alice know that he was busy completing a paper on what he termed "neurotic dysplasia" for the *Jungian Society Quarterly*. Alice rose from her chair and, with some mumbled words of gratitude, left him alone once more in the yellow silence of his office.

fifteen

The rain held off until the next afternoon, when the skies blackened, thunder echoed around the hillside campus, and the clouds finally let loose. Alice found herself with a few minutes to spare before her substance-abuse group at two, and decided to dash through the storm to the cafeteria for a quick lunch. She'd slept badly again that night, and eaten breakfast ridiculously early, at five-thirty, and she was starving. But the library was at the other end of the Freeman Building from the cafeteria, and, ravenous as she was, Alice thought she might swing by the periodical room to see if she could find out something about Brendan Hurley from the newspapers. She occasionally retreated there for a quiet moment during the day.

Mrs. Alfonzo, the occasionally nosy reference librarian, had her back turned as Alice made her way past the counter. This was just as well, since Alice didn't feel entirely right about coming in, especially with her jacket all soaked. It felt a bit like sneaking around behind her patient's back, and a very tedious ethics class at BU had made it quite clear that "amateur sleuthing," as her professor termed it, was not part of a psychiatrist's job description. But, she reassured herself, it might help the progress of their therapy if she could establish the reality of Mrs. Bemis's startling assertions about the corpse. It would place their discussions, which often seemed evasive and unsure, on a firmer footing. And, besides, she had gotten so curious . . .

Alice passed through the swinging glass door to the periodical room—mercifully empty of people at this hour—and spotted the rack with various dailies hanging off long wooden poles. She found the day's *Globe,* plucked it off its hooks, and set it down on an adjoining table. She paged through the paper. No word about any corpse washing up in Duxbury, or anywhere along the Massachusetts shoreline, for that matter.

She returned the *Globe* to the rack and, glancing around, she noticed a stack of papers in a bin under the window. She dug through and pulled out the *Globe* from the day before, which didn't yield anything, either. Nor did the previous day, or the fat Sunday edition a few inches deeper down in the pile, or any of the previous dailies from the previous week or the week before that. It wasn't until she went all the way back to the Sunday paper from the morning after the body was first discovered that she found any reference to it. And she might have missed that if she hadn't been searching so carefully. It was on page six of the Metro page, in the "New England Round-Up" section, below news of an incipient teachers' strike in Springfield. It ran under the headline "Floating Corpse found by Duxbury Pier."

Alice glanced around to make sure that no one had come in, then she took the newspaper back behind a long metal case laden with some gerontology journals. She spread the paper out on the table and read about the discovery of the body, which was described as "heavily mutilated." Most of the information was what the orderlies had mentioned. The body had indeed been discovered by a couple of kids who had gone swimming during a party in Duxbury. The body was believed to be that of Brendan Hurley, but no further information was available. The identification was based on the fact that a man of that name and roughly that description had been lost at sea after a sailboat accident three days before. The *Globe* noted that another man was believed to have been in the boat, too, but he had yet to be found. There were very few other details: the pier's owner, Cyrus Brewster, was a retired State Department official from the first Bush administration who now served on Duxbury's board of selectmen; one of his grandchildren, visiting for the weekend, had thrown a party that Saturday night. Alice guessed that Brewster's wealth might have accounted for the paucity of information on the incident. The police had described the body as that "of a white man, six foot two, approximately fifty years old, clothed only in 'a pair of tattered men's briefs.'" Several fingers were missing, and the face was "indistinct." A local marine biologist attributed the disfiguration to the work of sea creatures. "They can be voracious, especially the crabs." As to the cause of death, Duxbury police chief Alan Corbett was quoted as saying: "We have no reason to suspect that this was anything other than a boating accident attributable to inexperienced sailors in heavier than normal seas."

The story was brief, and Alice read it a couple of times. How did Mrs. Bemis know this man, and why would she refuse to tell Alice anything more about him? Who was this Brendan Hurley to her? A final distressing thought occurred to Alice. Could Mrs. Bemis herself have been involved in the death in some way?

When she returned this section of the paper to the stack of old dailies, she noticed that there were some tabloid *Herald*s mixed in as well. She plucked out the plump Sunday edition from the morning after the body's discovery. Its coverage ran bigger, on page twelve, with a blurry photograph of the Duxbury pier where the body was found and another, clearer one of the Brewsters' house. It played up the more lurid aspects of the tale—describing the "deep and angry claw marks across the legs and chest"—and included the fact that the teenager who discovered the body was herself "skinny-dipping" at the time. But it added no further information about the cause of death, or the identity of Brendan Hurley. After that, both papers had apparently lost interest in the story. Even the *Herald* included only a small item in the paper three days later, saying that, because of the prevailing tidal currents, Hurley's corpse was now presumed to have drifted over from Marshfield, one town to the west, where the sailboat, a seventeen-foot Laser, had in fact been rented, thus switching responsibility for the investigation to the department there. But there was no further information on the cause of death. The *Herald* mentioned a Marshfield detective named Frank LeBeau. Alice wrote down the name on a strip of the newspaper and stuffed it in her pocket.

"Why, Alice, I didn't see you come in," Mrs. Alfonzo said cheerfully as Alice crossed by the desk on her way out. She looked out at Alice through her bifocals, which she wore on a slender chain around her neck. Her computer screen colored the lenses an eerie blue. "You find what you need?"

"Why yes, thanks."

Damp and sheepish, her fingers smudged with newsprint, Alice braced herself for more questions, but there were none, and she left the library as quickly as she dared. She had barely five minutes before her class.

Hurrying into the cafeteria, she noticed Victor ahead of her in line, pondering the entrée choices. He was still in his raincoat, and he had an umbrella under his arm. Alice slipped past him, grabbed her usual coffee yogurt, added a banana, and handed the cashier a crumpled five-dollar bill. The cashier laboriously smoothed it out and made change. Alice took a seat at an empty table by the window and tore open the yogurt. She had nearly finished eating when Victor approached carrying a lunch tray.

"Mind if I sit down?" he asked, pursing his lips in that nervous tic of his.

"Please." Alice gestured toward the free chair across from her.

Victor eased himself into it, withdrew his napkin, and wiped off his glasses.

"Get what you needed from the library?" he asked.

Alice looked at him a moment to see if he knew more than he was letting on. He'd directed his attention to his pasta, oblivious to her gaze.

"What are you talking about?"

Victor dabbed at the corner of his mouth with his napkin. "Alice, I saw you burrowing into the old newspapers."

"Are you following me?"

"I saw you through the window." He took another bite. "While I was coming here."

She'd tried to be so careful, but the windows by the periodicals reached clear to the floor. "So?"

"That's not like you."

"This is interesting to me, Victor," Alice replied huffily. "Tell me, what am I like?"

"Okay. One point for you. But I did the intake on Madeline, remember?" His voice turned solemn, penetrating. "She told me about the body in Duxbury. Just in passing. Wouldn't elaborate when I returned to it." He dug into his pasta. "I left it out of the report, but I was curious, too. It's the kind of thing that sticks with you, isn't it?"

Alice wanted to reach across the table and grab the pudgy creep by his fat cheeks. "What are you telling me, Victor?"

"I'm telling you, I left it at that." He looked at her with his sad eyes. "Alice, the Massachusetts General Laws have something to say about this. It's about privacy."

"Oh, please."

"I'm serious! You aren't supposed to go outside that room. Everything in that room stays in that room. Everything outside stays outside. That is a cardinal principal in psychiatry."

"Well, thank you for the information." She put her empty yogurt container on his tray, and marched out of the cafeteria, scowling. Fucking Victor, with his fucking Harvard Medical School degree.

• • •

She'd pushed open the door and was headed out onto the walkway, relieved to be out in the wind, when she heard Victor calling her name. He rushed up to her, the tails of his raincoat flapping. "Wait a second, would you please?" he shouted.

"Why?" She kept right on going outside into the swirling air. "So you can question my ethics again?"

Victor followed her through the door. "Look, I didn't mean to come down so hard on you." He gulped in the air, although it had not been that long a run, and raised his umbrella over her.

"Oh, it just slipped out?" Alice teased. The rain was pouring down. "If I believed in unintended consequences, I'd be in another profession." She set out, but less quickly now, as she was glad to stay dry.

"All right, calm down."

"I'm perfectly calm," Alice snapped.

"Look, there are other ways to get at what you're after. You want to find out something, you don't just call up and ask. It's like anything. It's like psychiatry, for God's sake. Directness isn't always a virtue. I had a case once—" He stopped himself, glanced back at Alice. "Just don't identify yourself, don't say anything about—"

Alice whirled around on him. "Victor, Jesus, you thought I was going to *call* someone about this?"

Victor looked quizzical. "You're saying you're not interested in the connection?"

"There are *statutes,* Victor."

Alice thought she discerned a brief, uncomprehending look in Victor's eyes. But he plowed ahead all the same.

"Well, keep it vague, hypothetical," he told her. "That's all I'm saying. What if—blah, blah, blah. That way you won't get in trouble."

"*If* I was interested, you mean?" She could hear him breathing through his nose over the sound of the rain thudding against the umbrella.

"Right. If."

sixteen

Back at Nichols, Mrs. Bemis was lying on her back in bed, a blanket pulled up under her chin. Outside, the rain lashed the windows, but the old woman looked very cozy and, with the corners of her mouth upturned, oddly pleased. She seemed to have retreated into a happier part of herself.

"Mrs. Bemis?" Alice laid her hand on the old woman's shoulder, felt again the slim bones within as she gently tried to shake her awake. "Mrs. Bemis? It's past three. We were going to meet at three, remember?"

The woman opened her eyes and looked at Alice, from faraway, it seemed. Then she pushed at Alice with her hands, a gesture that startled her. "No," Mrs. Bemis told Alice. "No. Not today. No. I'm too tired. I can't. I'm sorry."

"But there is something I'd like to discuss."

"Go away, would you please?"

Alice turned to Rita, who was watching from the doorway. Rita shrugged.

There had been a crab apple tree in Alice's backyard when she was growing up. The tree was very old and gnarled, and it had grown up by a wire fence that was long gone by the time Alice had come along, all except for one strand of rusty wire that was deeply imbedded in its trunk. Something cold, hard, and sharp cut deep into Mrs. Bemis, Alice imagined, and now lay buried deep inside her heart. But what? Dr. Maris had guessed, in that rambling way of his, that there might have been some abuse in her past. Alice was certainly familiar with the tight knot of anger of abuse victims. But what she sensed more at the center of Mrs. Bemis was a wistfulness, a longing. Regret. Alice thought back to the other moments when Mrs. B, as Alice had started to think of her, had suddenly tuned out—the first, strange interaction over Alice's hair, and the tenderness with which she had touched it. Thoughts of loss—they seemed to send her off, too. Those "mistaken things"—such an odd expression. Why did they matter now?

Alice checked in with Mrs. Bemis again a little before five, but she was sound asleep, snoring lightly as she lay on her back. She decided to let her rest and left work on time for once to do some of the grocery shopping she normally put off. After everything was put away, she thought she'd catch up on the phone with her mother, while she was feeling reasonably fresh.

Her father answered, as grumpy and monosyllabic as always. He passed her on to her mother, who'd just come in from the garden. "She's been wanting to talk to you," her father said.

"Sorry I haven't called back sooner," Alice began when her mother came on the phone.

"That's all right," her mother said wearily. "It's just that—"

Alice slumped down on the edge of her bed; her mother's tone was enough to convey her meaning. "It's the Grand, isn't it?"

"Yes, but I—" She hesitated, which was maddening. "Well, I wasn't sure you wanted to know. Way up there in Boston."

"Of *course* I want to know."

"When you didn't call back—"

"Mom, *please*. What's happened to the Grand?"

Her mother took a deep breath. "She's had a stroke."

"Oh no."

"She's still alive. I mean, she's breathing." Alice's mother had always felt overshadowed by the Grand, who'd been so much more vibrant, and more loved. The Alzheimer's had only made that dynamic worse—now, on top of everything else, Alice's mother had to watch over the Grand in the nursing home, receiving nothing in return. "The doctors say it could be months."

"I'll come see her," Alice said. It had been a while since she'd been back to Latrobe. Not since she'd started work at Montrose.

"That might be nice," her mother replied glumly. "We'd like to see you, too, of course."

"Let's plan on it, then," Alice declared. She had meant to see the Grand for the longest time. But, the truth was, her last visits had been depressing. The last time, the Grand was literally tethered to the bed to keep her from roaming off. Temporarily, the nurses assured Alice: some weeks back, the nurses had found the Grand out on the sidewalk in her pajamas, mumbling that she had to take a book back to the library. No book was in her hand, though, and the nearest library was ten miles away.

The conversation continued a little longer. Her mother mentioned a drought, and a neighbor's daughter who had gotten married. But Alice was scarcely listening. She kept seeing the Grand, that terrible vacant look where once there had been such vitality.

•   •   •

In the morning, Mrs. Bemis was sitting by the window, listening to an aria on the radio, concentrating so heavily on a mournful soprano that she didn't seem to hear Alice come in.

"Oh, hello," Mrs. Bemis said when Alice came into view. The radio was still playing. *"Madame Butterfly,"* she said, snapping it off. "Puccini, you know. One of the few my husband could bear."

In the circular room where they'd been meeting lately, they'd been sitting on metal chairs, but Alice realized that there was a comfortable chair off in the corner, and she offered to move it over for her patient.

"I'm fine," the old lady protested.

Alice slid it over anyway. "Please."

Mrs. Bemis held out for a long moment, surveying the soft chair. "All right," she said, a note of regret in her voice. "If you want." She sat down, eased herself back.

"Better?" Alice asked.

She seemed to be working hard not to acknowledge the improvement. "I suppose," she said finally.

Alice took a seat on the folding chair across from her, asked how she was doing.

"Fair, I'd say," Mrs. Bemis replied without elaborating. Alice let the silence expand, then tried to dig out a little more by asking about her sleep, any physical symptoms, side effects of the antidepressants, whether she'd been thinking about Chris B. None of this triggered any particular response. Alice saw again how deeply Mrs. B's gloom could settle into her, hardening the lines of her face, causing her eyes to droop. "You've borne your sadness for a long while, haven't you?"

Mrs. Bemis rested her hands in her lap, the faint light from the windows reflected in her pupils. "It's like those clouds," she said. "Heavy, some days. You keep waiting for rain, but none comes, just darkness. Even—even at noon, a darkness."

"And that's what you're feeling now?"

A nod.

"And have been for a long time?"

"On and off, yes."

Alice thought she'd bring tears. She almost wished she would. Mrs. B was, perhaps, too strong for her own good. She might have found release in a good cry. Just as Alice had herself after Ethan had attacked her so cruelly with the scissors. Best not to think about *that*.

"Tell me about your family, would you? I've meant to ask you more about them."

"I told you, my husband is—"

"No, I meant your original family, your parents."

"They're dead," Mrs. Bemis interrupted. "There's no point talking about them."

Alice brought her chair closer to the old woman. "Why not?"

"There just isn't."

"Did you like them?"

"Well enough."

"It doesn't *sound* like you liked them."

Mrs. Bemis looked over at Alice. "Why don't you tell *me* something for once? Just for variety. Do you like *your* parents?"

Obviously, the question was too complicated for a yes or a no, as Mrs. Bemis must have known. "Well enough," Alice said, and smiled, hoping Mrs. B would join in the joke.

But she didn't. "My mother had her difficulties, as you know. But my parents were both very fine people," she said instead.

"I hear distance when you speak that way. Do you intend that?"

Mrs. Bemis weakened. "We weren't particularly close, no. If that's what you mean."

"Even though you were an only child?"

"Or because of it. My parents were older, you see. I'm not really sure they were prepared for me."

"How do you mean, 'prepared'?"

"Older people get set in their ways. The young can be unruly. Provocative, you might even say."

Alice looked at her more intently.

"In the things they do."

It made her worry that possibly Dr. Maris was on to something with his suspicion of some early trauma. She'd been reluctant to press; the time had not been right. But clearly this was the moment. "Now, Mrs. Bemis, I have to ask—did your father hurt you in some way, abuse you?"

"'Abuse'?" She looked mystified, as if she didn't know the meaning of the term.

"Sexually." The word sounded explosive even to Alice.

"Good God, no." Mrs. Bemis brought her hands down on the arms of her chair as if she needed to reclaim her balance.

"You're sure?"

"I'd know, wouldn't I?" She smiled slyly, savoring her victory.

"Of course you would," Alice conceded. "But there are plenty of stories in the psychiatric literature of patients repressing—forgetting—such material."

"Perhaps I am," her patient said. "But I doubt it."

Alice let that sit. "Do you see your parents when you leave me?"

Mrs. Bemis reared up. "When I *what?*"

"When you tune out. You leave me, you go back somewhere, I can tell."

"I don't go anywhere. I stay right here." She looked about. "Unfortunately."

There was a pay telephone downstairs in the Freeman Building, where Alice could make a call without anyone noticing. After the substance-control group, she consulted the telephone book and found a number for Peter Needham on Deaver Lane, in Milton. Number 12A. That must be Mrs. Bemis's house. Alice pictured him in a back room somewhere, in what once must have been the maid's quarters. She dialed the number. A machine answered, a grizzled male voice saying this was "Pete," and offering the chance to leave a message. Alice was about to do so when she herself hesitated, unsure of what to say, or ask. How she should identify herself was a problem, too. "Dr. Matthews" would only lead to questions about what kind of doctor, and where. Alice Matthews would be much better, but that might lead to questions of its own. Besides, hadn't Victor advised against being so direct? This Pete might get in touch with Mrs. Bemis and then there'd be trouble. For some reason, the name of her next-door neighbor from Latrobe, Debbie McGill, popped into her head. Alice used it, and was asking Pete to call her please at her home this evening if he had a chance, it might be helpful, when she heard a click and a man's voice came on the line. "Who's this, do you say?" he asked.

"Debbie McGill," Alice repeated. "I'm—I'm a friend of hers from the horticultural society. I was calling about Mrs. Bemis."

"Who'd you say you were?" The voice sounded suspicious.

"A friend," Alice said, deliberately not repeating the name. "From the horticultural society? She's been helping me with my orchids."

"Has she." Only slightly less suspicious.

"I've been trying to call her because I wanted to ask about a friend of hers."

"And who's that?"

"Brendan Hurley."

Silence on the other end of the line.

"What do you want to know about him?"

"Just how I might get in touch with him."

"And why's that?" Definitely suspicious now.

"Mrs. Bemis told me he knows about a certain fertilizer—"

"Brendan? About *fertilizer?*"

"That's what she told me."

"*Brendan Hurley?*" he repeated.

"Yes. Brendan Hurley."

"He's dead, you know."

"Oh, no, I didn't. Gosh, I'm sorry to hear that."

"Boating accident. Very upsetting to the missus."

"I'm—I'm awfully sorry to bother you," Alice said, and she hung up the receiver, then glanced around to make sure no one had seen her.

It was still cloudy after the morning's thundershower, but no more rain was coming down, and Alice hoped a quick walk before her afternoon psychopharm conference might clear her mind. A stroll down to the old stables by the West Gate, perhaps? Alice had loved horses. Riding lessons for her were about her parents' only splurge. She missed the days when she could communicate everything she needed to with the pat of a hand, some gentle words, or a few clicks from the back of her mouth.

The Montrose grounds weren't anything like the old photographs, when every corner bloomed. Now, only the forested Concord hills, an enticing green even in early September, offered much to the eye. Around her, the still inhabited Montrose buildings rose up like tombstones, barely softened by landscaping, while the abandoned ones were consumed by their ivy. As she made her way down the asphalt path, Alice wished she could have asked Mrs. Bemis to join her. Not the Madeline Bemis who was languishing in her bed, too frail seeming today to go out, but the one who was like that high elm leaning over Danzinger, its wet bark glistening. Someone tough and graceful, ready to take on Prince Charles over cocktails. The former Mrs. Bemis. Before sorrow had overcome her.

The thought of Brendan Hurley needled her as she scudded along in her clogs, her linen suit flapping. That caretaker certainly made it sound as if Mrs. Bemis knew him quite well. Not through gardening, though. She'd figured out that much. A friend? A handyman of some sort? A relative, perhaps? Alice found the idea of Mrs. Bemis linked to Brendan's disfigured corpse upsetting, like a creepy image from a horror film. She couldn't get it out of her head.

Alice breathed in the cool, wet air. The stables loomed up, their graying beams glazed with rain. For all the building's faded grandeur, it reminded her of Hank's Stables, where she'd gone to ride as a kid, a drafty old barn that smelled of oats, manure, and horse sweat. It had a stableboy, the furtive Lars Cooper in his cowboy boots who had become—after a sloppy kiss and a few dusty fingers slipped under her bra—Alice's first boyfriend. Six months later, he'd left for California without telling her, but there it was.

Alice pulled open the door. The horses were long gone from the Montrose stables; grimy lawn-mowing equipment was in there now. In the dim light, she sensed the openness of the space, the heavy, exposed beams, the knockabout feel. It was enough to bring back the flicking tails, the shiny leather saddles, and the thrill of Lars glancing over.

But—all the pangs in a lifetime as long as Mrs. Bemis's. Lars was a disappointment, certainly, hardly a disaster. It began, it ended. But, here in the old stables, thinking of Mrs. B, Alice had the sense of how, in a certain more ruminative mind, such closure might not be possible. For such a person, time might continue ceaselessly to unfold, one generation giving way to the next. The seeds yield their fruit, which drop more seed still. And so many harvests! Just the feelings—a feeling here creating another one there creating yet another somewhere else. Alice could scarcely imagine all the feelings of a lifetime—the worries, annoyances, mad crushes, irritations. Where they go, what becomes of them. All the things Mrs. Bemis must have said or done or felt, what they led to. How easily it can all go bad! Like Alice with Ethan. Something's a little off, and then worse trouble when you try to fix it, and then everything gets out of hand, growing and growing, until a moment, a season, a life that had once been perfectly fine becomes intolerable. Is that where Mrs. Bemis was—at intolerable? Would that account for her solitude, her sleepiness, her reluctance to meet Alice's eyes?

Alice ran her hand along the rough wooden post by one of the tractors. Brendan Hurley. Not Bren or Danny, but Brendan. That was so like Mrs. B, the formality.

From the stables, Alice looked back out at the grounds through the open door. The light was pushing through the clouds, covering the whole property with its honey.

It was almost four-thirty. Mrs. B's door was open, as always. She was sleeping again, on her side this time, with her knees up at a childlike angle. She had a light blanket over her that revealed the bony slope of her shoulders, her side, her hip. Alice peered at her in the half-light that filtered through the drawn curtains. Mrs. Bemis's face seemed tense even in sleep. The eyelids were quivering now, the eyeballs roving within. She smelled a faint sweetness in the old woman's hair, wondered what she saw in her dreams. Alice remained there for some time, watching, strangely happy just to be close.

seventeen

The rain started again as Alice left for home, and she paused a moment after she'd pushed open the front door of Nichols, wishing she'd thought to bring an umbrella. She thrust her hands into her pockets, and her fingers crinkled something. She expected a receipt, but it was that scrap of newspaper with the name LeBeau on it. She peered out once more at the downpour, contemplated her dreary apartment, the sleeping, troubled Mrs. B.

Could the detective possibly help?

Alice might be doing him a favor. The connection to Mrs. Bemis wasn't much, but it might be more than the police had to go on. And maybe the cops had some information of their own that could help Alice actually get somewhere with Mrs. Bemis.

She pulled the scrap of paper from her pocket again, smoothed out the folds.

• • •

At the pay phone again, Alice reached a lieutenant with the Marshfield police who told her she was speaking on a recorded line.

There was a pause, then a click, and a new voice came on. "LeBeau." This voice seemed lighter. "Can I help you?"

Alice girded herself. "I'm calling about that body, the one that floated up in Duxbury a few weeks ago. Are you handling that case?"

"Who is this calling, please?"

"I'd rather not give my name, if that's all right."

"Okay." A pause. "Yes. I'm handling it."

Hypothetical, wasn't that what Victor had advised? Okay: "What if I told you that a friend had some information on the case—"

"Who are we talking about here?"

"I'm afraid I can't tell you that—"

"Look, I don't have—" Huffy now.

"—over the phone," Alice continued. She was beginning to hate the phone—the distance, the confusion.

"—a lotta time here, okay?" the detective wound up.

"I'm saying I could *meet* you," Alice interrupted, her voice raised, her heart pounding. "In person."

"Could you," the detective said, softer this time. He sounded— amused.

Alice liked that. It took some of the pressure off. "I think I may know someone who knew Brendan Hurley quite well."

"Oh?" Skeptical, but interested now. Definitely interested.

It was pouring when she climbed into her car and drove out the east gate, and found her way to Route 3, gradually leaving the thunderstorms behind her somewhere south of Boston. But the image of Mrs. Bemis, asleep in her bed, kept filling Alice's mind. She wondered about the detective, what he'd say, what she'd say. Her only contact with the police came with speeding tickets, when she was not at her best. Those cops remained faceless and impatient no matter how much she said she was sorry, that she'd never do it again, as her father, always fearful of the police, had once counseled her.

The Marshfield Police Department was past Arnie's Bakery, on Route 22, just as Detective LeBeau had said. It was coming up on six as Alice stepped out onto the still warm asphalt of the parking lot. The air was steamy, laundromatlike. But it worked into her joints, relaxed her.

The police building itself was a gray slab of concrete, set back from the road. Inside, the sergeant at the desk was bent over a well-thumbed paperback. He directed Alice upstairs with a nod of the head.

Detective Frank LeBeau's office was the third one on the right down a narrow, paneled hall. The door was open, and Alice could see him laboring at a computer keyboard. The keys clicked slowly, punctuated now and again by a whispered oath. LeBeau was tall, early thirties, somewhat stiff looking, and his narrow, freckled face was crowned with a thick swatch of red hair that reminded Alice of a lighted match. Behind him, an air conditioner whirred and gurgled without having much impact on the mugginess that had wet LeBeau's brow and darkened his underarms.

Alice knocked on the door frame. It took LeBeau a moment to look her way. "Yeah?" he said wearily.

Alice poked her head inside and tried for the cheery smile she used with new clients, but couldn't quite manage it. "I spoke to you on the phone."

"Oh yeah, the one with the friend." He didn't sound wildly thrilled, but he stood up, ushered her inside, and then dragged a folding chair over to his desk for her. "Have a seat, why don't you."

Alice settled herself down on the cool metal. Unlike the other offices she'd glanced into, this one didn't have any framed snapshots or softball trophies or other personalizing details, just a big town map on one wall. "New here?" she asked.

"Yeah." He smiled, gently nodding his head. "Couple months." He chuckled. "Still can't get used to seeing the sea out there." He gestured out over the parking lot, where a sliver of ocean was dimly visible in the shimmering distance between a couple of industrial buildings. "I'm a mountain boy. Vermonter."

"So why'd you move?"

Some of the light in his face went out. "How long you got?" LeBeau pulled himself in closer to his desk. "So. Brendan Hurley. Got the photographs right here," he said, slapping a hand down on a manila file on his desk. "Maybe you want to see what we're dealing with. Guy's dead, you know. No kidding around. It's kinda ugly." He spilled the photographs out of their onionskin sleeve and onto the desktop for her.

There were maybe a dozen shots in all. Glossy five-by-sevens. The first few showed the body in the water. By the pier, Alice figured. The shot must have been taken almost straight down, because the light from the flash made the black water sparkle. The body itself was mostly submerged, with only the shoulders and back clearly visible, and it seemed barely human, just a slab of waterlogged meat. The next photo was taken from low in the water, off to one side, and showed just a bit of the bare back that crested above the water, with the pier behind, and a portion of the lower legs of the different investigators. From that angle, the body looked almost abstract, just a gleam of light, except for the hair billowing in the water and one partly chewed ear. Poor Brendan. *Whoever you are.*

"You okay with this?" LeBeau asked.

"I'm all right," Alice said. She'd seen cadavers in medical school, and watched patients expire on the operating table. But then again, none of them had been partly eaten.

The others pictures had been taken after the corpse had been hauled up onto a sheet on the dock. Alice could almost smell the rot, see the flies buzzing about the carcass. A policeman's face got into one of the pictures, and Alice could see the distress in it. Only loose strips of puffy tissue hung where Brendan Hurley's face should have been. One eye had been completely gouged out, the other was blobby and distended. And there were some deep gouges on his chest and shoulders where the crabs had clawed it. That thought reached inside Alice, made her head go cottony. The torn flesh, ripped by claws and pincers. The anonymity of it. The way this poor person had been turned into just a body, just meat. And Mrs. Bemis involved somehow.

"That's pretty much all we've got," LeBeau said, closing the file. "Pretty, huh? I feel bad for the kids that found him."

"The swimmers?"

"The girl, especially. Wasn't wearing a suit, even. Rubbed up against this thing. Can you imagine? God."

"I heard there was another man on the boat," she said, to change the subject.

"Yeah, we're looking into that. He hasn't turned up, and this guy here isn't talking. But we're still checking it out." LeBeau closed the file again. "So, you got some background for me?"

Alice returned to her chair, took a breath. If she could just figure out what to do with her hands, the rest would be easy. Fold them in her lap? "Look, Detective, I'm not really sure I should be here."

"And why's that?"

"Well, I'm a psychiatrist." The word sounded strange to her in that small, bare detective's office. "At a psychiatric institute." Stranger still. "I've come, well, I've come because of something I was told by one of my patients."

"Okay."

He said it so gently, so noncommittally, that Alice had to smile. "What?"

She liked the openness she saw in his face just then. "Maybe you should be a shrink, too."

"Oh?" The detective pulled one of his long legs up off the floor and crossed it over the other one, revealing a revolver in a holster around his ankle. "So why's that?" It seemed like a genuine question.

"You're good at staying calm."

"You haven't told me anything that means anything to me yet," LeBeau told her, twisting a paper clip. "Who knows, once you do, I might jump out the window."

"Somehow I don't think so."

"Well, that is a comfort to me."

Alice couldn't tell if his jokes were meant to draw her closer, or to keep her at bay. Some sweat on her palm was causing her cut to sting again. She dried her palms on her pants, and tried to remind herself that she was here for her patient. "Look, whatever I tell you, you have to promise me that it won't get me in trouble. Because, as I said, I really shouldn't be here."

"Sorry, but I can't promise anything like that."

Alice felt a pang of disappointment. "But I told you, I'm a *psychiarist*," she repeated with new emphasis.

"Well, we could all use a little of that, now couldn't we?" LeBeau got up, moved to the filing cabinet, where a large plastic thermos was perched beside a couple of glasses. He offered her some iced coffee. "Brewed it myself this morning," he told her. "I can't handle that hot sludge they got down the hall. Like goddamn lava or something."

Alice shook her head, but LeBeau poured two glasses anyway, and handed one to her. "Go on. Live a little." He handed her a packet of creamer, and a wooden stirrer. He settled back into his chair, poured in some creamer for himself, watched the whiteness billow through the dark liquid. "See, I can't promise you anything until I know what we're talking about."

"But I can't tell you until you promise me."

LeBeau thought for a moment. "Well, I guess we've got a little problem then," he said. He didn't seem to be in any hurry to resolve it.

The phone rang, and the detective reached for it. "LeBeau," he said. "Yeah." A pause. "You do?" Another pause. "Okay." Another, longer pause. He reached for a notepad, jotted something down. "Yeah, got it." He nodded. "Right, right. So—when's this going public?" Another nod. "Gotcha. Okay. Thanks." He set down the phone. He looked at the note he'd made, then ripped the sheet off the pad. "That was the state cops. More info on your floater," he said.

"Just then?"

"Yeah, we'd only had a name, pretty much. That's all they had at the boat company."

Alice must have looked perplexed.

"Where he rented the sailboat that went over. Fair amount of booze in the system." He glanced significantly at Alice. "We haven't released that, okay?"

"Sure," Alice said quietly.

"So now we've got an address, place of employment, the whole bit." He waved the note in the air. "We're keeping it quiet, though." He looked at her intently. "So."

The way he looked at her, she wondered what he could be seeing. Another potential informant, or was it something else? She could almost feel his eyes on her, probing. Her cheeks and forehead burned with a feeling close to shame, but when he looked away, she found she missed his gaze. "Okay," she said. "Okay."

She started to explain about Mrs. Bemis, whom she carefully referred to only as "a terribly depressed older lady." She described how she came to Montrose, which Alice likewise didn't name; how she'd begun therapy with her; how painfully blocked Mrs. B seemed. Talking to him didn't corrupt her the way she'd expected. She'd imagined that her skin would actually feel slimy. Instead, the talking seemed cleansing. She had the queer feeling that, as she talked to him, he was washing her, gliding a moistened cloth over her skin.

It was already hard enough to tell Mrs. Bemis's story without slipping up and revealing identifying details. Alice spoke haltingly, kept interrupting herself with explanatory asides, and then stopping again to clear some of those up. LeBeau listened patiently, his brown eyes never leaving her. She felt bashful when she finally arrived at the point. "What I mean to say is, she knew him."

"Well, so do lots of other people," LeBeau said.

"Yes, but he was important to her."

"How?" the detective asked.

"I spoke to her caretaker. He knew Brendan, too. So he must have been someone who went to the house. I thought if I could just find out a little more from you about the case, maybe I'd be able to help her." She stopped, put off by the coolness she saw on LeBeau's face. "I give you something, you give me something. Isn't that how it works?"

"Seems like a funny way to do therapy."

The remark stopped her cold. "Well, maybe it isn't exactly the normal way," she told him. "But maybe *she's* not quite normal right now." She had his attention now. "She's cut off from everyone. Cut off from herself, if you ask me. I suppose I could do the usual, drug her up, sit with her for a few more weeks or, I don't know, *months* doing the kind of stupid staring contest that passes for proper psychiatry with closed-down patients like her. Or I could try something that might actually help her. I don't have a lot of time here, Detective. My boss is leaning on me to get somewhere. And there was a suicide on the ward a couple of weeks ago. A college kid hanged himself. He was a friend of hers, too. I worry that that's in the back of her mind. Perhaps you know, a suicide can be contagious on a ward, and, believe me, I *really* don't want her to leave Montrose on a gurney." The words seemed to echo around the spare little office. She felt panic rise in her chest. Victor was right: the things in that room should stay in that room. She'd obviously overdone it. "I'm sorry. I should probably go. I don't want to waste your time." She stood up, headed for the door, and had it open when LeBeau stopped her.

"Hang on there a second, wouldja?" He eased the door shut. "Maybe you should sit down," he said.

She moved a couple of steps back into the room, but she remained standing.

"You write that out beforehand, or did it just come to you?"

Alice didn't feel like being teased. "Listen, Detective, I spent too many years in school for this. I've got work to do, all right? It's a bit of a drive back up to Cambridge. So if it's all right with you, I think I'll just go." She headed for the door again.

"Okay, just wait a sec," Detective LeBeau called out to her. "I'll stop jerking you around. I'm glad you came. Really. I wouldn't say that normally. You should see the whackos we get sometimes."

He leaned back against his desk, facing her. "Brendan Hurley, fifty-eight years old. Had an apartment in Quincy. Recovering alcoholic. Worked—when he did work—at the Pine Street Inn downtown. He drove the van that peeled the drunks off the sidewalk. Takes one to know one, I guess."

He handed her a single sheet of paper bearing the notes he'd made. "That's all we've got."

She took the paper from him, scanned the sharply angled letters.

"And it bugs me, too, if you want to know," he added.

Alice looked at him, surprised.

"Nobody gives a shit, pardon my language. Guy washes up dead, and people go, 'Okay, what else is new.' I just think we oughta try to figure it out a little. Guy deserves that much, anyway. Maybe he was murdered, who knows? But even if he wasn't, I think we ought to know what happened. Not just bury him and be done with it."

"You mean, there's been no investigation?"

"It's just me, pretty much. And whoever else I can drag into it with me, which is nobody." LeBeau reached out on his desk and lifted a pile of manila folders. "And there's all this other stuff I'm supposed to be handling." He pulled up one folder. "A supposed arson investigation on Grendell Street. Which sounds like a big deal, but it's really just a Dumpster fire that a neighbor's all excited about." He lifted up another folder. "A marijuana case involving a high school teacher." A third. "Guy slapped his boss around at a bar."

"Even if it's a murder?" Alice interrupted.

"Listen, I agree with you. But he's a nobody. That's the whole problem. Just another drunk."

"What about the other guy? The one in the boat?"

LeBeau shook his head. "Zip. Sharks could've got him. We don't know." He kicked back from his desk, crossed his legs. "Brendan's brother's a big deal, though. Michael Hurley. Ever heard of him?"

The name did sound familiar, but Alice couldn't place it.

"Computer guy. Head of a dotcom, one of the few that's still going. Telectronics.com. If it was him who was dead, maybe we'd have something. But this guy, Brendan—"

There was a knock at the door. "Frank?" asked a female voice.

"Yeah?"

A dark-eyed woman in a blue shirt poked her head in; her eyes met Alice's for only a moment before they locked onto LeBeau's.

"Just wanted to remind you, you got that meeting with the state people at eight."

LeBeau checked his watch. It was nearly six-thirty.

"Oh, shit. Yeah. Thanks, Kath."

She closed the door behind her.

"Department secretary," LeBeau explained. "Looks like I've got about an hour. Hey, I don't want to be a total pain. We can talk if you want. Grab a bite maybe before you head back?"

"If you want," Alice said, uncertain about just what she was agreeing to.

"Oh, and one other thing."

Alice braced herself.

"What's your name?"

She smiled, relieved. "Dr. Alice Matthews. But Alice is fine."

LeBeau offered his hand. "Pleased to meet you, Alice. I shouldn't have given you so much shit. I'm Frank."

eighteen

LeBeau had some calls to make, so he asked Alice to meet him at a seafood place, Katie's, down by the water on the outskirts of what passed for Marshfield's downtown. She found it easily enough, and took a seat on the deck out back under a blue awning. The air had turned balmy as the evening settled in, and the wind was up. It ruffled the awning's fringe, flapped the checkerboard tablecloth, and threw a few strands of Alice's hair across her face.

When the waitress came around, Alice ordered a daiquiri. "Virgin, please," Alice added.

"Yeah, I get that way sometimes," the girl told her.

Alice smiled, watched the girl retreat back through a glass door to the kitchen, then turned her eyes toward the sea. It was a hundred feet away, past a weedy lot that ended in a narrow beach where a few fat gulls were waddling. She could see some whitecaps out in deeper water, where the body had come from.

From nowhere, really. Alice thought again about how it had

floated in from the depths of the bay, scaring the hell out of a skinny-dipping teenager and sending Mrs. Bemis to her.

Her drink came, and as she sipped it, she looked back out to the water, scanning the horizon line between the dark sea and the fading band of brightness of the sky. It was from there that the body had come. What was that—two miles, three, five? A long way, in any case. But it wasn't just the distance. It was also the time. Brendan Hurley had come out of Mrs. Bemis's past. From deep in her past, Alice guessed, judging by the way she was so fixated on him.

Alice scanned the bay again, the distant waves. There—and here. Then—and now. They're always linked. That was the essence of psychiatry, wasn't it? Seeing the single coin of which these were the two sides. Alice had some more of the daiquiri, enjoying the fleeting sweetness on her tongue. There is no here, not really—no here that a there does not intrude upon. Right now, she felt the wind on her face, blown in from who knew where. And, as for now, it's the barest shaving of time, too slim even to detect. The present is gone before you can even register it. Alice felt again the gusty, evening air. The not-here, not-now rises up all around, pressing in, giving us our shape, telling us who we are. Alice didn't even have to close her eyes to bring her friends and family back to her—not just to her, but inside her. The Grand, telling rollicking stories to the spellbound kindergartner Alice once was; her parents, grumbling over after-dinner Sanka on the back porch in their small, clapboard house on Pearl Street; Lars, who ran his hand down her jeans that first time they'd touched, as if she were a horse and he were stroking her flank. Even now, at the end of a long day, she could picture all these people *so easily*. They were right here, right now. She was sure they'd speak to her if she said hello.

Alice was a few inches into her drink when LeBeau stepped out onto the deck. He wore a light windbreaker and he'd combed his hair, giving it a sheen. He walked a bit stiffly, as tall men tend to. His height, or maybe it was the ruddy brightness about him, held her eyes. Alice thought she detected some cologne on him when he approached her table.

"Sorry to make you wait," LeBeau said.

"Don't worry about it. It's nice out here. Gave me a chance to think."

"About?"

"Oh, nothing. People I used to know."

"Sea does that," LeBeau said. "It's like a fire in a fireplace up north. Gets you remembering." He took a seat across from her and flagged down the waitress for some cranberry juice, explaining he still had his meeting to go to. They both ordered the smoked salmon plate.

"Thanks, hon," he told the waitress, who smiled back at him.

"I've got more info on this guy Hurley," LeBeau said, setting down a file he'd pulled out of a zippered case. "Lotta faxes. Thought it might interest you." He glanced over at her, his brown eyes on hers. "Now, this is our secret, right?"

Alice smiled. "Of course," she said. She liked being in his confidence.

LeBeau glanced down over the facts, read off the high points. "Okay," he started in. "Grew up in South Boston. Down by the projects, 112 C Street. Rough neighborhood. Went to Southie. The high school, I mean. No college. Father worked for the city as a custodian of some kind. Mother a seamstress. They're both dead. Brendan never married—at least there's no record of it downtown. That Michael, at Telectronics, appears to be the only sibling. There was no missing-person report on Brendan, by the way. Nobody noticed he was gone. That a pisser, or what? One of my guys called Pine Street. They hadn't even realized he hadn't shown up."

Alice thought about Mrs. Bemis, so far removed from Brendan's world.

"That depressed lady of yours isn't from there, I take it."

"Hardly." She shook her head, impressed that LeBeau could track her thoughts. "She's a real WASP. Grew up in a big place in Dover. Lived in Milton for almost fifty years. I don't think she knows where South Boston is." Alice hardly did herself, but she was enjoying the detective's nuanced sense of the local geography.

"But she knew Brendan."

"Yeah. Somehow."

"Interesting."

The waitress came out with their fish. Starving, Alice lit into hers as LeBeau watched. "Okay," he said after a moment. "So are you going to tell me her name?"

Alice set her fork down on her plate.

"Okay then," he said, nodding.

Alice felt a twinge of reluctance as she looked over at LeBeau's eyes, so expectant. But she plunged ahead. "It's Madeline Bemis." She spelled the last name for him. "She's at Montrose. That's where I work."

"Oh yeah?" He seemed interested. "With all the movie stars? I read about that place."

"It's not really that glamorous," Alice said, remembering Ethan. She'd never seen any movie stars herself, but she'd heard about a couple of rock stars who'd been in for treatment a few months before she'd come. One had arrived in a limousine.

LeBeau took out a small black notebook from his jacket pocket and wrote down the words "Madeline Bemis" and "Montrose" in pencil. Then he looked up at Alice and added "Alice Matthews."

"You have a phone number where I can reach you?"

Alice gave him the number. "It's better if you don't call me at work."

"I understand." He jotted down her number. He tucked the notebook away and turned to his fish. "There. That wasn't so hard."

Alice thought about Mrs. B's name in his book, wondered if it was safe there.

She ate another few bites, deliberating. "You don't happen to have a picture of him, do you? I mean, before he washed up by that pier."

"Got a photo off his driver's license. Came through on a fax, so it's kinda blotchy." He turned his attention to the pile of faxes by his plate, flipped through the pages. "I tried to grab some things before I came. Yeah. Here we go." He handed her a sheet.

She wiped her hands with her napkin and took the photo from him. The picture quality was poor, just as he'd said. It showed a weary, sad-eyed man in an open shirt. The fax had darkened the hollows under his eyes, and blackened his hair, which was thick and bushy. So different from Mrs. Bemis, who was so resolute, so steely in her propriety.

"He got any family?" Alice asked, handing the fax back.

"Nope. None of his own, from what they're saying. Just the brother."

"You don't suppose he was the man out with him?"

"Now you're thinking like a cop," LeBeau said. "I checked already. Michael Hurley is very much alive. I talked to him just yesterday. He's back from a business trip to Pittsburgh."

Alice looked up at him.

"Way ahead of you. I checked that, too. He's been in a big conference down there. A lot of people saw him down there the whole time." LeBeau looked over at her. "So tell me about your patient, all right? Can you do that? It might help us."

"You're not going to talk to her, are you?" Alice asked.

"No." He paused. "Well, not yet, anyway."

"Look, Detective—"

"Frank. The name's Frank, okay?" Slight irritation, enough to hold Alice's attention.

"Frank, please, you've got to promise me—"

"It's got to be a two-way street here, okay, Alice?" LeBeau interrupted. "The woman might have some information for us. I'm busting my hump on this thing, and, as I told you, I'm not getting a lot of support. This isn't psychiatry. We may be looking at a murder here."

"But I thought he drowned."

"Any number of ways a person can drown." He paused a moment, appraising her.

It was frightening to hear him turn so coldly professional. For a fleeting moment, she was afraid she'd misread him.

She reached out a hand toward him, hoping he'd ease off Mrs.

Bemis, at least. "I understand. But, please, Detec—Frank. I feel protective of her. The whole idea about coming down here was to help her. I don't want her to get grilled."

"No one's talking about grilling," he said evenly. "That's not something I do." Then he softened. "Listen, I like you, all right? You're a good person. And because of that I've probably gone too far down this road already. But you've got to understand, this is a police case. We can't leave stones unturned here."

"That's what I'm hearing."

"Okay. So. What can you tell me?" He folded his hands on the table in front of him.

Alice didn't know where to begin. "Well, I like her." Strange that that was the first thing that came to mind. It was not at all the first thing she'd say about most of her patients.

"Because?"

She started to say that beneath Mrs. Bemis's coldly proper demeanor, she had a warmth to her, deep down, like some "ancient fire," as she put it a shade too poetically, that had never gone out. "But you probably just want to know what her connection is to the case."

"I want you to tell me whatever you want to tell me."

Alice smiled. "I probably just have a weakness for elderly women. I was extremely fond of my grandmother. I guess I tended to look past my parents a little, since—" She stopped, looked up. "You don't want to hear about this."

"No, I do, really, but—" LeBeau looked down at his watch.

Alice didn't want to seem so self-involved. "Sorry."

"No, I'm sorry," LeBeau told her. "All this rushing around."

"You really should be a therapist, you know," Alice continued, to try to patch things up. "You're a good listener."

"I just know when to keep quiet," LeBeau said, and he finished off the last of his fish.

But Alice knew that he needed to get some hard information out of her, and she cleared her throat, told him what she knew about the

fairly tight circle of Mrs. Bemis's associations: the horticulture society, the orchids, the Milton house, her late husband.

"So what's the link, do you suppose?" LeBeau asked finally.

"Between?"

"Your patient at Montrose and this dead man here."

"That's the thing," Alice said. "I haven't any idea."

"What's your guess, then? If you had to say, right now."

"I'm not sure I'm ready to say."

"But if you *had* to."

"Well, I'd guess it's in her family somehow," Alice said. "That's
the thing that comes through strongest. That he's some relative.
She's so desperate for connection. Resisting it, but craving it, too.
Husband's dead. No kids. She used to be very social, all these parties.
But now, the isolation—I just think it's eating her up." She fished
out the photograph again, stared at it. "But God, you look at him
and he seems so different." She looked at LeBeau. "I'm sorry, I don't
think I've been all that helpful to you."

"You never know what's helpful."

They'd finished eating. LeBeau glanced down at his watch, then
asked for the check.

"Can I ask you a question?"

LeBeau appraised her. "Sure. Go ahead."

"How come you're handling the case?" Alice asked. "You're the
new guy, right?"

"Just lucky, I guess."

"No, really."

"Nobody else wanted it, tell you the truth. Plus, I've had some
experience with unidentified remains." Alice tried to keep her face
expressionless. "I investigated a fire in a trailer park outside Brattleboro one time. Five, six trailers went up. Arson, turned out. Jealous
husband. He caught his wife shacking up with some guy, and lit the
whole place up. That was a big deal locally. And there was another
one, a murder victim in a septic tank. We had a pretty good idea who
it was, but we still had to go through the DNA and everything."

"That sort of thing bother you?"

"Other things bother me more."

"Like?"

LeBeau didn't answer.

"Like your marriage? That why you left Brattleboro?"

LeBeau looked at her for a long moment, but said nothing. He swiped his mouth with his napkin and put it down on the table in front of him. "C'mon, I want to show you something." He started to stand up.

"What?"

"Rexhane Beach. It's just up there a ways." He swept a hand up the beach, toward Boston. "Might help you get the lay of the land."

Puzzled, Alice stood up, too. "Why, what's there?"

"It's where Hurley and his friend put the Laser in. Thought it might give you an idea."

"Just to see it?"

"Listen, you don't have to."

"No, I'd like to. Really. It might . . . help, somehow."

The waitress came over with the check, and LeBeau took it from her. "You can get the next one," he told her. He paid cash, and left a nice tip, which Alice couldn't help noticing.

When they were outside in the parking lot, Frank told Alice to follow him. Then he climbed into his unmarked cruiser, and after waiting for Alice to start up, he drove slowly—considerately signaling well ahead of every turn—as he led her down the narrow Marshfield streets lined with weatherbeaten houses. Eventually, he turned in by a municipal sign that said "Rexhane Beach," and pulled into a broad lot. Alice followed him in and parked a couple of spaces away. A group of kids at the tiny Clam Shak there in the lot waved to him as he climbed out of his car. LeBeau waved back, and called out to one of them by name. "You're not gettin' in trouble again, Danny, are you?"

"Oh, no, Detective." Danny grabbed the teenager beside him. "He's the kid you gotta watch."

"Got it." LeBeau laughed. Alice admired the easy, confident way he walked, his jacket billowing in the breeze, his red hair fluttering. "It's over here," he said quietly. He led her across the pavement toward a narrow path that passed through a gap in the marsh grass on the ocean side of the lot. Alice's shoes slid about on the still warm sand as she followed him onto the beach. He stopped a few feet down. Some kids were swimming inside a rectangle of buoys out in the water, although the lifeguards had long since left their stations. "Down there," he said, pointing about halfway down the beach. "Just above the tide line. Some eager beaver was renting boats off a trailer. Brendan signed for the boat, paid cash, and gave an extra hundred for a security deposit since he didn't have a credit card. The rental guy didn't see anything suspicious. He thinks they may have had a cooler, but that was normal. Two of them, he says. Didn't get a name on the other one. Younger man, sort of athletic."

He paused, seemed unconvinced. "But we don't have a clue, really. They were supposed to come back in four hours. Guy figured they'd stolen it, since it was fairly calm that day. Plus, a boat like that's hard to tip over. And Brendan's friend seemed to know what he was doing." He turned to her. "We're keeping this out of the papers, right?"

"Yes, Frank."

"We're thinking that they may have gotten into a fight, or maybe they just fucked up royally. That happens. I hate boats, myself. You'll never catch me in one of them."

"Mountain boy, you said."

"Damn right."

"So the boat went in right here?" Alice repeated, looking down toward the water.

"Yeah, just about. Off a trailer, the guy said. He wheeled it back from that little road there." He pointed to a narrow asphalt track off the edge of the parking lot.

Alice tried to picture a boat heading out into the waves, then some trouble, the sail pitching about, someone going over the side.

The scene bore so little relation to the image of Mrs. Bemis lying in bed, her eyes shut.

"Thought you might want to see it," LeBeau said. "Thought it might help." He walked her back to her car. Alice didn't get in right away. Instead, she leaned against the side of her car a little, felt the cool metal through her clothes, and turned back to him. She sensed he wanted to tell her something more. And maybe he did, or maybe he knew she wanted to hear something more from him.

"You were right about my wife," he said, in a soft, newly uncertain voice. "She's still back up in Brattleboro." He paused a moment, watching Alice. "Sheila. We had a nice house in the foothills, a dog. I thought everything was set. Turned out she was in love with somebody else."

"I'm sorry."

"I found her with him. She stayed home sick from work one day, and I came back at lunchtime to check on her. I'd brought her some soup from this place I knew. I found her sitting with this guy on the rug in front of the fire. They weren't having sex or anything, just sitting together there, real close, holding hands." LeBeau folded his arms across his chest, looked downcast.

"It bothered you," Alice said.

"Yes it did. I threw the guy out. It got real ugly. Sheila started screaming, I started screaming." He paused a second, looked back at Alice. "I moved my stuff out the next morning."

"So you're separated?" Alice asked.

"I am. I don't know if she is."

"She with that other guy?"

LeBeau shrugged. "I really don't know." He glanced down at his watch. "Look, I better get going. I'm late, and I've bored you enough already."

"It's not boring, Frank."

He seemed to consider that for a second. "Maybe it's just boring to me." He headed for his car.

"You didn't tell me where the body floated up," Alice called after him.

He turned. "You mean in Duxbury?"

"Yeah."

He pointed down the beach toward Provincetown. "Down there a mile or so. Cyrus Brewster's place, on Spinney Street. But don't go bothering them. They're already plenty ticked off about the publicity. People like that don't like seeing their names in the newspapers. Not for something like this."

"Got it," Alice assured him.

He reached his car, opened the door. "Nice meeting you. We'll be in touch, all right? I want to figure this thing out. I guess you do, too."

"Yeah."

He rolled down the window. "And remember, the next dinner's on you."

nineteen

After LeBeau drove off, Alice sat in her car for a few minutes. The night had fallen, and a few stars were starting to peek out from the mist. The boys had left the Clam Shak; she was alone in her little car in the big lot where Brendan Hurley had passed through the very last day of his life. LeBeau was right: it did give her a feeling, brought her closer to this strange case that had so upset her patient. LeBeau had a toughness to him, yet he was insightful, and the kindness was there. He was like some high, stout tree growing in front of a house. Hardly an exotic, but it gave good shade. Then she stopped herself when she realized that that was the sort of thing Mrs. Bemis might think.

Alice still didn't understand Mrs. Bemis's connection to Brendan Hurley. If anything, the connection now seemed even more tenuous. Mrs. B didn't look like Hurley, didn't live anywhere near him, and they were from completely different backgrounds.

And yet, Brendan and his friend (if they were indeed friends) went to sea from the beach by this parking lot. For all Alice knew, the car that brought them might have been parked right here, where her car was.

If so, where was that car now? Surely people didn't take taxis to a beach like this. Could someone have dropped them off? Who?

Not Mrs. Bemis. That was impossible.

Wasn't it?

Alice wondered if LeBeau thought along these lines, if detectives always thought along these lines, every avenue forking, then branching out farther, creating a vast, frail web of tantalizing possibilities.

She thought of the other end of Brendan's final journey—the pier where the body had been found. Where had LeBeau said it was? Spinney Street in Duxbury? It wasn't far, and on her way back to Cambridge besides. What harm could it do just to see it?

When she switched on the ignition, she felt a jolt as the engine whirred. Here in this vacant lot, with the light dying all around her, the car seemed alive, pulling her. All she could do was let it go. She turned out of the Rexhane lot, headed down Dover Lane and back onto Route 20, toward Duxbury. She wasn't driving fast, not for her, but the streets were narrow and the houses flew by on either side. It felt like she wasn't moving ahead, but falling helplessly, sucked by a kind of gravity. The streetlights glowed to ward off the black sky, and, as she passed through them, the inside of the car flipped from dark to light to dark again.

Spinney Street was off Bay Avenue, by the Duxbury shore. The houses were large, imposing, and they were surrounded by lawns that were pools of deep green in the late evening. So unlike the neighborhood in Latrobe where she'd grown up. She pulled over about halfway down the street, shut off the engine, and waited a moment.

It was quieter here than in Marshfield, or in North Cambridge, or Latrobe, or most neighborhoods she knew. She imagined that this must be the quiet of money, the kind of quiet you have to pay for. She could just hear the gentle rustling of the water on the beach. Off to her right, in the wide gaps between the houses, she could see the ocean gleam in the twilight.

The Brewster house was the one at the far end, closest to the water. A photo had turned up in the *Herald* account, but the place seemed bigger now. She took a breath to calm herself, then stepped out of the car and closed the door quietly behind her, pushing till it clicked shut.

The air smelled of salt, and a slight breeze moved through the low bushes lining the street. Around her, the windows of the houses were open to the evening air, and as Alice made her way down the sidewalk, she could hear murmurs of conversations and the clinking of plates and glasses from the dining rooms inside.

Up ahead, the Brewster house was a shingled castle, with wide porches and white trim, and it stood out boldly against the graying sky. There were two cars in the drive, expensive ones, but the house was dark except for a pair of windows off the kitchen. The radiance spilled out across the lawn, illuminating a small flower garden. Hugging the shadows by a row of heavy bushes to the right of the drive, Alice crept closer, alert for any movement, any sound. Every thump of her heart told her that what she was doing was stupid and dangerous.

As she reached the end of the bushes, she could see the pier where the body had floated up. The low, angled roof of the boathouse stood out against the flat water of the bay, and, beyond it, there were a few sailboats swaying at anchor, their halyards ringing against the masts.

Alice waited, watched. Nothing moved in the house.

The garden was to her right, and there was a gate just beyond it, she could see, and a path through a field beyond that. It led to a boardwalk through the marsh, and to the boathouse beyond. Around her, the crickets throbbed, a loud ringing in her ears.

She advanced toward the gate, staying low. Closer, closer, across the grass. She found the latch, lifted, pulled the gate toward her. The hinges creaked, sending a wave of fear down her arms, to her fingertips. But there was no stopping now, not with the sea so close. She closed the gate behind her, and hurried through the field to the boathouse.

Just to see.

Yellow police tape blocked off the entrance to the boardwalk, with a strip across the top and then two diagonals forming an X below. Alice slipped under it. The boards gave some under her tread as she hurried along, eager to conceal herself in the shadows of the boathouse. The air was cooler down here by the water, and it pushed through her linen suit. The boathouse stood in the middle of the pier, but a slender walkway wrapped around one side.

A last nervous look toward the house. Nothing. Alice stepped around the boathouse, hugging the shadows cast by the moonlight, and approached the edge of the dock beyond, which she recognized from the police photographs. She was near where the naked girl must have fled from the water. Alice crept forward to the spot where the police photographer probably stood to take his grisly pictures of the floating corpse. The night was settling in; the air itself seemed to be slowly turning black. Beneath her, the water sloshed gently against the wooden pilings holding up the pier, washing over the steps that descended into the pale, translucent green below. Alice saw the police photographs again: the decayed body of Brendan Hurley, facedown in the brine; the close-up of the horrible, ripped-away face itself. The images startled her with their ferocity.

Who was Brendan to Mrs. Bemis? Was he family, after all?

She was lowering a hand to reach into the image from her mind, to touch the water in which the body had floated, when she heard a shout, and felt a radiance on her.

"Excuse me!" A woman's voice.

Alice turned toward the sound, her hand shielding her eyes from the bright light.

"Who's out there? Hello?" the woman called to her. "I can see you out there. Yes, you there. This is private property, you know. What are you doing?" The woman was coming closer, the light fixed on Alice.

"You shouldn't be there," the woman declared. "It's a crime scene, don't you know?" Then the light slipped off Alice as the woman shouted back up toward the house—"Cy! Cy! Come out here, would you? There's someone out on the pier!" A few more steps from the woman—Alice could hear them—and then a screen door opened with a screech.

"You out there, Ellie?" a man cried.

Two of them! The woman was nearly to the boardwalk.

The woman again: "Come down here, would you, Cy? There's someone on our pier."

"*Again?*"

"Come, would you?"

But then barking, from deep in the house, and a screen door banged, and the man again, distressed now, "Oh, *hell!* The dogs are out! Ellen!"

It was more than barking, more like a roar, a thunder of heavy paws on the lawn. Three dogs at least, maybe more, racing down the lawn toward the water, toward Alice.

"Call them, Cyrus," the woman shouted. "I didn't shut the— Cyrus! *Call* them!"

"Ranger! Duke!" Cyrus cried. But his voice was weak, old. It didn't slow the dogs. They growled and yelped as they charged down the slope toward Alice. They were coming, coming for her.

"Oh, *hell!*" Cyrus shouted once more.

Alice didn't look back again. There was no time. She had to get away. Now! She looked down into the water again. Yes. Into the water. Where the body had—Yes! Now! Alice kicked off her shoes, flung them into the water, then splashed down the ladder in her stockinged feet. The water was dark. And so cold!

But the barking, the pounding of the dogs, the jangling of dog tags—they were all coming closer. She swung herself around, scraping her hand on the rough post, and let go. The chill rose up her body as the wetness seeped through to her skin. She kicked the pier away, lurched out toward open water, stroking. Her head up, she could hear shouts, barking, but couldn't make out any words over her own labored breathing.

The water dragged across her body, pulling at her. She fought her fear, kicking and stroking, trying to propel herself along, the linen of her suit twisting around her. There was a splash on the shore, and more furious barking. She braced herself for a slash of claws, for teeth ripping her.

She hadn't swum in the ocean in years. And her sodden clothes were dragging her under. But there was a spit of land off to her right. Her car was back there, somewhere, on the street. She swam harder. Then a flash of brightness lit her up, and more shouts to the dogs and a "There—see?" Alice ducked under, felt the cold water freeze her cheeks, push against her eyeballs, tug her hair. Her cheeks puffed to hold the air, she kicked and stroked through the underwater silence, sweeping the water back. Her lungs begged for air, but she drove her arms ahead, again and again, through the silent blackness to get clear. Finally, she couldn't bear it a moment longer and she rose to the surface, but gently, cresting just once for a gulp of air and then descending into the murk again. She kept on, her pulse pounding in her ears, the blackness swirling all around her, as she thrust the water behind her. Again and again and again until every muscle ached and, starved for air, she rose for another breath. Then longer strokes, over and over until finally her fingers scraped on something. Frightened, she yanked her hand back before she realized it was a rock from shore, and she calmed herself and straightened and pushed her feet down and felt the rough bottom through her spongy socks.

She glanced back: the light was flashing across the water now, but away from her, out toward the boats at anchor in the deeper water. Dogs were thrashing about, but they were still some distance away. "Ranger!" the woman was shouting. "Duke! Queenie!" And the man was yelling, "Who's there? Did you see?"

As quietly as she could, Alice stumbled toward the shore, staying low, sucking in the air. The ground was just muck, and she sank in a few inches with each step. Still, she slogged on up to the marsh, which stank of stagnant water, and she pushed ahead until she came to a field, and then to a sloping lawn by a tennis court. The shouts, the barking were well away now, and she was nearing a house, a big shingled one. Snatches of conversation drifted out from open windows as she hurried across the lawn, then slipped through a line of fruit trees and saw the street again. The barking again, louder now. She broke into a run, although her lungs burned and her clothes hung on her like weights. The dogs came into view when she reached the sidewalk. Huge ones. Mastiffs, maybe, or German shepherds. Three of them, all coming for her. And an older man behind—Cyrus—yelling for them to stop. Stop! Or was it for *her* to stop? She kept on, her stockinged feet slapping the rough sidewalk. She reached her car, jumped in, sloshing onto the seat in her sopping clothes, and slammed the door behind her just as the first of the monstrous dogs leapt up on the side of her car, scratching the paint with its claws. Other big angry heads bobbed up onto the window, their bared teeth glinting. She hit the horn to scare them, but they kept right at it, scraping, howling, wanting to kill. She turned the ignition, and the engine rolled over once. "God*damnit!*" The man was coming for her now. She could see him through the windshield, coming slowly. He was not one to run. She pounded the dashboard, then tried the key again, and this time— oh, thank God!—the car came alive. She threw the car into reverse, dogs squealing as the car slithered away. She didn't hit the lights till she reached the end of the street, when her headlights caught the older man again at the far end. He was staring at her, his eyes shining.

The whole way back up Route 3, her entire body quaked, though whether it was from fear or from the cold she couldn't tell. She turned on the heater in the car, and warm air blasted at her through the vents, but she still couldn't keep from shivering.

What had she been thinking? What had she done? The questions careened about inside her head like the headlights of the oncoming cars, zooming at her, then whizzing past.

To get to Cambridge from Route 3, Alice would take the turnpike to the Allston exit for Storrow Drive. But Alice let the Allston exit go by, continued on through two sets of tolls to 128, and then went north to Route 2, and west from there. It was well past nine o'clock, but she had to see Mrs. Bemis once more before she could sleep tonight.

Her clothes were still damp in the crotch and under her arms. But she didn't care. She slipped on some flip-flops she'd left in the trunk after a trip to the beach with Ethan and made her way to the front door of Nichols.

She swiped her card for the keyless entry. "You're in a little late, aren't you?" the security guard told her.

"I forgot something," she replied, and kept going to the elevator so he wouldn't ask what. Marnie was on night duty in the nurses' station. "Well, hello," Marnie called out to her through the open door. "I thought you went home early." She took a closer look at Alice as she swept past. "Jesus, what happened to you? Get caught in a washing machine?"

"Thunderstorm."

"But it cleared off."

"Not where I was."

Marnie wagged a motherly finger at her. "I keep telling you, get an umbrella."

Alice kept on toward Mrs. Bemis's room.

"What are you doing here, anyway?" Marnie asked.

"I thought I'd check in on Madeline. I keep worrying about her." Alice continued down the corridor, her flip-flops smacking against her heels.

"Love the shoes," Marnie called out from behind.

Alice ignored her.

Mrs. Bemis's door was open, as always; but the lights were off as Alice stepped quietly into the room. Mrs. B was lying on her side, away from the light from the hall. Alice leaned down to her. Her patient's eyes were shut, but Alice could see her eyelids flutter as her pupils roved about inside.

Alice told herself she'd just stay a minute, but she pulled up a chair from the other side of the room, then took the spare blanket from Mrs. Bemis's bed. Gathering it around her, she sat down, tucked her feet under her, and, still shivering, watched her patient sleep.

Maddy

twenty

When she climbed back up the trellis into her room that night, Maddy went straight into the bathroom to take off her clothes and wash herself all over. Her skin felt strange, though, especially the tender parts. She kept feeling Gerald's hands on her. Had he left some mark? She drew a hot bath and washed herself thoroughly, scrubbing hard with the cloth, even though that reminded her of Gerald all the more.

She slept poorly that night. There were terrible, loud noises in her dreams, like thunderclaps, or bursts of gunfire. She couldn't tell just what. She kept waking up with a jolt, her skin drenched with sweat. Its salty, wild smell sent her back to the hayloft again, and to that full feeling she'd had when he entered her, and then to Gerald's face over hers, bobbing in and out of focus as the sensation flooded her . . .

When the first light of dawn broke through the edges of her window shades, she lurched up—and saw the pile of Ronnie's letters on her bedside table. The sight of them hurt. She plucked the top one off the stack, and then the next, and the next. Before, he'd seemed so far away; but now, if she shut her eyes, she thought she might be able to reach out and feel the light stubble of his beard, slip her fingers into his hair. Ronnie's letters weren't the most evocative—they were straightforward, matter-of-fact, like him. But, as she read, she could almost hear his B-17 engines, the boom of anti-aircraft cannon, the scream of dying planes tumbling from the sky. As the light filled the room, tears pricked her eyes, and she went to her desk and wrote him a long letter, full of feeling, that called him "dear Ronnie" and "my one true love" several times. She did miss him. She missed him terribly. She did! Even her handwriting reflected that, she was sure. Her *a*s and *o*s, so nicely rounded, looked as if they were absolutely filled up with her love.

She told him how the roses were starting to bud around the fountain, and how her mother had been so busy lately, and how lonely she was so much of the time without him. She didn't say a word about Gerald, of course. She had already decided that what had happened between them had simply not happened at all. It couldn't have happened. That was all there was to it. Otherwise, she might just— She might just—

No, better not think about that. It was Ronnie she loved.

Her hero. That's what he was. Her savior, even. She felt reassured of the amplitude of her love as she folded the many crisp pages of her personal writing paper, Shreve's very best, with her initials swirling across the top of each one. All the pages made for a very fat envelope, and she covered it with three-cent stamps—probably more than necessary but Maddy would take no chances—and carried it outside to the mailbox on the corner that very moment. It was only a little past dawn, and it was quiet and a bit lonely out on the sidewalk. But the letter itself gave her purpose and strength, and when she finally reached the blue mailbox, and pulled down the heavy handle, she brought the envelope to her lips for a parting kiss before she sent it off.

Despite her letter, and all the good feeling it gave her, she kept thinking about Gerald, kept wondering what was going through his mind during that long silence together in the barn—when her own mind was spinning like a top! Did he love her? Did he dream of her last night?

Love. She'd never even heard the word spoken out loud—not with its real meaning, anyway. The closest anyone came was her mother exclaiming into the phone: "Oh, I'd *love* to go"—to some party she was bent on avoiding. But I love you? Love being with you? Never.

And she'd felt that love, for the very first time, with Gerald. When they were together on their walk, and then dancing, and then in the barn, when he was touching her, and then moving in her, inside her where the deepest feelings are, it was all so much! Why had she never felt so much before? It was unexpected, improbable, and wrong, all wrong, but her passion for Gerald—God! She had to see him again! She'd throw herself at him. She would! Kiss him, on the lips, right there in front of everyone. Oh, the things she would do for Gerald, he was so slim and strong and soulful with that voice of his that was like singing. She would live with him. Oh, yes! She didn't need all the fancy furniture, the beautiful carpets, even the gardens, although they were heavenly in the spring. She could do very nicely in a spare room with bare floors somewhere, in Jamaica Plain even, so long as he was there. She'd wear rags for him. She would! What do nice clothes matter, really? It was absurd the amount of time—and money—she spent on them, and for what? Clothes only hid a person.

Father would be furious, and Mother, too. They'd cut her off without a cent, but it wouldn't matter, not really. Not in the long run. It would be good for her! She wouldn't starve. She'd work. Work with Gerald, that's what she'd do. She'd help him build his landscaping business. She could weed while he tended the grounds, mowing and planting. They'd be partners. She'd love that! Getting her hands into the soil, seeing her efforts bloom. Money was nice, of course it was. But everybody worried about it far too much. Love was so much more important, the real kind of love, where you actually felt something for another person, and didn't just stay with them forever out of convenience or propriety or—

"There you go, then," he'd said to her as he'd gone back down the narrow stairs alone. It was his idea, but she'd agreed (reluctantly) that it was sensible not to make too much of a commotion. And he had left her there in her white brassiere and pink underpants, picking the hay out of her beautiful cashmere sweater.

The worry stabbed her: Did he love her at all?

Those days were hectic, since her mother was frantically busy lining up a bridge tournament at the club to support the war effort. Maddy had only a few moments with her, but she took the opportunity to ask her mother if by any chance she imagined she would be employing "that Irish boy" any further.

Her mother was putting something in her pocketbook, and she didn't look up, which was just as well, since Maddy was afraid of what her mother might see on her face.

"I don't think so, dear," her mother said. Amazingly, that relaxed Maddy a little, since at least she knew now, but then her mother startled her by adding: "Goodness, what a curious question."

She'd tried to stay by the phone, so that she could quickly pick it up if Gerald called. But he didn't call. And she realized that she couldn't call him, because she didn't know his number, and couldn't look it up because he'd never even told her his last name.

And why had she never asked?

She thought she should go back to Jamaica Plain. Find his house again. She hadn't noticed the names of any of the roads, but how many could there be? She remembered a few of the shops, and, yes, though most of the houses did look the same, a few had been distinctive, because they were larger, or had some design on the shutters. She'd find her way back. She was certain she could.

But her mother stayed in the house all that Sunday, and she seemed to be watching her more closely than usual, asking where she was, what she was doing. Did she suspect something? Oh, it was damnable! She should have just dashed out of the house, run into town, and hired a cab. You could usually find one by Mr. Beebe's. She'd have driven back to Jamaica Plain, found Gerald's house, with that big barn behind, thrown herself at him, and never left him again. She thought about that, over and over, each time scrunching down on the idea so hard that it seemed to tighten inside her until in the end it was a bright diamond within her.

But she did not do it.

Why?

That night, her parents had the Scotts again for dinner, and she had to stay in the whole evening, and even play her mazurkas for them after dessert. She exclaimed about how hot it was and opened the windows by the driveway. She hoped to hear the squeaky grumble of Gerald's Pontiac idling on the street, waiting for her. But she didn't. At bedtime, she told her parents she was taking a walk to calm herself after all the excitement. Just for a few minutes, her mother said. She went out to the road, hoping to see the Pontiac waiting for her.

When she returned to Miss Southwick's the following week, Maddy kept to herself more than usual. She fretted about Gerald constantly. Where was he? Why hadn't she seen him? Why hadn't he called? Come by? Would she *ever* see him? Would she *never* see him? It made her worry about herself, and the feeling, all black and pitchy, built up inside her, covering over the bright diamond that was her perfect plan to run off with Gerald. It made her feel heavy, to have so much inside; when she was around her friends, she didn't have any of her usual bounce.

She had resolved to say nothing to Ellen. What she'd experienced was too profound for the kind of idle conversation that Ellen engaged in. But, with her pert nose and keen eyes, Ellen was a bloodhound for the little changes in people, and she kept telling Maddy that she seemed different somehow. She must have said that a half dozen times, with varying degrees of inflection over the course of the week, until finally, on Friday afternoon, Maddy couldn't bear it any longer. She grabbed Ellen's hand and took her around the corner of the hallway after biology class. (They had been dissecting salamanders, which was hideous.) After swearing her to secrecy, and then insisting that she *really meant it,* that Ellen could tell *no one, not one single soul,* Maddy told her about Gerald and what they'd done together in the hayloft.

Ellen's face went white for a moment, and her eyebrows rose and her mouth opened, although no sound came out. And, seeing that, Maddy herself nearly broke down, too, reminded once again of the horror of it all.

"But—but what about Ronnie?" Ellen finally said.

Maddy almost slapped her. "Oh, Ellen, *God!*" she exclaimed. As it was, she turned abruptly away and, choking back the tears, ran down the corridor and up the stairs to her geography class.

When she got home, Maddy felt terribly burdened, and she retired to her room. She scarcely ate anything all that weekend. Gone were the nights when she would remove her nightgown to let the wind blow across her body, or slide her pillow up between her thighs. Now she huddled in bed, sick with dread. Every time she closed her eyes, she felt Gerald's hands on her again, only this time they didn't release the soft pleasure that she had, in fact, taken from his touch, but a searing sort of pain. There weren't just two hands, but many more, and they pried and scraped and scorched. She'd scarcely seen his sex. It had scared her to rest her eyes on it. Now, in her mind, she saw nothing but. It rose up before her, long and hard and a violent red.

A week went by, or was it two or three? Maddy drifted through her life as if it were someone else's. She felt huge but weightless, like one of those dirigibles, a being without force or consequence just drifting along. Her mother took notice, and, with some concern, declared that perhaps she wasn't eating enough. Her father decided she should get out more, take a walk perhaps. Maddy hardly heard them. She stayed in her bedroom. The letters from Ronnie came even faster and were thicker than before, now that Maddy had delivered herself of that huge letter of hers, which Ronnie called "quite something." Just his usual exuberant vagueness, probably; nothing worth thinking about. But Maddy was afraid that even he had sensed a change in her, just as her parents had.

In one letter, Ronnie noted that he had completed his twenty-third mission, a risky side trip to drop emergency supplies to a company of infantrymen that was pinned down in the Italian Alps. Originally, he'd had only to finish twenty-five to complete his tour of duty, and Maddy could tell that his anxiety had risen, along with her own, as that magic number drew near. But perhaps a week before (her dates were getting muddled) General Dorris had informed the men that they could not be spared, now when the outcome of the war still hung in the balance. The number was being pushed up to thirty-five. How Maddy's own heart thudded to read that news! It was queer, impossible to figure, but at moments she was eager to see Ronnie again, nearly desperate. She needed his familiarity, the way he didn't push himself on her, not like Gerald. Maybe love wasn't all that important. Maybe love just got you into trouble. Maybe liking was better, safer, more reliable. She liked Ronnie well enough. And she was desperate to get back to that easy, nice, comfortable place where they had been together just before he left. But then suddenly she wasn't sure she could face him, not just yet, not until she'd settled things with Gerald one way or the other. So she wrote Ronnie to be brave "as you always are," and that she was sure that he would be "absolutely fine." She'd signed that letter, "Love, always, your Mad Mad Maddikens who is Mad for *you.*"

The next morning was a Saturday, and, after taking her toast and morning tea in the dining room, she found Bridget at the big kitchen table polishing the silver. That was normally a peaceful, mindless task, and Bridget, who had been watching her warily for some time now, seemed more relaxed with her than usual. So Maddy asked Bridget if by any chance she remembered that young Irishman, the workman, Gerald, who had come to the house. Bridget set down the spoon, looked up at her, and seemed to hunt for something in her eyes. "Now just why d'you ask?" she said in a way that was not at all casual.

"I'm curious, that's all," Maddy replied as airily as she could. "I thought you might know him."

"He's not a fella you should be thinking of." Bridget's small mouth seemed all the smaller now that she was being curt.

Maddy thought quickly. "But he invited me dancing."

"I wouldn't mention that to your parents if I was you. Going dancing with an Irish lad. You'll be giving them both heart attacks."

"Well, do you at least know his last name?"

"What, so you can phone him?" Bridget's eyes flashed. "You're not going to be phoning a boy like that."

"And why's that?" Maddy felt faint with distress, but she was determined not to let on.

"Because I'll bet you he's got no phone! Which is another reason you shouldn't have anything to do with him."

"Do you even know his last name?" she repeated.

"Can't say as I do," Bridget replied, and with a crash, dumped all the silver into a tub for rinsing.

• • •

Twice, Maddy went back to the barn to see if, by chance, Gerald had left some trace of himself there, something to help her find him again, or at the very least to remember him by. Only the second time, several days after the first, could she bring herself to climb the narrow stairs to the hayloft again. It was darker than she had guessed it would be in the daytime, and the upper corners of the ceilings were thick with spiderwebs, where the rafters ran across. But her eyes were drawn to the pile of marsh hay in the corner. A few bits of it were strewn across the floor. The sight froze her. She and Gerald must have scattered them that night when they made love. The pile itself was still hollowed out, like a nest.

She picked up a piece of the straw, wondering. It felt so strange in her hand, so stiff and unpleasant. She couldn't quite imagine that her bare skin had willingly, eagerly, lain against such stuff—and against him. She held it for some time, then finally remembered herself and tossed it back onto the pile.

Ancient history now. It was over. Over, over, over, over. Best put out of her mind completely.

No, more than forgotten. Obliterated. Removed from existence, every last trace of it. With her hands, she scooped up some of the hay to restore the pile to its original shape, filling in the hollow the two of them had made. She did it carefully at first. But then, as the memory deepened of what they'd done, and how much it had meant to her and how much it hurt to recall, and how absolutely nothing had come of it except pain where the love once was, she grew rougher, and soon she was actually slapping at the hay with her hands, and she was using her feet to stomp on it and kick it, too. Her blows sent the hay every which way, and spewed clouds of chaff into the air. In her anger, she imagined it was Gerald himself she was striking—great, whacking blows to his side, his chest, his thighs. But then it seemed to her that the hay pile really *was* Gerald—Gerald with his beautiful, soft, pale skin, like a baby's almost—and her heart filled with sadness, with pity for him, and for herself, and she relented, and, seeing the awful mess she'd made, wearily tidied up the pile once more.

When she had finished, she glanced about, hoping to spot something of his—a coin, a scrap of paper, a note of some sort. Surely he'd leave something for her. He wouldn't just go. Take from her the most intimate, the most prized thing a girl had, would *ever* have. Surely, he'd leave a note of some kind, a remembrance. He had to. Her Gerald. Her beautiful Gerald. After what they'd done together?

She checked around the floor, searched through the hand tools spread across a worktable in the corner. But there was nothing, absolutely nothing, and her heart felt as heavy as a rock when at last she descended the narrow stairs once more.

For some time, her stomach had been feeling queasy, at odd times, like first thing in the morning before she'd had a chance to eat anything at all. She assumed that she'd picked up a germ from school. It troubled her, too, that her period hadn't come, and she'd always been so regular. Month in, month out, her "letter from Aunt Suzie"—as she and Ellen termed it—had always arrived faithfully on the twenty-eighth day of her cycle, a fact that was duly recorded with a tiny red dot in the upper-right-hand corner of her daily diary, which was otherwise devoted to reminders about haircuts, brief notations about her small round of activities, and occasional silly speculations about odd things like whether certain school chums really liked her or whether she'd be happier if she had a brother or a sister.

Her regularity had always been a point of pride. It suggested consistency, steadiness—virtues she had always aspired to, but generally lacked. But now, in a mounting panic early in May, she stumbled to the table by her bed, jerked open the drawer, and plucked out the diary from its hiding place way in the back behind the Bible her aunt Dot had given her for her confirmation. She opened the book to that day's page, marked by a golden string, and then flipped back through the previous pages to find the last time she'd made a tiny red dot. She had to go back and back *and back* all the way to March 17!

Oh, God, oh, God, oh, God, oh, God. The prickles rose in her chest and traveled down her arms and all the way out to her fingertips. There must be some mistake, she said to herself, there must be some mistake, there must be—

Just then, she heard her mother clipping the dead blossoms off the daylilies along the side of the house, below her window. The steady rhythm reminded Maddy of Gerald working. She squeezed her eyes shut and began to cry.

Maddy didn't come down for dinner that evening, and when her mother came up, she found Maddy in bed with the shades drawn.

"Darling," she exclaimed. "What is it?"

Maddy said nothing, which must have worried her mother all the more.

"Maddy?"

"I don't feel well." She had hardly any voice.

Her mother sat down on the edge of the bed, and placed a hand on Maddy's forehead. "What's wrong?"

This time Maddy fell silent.

"Not some female trouble again, is it?" her mother asked soothingly.

Maddy had confided in her about some cramping back in the fall. She was surprised that her mother remembered. Maddy nodded, wishing that was all it was. Her head rustled against the horsehair pillow.

"You're worried about Ronnie, I know," her mother said. She stroked Maddy's hair, and there was a warmth to her voice that Maddy rarely heard; it hurt to hear it now when it was so misplaced. "I'll have Bridget bring up some soup and a bit of toast. That should go down easily enough."

Maddy rolled away from her with a heavy sigh even before she had left the room.

"Poor dear," her mother said as she closed the door behind her.

• • •

Bridget appeared with the tray a short time later, and she set it down on the table by the bed. Maddy said nothing, although she knew that was ungracious, and she made no move toward the food.

"Sick, are ya now?" Bridget asked with a marked coolness in her voice.

Maddy continued to lie on her side. She held a small pink stuffed rabbit in her arms. A comfort from her earliest childhood, and one she desperately needed now. She could see Bridget scowling down at her.

"Go away, would you please?" she told her.

The maid's eyebrows jumped, which was gratifying.

"Don't go blaming *me* for your folly," Bridget snapped.

Maddy's heart slammed against her chest as if it might split her open. "What's that supposed to mean?"

"I think you know. You and that fella. You'll have the devil to pay."

"You don't know! You don't!" Maddy screamed, and she hurled her pillow at her.

Bridget let the pillow smack harmlessly against the wall behind her, well below a watercolor of Notre Dame in Paris. "Calm yourself, child," she angrily cried out. "What's done is done."

Without another word, Bridget withdrew, shutting the door behind her, and plunged Maddy into the shadows once more. A sadness, a bitter, mournful sadness, gnawed at her insides like acid. She drew her rabbit to her face for comfort as she lay her head back on the hard, pillowless mattress. She was just a child herself. Just a child! How could *she* have a—? She couldn't complete the thought before she started to moan, a terrible, low, breathy sound that came up from deep in her chest and actually hurt. To calm herself, she squeezed her rabbit tightly to her mouth, pressing her dry lips against the soft, artificial fur, until the dear old stuffy was drenched with the tears that poured down her cheeks. Then—

In a fury, she tossed the animal across the room, smacking it against the far wall above the mantelpiece. It whacked a small photograph of her mother as a child, wearing a bonnet. The picture did not fall, but Maddy would not have cared if it had. She threw the covers off the bed and yanked up her shirt, pushed down her pants and underwear, and clutched her belly, the round part just above her pelvis, and she gripped the soft flesh that Gerald had so admired, digging in her fingernails until it hurt. She drove the heels of her hands into her belly, too, then pushed the roll of flesh down her abdomen toward her bony pubic mound. She did this over and over, the flesh turning red, then white, then red again. Her face tightened with effort, the air cutting through her clenched teeth; she dug and pushed, dug and pushed, trying with all her might to shove the vile creature that had entered her body out the way it had come.

twenty-one

Days went by. Days without any day at all. Just endless, dark, solitary, frightening night.

One morning, a rap at the door. It must have been early, since Bridget hadn't yet brought up her breakfast tray. Maddy lifted her head off the pillow at the sound. She must have been sleeping, although she had no feeling of rest, just the tight, anxious weariness she always felt these days. The room was blurry, and it spun a little.

More knocking. Then a voice. "Madeline?" It was a deep voice—Father's.

She held her silence, worrying.

The door opened, and Father came in. He was wearing a gray business suit and a striped necktie, and his fine English shoes clicked on the walnut floor as he briskly crossed the room. In a rapid, enthusiastic motion, he raised the shades on either side of her bureau, and the morning light streamed in, blinding Maddy for a moment until she covered her eyes with her forearm. She did not speak, but reached for her pillow and hugged it to her head, craving the silent darkness of caves, of tombs.

A firm hand at her wrist, and the pillow rising off her.

"You need to get up now, Madeline." A steely voice that Maddy rarely heard.

She squinted up at him. Her father was not tall, but he seemed immense as he stood over her.

"I've made an appointment for you with Dr. Eldridge."

Maddy blinked, uncomprehending. *Dr. Eldridge?* Her doctor was the nice, cheery Dr. Glaws in the medical building across town.

"He's a good man," her father said. "A specialist."

"What about Dr. Glaws?" Maddy asked.

"Dr. Eldridge specializes in older children. He's especially good at talking to them, finding out what's wrong. I spoke to him over the weekend. He thought it would be a good idea if you came in to see him this morning. We agreed on eight-thirty. I should have told you before." He went to her bureau, pulled open the middle drawer, and grabbed a shirt for her, a sleeveless one. That was a shock: Father's hands in her bureau drawer, touching her clothes, especially that shirt, which she would never wear to a doctor's.

Words came to her, finally: "I can dress myself, thank you." A dry, raspy, early-morning voice that should have told him she was sick.

"Of course you can." He went to the closet, found a pair of slacks, and tossed them onto the foot of her bed. "There. That should do." He turned to her. "Hurry up now. We don't want to be late."

Maddy shifted back in bed and leaned up against the headboard to gain a little height. She did not pull the sheet up over her, although her nightgown was so thin she would normally never be seen in it by anyone. She remembered how Gerald had gazed at her bare front so hungrily. Father was nearing the door when she called out to him, "Why are you *doing* this?"

He turned to her one last time, deliberately, his jaw set. Every hair in place, as always. "You need to get up, my dear. You can't stay in bed like this. You just can't."

"But I don't feel well!" Maddy declared with a force that enlarged her father's eyes for a moment and moved him back slightly from her bed.

"No need to yell, darling." He was all civility, but Maddy could hear the irritation in his voice. "That's why we're taking you to the doctor."

"But I don't want to go, don't you see? I don't want to."

"I'm afraid you must."

It was his business voice; she'd heard it addressed to others, but never, ever to her. "Where's Mother?"

"I'm here, darling." That was a shock. Her mother was there in the doorway, neither in the room nor out. Her voice lacked all warmth. Had she been there the whole time? How could Maddy not have noticed? Was her mind fading, along with her body? Why hadn't her mother come in, said something?

"Mother! *Please!*" She might have reached for her, but that was not Maddy's way. Her arms might have been pinned to her sides. Maddy looked from one parent to the other. They stared back at her like fish from a fishbowl—transfixed, but without understanding, or any sign of love.

"Why are you looking at me like that?" Maddy asked.

Her mother glanced at her husband—a moment of silent complicity—then each of them turned slowly back to Maddy.

Her father spoke for both of them. "We're concerned about you, that's all." It wasn't the words, it was the tone—the steely coldness—that hurt.

They went in the Studebaker. Father driving, Mother riding beside him. Maddy in the backseat, looking out the window, determined to believe that none of this was happening. As they drove along the Jamaicaway, she wondered just how badly she would be hurt if she threw herself out of the car. The door was unlocked. It would be so easy. With luck, she'd hit her head on a parked car, on one of the shiny chrome bumpers, perhaps. That would end everything. But what if she didn't die, just lingered on as a useless cripple, with hideous scars all over her body?

The parked cars went by, one after another. She reached for the door handle, felt the cool metal. It would have been so easy. But she could not bring herself to jump.

Dr. Eldridge's office was in a brownstone on Commonwealth Avenue. He was a tall, frail man who liked to touch his fingertips together as if he were cupping his hands over an invisible ball. He wore a white coat, wire-rimmed glasses, and a priestly expression. Maddy's father went into his office with him for a few minutes, the door shut behind them. Her mother took a seat in the waiting room, and Maddy did, too. But they said nothing, and Maddy's mother, ghostly despite her bright summer dress, leafed through a *McCall's*. Maddy herself felt sick, and she was afraid that she might throw up this time, but she held on and the feeling passed without her mother noticing.

Then Dr. Eldridge came out and said to Maddy, "Is this the young lady?," and Father nodded. The doctor placed his arm on Maddy's back for a moment. The arm was heavy; it weighed on her, frightened her, controlled her.

He ushered her into his office, which bore an impressive array of framed diplomas on the wall. Maddy sat in a wooden chair across from his desk, and he pulled his own chair around in front of her, which she found somewhat forward and off-putting. He had a spongy sort of voice, but he spoke genially enough as he asked her the expected questions about how long she had been feeling ill, and whether she had any specific pains anywhere. To answer the latter question, Maddy thought of pointing to her heart, since that was the part of her that hurt the most. Instead, she shook her head, no, and kept her hands in her lap. He went through a variety of medical questions, and then he branched off into topics that Maddy didn't find particularly germane, like how she got along with her friends, how she was doing in school, and whether she was enjoying her various activities. Still, she appreciated the distraction from her real worries, and she thought she might possibly enjoy her time with Dr. Eldridge after all.

But then he said, "Look at me, Madeline, would you please?" And she realized she hadn't been. (She had been studying the branch of the tree out the window, which was dipping and swaying as some squirrels dashed along it.) She stared at the bridge of his nose, on which the center of his wire-rimmed spectacles rested. It was the one part of his face that bore no expression, unlike the eyes that seemed to be aimed at her like guns, or the mouth, which turned down at the edges to reflect, she sensed, suspicion. No, the bridge of his nose was completely neutral, and she required neutrality on his face when she responded to the question that she could feel in the pit of her stomach was coming next.

"Let me ask you something, Madeline, would you mind?" Dr. Eldridge paused as a wave of pins and prickles spread throughout Maddy's chest. "Do you have any reason to think you might be pregnant?"

She tried to clamp down, say nothing and do nothing to give herself away. But a tear pooled in the corner of her right eye for a moment, and then spilled down the side of her nose before she swept it away with a fingertip, all of which she hoped desperately he had not noticed. "No," she said. "Of course not."

"You're sure?"

"Yes. Absolutely. I'd know, wouldn't I?" For this, she managed a faint smile.

Finally, a smile out of him in return. "Well, then," he said, standing up. "Good. Perhaps we'll do a quick physical, if you don't mind. See what we can figure out." He handed her a hospital johnny to change into—a drab, green, wrinkled cloth that didn't seem as if it could possibly cover her—then stepped out of the room for a moment to give her some privacy. She wasn't sure she was supposed to take off absolutely all her clothes, but she did anyway. Although the day was actually quite warm, she felt chilled as she set her various garments in a little pile in the corner, with her socks draped over the top and her shoes beside them. Her fingers trembled as she tried to do up the laces on the johnny, and her heart pounded, and sweat was gathering under her armpits, which she hoped wouldn't smell. She was still tying, but she was decent, when Dr. Eldridge knocked on the door.

"You can come in," Maddy said. "If you want."

The door opened. "Ah, there we are," Dr. Eldridge said.

She clamped her legs together—she felt so exposed!—and held her elbows close to her sides.

He turned his back to her for a moment, but she could see he was donning a pair of rubber gloves. "I thought we might start with a pelvic exam," he said, his back still turned.

She glanced up nervously. She'd never heard the term.

"It's just routine." He turned back to her, his hands encased now in rubber gloves. "You're not feeling any discomfort down there, are you?"

"No," she assured him. "Not at all."

"Period on schedule?"

She'd never discussed such things with Dr. Glaws. She became acutely aware of the sweat filling her armpits, and her heartbeat was like thunder.

He was looking directly at her now. "Is it?"

She hadn't realized she hadn't answered. In fact, she'd forgotten the question. "Is what?"

"Your period, is it regular?"

"Oh, yes, that." Her heart was going to burst out of her chest, she was sure. "Yes. Quite. Quite regular. Yes, thanks."

"Good," he said. He directed her to sit on the end of the exam table and slide her feet into a pair of metal stirrups on either side of the end. She had never seen such a contraption at Dr. Glaws's office. She really did not want to open up her legs at that angle for Dr. Eldridge. But he stepped closer to her and tapped the inside of her calf. "Please," he said.

She relented, but a clamshell would have opened up more easily. The stirrups were ice cold, and they dug into the soles of her feet.

"That's the girl," Dr. Eldridge said as he stood before her between her knees. Her thighs tingled, just to have him there so close.

"Now just relax," he told her. "We'll have a quick look." He reached up under her johnny to press a hand down on her pelvis while he slipped the fingers of his other hand right up inside her. She gasped to feel him there, all cold and rubbery.

"Easy, now, Madeline. This will just take a moment."

But she couldn't relax, not with him pushing up inside her, probing, probing, with his gloved fingers. Going just where Gerald went, trying to find traces of him there. She tried to see something in his eyes, but his face bore only the look of intense concentration, as if he'd lost something inside her, and he was searching for it. He poked and probed for an eternity, it seemed. But then he suddenly withdrew his hand again, and yanked off his gloves and laid them down on a table beside him. "Yes," he said gravely. "It's as I thought." But now the look on his face twisted her stomach into a knot, and her skin went cold all over.

"What?"

"You're going to have a baby, Madeline."

She almost didn't hear him, at first. Or rather, hear that it *was* him who uttered these words. For they were words that she had said to herself a thousand times. But no, the words were outside her, and they would spread farther outside her. They'd spread like seeds in the wind, sending up hideous shoots everywhere. Shoots that would yell to the world what she had done. Even in England, they would know. Even in the sky over Germany they would know.

That thought was vast, and it overwhelmed her. It emptied out her body, and hollowed her mind, and gave her a fearful buzzing in her ears, or possibly deeper inside, right in the center of her brain, and that's when her head started to tingle and the whole world started to tilt, to slip away. Maddy had been staring intently at the bridge of Dr. Eldridge's nose. But as her head lightened, the nose left her for the whiteness of the ceiling, then the whiteness started to blur and wheel about, and she was conscious of a coolness on his skin and her teeth felt strange and then she emptied out altogether and slumped down, down, down, and there was, blessedly, nothing. Nothing at all. Until—

A scratchiness underneath her, and her mouth all puffy, and she was on her back on a white sheet, with a light blanket over her and her parents standing beside her, both of them, which did awful things to her stomach. For a moment she thought she was dead, and that was a comfort, but then she realized she couldn't be, not like that. Her mother's eyes were rimmed with red and the corners of her mouth pointed straight down toward the pits of hell where her gaze consigned her daughter, and her father's face seemed to have been set in stone. His hands gripped a metal bar on the side of her bed, his wedding ring a glint of bright light.

"How could you?" she heard her mother say.

She looked away from them, hoping to find a window, or someplace where it would be happy for her to look. But there was none.

"How *could* you, Madeline?" her mother repeated.

But this time, when she swung her head back to them, her parents were hard for her to see, because her eyes had gone filmy and her tears were spilling back sideways toward her ears, annoying her as they went. And she couldn't reply, not that she had anything at all to say, but because the only sound she could make was awful gasping noises from the bottom of her throat.

She didn't stay there in the doctor's office very long. She heard Dr. Eldridge tell her parents, "She's had quite a shock just now, as you can imagine."

"And you're sure."

"Oh, yes. Quite."

When Maddy was finally strong enough to get up off the bed, a nurse helped her into the waiting room. There she saw Dr. Eldridge shake her father's hand and clap him on the back, all without a word between them. Like the greetings people give at funerals.

The three of them said nothing in the car on the way back home. Not a word. Once they had returned to the house, Maddy's mother helped her up the stairs to her room. Maddy was glad to return to her room, to its silence. She did not pull the shades, though. She could face the light, actually welcomed it, now that her terrible secret was out. She drew up a chair to the window, a tall window that reached nearly to the floor. And from her seat, she could see the lawn and all the trees and the flowers that were blooming in the garden. She sat stroking her stuffed rabbit in her lap, and, for the first time, it actually pleased her to think that there was something growing inside, that Gerald's tiny little seed would soon flower.

She was still sitting there an hour later when her father came into her room again.

"We've made some arrangements," he told her.

She clutched her stuffed rabbit. "Oh?"

"We'll be sending you to Colorado."

Maddy gasped and hugged the rabbit to her. She didn't care if her father saw. She thought of snow, of craggy mountaintops, of distance. "Why?"

"Well, you can't stay here, God knows," her father said irritably.

It was astonishing. Each thing her father said was stranger than the previous one. "But——"

"Goodness sakes, child. Don't you have a brain in your head? You're *pregnant*. You're going to have a baby. You can't do that here. We can't have you walking around town with your goddamn belly out to here."

She flinched; he'd never used such language with her before. She was determined not to cry. Absolutely determined. She clutched her stuffed animal to her, concentrated her feeling for her dear old stuffy who had seen her through so much.

"But where will I stay?"

"There is a home there. Outside Denver."

"A home," she repeated. Her brain was not working well.

"Yes, for unwed mothers."

"You mean I have to stay there until—"

He nodded. Once, sharply.

"But that will be months!"

"Of course it will."

She turned to him. He looked so cold and serious. "Where's Mother? I want to talk to Mother." She stood up, started to head toward the hall, but he grabbed her shoulder. His fingers pinched where they dug in.

"She's resting, I'm afraid," he told her.

"But—" She started to struggle with him, but he held her firmly in his grasp.

"This has been very difficult for her," he told her. "I'll speak to your mother later, when she's feeling better."

"I can't—?"

"Not just yet, Madeline. It would be better if you didn't."

She slumped into her chair, drew the rabbit to her cheek, worked at not crying.

"Now, Madeline." He came around toward the window to look at her from the front. "Were you . . . forced?"

"No."

A pause. Then a terrible voice: "Well, then, what in *hell* were you thinking?"

She tried to cling hard to her rabbit, hoping that it would hold her together, but the bitter anger of the question came at her like a bomb.

"So you just threw yourself onto your back?" he demanded. "Spread your legs for him, did you? Is that it?"

She started to whimper.

"Is that how we raised you?" He glared at her. "Is it?"

With that, Maddy somehow slipped off her chair, and tumbled

onto the floor, gasping and wailing. Still the barrage continued—louder and closer. "Didn't you think for a moment that an act like that might have consequences? Good God! Pregnant—at seventeen! My own daughter! And unmarried! Why if my parents were alive— I should take you over my knee! I should give you a thrashing from here to next week!"

She tried to rise but he pushed her head down with his hand. It was probably not meant to be hard, but his fingers dug into her hair, and he bent her neck as he pressed against her with the flat of his hand. It seemed like something you'd do to a dog. She wasn't a person anymore. She was merely an object of scorn, a thing. A nothing. The thought went down deep into her and it set off feelings that were ready to explode, like how much she hated him, and how much she hated being in this house where nothing ever happened, and how much she hated herself. The hate rose up now, huge. It filled the bedroom, with its fireplace, European watercolors, and complete set of the works of the Brontë sisters. "Well, do it then!" she raged. "Go on!" And she jumped up and shoved a hand down her front and yanked open a button on her slacks, and then ripped down the zipper, and she pushed the pants down to expose her bare behind and swung it around toward him, up toward his eyes, so he'd really see it, really be shocked. "Hit me, why don't you! Hit me, Father! Do! Do! I deserve it!"

Mr. Adams recoiled in horror, and he staggered back from her. "Oh, you disgust me!" he shouted. He went to the bed and pulled off the bedspread, and threw it at her. "Cover yourself up. Don't be revolting."

"*I* disgust you? I do? It's all me, is it?"

Mr. Adams stared at his daughter. She made no move to cover herself, even though she was aware that the top of her pubic hair was perfectly visible to him where he stood before her.

"It takes two, you know, Father, if you haven't heard." She balled up the bedspread and threw it back at him. It landed on his shoulder, and draped him vaguely like a Roman toga. "Two!"

To her surprise, her father made no effort to remove the cloth from his shoulder. Instead, he stood motionless before her.

"It's the boy Ronnie, isn't it," he said at last.

It wasn't a question.

For the first time, Maddy sensed weakness, vulnerability. She moved to exploit it, to twist the knife that, to her joy, was already in deep.

"Yes, Father," she told him. It thrilled her to see on his face how much that hurt. To see him take some of the pain that had been hers alone for so long. "It's Ronnie. It's him. Yes."

Her father stared at her, his jaw tight.

"He took me into the barn one afternoon when you weren't here, and Mother was at the club," she told him. "He took me upstairs."

"That's enough now."

"It was just once, Father. It only took once."

Maddy's father seemed to lose his balance for a moment, but he quickly righted himself. "Well," he began, but no other words followed. He started to move away from her, sideways at first, awkwardly, still keeping an eye on his daughter, who seemed to be a stranger to him now. At the door, he grabbed on to the knob as if it might hold him up. He paused there, gathering strength to carry out the heavy load of everything he'd learned. Then he left the room, shutting the door tight behind him.

The bedspread was on the floor beside Maddy, where it had fallen, and she reached for it, then gathered up her stuffed rabbit from the floor by the window. She kissed the bunny on its nose and face, then pressed it up against her cheek. She should have felt victorious, but she didn't. She felt exhausted and sadder than she ever had. She lay down on the floor and then spread the bedspread over herself like a pall, covering her whole body from her feet to her face. She lay there underneath, her hot breath puffing up the light cloth, and wished with all her heart that she was dead.

twenty-two

The heat flushed her cheeks, her scalp. A dry, raw heat that blew up from the canyons along with a fine red dust that coated her skin and came between her and everything.

It was such a long, hot, awful summer, that summer in Colorado, made all the worse because it was so dry. There was no rain, nothing green. Back home, Maddy had always been able to take refuge in the big swimming pool at the club, or at the seashore in Nahant. But here, the few creeks had long since dried up, and the only lake was two hours' drive down into the valley.

The Golden Home for Unwed Mothers was a drab, stucco building on a high ridge up a steep, twisting road that proved almost too much for the bulky taxi that delivered Maddy, with her two fat valises, from the Denver train station after an exhausting four-day journey by sleeper from Boston. She was wearing her lightest summer clothes, and the heat burned right through them. Her skin had turned as pale as death, after she'd been stuck in that blasted compartment of hers with a shade that only went up halfway, while the train rattled and shook, rattled and shook, day after day after day across the country. It chugged through the big brown cities of the East—Albany, Buffalo, Cleveland, Chicago—and then whistled across the great, flat, yellow plains with their silos and cattle and tumble-down houses, and up and up to the edge of the craggy mountains, barely visible from her window, where it lurched to a halt in Denver just as a ruddy dawn was breaking, tingeing the valley with its blood.

The home was in the foothills of those mountains, on the remote upper edge of Golden, with its nothing downtown and movie theater boarded up for the war. Or so the taxi driver said, picking some loose tobacco off his lip as they drove past. The war explained everything. The home had once been a small, cloistered monastery for Franciscan priests, but the Depression had ended that. Some Methodists bought the property, and the "unweds" moved in. Teenagers mostly, but some in their early twenties. A few of the unweds were well-off like Maddy, but only a few. The shame of an illicit pregnancy apparently was not confined to what her father called "people like us."

Up high under the big Colorado sky, they were alone with the boulders and the dirt and whatever pale grasses could survive the dry summer heat. It was nearly silent up there. That's what Maddy would always remember. It's what gave the heat its hellish force: the lonesome, haunted silence—the silence of the desert, broken only by the merciless wind that whistled through, kicking up the dust, and by whatever drabs of conversation the girls could generate.

That first blistering June afternoon when Maddy arrived, a dozen girls were sprawled out in the shade of the few straggly aspens on the dusty grounds, fanning themselves, their sun-blotched faces slack with the heat. The girls barely stirred as the taxi pulled up, and they watched, without a word, as Maddy struggled with her suitcases to the front door. The wood on the door was dry and splintered, and Maddy knocked carefully, lest she burst a knuckle on it. Her knock was answered by the matron, Miss Morely, a narrow figure with a blade of a nose and pinprick eyes, who welcomed Maddy with a single shake of her slender hand. She shouted for Pammy, just thirteen, to show Maddy to her room upstairs. A freckled little thing grossly deformed by pregnancy, Pammy led Maddy upstairs to a big bedroom with six cast-iron beds. "This is yours here," Pammy said, smacking a hand down on the slim mattress and sending a cloud of dust into the air.

At least her bed was by the window, with a view out across the valley. Denver, which wasn't much in those days, was vaguely visible through the haze. The bedroom walls were knotty pine; the black eyes were everywhere.

The first question anyone asked Maddy after her arrival, the first real question, came when Maddy was helping set the table for dinner that evening while Miss Morely was overseeing the stew, out of earshot. It came from Toni, the saucy one, who was seven months gone. She made a playful swipe of Maddy's lower abdomen, trying to feel how far along she was. Then she asked, "So, was it fun?"

Maddy was too appalled to answer. The other girls tittered, all eyes.

Toni's bed was next to Maddy's, and later that night, she whispered to her, "Now, me, my Eddie knew how to touch a girl."

That got them all going, all except Maddy. It was sex that brought them all there, after all, and sex was the secret language they all shared. The sallow-cheeked Julie; the monstrously heavy-breasted Mary-Anne; even the ridiculous Genevieve who, two months later, would insist on wearing makeup and eye shadow right into labor. Several of them joined in, quietly offering up the details of their own deflowerings—the places, the boys, the things they said. Mary-Anne's lover had lit a candle; Genevieve had coupled in the mud with a younger cousin after a rainstorm; Julie's boyfriend had talked dirty to her the whole time. But not all spoke of such things. Pammy, for one, never said a word, just stared. It was only later, long after Pammy was gone, that Maddy learned—from Julie, in a horrified whisper very late one night—that the little girl had been raped by her father.

In nagging voices, the more vocal girls demanded Maddy's details, reaching out to her in the semidark with their ratty hands. Maddy said nothing. She could tell they thought she was an old stick. They had their games of hearts and crazy eights and solitaire, their endless chores (sweeping, mopping, dusting), the fun they took in pinching each other, or yanking hair, to get a shriek. But not with Maddy. From the very first day, she was the silent one, even more than little Pammy, Maddy's secrets closed up within her. She could tell she was a fixture to them, nothing more. Like the door to the front-hall closet that wouldn't close, or the toilet that sometimes ran all night.

Maddy hardly slept that first night. An angry wind whipped up from the valley, rattling the windows, knocking the shutters against the dry stucco walls. Or was there no wind at all, and ghosts banging on the sashes trying to get in? Her mind lurched and spun with worry as her past whipped around inside her. She saw Gerald again, bending over her, pressing against her. Then her father, so stern. Her mother, with that terrible pinched expression she wore whenever Maddy drew near, the hollowed eyes. Then Ronnie, helmeted and shivering. Then all of them again in a whirlwind. Maddy's mind leapt from one to another, fretting fitfully about each. What would they do to her? What had she done to them? She tried to lose herself in other, happier thoughts: clouds drifting across a summer sky, daffodils bobbing in the breeze. But it was no use. Her mind wouldn't hold. She tossed about in her bed, kicking the covers this way and that, her body oiled with sweat, desperate for daylight to free herself from her dungeon of black fear. The moment the first rays of sunlight finally streaked across the bedroom, Maddy lurched up, exultant to have survived the night.

She glanced about, saw that everyone else still slept, noisily, their limbs splayed at odd angles on their beds. Still in her nightgown, damp across the back and under the arms from her night sweats, Maddy sneaked downstairs and went outside, barefoot, in search of privacy.

She found the rocky path that led up the ledge to a small stone chapel with a steep spire. The monks had prayed there. The rough pebbles dug into her soft feet, and some thorns ripped at her ankles, but Maddy pressed on to the heavy door and pulled it open. It was cool inside and dim, with muddled rainbows slicing down from the stained-glass windows. The cross had been removed from the altar, and all the hymnals were gone from the pews. Still, Maddy dropped down to her knees, put her hands together before her face to pray for herself, for her baby, and for her future. She longed for Gerald's touch, just once more. Just once! A gentle, soothing, warm, lovely touch. He had touched her like that, hadn't he? It had been love, hadn't it? She had to cling to that. Had to! The cool air rose up between her legs, and she opened the buttons of her nightgown and looked down at herself, the soft flesh that parted into the breasts that Gerald had exclaimed over. She reached under the fabric and cupped a hand under her left one, its plump whiteness crowned with a circle of brown at its tender tip. Just to see what Gerald had seen, that was all.

She raised her right hand and, with her fingernails, raked long white lines down the soft flesh to the tender nipple, over and over, until the white lines turned to angry red streaks that hurt. Then she took the nipple itself, touched it lightly with her fingertip, trying to remember the feel of his wet tongue against it, and then, in a sudden rage, she pinched it with her jagged fingernails until she gasped with a hot pain that shot down to her crotch. The pain surrounded her, filled her, just as Gerald had. She took the other breast, and treated it the same until the tears welled in her eyes. Then she raised the nightgown over her head, placed it on the pew beside her, and, dropping down onto her knees once more, she lowered herself to the icy floor, as Gerald had lowered himself onto her. And she splayed herself out, pressing herself against the stone, her cheek, her breasts, her pubic bone, her thighs, the tops of her feet. She moved against the cold stone floor as Gerald had moved against her.

She was the floor, the stony bottom of this barren place where God had left.

• • •

Ronnie. For weeks, Maddy wondered about him as she drifted through her days at Golden. His letters had ended the very day of her outburst at the end of May. Not a single aerogram had come into her hands. Not one. An outcast in her own house, she didn't dare ask her parents about it. Not after what she'd said. She assumed that her parents had simply kept any further letters of his from her, believing that it would be best for everyone if this relationship were terminated. Maddy could picture them dropping the precious, slim aerograms into the trash or burning them in the fireplace, making a small bonfire of their rage, before the letters could reach the silver dish in the front-hall table that held the day's mail.

Or perhaps her father had brought an end to the missives. Just a quiet word or two from him to Ronnie's father at their club, the Somerset, one evening over drinks. A nod of the head from Mr. Bemis and it would be done.

At first, Maddy didn't miss hearing from Ronnie. She had so much on her mind, Ronnie's silence—forced as it might have been—was a blessing. It brought her some peace, quieted one front of the three-way war between herself, Gerald, and Ronnie that was raging in her head. But as the days turned into weeks, and then the weeks mounted, and she had not heard a word from Gerald—indeed, had begun to resign herself to the fact that she never would—Maddy started to miss Ronnie's letters. He had, after all, been so steady in his devotion to her, and she could think of no one else of whom she could say the same. And entirely blameless in this whole miserable affair. An innocent! He was like his handwriting, slanting forward so optimistically, no matter what, and always completely legible, even in dim light. And for her to have said what she had about him, to have lied, to have treated him abominably! It was unbearable! If only they could return to the old days, when he adored her . . .

And to think he still had the lock of her hair!

Her parents wrote her. Both of them sent regular, cheery letters that might have been written to her years before, when she was at summer camp. Not Whistling Pines, but Wokenoki, the one for grade-schoolers that had preceded it. Her mother reminded her to stay warm and to get her rest. And her father dashed off absurd notes about playing mixed doubles with the Baumgartens or recounting the latest biography on his bedside table (usually of some nineteenth-century British admiral). In one aside, her father did let Maddy know that he and her mother had put out word that Maddy was suffering from a preliminary form of tuberculosis, and that she had gone west to a special clinic in the mountains to ward off a full-blown attack. The official line was that her condition was potentially dangerous, but that her doctors were confident that, with the excellent medical care available to her, she would recover beautifully. Absolutely no one was to contact her since complete isolation was essential to her cure. Indeed, it was best not to mention it to her later, when she returned, either, since fussing about such a thing could bring on the symptoms. And, of course, any visit was out of the question, owing to the contagiousness of the disease.

Maddy was impressed that her parents could be so deceitful. She'd certainly heard of tuberculosis, the dreaded TB, but she had no idea what it was, exactly, or how it was transmitted, and she doubted that any of her friends did, either. It did sound serious, though.

Only Ellen knew the truth. She hadn't forgotten Maddy's outburst in the hallway at Miss Southwick's. Somehow she had discovered Maddy's address, and she sent her letters to the post-office box in town that the home used for correspondence—wonderfully gossipy ones that lifted Maddy's spirits immeasurably. To Maddy's astonishment, Ellen let on that she was full of admiration for what she had done, and pleaded with her to write a long letter telling her *exactly* what sex was like (not that Maddy ever did), stunning confessions about what she herself would someday like to do with a boy, and assurances that Maddy's secret was safe with her forever.

All that was startling enough, but it was the third letter from Ellen that threw her. "I assume you've heard, by now, about Ronnie?" it began.

Ellen's details were sketchy. She knew only that Ronnie was in the hospital in Easterbrook, a small town in the south of London. He'd been there for months, ever since his plane had crashed-landed in the fog. It was an elaborate story, and Maddy had to read it through several times to assemble all the details. Ellen was not the most direct writer. But of course the whole thought of Ronnie, hurt, in the hospital, made Maddy's mind heave. Apparently, the plane had a new pilot, Reg, who had, Ellen said, "made everyone nervous because he was so skinny." That was the sort of detail from Ellen that Maddy had trouble making sense of. This Reg had only been with Ronnie's crew for three or four missions when they'd encountered some Messerschmitts on a bombing run over the Ruhr Valley. To escape, Reg had taken the plane almost straight up—and then blacked out from the heavy gravitational forces. "I'm told that's common," Ellen wrote with the kind of knowing certitude that Maddy found maddening. Ronnie had had to take over. It wasn't clear what happened after that, whether the plane had been damaged somehow, or if Ronnie himself had been hurt in the Messerschmitt attack, or what. But Ellen had heard from Ronnie's parents, who told a cousin, who told her, that Ronnie had, over the orders of his squadron commander, immediately headed back to base in England. A thick fog enshrouded the coast, and—this was the part that simply was not clear—Ronnie must have lost his bearings, because he came in low and wide to the landing strip, and caught a wing tip on a haybarn a good half mile from the runway. A length of wing sheered off and the wide B-17 spun and crashed down crosswise into a barley field and burst into flames. Ronnie's hatch was the only one that would still open. He unclipped his harness and tumbled out. The fire was all over him, but he rolled to snuff it out as soon as he hit the ground. He was horribly banged up, but he managed to crawl away, pulling himself on his elbows, before the flames reached the fuel tank and the plane exploded behind him.

Ronnie was the sole survivor. He'd broken an arm, and several ribs; damaged several internal organs (Ellen was unsure just which but thought the kidneys were among them); and had third-degree burns all over his back and neck. But he was alive. All six other crew members perished—either in the crash, or in the fireball that followed.

It was Ronnie's forty-fourth flight, one shy of completion.

Ellen being Ellen, she let Maddy know that she wasn't sure the weather had all that much to do with the crack-up. "You know how he is under pressure," Ellen wrote, which, in fact, Maddy did not know. Angry at the insinuation, she wrote asking Ellen to be clearer, and her friend replied in a looping, blasé script that Maddy found infuriating: "He's very high-strung, you know. Very hard on himself." Then she added, in words that hit Maddy in the face, "Not at all like you."

How did Ellen presume to know what she, Maddy, was or wasn't? Did she have some sort of psychological X-ray machine that would allow her to see inside people?

Maddy was in the chapel, in the pew up at the front. She often read her mail there, since it was about the only place that was at all cool where she could count on being alone. She was nearly quaking with anger and frustration, thinking of the prim and faintly obnoxious Ellen, who'd never done anything, ever. How had she, Maddy, ended up with *her* as a best friend?

But mostly her thoughts hung on Ronnie. God! A fear dropped through her—had Ronnie been thinking of *her* when his plane went down? Back in the spring, when she'd fretted about him so, she'd sometimes had the queer thought that Ronnie was up there fighting for her. Not for victory, not for peace, not for survival. For her. For her heart. Her *body*.

When she looked through the correspondence, she could tell that the accident had happened the first week of June, maybe a week to ten days after Maddy's furious confrontation with her father. Had Ronnie gotten wind of what she had done with Gerald? Was he distracted, upset, angry? Was it all her fault he'd crashed?

Maddy asked Ellen to get Ronnie's address for her, and Maddy sent him a long letter, telling him how sorry she was to hear about what had happened to him and begging for him to write her. She kept up the fib about TB, but told him not to worry about that, since *she* didn't at all, and she gave him the address of the home's mail drop. She would write him back *immediately,* she promised. She signed it "love," with the word underlined three times.

She soon received an aerogram back, which she read, as usual, in the chapel, by the light of the small rose window. The letter itself had been written this time with Ronnie's left hand, in wobbly capitals that reminded Maddy of ailing stick figures, and had none of the clarity and force she was used to. The letter was full of apology for "failing" her. She was right to have "withdrawn" from him. (What did he mean by that? What did he know?) He'd been a lousy airman, he admitted. Absolutely lousy. His mind fogged when it should be most clear. He was unreliable. That's why his first pilot, Smitty, had bugged out; he'd lost confidence in him, and confidence was everything when you're up there at fifteen thousand feet. Ronnie was scared, cold all the time. All he could think about was how he was going to die. He was sure he was going to die. That's what the cold was—it was him slowly dying, starting with his feet. All the other copilots had long since become full-fledged pilots. "Even the really crappy ones." But not him. That last flight—it was his chance to show what he could do. But he'd been up there, and it was so gray everywhere, and that new man, Reg, was slumped over the controls, unconscious, and everyone was shouting at him, and he couldn't see. The instruments were right there in front of him. But he couldn't see! The letter closed:

> *I lie here thinking of you, Mads. I wish so much that you were here with me. I guess we're two broken people.*
>
> *That's what war does. It breaks people apart. If not their bodies, then their souls.*
>
> *I may not be the best man for you, Mads. I know that. But I do love you. Lying here, I can't think about much else besides you. I hope*

you haven't left me, Mads. Write me again, won't you? Tell me you
love me, won't you please (even if you don't)?

>   *Sincerely,*
>   *Ronald A. Bemis*

The light in the chapel was never strong, and it was fading when she read those words, but they cut into her all the same.

She was squatting on a boulder by a dusty juniper bush, her writing pad between her legs, forearms gently rubbing her swelling belly as she wrote her reply.

> *I do love you, Ronnie. I do, I do. And I will never leave you.*
>
> *I feel terribly weak most days, but the doctors here are encouraging. They tell me I'll be strong again one day. And I will be. I'd feel so much better if I knew that you were there, waiting for me, when I finally come home.*
>
> *You will get better, won't you, Ronnie? For me?*
>
> *Ask me, Ronnie. Ask me to be yours. I wish you would.*
>
>   *Yours always,*
>   *Maddy*

Maddy did not tell her parents her plans. They must have heard through Ronnie's parents, for they wrote to her a joint, astonished letter in September. They didn't mention her "condition," as they'd previously termed it, nor allude to the fact that, in their minds, Ronnie himself was the cad responsible for it. It was a brief letter, asking merely if she was "sure." It was clear enough that they viewed the prospect with alarm, given Ronnie's misbehavior, but the young couple's intentions were public by then, and, for appearances' sake, Maddy's parents had no choice but to go along. "Yes, I'm sure," Maddy wrote back. "I've never been surer about anything."

"We wish you happiness then," her father replied a week later. The letter radiated coldness. This time, Maddy's mother did not sign her name, or add any of her customary cheery asides about the weather.

Maddy said nothing to Miss Morely of her engagement. She mentioned it only to Julie, who had by then become her only confidante. Maddy had poured out her heart to her one sleepless night in the fall, Julie, a dark-haired girl whom Maddy regarded as a beauty. Julie had wished her luck, and given her hand a squeeze. That was encouraging. Despite her parents' distress—or was it because of it?—she was pleased to think of her betrothal to Ronnie as the hot summer turned into a cool, bright fall and then the first snows fell in the mountains.

twenty-three

Inside, the baby grew. But she did her best to forget about that. She might be doing the dishes, or sweeping up, or folding laundry, and she would be thinking only of her poor broken-up Ronnie, who she was sure was thinking of nothing but her. And she'd be happy, thinking that he needed her. No one had ever needed her before. Only at night, as she lay sleepless in her bed by the window, the other girls breathing heavily around her, only then did she think of Gerald again. So slender and gentle, with his darling foot. She wished he could be hers just once more before she married Ronnie and was gone from Gerald forever.

She felt the baby's first kick that fall, in October, when the days had finally cooled. A tiny blip in her belly, like a muscle quivering, beside her navel, which was flattening as her womb grew. She was lying on her back on her cast-iron bed. A cold moon rose over the mountains, brightening the curtains. She was six months along, not too large. But she felt a ripple from underneath, and she brought her hands down to cradle her belly.

Until then, the fetus had been a thing. Barely animate, soulless. A creature growing inside her, a kind of parasite. But with that first tiny blip—an elbow? a knee?—it was a baby, *her* baby. A little her. Maddy was just *sure* it was a girl. That first knock had seemed so tender, feminine. Lizzie, she decided to call her, after a friend from grade school who'd looked up to her, imitated the way she dressed, and even said the same things sometimes, before moving away one summer. She told Julie that, and, to Maddy's annoyance, Julie decided to call her child Sam after a black cat of hers that had run away. No child of hers would ever be named for a cat, Maddy told herself, as she imagined dressing her Lizzie, tying bows in her hair, singing her lullabies.

Julie went first, in December. Her water broke when she was at the sink doing the breakfast dishes. She was all packed, but it still brought tears. Miss Morely told the other girls to gather up her things. She'd drive her to the hospital herself in the Ford pickup. Before Julie left, Maddy gave her a kiss, and then grabbed her hand and brought it to her cheek when the kiss didn't seem to be enough. They'd exchanged addresses in the weeks before, and Maddy promised to write, but it shocked her that Julie couldn't seem to focus on that, on the future. She seemed so scared. And that scared Maddy, too.

Her own time was near. As the winter settled in, Maddy felt so heavy and slow and exhausted. Just to draw breath was a struggle. Time slowed and bent and sometimes broke. She was there at Golden, in the big, wind-whipped house, with its views of the whitened plain. Of course she was. But, sometimes, when she closed her eyes, she was in Dover, upstairs in the hay, her nostrils full of it, and of him, of Gerald. And, when she tossed her head to free herself from that memory, she was in Ronnie's all-white hospital ward at

Easterbrook, too. She'd asked Ronnie to send word of the view out his window, so she could see it, too. The reply came back—"No window, only a door, usually closed, to the main hall." And so she'd focused on that door. White, she imagined, with panels, and two hinges on the side. Once, in a dream, she nursed Ronnie from her breast, his beard scratchy, his hands clutching her. She woke up sweating. The skin on Maddy's abdomen was taut and almost shiny; her breasts were huge, the nipples spreading. Her baby was inside. If she pressed down here, she could feel the head; there, the rump.

Christmas came and went without much festivity beyond a droopy pine in the corner of the common room. Her parents sent her a prayer book. She felt a sting when she opened their package, wrapped in bright red. Ronnie sent nothing—until a week later. A tiny box, which Maddy opened with trembling hands. The other girls gathered around her, much to her distress, and they all gave a shout when she discovered a ring inside. A single, large diamond, set in gold. "A new beginning . . ." Ronnie wrote in the card. Maddy slipped that in her pocket.

The ring didn't fit over her newly pudgy ring finger. She put it in the cabinet by her bed. She couldn't think about Ronnie now. Her back hurt, her knees. The other girls kept their distance, but they talked about her. She could tell because the conversations always stopped when she drew near. She would be the next to go.

Finally, a snowstorm, a quietness that descended from the sky, whitening the valley. For two days it snowed. Then the silence was broken by the buzz of an engine, chugging up the hill. A doctor coming for her? A minister? Out in the driveway, a car door opened, then shut with a thump. Curious, Maddy climbed out of bed, her wide hips rolling, went to the window. A large woman was coming across the drive in tight, uncertain steps. Her blue coat was dusted with snow. A small handbag gripped by mittened hands. A man following behind with a suitcase.

Bridget. The maid from back East. What was *she* doing here?

The door creaked open downstairs, the latch clattering. Quiet greetings. Then a heavy tread on the staircase, and a knock on Maddy's door.

Maddy wanted to hide, but there was no place to go.

"A visitor for you, Maddy," one of the new girls called from the hall outside. The door opened, the light shone in, and Bridget entered. Maddy could sense Bridget's taking in her fat face, swollen belly, and hair that had lost its shine.

"My, my," Bridget said.

Maddy's water broke the next morning, and right away the pains started, terrible jolts that began between her legs, as if she were being stabbed by a jagged blade, and then surged up into her belly, around her back and down her thighs. Bridget was with her. Maddy grabbed for Bridget's hand, and squeezed her fingers—until Bridget irritably yanked her hand away. "What were you expecting?" Tears flooded down Maddy's cheeks as she squeezed her hands into fists. "But it hurts!" she wailed.

At the hospital, a nurse wheeled her down the corridor to a waiting room that was large, white, and cool, with immense windows that gave views of the downtown that looked drab even when snow-covered. The pains were just a few minutes apart now. Maddy breathed slowly, trying to ride out the pain. But the stabs came faster, plunging deeper and harder inside. They'd leave her gasping and desperate. She twisted her head this way and that, drove her fingernails into the outsides of her thighs. She'd had no idea it would be like this. She'd scarcely recovered from the last one before the next one came. "Give me something?" Maddy pleaded. "Please, you've got to give me something!"

But there was no nurse there. Only Bridget, in a hospital gown of her own. "Just you wait now," Bridget said calmly.

Maddy couldn't squeeze the words out. Another pain had come, and Maddy screamed so hard she thought she'd rip the corners of her mouth. She was shifted to a bed and rolled into the delivery room where a blurry head, crowned with a nurse's white cap, loomed over her. "Shush now." A prick in her arm and everything went gray and dim.

The grayness lifted, and through the fog a pair of cold, gloved hands reached between her thighs, her knees wide on either side. She fought through the wispy tendrils, through the terrible ripping, to see the child those hands reached for. Her Lizzie. Gasps, desperate breathing, then a matted head, glistening shoulders. The doctor had reached in and then, in a rush, she was hollowed out, and heard the word "boy." As groggy as she was, Maddy knew that could not be right. Then a clear look at the little body smeared with her blood, the pouting mouth, and tiny fingers curled to greet the air, and a cord curling out—and some extra flesh dripping between the legs. A boy indeed. A tiny Gerald. She reached for him as she'd reached for his father. "Gerald!" she cried. "Gerald!" But Bridget was there in her gown, and she said, "That's enough of that now."

"Let me hold him, would you, just once," she pleaded. "Please!" It took all her strength to force the words out. She was floating on a sea of pain.

"It wouldn't be right, dear."

The nurses washed the baby and bundled him up in a long white cloth. He cried when the cloth came down around him, but then he quieted. A good baby. A wonderful baby. So sweet, calm. Her Gerald, come back to her at last.

And Bridget said, "There, you see? It's better this way. Much, much better." And then she'd turned and blocked Maddy's view of the boy. "It's all done now. It's finished." Maddy reached out, pushed her hands against the maid's wide back, trying to move her aside, to clear a sight of her Gerald. Everything was swinging around, and nothing clear. Maddy rolled, trying to get down off the bed, her arms flailing. Anything for her Gerald. Her baby Gerald. She could feel herself tipping, then falling as the bed slid—or was *she* sliding?—

and then voices, and strong arms held her tight and lifted her back onto the mattress. "There now," a voice said. "That's better. Yes."

"Gerald," Maddy shouted. "My baby!"

"Should we give her a little more?" asked a nurse.

Maddy kicked, struggled against them, but it was no use, she was so groggy and feeble, and she was getting heavier by the moment, she was turning to stone. And her Gerald—her baby!—was moving away from her in Bridget's arms, and out through a pair of double doors, away from her, away, away. And there was nothing to do, as darkness descended, but draw her knees up, wrap her arms around herself, and hug the hollow, the empty hollow of herself, that was left behind.

Alice

⤚ twenty-four

When Alice finally returned home that night, her hair all matted and her clothes still damp in spots, her apartment seemed larger than she'd remembered, and it seemed to belong to someone else, someone she barely knew. That chair, the brand-new one, in front of the TV. Was that *hers?* Whatever had happened to the lumpy one she'd bought cheaply from Jenna, her cheery Penn State roommate? She missed that chair. That chair was her.

She heard Fido rustling about in the mouse house in the kitchen. She went in to him, flipped on the light, and found the mouse burrowed under a pile of shavings in the corner, where he liked to curl up with his back against the glass. Alice pulled him out and pressed him gently against her cheek. "Hey, buddy," she said quietly, then took pity on the sleepy mouse, with his twitchy whiskers, and set him back down in his cage once more with a pat of her forefinger.

She crossed back through the living room to her bedroom, but it felt wrong somehow, even aside from the ripped quilt on the bed. It seemed as if there was something extra in the room, an emotional weight that went beyond sorrow, all the way to a physical unease, a dread, that she felt on the back of her neck and all up around her shoulders, which were sticky from the seawater. She'd had some wild times here with Ethan. Sex that would leave her actually pulling on him, hoping for more. Her old neighbor Debbie would be shocked to hear about the things she'd done with Ethan, she who was the last surviving member of the Never Been Kissed club until, at fifteen, Lars had surprised her that afternoon in the horse barn. Was she paying for her wildness now?

"Ethan?" she called out. "Are you here?" She waited for a second. "Are you?" When there was no answer, she added, more quietly, "You bastard. I should have reported you to the police."

She returned to the kitchen, picked up the mouse house and brought it back to the bedroom, and set it down by her bed. Tonight she was not sleeping alone.

She didn't always bother to draw the curtains when she changed, but she did this time. Drew the curtains *and* pulled the shade, and then checked the locks on her apartment door before she stepped back into the bedroom, shut the door behind her, and peeled off her clothes. Her bra stuck to the undersides of her breasts after her swim; it came off with a light sucking sound that she might have thought funny any other time. The band on her underpants had nearly congealed to her waist. And she smelled of the sea. Also of fear, a foul, oily scent. She went into the bathroom, ran a hot bath, and took one of her new towels down from its hook. She wetted it in the tub, then brought it, steaming, slowly all over her, reddening her flesh, especially around her shoulders and the back of her neck where the fear still was.

She pulled on a T-shirt that went halfway to her knees, glad to feel the soft, dry cotton against her skin. She brushed her teeth, used the toilet. Then she checked the locks again, wondering, idly, how many times you have to do that to be diagnosed with OCD. Finally, careful not to trip over the mouse house, she made her way back to bed, pushed the torn quilt aside, and slid under the covers.

With the lights out, she watched the shadows cast by the cars on the street slide across her ceiling, heard the occasional creak of the floorboards and spastic rumbling in the pipes. She was drained, but too jumpy to sleep. She curled up on her side, tucked her hands under her cheek, then tried her other side, then sprawled out on her front with her leg poking out from under the covers.

She kept feeling the water on her, like so many cold, wet hands touching her, grabbing her, pulling her under.

Alice must have slept, because it was suddenly light everywhere and a buzzer was going. A fright shot through her that she'd overslept, until she remembered that this was Wednesday, her late day, when she wasn't due in until noon, thank goodness. She let her head plop back into the pillow, but then the buzzer sounded again, more insistently this time, and she realized that it couldn't be her alarm clock because she hadn't set it. No, the buzzing was from the front door.

She threw on her bathrobe and, after checking through the peephole, she opened her apartment door and stumbled down the creaky stairs in her bare feet.

There were two panes of glass at the top of the front door, and, as she was coming down, she thought she caught a glimpse of red hair in one of them. She tightened her bathrobe, swept the hair back off her face, squeezed her eyes shut a couple of times so she'd look a bit more alive, and yanked open the door. It was the policeman, LeBeau, all fresh looking in a short-sleeved shirt and khakis. He seemed like a giant there on her front step, and not a jolly one, either, in his aviator-style dark glasses, his jaw clenched.

"Hi," she said.

"I've got something for you." He lifted up a brown plastic bag.

"A present?"

"Not exactly." He reached in the bag and pulled out a woman's clog—*her* clog, the leather darkened and curled by its exposure to the sea. "This yours, by any chance?"

Looking at it, Alice felt the chill of the water on her again, and her body shrank into itself.

"The Brewsters found it by their pier this morning. Said they'd seen somebody down there last night. A woman, they thought. Twenties, maybe. With short hair." He eyed her hair, which was still thick with salt. "Kind of like yours, as a matter of fact." He paused a moment. "They were pretty pissed off, Alice."

Alice didn't like having this conversation out on the front step, in her bathrobe, with people going by. "Maybe you should come in for a second."

"I thought we *talked* about this," LeBeau said, his voice rising.

"Please, just come in for a second, would you?"

He was all eyes inside her apartment. He'd taken off the shades, and his glance went everywhere—through the open door to her bedroom, with its tangle of sheets and her mouse on the floor; to the framed black-and-whites of Debbie and some other Latrobe friends on the wall behind the white couch in the living room; the stack of Motown CDs on top of the CD player in the corner; the view of the other triple-deckers out the window. She couldn't tell if his nosiness was just the way cops were, or whether he was being a guy trying to figure a girl out.

If only she'd had a chance to get dressed, brush her hair. With a flutter of her hands, she straightened up the *People* magazines and psychiatry journals on the glass table in front of the couch. But she was probably just making the mess worse by drawing attention to it.

LeBeau was by the TV. Her clog was still in his hand, and he was swinging it about.

"Maybe I should take that," she told him.

"So it is yours?"

"Yeah, it's mine." She met his eyes, which were colder than she'd like. "I guess that makes you Prince Charming." The detective didn't smile. "That's a joke, Frank. What do you want? Should I try it on? Or do you want to take me straight to jail?"

"What the hell were you thinking?"

"I *wasn't* thinking, okay? I just went there." She pulled the bathrobe tight around her and sat down on the chair. "That never happens to you?"

Frank said nothing back, just watched her.

"Well, it happened to me," Alice went on. "I thought it would help me figure some things out."

"Like how to get everybody really steamed?"

"No."

"Then what?"

"Like who the guy was, and what he was." She looked up at his face, saw no comprehension whatsoever. "I was just trying to put a few things together about this patient of mine. That okay with you?" She tightened her fists in exasperation. She wanted to pound on his chest, his face, anything to try to get through to him.

This time, LeBeau spoke softly as he looked down at her. "Alice, listen, I want to understand it, too, all right?" He let that sink in. "I'm just going about it a little differently."

She stood up, took the clog from him. It was still slimy on the inside, and the leather had been whitened by the saltwater. She let it hang off her index finger. If she'd had the other one, she'd have smacked them together to get some of the crud off; but, all alone, the shoe just pendulumed pointlessly in the air. She looked at him, distressed by the bafflement on his face, as if he'd seen some real lulus in his day, but this girl . . . She was going to be quite a story back at headquarters.

"Let me get dressed, okay?" She swept past him, went into her bedroom, and yanked on a pair of jeans and a T-shirt and gave her hair a few brisk strokes with her brush.

"They were coming with *dogs,* Frank," she shouted back to him through the door. "Huge ones. I had to get out of there, or they'd have ripped me apart."

"Wait, you *swam* away?" Incredulity now.

"Well, yeah." She stepped back into the living room, still brushing. She thought he knew that. "That's why I had to take off my shoes."

He chuckled at that—a relaxing, back-country sound.

"What?"

"I was just picturing you out there, that's all."

"I'm not much of a swimmer," she told him. "I could hardly swim in my clothes."

"Well, maybe you should've chucked them, too."

Alice just looked at him, trying to gauge exactly what he was suggesting. "I don't think so," she told him, glad to have caught him out for a second. "It was *Duxbury,* Frank."

This time, LeBeau paused before he chuckled again. "Well, you got that right." Then something behind her captured his attention. "What the heck you got there, a hamster?" He looked through the open bedroom door behind her to the mouse house on the floor.

Alice explained about Fido, glad to be able to talk about something besides criminal trespass. She told him how she'd saved the mouse after a lab experiment. "I guess I got attached."

LeBeau stepped closer. "Look, I didn't mean to come down on you too hard. It's just that I got an earful from Duxbury."

She brightened. "You want some coffee? I was going to put some on." She could see him hesitate. "Come on. It won't kill you." She went into the kitchen, pulled out a chair for him at the table by the window. He settled himself down uneasily, his knees up because of his height. It was different to have him in her kitchen, as if some line had been crossed. There was a nice view of the stone Catholic church, with its bell tower, from there, but she could feel his eyes on her back as she put the kettle on.

"Maybe I haven't been making the best decisions lately," she admitted, glad she was facing away from him so that he wouldn't see her blush.

"You seem to have gotten in a little deep with this depressed lady of yours, if that's what you mean." Frank settled back in his chair; she could hear it creak. "Of course, I'm not in your business. So maybe I don't know what's normal."

"It's not just her, Frank." She could sense the silence behind her, the attention. "It's a lot of things." She started to tell him about her grandmother's stroke, and Chris B. Then she bit her lip. "Plus, I had this big scene here with my boyfriend a few nights ago." She peeked back at him to see how this information was going down. He was fiddling with her salt shaker, a small blue porcelain one that didn't match the orange plastic pepper shaker.

"We broke up," she told him.

"Bad?"

"He cut me with a pair of scissors. Look." She showed him the scar on her palm.

"I thought psychiatrists were supposed to stay in control."

Alice frowned. "Yeah, me, too."

"Any connection, you think?" Frank asked.

"Between—?"

"Between the boyfriend and this Mrs. Bemis of yours? Can't fix one, you try to fix the other?"

Alice looked back at him, impressed and annoyed both. "You think you know a few things, don't you, Detective?"

"I just try to pay attention."

She looked at him. "And tell me, what do you see?"

"Someone who's trying pretty hard. But you can't fix everything for everyone, you know."

"No?"

"No."

"That's the cops' job," Alice teased.

LeBeau smiled. "Yeah. That's *my* job."

Alice got two mugs down from the cabinet. "Still, it scares me I didn't see the scissors coming. I mean, that somebody I cared about could do that. Could *cut* me."

"People can stun you, believe me. Even the ones you think you know." LeBeau pushed back from the table. "I sure didn't expect Sheila to turn on me. And we'd been together seven years." He crossed his legs, pulling one ankle up over the other knee. "But now listen, call the cops if he bothers you again. That's what we're there for. Promise me?"

"But how would that look, me a psychiatrist, with an M.D. from BU, phoning in a domestic-violence complaint?"

"You wouldn't be the first, believe me."

"Well, thanks for the advice, Frank." She liked the sound of his name there in the kitchen, with coffee brewing.

"And you gotta quit with this sneaking around, okay?" A roughness returned to his voice. "And stay away from crime scenes. That yellow tape, Alice? It means don't go there."

"I know, I know." The water was boiling now, and she turned back to the counter, saw the instant Medaglia d'Oro, which was all she had. "Oh shit, you're going to hate this stuff." She spooned some of the crisp granules into a mug, flooded it with boiling water, and set it down in front of him. "Is that why you came up here, just to give me my clog?"

He stirred in some sugar, took a sip of the coffee. "Actually, I got an interview set up with the younger brother, Michael Hurley. There were all sorts of scheduling problems. And my boss kept saying, 'Don't bother,' and 'Do you really have to,' and all this." He set down his coffee mug, which had a dalmatian on it in honor of a dog from Alice's childhood. "We're getting together at his dotcom in about a half hour." He glanced at his watch. "Me and a couple of the state guys I got interested in it."

He sipped the last of his coffee, and set the mug down. "Oh, I didn't tell you. I got the name of the man he went out in the boat with. Harry Brandt." He spelled it. "Ever heard of him?"

Alice shook her head. "So he turned up?"

"No, not yet. Sharks probably got him. Or whatever the hell's out there. Family finally put out a missing-person's report, and it matched the description the boat guy gave. Mustache was the giveaway. That and muscles. Brandt was extremely muscular, worked out a lot."

"And the link to Brendan?"

"Seems they worked together at Pine Street four or five years ago. Then Brandt went off to an HMO as a receptionist. I spoke to his sister late last night. She's out in Spokane. She didn't sound too distressed about his disappearance. Flaky, I got the impression. She'd never heard of Brendan."

"Did you—"

"Ask her about Madeline? Yeah."

"And?"

"Never heard of her, either."

Alice took a seat at the table across from him. "So that's all, Frank?"

He looked puzzled.

"About your coming up here? You just wanted to chew me out about the clog?"

"I'm not digging around just for the hell of it, if that's what you're asking."

The words hung there between them in the small kitchen with its yellow cupboards and ticking clock.

"Like I am, you mean?" She nearly reached for him, to help him see, but a hardness had come over him, a kind of glazing. He was turning back into a cop again. Alice turned away from him, glanced out the window toward the church across the street, its narrowing spire topped by a slender cross.

"I thought you said I was a good person," Alice said evenly.

"Okay, look, I'm sorry."

He was so close, there at the narrow table, she could smell him—sweaty in the heat, strong. She felt the sunlight on her, angling onto the outside of her arm, the side of her neck. She turned from him slightly, trying to resist.

"Maybe I'd better get going," he told her, standing up.

Alice swept the hair back off her face to make the prospect of his staying more appealing, but he pushed his chair in, under the table, without noticing. He brought his mug over to the sink, started washing it out until Alice told him she'd manage all that. He quickly dried his hands on the dish towel that hung off a drawer pull, and made for the door. He had his hand on the knob when he turned back to her.

"I'll call you, okay?" he said.

"I want to hear what you learn about Mrs. Bemis. Promise me?"

"Sure." He looked at her again, just once. It was just a flash, and then the door was shut again, and he descended the stairs with a clatter of his heavy cop shoes.

twenty-five

Alice had taken a quick bath, and, wrapped in a towel while her hair dried, she was at the sink washing out the coffee mugs when the phone rang about fifteen minutes later. It was Frank. From the crackling, she could tell he was calling from his cell phone.

"There's something else," he told her.

Alice braced herself.

"Truth is, I didn't have to go along on this interview. That's what I wanted to tell you. The state guys were gonna handle it. But I thought, well, there might be a few things you'd want to know."

"Me? That *I'd* want to know?"

"For that patient of yours."

She had been drying the dalmatian cup. She set it down on the counter and dried her hands on the dish towel. She took the receiver in both hands. "So reaming me out about my shoe was just an extra?"

"Don't start, all right? The boss is giving me enough problems. If he knew I was getting involved with a psychiatric case, he'd—well, let's just hope he doesn't find out." He paused a second. "So, like, what questions? You must have something you want to know. I should've asked you before. But I guess I was too busy being a prick."

"These state policemen—they're friends of yours?"

"I trust them to keep their mouths shut, if that's what you mean."

"Okay." Alice's mind shifted about, trying to land on something sensible. She told him she was primarily interested in the connection between Brendan and Mrs. Bemis. Had Michael ever heard of Mrs. Bemis? That would be good to know.

This question was greeted by silence on the other end of the line.

"Frank?" Alice asked, afraid the connection had cut out.

"Just making a note."

"Well, don't go off the road." She pictured him struggling with a notebook.

"No, no. I got this pad stuck onto the dashboard. Anything else?"

"Or, I know—" She added excitedly, "Does he know if Brendan ever worked in Milton? I talked to Mrs. Bemis's caretaker, and got the impression Brendan had been there a few times. He wasn't a gardener, I know that. Was he a workman of some kind? A laborer, maybe?"

"On top of his Pine Street job, you mean?"

"Or before it."

"Okay."

"There might be a psychiatric angle to it, too," Alice went on. "Maybe they were in some support group for something—alcoholism, maybe, or depression. There's no mention of such a group in her file, but it's a possibility."

"I'll try to see if I can work that in. Anything else?"

But that was all she could think of, at least all she could think of while he rushed along in his cruiser, sounding impatient.

"All right then," he said, noisily ripping the page off the pad.

"Oh, and Frank?"

"Yeah."

"Thanks."

• • •

Alice still had almost an hour before she needed to drive to Montrose. She'd been thinking about how cooped up Mrs. Bemis must feel in the hospital. Back when she'd felt so confined, her first year at medical school, when it seemed that she spent all her time slaving over her books, she'd started smoking unfiltered Camels. It broke the monotony of those endless pages of facts to cram into her head, and allowed her at least the illusion that she was still free. She'd noticed that Mrs. Bemis hadn't been smoking, and she certainly wasn't going to sneak her a pack of cigarettes. But she did remember the chocolates that she'd relied on to break the cigarette habit that spring. French chocolates. Seductive little squares, all individually wrapped in black. Her friend Kristen had put her on to them. Ridiculously expensive, hard to find— and, for these reasons, far more sinful than any cigarettes. Kristen had bought Alice a box for her birthday, and they were heavenly. It was a soft sweetness that somehow penetrated the soul, and Alice, who had started in with Dr. Horowitz by then, had joked that, in terms of sheer oral pleasure, they were worth at least six months of therapy.

There was a place in Harvard Square that sold them, and Alice thought that, if she hurried, she might be able to pick some up. It would be nice to surprise Mrs. Bemis. The Grand had always been an excellent one for presents—trifles mostly, but thoughtfully selected. Chinese rice candies, museum postcards, romance magazines.

Alice was in luck, the store had an entire bowl of them out on the counter. Alice scooped up a handful, paid the cashier, and practically danced out of the store, she was so pleased. As she made her way back to her car, it was just shy of eleven-fifteen. Frank might be done with his interview by the time she got home. Maybe he'd leave a message on her machine?

"Glad I caught you," Frank said, his voice riding over some highway noise. He'd left his cell number on her tape, said he had something for her.

"So——" Alice prompted, eager to hear his news.

"So we saw Michael Hurley," LeBeau started in. "Seemed like a good enough guy. He runs Telectronics, you know. CEO. You wouldn't guess it, though. He was wearing jeans and a T-shirt. I mean, cops dress better than that on their days off." He paused a second. "Job like that can't be easy on him, the dotcoms being what they are."

"And his older brother dying."

"Hard to tell how close they were. But, yeah, he'd taken a few days off to get his stuff back together. Then he was out in California. This was his first day back on the job. Didn't have much time for us."

Alice needed to hurry this along if she was going to make her twelve o'clock appointment with Mrs. B. "He say anything about Mrs. Bemis?"

"Didn't get into that until the end. State guys looked at me kinda funny when I brought her up. I could see them thinking, 'What the hell?' But they're good guys, pretty much. I worked another case with them this spring. Stolen-property thing, involved a huge warehouse in Hingham. It was in the paper."

"But Mrs. Bemis, Frank?" Alice interrupted. "I'm sorry. I'm in a bit of a rush here."

"Well, you tell me. He started to blow me off, said he didn't know anyone by that name. But then I described her, an older woman, mid-seventies now, maybe a little starchy, and all that. And he said no, no one like that. But then I said, maybe when she was younger. Who knows, this thing may go back. So he thought for a second and said, 'Well, there was one time,' and then he gets into it. Says there was a young woman, quite attractive and kind of proper, that came around once way back when he was a kid. Just once, though. I'm surprised he even remembered, frankly. But it was a weekday, and Mike was home sick from school, which was unusual for him. He was all alone in the house, with his dad off doing his custodial work at the courthouse and his mother working wherever she worked."

"Seamstress, I think you said."

"Right. Seamstress. Okay. Mike figures this was seventh grade, eighth grade. This young lady comes to the door, pretty well dressed. 'Like for church,' he tells me. Remember, this is down by the projects where people never get dressed up except maybe for a funeral."

"Got it."

"Michael can see her from his bedroom, coming up the walk. She's obviously not expecting anybody home. She doesn't ring the doorbell or knock or anything, just slides something through the mail slot. He hears the slot bang shut. So Mike gets curious, hops out of bed, goes down, and there's an envelope there with Brendan's name on it. Just that, 'Brendan.' Underlined. And then, get this, through the window he sees a woman about to get into her car. She's a little younger than his mother, he figures. Maybe thirty. He opens the door, shouts to her, 'Brendan's at school, you know.' And she says, 'Good for him.' And then she gets back into her car. Real nice car. No rust, which I gather is unusual in Southie."

The cell phone started to buzz, distorting Frank's voice for a moment.

"You're breaking up," Alice said, afraid she was going to lose the connection. "Can you hear me? Frank?"

"Yeah, I got you," Frank said calmly. "But here's the thing. When Mike holds the envelope up to the light, he sees there's money in it."

"And?"

"He rips the thing open and there's like a hundred bucks in there." Frank laughed. "He pockets it. No love lost between those two."

"Did Brendan ever find out?"

"Yeah, beat the crap out of him. That's another thing that helped him remember."

"So Brendan was expecting the money?"

"Sounds like it. Mike never saw the woman again."

"She learned to be more careful."

"Maybe."

"Who'd he think the lady was?"

"Figured it was somebody from church. He never asked who. Probably didn't want to know."

"Or he figured Brendan wasn't going to say."

"That, too."

twenty-six

At Nichols, Alice stepped quickly out of the elevator, annoyed with herself for being late. The lift opened directly onto the common room, a spare space with a dried-up spider plant hanging in the window and a TV mounted on a deep shelf in the corner. Lana, a sad teenager who'd cut long slices with a meat knife across her thighs, was staring up at the TV beside Charles, the hot-tempered accountant from Alice's anger-management class. Both of them wore somber expressions as they watched, mesmerized by a loud, clanging game show.

She was just thinking that such a scene would set off someone like Mrs. Bemis, when, to her surprise, she saw that Mrs B was, in fact, *right there,* sitting in a Naugahyde chair directly before her. Quite refined this morning, too, in a summer dress that an older person might wear to a garden party. She looked lovely, even, the light through the window playing up her prominent cheekbones. But anger glinted in her eyes.

"I was waiting for you," Mrs. Bemis told Alice. The clipped propriety again.

"But I don't come in until twelve on Wednesdays."

Mrs. Bemis looked down at her watch, adjusting the distance of her wrist to bring the time into focus. "Yes, and it's eighteen minutes *past* twelve."

"Well, come on then," Alice cajoled her, reaching down to help her elderly patient out of her chair. But Mrs. Bemis refused any assistance. Instead, she placed her hands on the wooden arms and rose on her own. "There," she said with a note of triumph when she was on her feet.

Alice patted Mrs. Bemis's back, feeling again the iron in the old woman's bones, and together, they passed through the double doors to the corridor, toward Mrs. Bemis's room. But Alice noticed Marnie through the window in the nurses' area and asked her patient to go on ahead. "I'll be there in a moment, okay?"

"All right." Mrs. B continued on down the corridor, her head down. She walked slowly, elbows out, like a farmer. "But don't keep me waiting too long," she said over her shoulder.

In the nurses' room, Marnie was filling out a report. She glanced up at Alice. "Madeline's been looking for you."

"She found me." Alice shut the door behind her. "Any idea why she was all dressed up and waiting for me at the elevator?"

"Looks as if you're getting through to her. She asked for you last night, and again this morning. 'Where's Dr. Matthews?' 'Where's Dr. Matthews?' 'Is she in yet?' 'When's Dr. Matthews coming in?' She wouldn't do any of her usual groups. Wouldn't *touch* her food. She insisted on parking herself right there by the elevators."

"No explanation?" Alice asked.

"She missed you, I'd say."

Both of their usual therapy rooms were occupied, so Alice met with Mrs. Bemis in her bedroom. She was sitting on the side of her bed, her hands warring with each other in her lap. Around her, the bare walls seemed particularly bleak compared to the gay print of her dress.

Alice took a seat across from her. "Oh!" Alice declared, digging into her handbag for the small plastic sack from the sweets shop. "Here. I brought something for you." She pulled out one of the square chocolates. Individually wrapped in luscious black paper, it might have been a tiny Christmas gift. "It's French."

"What in heaven's name—"

"Chocolate, Mrs. Bemis. Dark chocolate. I was addicted to them in med school. Better than cigarettes."

"How would *you* know?"

"I smoked."

That got her patient's attention. "You did?"

"I've done a few 'mistaken things,'" Alice added with a sly smile.

Mrs. Bemis's eyes let Alice know she caught the reference although she said nothing.

"Please, try it. I know you haven't been smoking and—"

"Oh, no. I couldn't possibly. It wouldn't agree with me." Mrs. Bemis must have noticed that Alice seemed a little hurt, for she added, more softly, "Actually, I've never liked candy of any sort. My mother was always dead set against it. She was always concerned about my smile, you see. She thought that a bright smile was the mark of good breeding. I thought it more likely to indicate idiocy, but I went along."

"Then try it," Alice said, offering her the chocolate once more.

"I'm sorry. I became persuaded, you see. A mother is always right."

Alice put the candy down on the table by her bed. "Well, in case you change your mind later."

"I won't," Mrs. Bemis said, crossing her arms in front of her.

Alice settled back in her chair, uncertain as to just how to proceed. "Are you all right?" she asked. "You looked nervous in the common room this morning. And the way you're fighting with me just now."

Mrs. Bemis bowed her head to stare down at her black shoes, which were tight together on the floor, the laces drooping. "I was—" She looked away, toward the window, then, with a grimace, swung her head back down toward her feet again. "I was worried about you, that's all."

"I'm sorry I was late," Alice told her.

"I suppose I have—" It seemed like torture for Mrs. Bemis to speak. "Come to—" She stopped again. "Well, to depend on you. Somewhat."

"I feel that from you," Alice assured her. "It's all right. It helps me."

Another grimace. Mrs. Bemis seemed to hate the words she was about to speak, and to want to fight the person within herself who was determined to speak them. "But I didn't want you to get all involved in—" Her voice trailed off. "You know."

"Brendan Hurley, you mean?"

Mrs. Bemis seemed to be startled to hear the name from Alice's lips. "Yes."

Alice moved her chair closer to Mrs. B, deliberately invading that sphere of privacy that, out of primness or self-protection, the old woman always drew around herself. She edged back now as Alice leaned close.

"How do you know him, Mrs. Bemis?" Alice asked gently. "Why do you care about him so much?"

Her patient stared silently back.

"It might help me to know why his death is so troubling to you."

The woman turned away from Alice, to the window, as if dashing for cover in the trees.

"Mrs. Bemis?"

Still nothing.

"I'd like to try something, if I could. Give me your hand, would you?" Alice asked.

Mrs. Bemis peered dubiously at her for a second. "My hand?"

Alice nodded. "Please." She reached out to her patient.

Mrs. Bemis extended her left hand toward her, fingertips wobbling. A slender wedding band hung loosely off her fourth finger.

Alice took Mrs. B's hand in both of hers. The skin was cool and paper-thin; it slid over the knuckles like silk. "This is about trust, Mrs. Bemis. I want you to trust me, okay?"

The old lady nodded silently, her eyes locked on Alice's.

"The other day, you told me that you knew the man who drowned in the water off Duxbury."

"I shouldn't have said anything."

"Well, I'm glad you did. It may help me to help you."

Mrs. B dipped her head as if to acknowledge praise.

"Now, tell me. Did you know him?"

Alice could feel Mrs. Bemis pulling her hand back slightly. Not a hard tug, more a flinch.

"Mrs. Bemis—please?" Alice asked, stroking her hand to soothe her. The skin was crinkly, with none of the buttery softness of Alice's own. Alice could feel the tension in the fingers, like a pull shade that's about to snap.

"But I—" Mrs. B looked up, a flash of fear in her eyes.

"I think it would help you if you could talk about this. It's obviously bothering you a great deal. You said you were concerned about me. Were you afraid that I might be hurt somehow?"

"Possibly."

"Can you tell me how?"

"I don't *know* how."

"So what makes you think so?"

Silence.

"Do you know how Brendan died?"

"Not for sure, no." Mrs. Bemis paused. "I believe he drowned. That's what they said on the news."

Alice squeezed Mrs. Bemis's hand. "Please, tell me *how* you know him?"

Silence, but she did not let go of Alice's hand.

"Have you known him long?"

Nothing. Mrs. Bemis's eyes were fixed on the floor. In Alice's hand, Mrs. Bemis's hand seemed suddenly lifeless, as though the remaining vitality in it had slipped away with her gaze. The way Mrs. Bemis's shoulders were slumped, her whole body seemed crushed by a great weight that seemed to come down from the sky and load up onto every part of her.

Alice stroked her hand.

"I used to watch him sometimes." Mrs. Bemis spoke quietly, as if in a dream, and Alice sensed she was being taken into new terrain, a strange, featureless place like the blurry underwater that Alice had seen as she swam so frantically from the dock.

"I watched him wrestle. At his school."

"You went inside?"

She nodded. "I was curious." She paused. "To see him."

"But why?"

Mrs. Bemis looked back at Alice, blankly.

"Why what?"

"Why did you want to see him?"

"See who?"

Had Mrs. Bemis truly lost track of her thoughts? Did the vacancy come over her with no words or images attached—just a sudden patch of nothing? Or were there memories, unspeakable ones, that triggered it, as if her past was playing right now, like a movie in the dark theater of her mind?

"We were talking about Brendan Hurley," Alice repeated.

Mrs. Bemis glanced about, as if searching for a memory in the air somewhere. Then she rapped on her temple with the knuckles of her free hand and gave out a gasp of frustration. "I used to know things. My husband thought I used to know *every*thing." Mrs. Bemis gave her an aggrieved look, as if she might actually cry. But then she rallied, and shot Alice a brave smile.

"Sometimes we forget things because they're too painful to remember," Alice said. She let that sink in. "I asked about Brendan Hurley."

"Oh, yes." Mrs. B looked at Alice sorrowfully. "Him." She hardened into a statue of herself—bemused, expectant.

"What was his connection to you?" Alice probed. "Was he a friend? Someone you knew through church? Was he—"

"There was no relationship," Mrs. B interrupted. "None." She shrugged, her dress bunching up at the shoulders.

Alice's mind reeled. "Then how—"

"I don't especially enjoy these questions," Mrs. Bemis said sharply.

"Well, I'm not sure I like your answers," Alice shot back, to her immediate regret. It was with dismay that she saw Mrs. Bemis pull back slightly from her grip, and her shoulders rise. Alice was about to apologize when—

"Please," the woman cried out. "Please, don't— Don't be frustrated with me. Of course I *knew* him. I told you, I used to watch him play his sports. He was a wonderful athlete, always getting his name in the paper."

"So you were just a—just a fan of his? Is that what you're saying?"

Mrs. Bemis looked at Alice with new appreciation. "Yes. A fan. That's what I was. I was a fan."

Alice would have liked to push, but she didn't quite dare. This wasn't a cross-examination. Push too hard and you run the risk of breaking the bond of trust, of sympathy, that therapy requires and that Alice had worked so hard to create. So it was with some relief that she heard a knock on the door. It was Victor, reminding her of their regular Wednesday psychopharm conference. Alice released Mrs. Bemis's hand, and let her head slump back onto the pillow.

Before she left, though, Alice quietly placed two more pieces of chocolate on the side table, just in case, once she tried one, she wanted more.

twenty-seven

Alice was exhausted that night, and she went to bed at a little past nine. But the phone rang as she climbed under the covers. It was Frank. "Got a little more background on the other guy, Harry Brandt. I told you how they used to work together at the Pine Street Inn. Well, I finally tracked down Brandt's wife." He waited a moment. "She's really worked up over it. Flew into a rage when I mentioned Brendan Hurley. She thinks he's a devil."

"Why?"

"Bad influence. He was always taking Brandt out to card games, the dog track, strip joints, stuff like that. They played pool, too. Apparently, Brendan was pretty good. It was nothing for him to come out of there with a hundred, hundred fifty bucks in his pocket. Then blow it all on booze and lottery tickets. Played his number every day for thirty, forty bucks. Got Brandt into it, too. Which did not please his wife. But Brendan always thought that one of them was going to get lucky."

"Did they?"

"Not as far as I know."

There was a pause on the line. Frank spoke a little more quietly this time. "I also wanted to make sure that that ex of yours isn't causing you any more grief."

"No sign of him so far. But thanks."

"It's a cop thing. Worrying. It's part of the job."

"Maybe you should try therapy."

"You offering?" he asked.

Alice had to laugh. "Good night, Frank."

twenty-eight

*M*rs. Bemis had wrapped a silk scarf, bright yellow, around her neck—to keep the sun off, she'd said. It made her look dashing in an old-fashioned sort of way. Above her, gorgeous, puffy clouds sailed across a sea of blue. She seemed to gain strength from the brisk air, the great trees casting a kaleidoscope of shadows on the path at their feet.

On this, their first walk outside, Alice let Mrs. Bemis choose the way, and she started down toward gabled Danzinger, drawn to the small garden flanked by azaleas along the wall there. She moved jauntily at first, but slowed as she approached. "Oh, dear," she exclaimed as her eyes fell on a clump of wilted zinnias beside a bed of leggy impatiens, thick with weeds. "I do miss my roses."

"They don't have much money for gardening," Alice explained.

"Beauty doesn't have to be *expensive.*" Mrs. Bemis landed scornfully on the last word. "All it takes is a little attention. My heavens, when I revived our garden in Milton, it scarcely cost a thing. I had to show Ronald every last receipt, that's how I know. But so many things can be grown from seed, my dear. Many of my orchids, for instance, I'm very proud of that. And some gardening friends gave me things—some marvelous blush roses I still have, and a tiny peach tree that one of them had no room for. And lots of flowers were wild—foxglove, hollyhock, sweet william. Simple flowers, certainly, but absolutely adorable. I'd love to show you sometime."

"I'd love to see."

Mrs. Bemis was suddenly interrupted by the sight of the stables at the end of an asphalt path that cut diagonally across the grounds. Her eyes lingered on the old building, with its rough, crisscrossed beams. "Now, what on earth—?"

Scarcely waiting for an answer, she ambled slowly toward it, pausing only once to exclaim over a few spikes of purple larkspur peeking up by the edge of the path. The large doors were open, and Mrs. Bemis stepped inside ahead of Alice. If she was expecting something in particular—an old Model T, a horse or two—she didn't say so. She merely glanced about at the various pieces of gardening equipment that were leaned up against the walls, or mounted on hooks higher up. The grounds crew must have been out with the lawn mowers, for the floor was nearly empty.

"Chilly," Mrs. Bemis said, drawing her bare arms about her. She glanced about, seeming to savor some idea or recollection about the place.

"It's nice on a hot day, though," Alice replied, adding that she often came here on her break. She nearly told her about Lars, but decided against it. "Did you ride?" she asked instead. Alice enjoyed the thought of Mrs. Bemis astride some stallion, galloping across a field.

But Mrs. Bemis was gazing up toward the hayloft, her eyes on the cobwebs draped from the rough beams at the corner.

"Mrs. Bemis?" Alice prompted. "Did you?"

"Only a few times," she finally replied. "I was never much good at it."

"Where was this?"

"Where was what?" Mrs. Bemis's eyes lingered on a couple of loose bales of hay that were stacked in the corner beside a tool bench. A few bits had spilled out onto the floor, forming a kind of patchy rug.

"Where you rode."

"Oh, that. At camp. Whistling Pines."

Even in the dim light, Alice could see that Mrs. Bemis had turned pale.

Concerned about her, Alice stepped closer to her patient. "I hope I haven't tired you," she said and reached for Mrs. B's elbow.

"It's just the air in here." Mrs. Bemis waved a hand in front of her face. "It must be carrying a mold."

Alice touched the inside of her elbow, felt the cool flesh. "Let's go back outside then, shall we?"

Mrs. Bemis did not resist. Rather, she seemed to lean on Alice somewhat, as if, in fact, she depended on her. Alice slid another hand around the old woman's elbow.

"Yes. Outside. Please." Mrs. Bemis seemed as if she might faint, and Alice guided her back toward the open door.

Outside, in the brightness, Alice cautiously led Mrs. Bemis back toward a stout bench on the path up to Nichols. It was out of the sun, in the shade of one of the few elms left on campus.

"Yes, that's it," Mrs. Bemis said, easing herself down. "Just let me rest here for a moment. Goodness, I don't know what came over me. I felt weak all of a sudden. I'm glad you were there to catch me."

"Something happened at the camp?" Alice asked.

Mrs. Bemis did not seem to grasp the question. Her eyes were on the far horizon.

"*Something* about the stables troubled you," Alice persisted.

Mrs. Bemis waited a moment before speaking. "Yes," she said. "Many things."

"Such as?"

"Oh, Dr. Matthews, I *can't*—"

"Please. Tell me."

"But it's nothing. Nothing that could possibly matter to anyone. The long ago, the insignificant, the pathetic. It's nothing, I tell you. Absolutely nothing."

"It's not nothing. It's your life, it's why you are the way you are."

"Mad as a hatter, you mean?"

Alice ignored that. "Please, Mrs. Bemis. Tell me, would you? Let me decide if it's nothing."

"I was just—I was just remembering a letter I received at camp. Nothing, you see?" She turned to her with a victorious smile.

"From?"

"From my husband. My future husband, I should say. Ronald. My very first letter from him, as a matter-of-fact. He asked if I would 'go' with him." She said the words archly.

"That doesn't sound like nothing to me. The first exchange with the man you married?"

"I suppose it was a beginning," Mrs. Bemis admitted. "But it was so slight, and my dear, if you'd seen the letter. He signed it, 'Sincerely, Ronald Bemis.'" She smiled. "Can you imagine? He was fourteen! I'll never forget that."

"And what did you tell him?" Alice asked.

Her face darkened. "I told him I would." She stared back at the stables. "I should have said no. It would have been so easy to say no."

"But you said yes."

Mrs. Bemis nodded, her eyes still on the stables.

"What happened? What went wrong?"

Mrs. B turned to Alice, anger on her face. "What went—? What went right? That would be easier to say."

"You weren't suited?"

A shake of the head. "He didn't care about me, apparently."

"Why not?"

Mrs. Bemis shrugged. "We were different people, going separate ways, I guess." She sighed. "He simply went where I could not follow."

"Your husband?"

Mrs. Bemis turned sharply to Alice. "My——?"

"Husband," Alice repeated. "Ronald. We were speaking of Ronald. He left you?"

"Why yes, I suppose he did, in a way."

"When?"

"Who can say? When does disappointment begin?"

"But you were a beautiful, talented woman. Your garden, your orchids. Ronald should have been proud of you."

"Proud?" Mrs. Bemis craned her head around to look at Alice. "'Proud' was not in his repertoire. He was too——too embattled. He was all banged up from the war when I married him. Braces on both legs. Hideous things. I was only eighteen, you know. A scandal!" Her eyes flashed, as if she enjoyed the recollection. "Why, my dear, you look so serious. I didn't mean to alarm you." She patted Alice's knee. "Do you know what he asked me before he went off to the war?"

Alice waited.

"He asked for a lock of my hair." She looked intently at Alice. "You remember, weeks back, when we first met, and I wanted to touch your hair?"

"Yes, of course."

"Your hair reminded me of that moment with him, or, perhaps I should say, *you* reminded me of it." She fixed her gaze on Alice. "I see things in you. You and I, we——" she stopped.

"What?"

"Oh, heavens. No point going on about *that*." Mrs. Bemis smiled. "I ate those chocolates of yours, you know. All three of them. I had one yesterday after dinner, and then two more this morning. Before breakfast!"

"I'm glad. I'll have to give you some more."

"Oh, don't. I'll have to go on a diet. But they are delicious."

"Aren't they?"

"Still not as satisfying as a cigarette, though."

"I know," Alice agreed mournfully.

And she turned to Mrs. Bemis, whose eyes were in the trees.

Maddy

≻—   twenty-nine

I t was just one brace, actually. A thick metal band, hinged at the knee, that he clasped onto his thigh with a leather belt. It chafed him, especially in the cold weather when his skin was dry, accentuating his limp. So odd, that poor mangled leg of his. The kneecap, thigh, and shinbones had all been shattered like crockery when his plane slammed into the barn. There were so many breaks, the bones never set properly, and the joint was nearly useless now. At first, the sight of his bare leg—puckered with scars—had filled her with sympathy. She wanted to kiss it and stroke it with oils, especially the rough, red band at mid-thigh where the brace rubbed. That poor leg—the asymmetry, the clumsiness—was simply part of Ronnie. She should have accepted it, possibly even loved him for it, but it hardened her to him instead. She grew impatient with the way he moved, shuffling along with his cane like an old man. Hated him for it, positively hated him. And she hated herself for that.

• • •

It had been a small wedding at St. Paul's, in Dover, a stone fortress with a high steeple that her father's family had always belonged to. The minister was the hunched-over Reverend Edgars, the great favorite of her father's who'd come to lunch that day Ronnie had snipped off her hair. The service went by in a blur, even the pivotal moment when she had to "give herself"—such an odd expression— to Ronnie, and the fumbling exchange of rings, and the awkward, lunging kiss. She didn't quite grasp that this was marriage—holy, permanent, binding matrimony. Or perhaps that was all she grasped. Either way, the church bells were suddenly crashing above her as she emerged from the chapel, a wife, with her husband hobbling beside her. She cringed as the rice tossed by some of her younger cousins rained down on her. The reception was held in the massive white clubhouse that was like an ocean liner trapped in an ice floe of fairways. The reception was not excessive; nothing her parents ever organized was. Still, Maddy couldn't help thinking that their restraint—the few guests, the small cake—reflected their misgivings about her choice of groom. She hated their being so cold to Ronnie, with their teeth-baring smiles, the ones that cut.

Ellen was Maddy's maid of honor, and she got drunk on champagne and made a fool of herself with a cousin, an untrustworthy boy named Henry Rollins. She let him kiss her on the lips, right by the punch bowl, which caused Maddy's aunt Edith to flush with distress. Maddy had been worried about the dancing, what with Ronnie's brace, but the two of them shuffled about a little to Phil Stevens's band, which played at all the best parties these days according to Ellen. When Maddy drew close to Ronnie for their first waltz as Mr. and Mrs. Ronald Bemis, she felt a film of sweat behind his neck, below the hairline. Still, she clung to him as tightly as she dared, grateful that he was there.

When their dance was over, he kissed her on the cheek and told her he was going to get some air. And then he stepped out toward the patio off the end room, by the ninth hole. Maddy's father stepped in for a foxtrot from his "little girl," as he called her. (He must have had a couple by then.) After everything, it pained her to move with him, his body so close to hers, forcing her to conform to his errant sense of the beat, and it was a relief when her balding uncle Harold tapped his brother's shoulder and took her for what he termed a "spin" about the floor. When the band finally took a break, Maddy needed some air herself, and she went outside to look for her husband.

He was standing by a pillar, looking out at the bare trees, and he was smoking, which she'd never seen him do before. More than smoking, he was giving a Lucky Strike a fierce pull, hollowing his cheeks, drawing the smoke deep into his lungs. And he was talking to her cousin Lucy, at twenty-one a full three years older than Maddy and a well-filled-out Radcliffe senior besides. He was telling her about the war, a topic that he rarely broached with Maddy. She heard the word "Krauts," which she hadn't heard before. Lucy seemed to find him fascinating.

"Ronnie?" Maddy asked, which was imbecilic.

"Oh, hello you," he replied. A strange formulation. British, perhaps? It reminded her, yet again, of how little she knew this man.

"You all right?" she asked. "I don't like thinking of you out here in the cold." It must have been nearly freezing out there.

"I'm fine," he told her. "Just came out for a smoke. Lucy had some cigarettes."

Lucy looked from one to another, then reached for Ronnie's hand and gave it a squeeze. "Perhaps I need some more punch."

Maddy watched her go, back through the double doors to the ballroom. The music had started up again now. It seemed to be coming from another world.

"I didn't know you knew her," she told him.

"She offered me a cigarette, that's all."

"Well, the Scotts would love to see you," Maddy replied. "You remember the Scotts, don't you, darling?"

He let a spurt of cigarette smoke go toward the trees, then looked over at her. "Come here for a second, would you?"

"But they're expecting—"

He must have drunk a bit of the champagne himself, because he reached for her and grabbed her around the back. She froze, speechless. Her dress was thin, and she could feel each cool finger pressing into her back. Then he tried to kiss her. He did it fumblingly, as if uncertain as to just where her mouth was, but caught the corner of her lip, sucking it into his mouth, he was so voracious. She could taste the tobacco smoke on him.

"Not—not just now, okay, Ronnie?" She wriggled loose from him.

"You're the boss," he said. He took a last pull on his cigarette, then, with his third finger, flicked it out off the porch, toward the lawn.

She backed away from him, staring at the slim, haunted figure she'd married, and returned to the party.

Did he know?

The wedding trip was to Niagara Falls, but, because of last-minute changes in the railroad schedule, they weren't able to leave right away. Instead, they went from the country club to Copley Square, where they passed their first night together in the Copley Plaza, overlooking the bristling Trinity Church and, across from it, the massive public library that might have been built for a doge. Ronnie himself had made the arrangements, and Maddy was surprised to see how small the room was, and how big the bed. She had never seen a bed so big.

"Try to imagine it's Florence," Ronnie said when Maddy went to the window to look out at the square below. There was a new tone there, a dry bitterness that she didn't like, but it was too subtle to respond to. They would have gone to Florence if it hadn't been for the war. It was his mother's favorite city, Ronnie had told Maddy more than once; his mother had taken him there on a grand tour at sixteen. The previous summer, he'd seen it again at ten thousand feet when they'd swung southward after his rescue mission in the Italian Alps.

Maddy's head was still spinning from the party, and she told Ronnie that she'd feel better if she took a bath—and then was stunned when Ronnie said he'd prefer it if she didn't. "I've waited too long as it is," he told her, turning away to jerk the curtains closed.

"But—but it was so hot in that room, I'm sweating so much it's indecent," Maddy stammered, appalled by his peremptory manner. "Really, Ronnie, I should bathe first, or at least wash." She'd planned to take a steaming bath, then, on Ellen's advice, to dust herself lightly with talcum powder. She'd smell so fresh.

Ronnie turned around to address her straight on. "I'd rather have you as you are."

"Have me—?" Was this the way men spoke to their wives? Had her father spoken this way to her mother? She wished Ellen were here, or Julie, or someone, to offer advice or *something*. But of course she was alone here with Ronnie.

"Yes. As you are," Ronnie repeated.

"But I'm dirty," Maddy said.

"Yes." Ronnie settled down into the big chair across from her. "I expect you are. But that's all right. Don't you worry."

He watched her undress, which she did shyly. Just watched, nothing more. Before leaving the country club, she'd changed out of her white satin wedding gown, which had been her grandmother's, and into a loose dress with a floral print. It buttoned up the side in a way that she'd considered quite racy (and Ellen had agreed). She'd imagined that Ronnie would help her out of it. She'd pictured him popping the buttons one by one, delightedly.

Now, it brought her pain to undo the buttons herself, and drape the beautiful dress over the chair by the wardrobe, as his eyes bored into her.

"Maddy," he commanded. "Turn to me, would you mind?" He was staring; she could feel it. "And stand in the light so I can see you? I've thought of this moment for such a long time. Dreamed of it."

"Ronnie, please." Maddy did not like making a display of herself. Not to him. Still, she turned back to him and, fighting her humiliation, she unclasped her brassiere. She continued to hold it tight to her chest with the insides of her arms.

"Madeline." The tone was insistent. "I'd love it if you'd—"

She lowered her arms, letting the brassiere flutter to the floor. She dropped her eyes, unable to meet his gaze.

"All right. Yes. Beautiful. Just beautiful. The rest now. Please, dear?"

"Ronnie, for goodness sake, I'm not a showgirl." Maddy wished there were some escape. She wanted to run into the bathroom, or pull her bathrobe over her, or grab a towel even, and flee into the hall. But this was her wedding night. That was impossible. Everyone would know.

"And stay in the light, would you?"

She hooked her fingers under her underwear, felt her skin dimple where her fingertips went in. She looked once more into his eyes, hoping he'd relent, or laugh, or show that this was all a misunderstanding. But no, his eyes were as hard as ever, staring.

"That's right. Yes," he said.

She quickly lowered her underpants, hurrying to be done with it. The elastic band seemed to scrape her sides as the underwear descended, revealing herself completely to him. She stepped out of them, stood there naked before him. But, more than naked, she felt small, exposed, helpless. All skin, nothing to hide behind. Just her.

"Yes, very fine," he said.

She knew what was next. She retreated to the bed. She slid under the sheets, which felt rough and heavy, almost binding, and they pressed down on delicate places where she had never felt the weight of sheets before. She lay on her back, with her legs together, and her toes pointed, as she stared at the white ceiling. He took a while to remove his own clothes. She could hear his breathing, the sound of zippers, cloth sliding off him. It seemed to be a labor. Finally, a squeak as he removed his brace, and then a thump when he placed it on the rug. He slid off his own underthings, and then, in a slow, uneven gait, he came for her.

Maddy felt the mattress give as he lay down beside her, and then he rolled toward her, and draped his good leg, the right one, over the two of hers. His penis, stiff and thick, pressed against the outside of her thigh. She continued to stare at the ceiling, her eyes following the curve of the unlit chandelier. He'd kept his own shirt on; it rubbed against her. He was sensitive about his scars, that's all she could think. His tuxedo shirt, very starchy. The buttons pushed into her skin. After the baby, she was so tender, so raw. She wanted to tell Ronnie, to ask him to go slow. But— she couldn't! How could she ever explain? Yet she felt that the lightest touch would make her scream.

Gerald had caressed her beforehand, kissing her breasts, even sucking on her nipples, which nearly made her laugh it was so surprising, and then gliding his thick fingers into her a few times before he slid himself in. It did hurt, at first. But, eventually, his touch had warmed her, eased her, turned her body into something languid, fluid, hardly a body at all. But Ronnie did not touch her nearly so tenderly. He was too eager, desperately so. He seemed like one big, hard thing. He slid his knees between her legs, opening her. When he shoved himself into her, his thing was like a poker that jabs into a fire. Jab! Jab! Jab! He didn't mean it, she was sure. He couldn't! But it took everything she had to keep from screaming. She was dry, unready. And afraid he'd tear her open, rip apart the place through which the baby had come.

Did he know?

The chandelier had smoked glass, in a flower design. As she stared up, it seemed to bounce and flutter with every thrust of Ronnie's into her. It hurt—hurt so much! She was sure he'd draw blood. Any moment, she expected to feel a sticky wetness spilling over her thighs. She must have been shouting, someone was; she could feel the vibrations in her chest. Ronnie was grunting, right by her ear, and his mouth was wet and his beard was rough, and he scratched the side of her face, up by her temple, with his hand as he pushed into her, over and over. The joints of the bed strained, the bedsprings squealed. But he said nothing, just grunted, as if his mind were far away, up in the sky somewhere, and only his body was here, slamming into her.

She thought he'd split her open. She started beating against his wide back with her tightened fists, and then grabbing at his shirt with her sweaty palms as the red-hot pain shot through her.

Someone was pounding on the wall—or was it the bedpost smacking against it?

"Ronnie! Ronnie! No! Enough! Stop! Please! Please!" she gasped, every muscle tense, straining, trying to push him off, make him stop, stop, stop hurting her. She brought her hand to his face, sliding around his chin, to push at him, to push him away.

But he wouldn't stop, or couldn't. He continued on, groaning and straining, as if he were in agony, too, and relief lay ahead. She couldn't imagine that anyone would be so desperate, so needy. It was as if he was charging up some endless hill. He kept going and going, lost to her. Finally, with a strangled sort of gasp, Ronnie reared up, his neck veins swelling, and, with a tortured look, he gave out a fierce, angry cry, like that of a soldier pushing a blade home.

When he was done, she pushed him off her—his shirt was nearly soaked through with sweat—and went into the bathroom without a word. She locked the door behind her and drew the bath. She made it as hot as she could bear. There was a scrub brush, and she scrubbed herself red, trying to remove the stain of what he'd done.

•　•　•

"He didn't even say anything?" Ellen asked her the next afternoon. They were having tea at a little place on Newbury Street. Ronnie was at the bank, attending to his accounts.

"Just, 'Face me, would you?' or something like that. I don't exactly remember."

A small smile crept at the corners of Ellen's mouth. "I wouldn't have guessed that. Not from Ronnie. I didn't think he'd ever say anything like that."

"It was awful," Maddy cried.

"But it sounds so racy," Ellen replied, obviously not grasping her friend's distress. "I'd love it if my husband wanted to look at me." She twisted her shoulders in a way that gave her breasts a shake.

"Oh, Ellen, you wouldn't. Not like that."

"Like what?"

"The coldness. He didn't ask me, he *told* me. Practically ordered—" Maddy stopped, realized that she was speaking entirely too loudly on such a subject with other people about, then dropped to a whisper— "practically ordered me to take off all my clothes and then stand in front of him while he—Ellen you cannot repeat this to anyone, do you hear?—while he *inspected* me."

"Inspecting you for what?"

"Wake up, would you!" Maddy put down her teacup. "I think he knows."

Ellen's face went white. "Oh, Maddy!" She brought a hand to her mouth in shock. "Seriously?"

Maddy nodded.

"But he couldn't!"

"*You* know."

Her friend's eyes widened. "But I—I've never said a word."

Maddy scrutinized her. The white skin, the cherry-red lipstick.

"And I wouldn't!"

"There are many ways of telling, Ellen."

"Oh, pish-posh."

Maddy didn't know how, or why, or to whom. But Ellen had let something slip. If Maddy had not already become the subject of stray gossip, of heartless rumor, she would soon. It would encircle her like a noose, and tighten. She could sense it. Some people knew about her; how many, or who, she couldn't guess. But some people knew already, and more would soon. Henceforth, whenever she walked into a room, or down the street, or stepped onto a train, someone would look at her differently for knowing something about her that no one should know. Ellen was not her friend, Maddy realized with a thump of her heart. No one was.

Ellen must not have realized how far she had fallen in Maddy's estimation, because she set down her teacup and looked kindly at her. "You do like Ronnie, don't you?" she asked imploringly. "He's very handsome, you know. Even after—well, you know. He's not that bad, is he?"

Maddy stirred another lump of sugar into her tea, forgetting she'd used two lumps already. "He's fine, Ellen. I'm sure he'll be a wonderful husband."

Ellen set down her teaspoon and looked at Maddy. "Well, I'm very glad to hear it. I was starting to worry."

But Maddy didn't care what Ellen thought anymore. She'd never fallen in love with a stranger, never been sent away from home to give birth, never given up her child, never married a man she did not love. Her gaze had gone past Ellen to the window, where she took solace from the street trees, just beginning to bud.

Out on the street again, Maddy walked with Ellen to her train, since Ellen wanted to stop in at the perfumer's by the station. Ellen gripped her arm and said there was something else that she wanted to ask her. Maddy slowed somewhat, but Ellen gave her arm a pat and told her to relax.

"Whatever became of—him. Do you know?"

"Of Gerald?" she asked.

"No, not him, silly goose. I assume he's long gone."

Maddy turned away, ice in her heart. Anything to avoid Ellen's insipid smile.

"The *baby*."

Maddy saw again the tiny bundle in white, being whisked out the double doors.

"Aren't you curious?"

At first, Maddy didn't think that Ellen was entitled to an answer. "He's in an orphanage somewhere, I suppose," she said vaguely.

"That's it? That's all you know?"

"No one sent me a postcard, if that's what you mean. 'Hi, I'm in Milwaukee! Write me a letter!'"

"I know that. I was just wondering—"

Maddy plucked her arm free from Ellen's grasp. "Well, *stop* wondering, all right? It's over! Finished and done with." They continued to walk along together, but only because they were both headed in the same direction. And they went the rest of the way to the train station in silence.

thirty

*M*addy and Ronnie left for Niagara Falls the next morning. It rained for all three days of their visit, producing great torrents of water that sloshed down the cobblestone streets on the Canadian side and made it impossible for the newly wedded Bemises—would she ever get used to that name?—to go outside for more than a cab ride to view the great roaring falls briefly, under a stout umbrella. Maddy would have liked to take a walk, rain or no, but Ronnie told her that, unfortunately, walking was an ordeal for him even in the best weather; when she persisted, begging him for the third or fourth time, he admitted he was afraid he might fall. He said it so forcefully, she nearly cried. She'd brought a pack of cards, thinking she might teach Ronnie some of the games she'd learned from the girls in Colorado, but he was buried in a book about Thucydides, or perhaps it was actually *by* Thucydides, so she played solitaire instead, and read a few of the Canadian women's magazines, as dull as they were, and wished she could call Julie, whom she'd come to miss acutely. But she was unsure of the phone number, and it was long distance, and, from this side of the border, international besides, and Ronnie discouraged such expenses, although, as far as she could tell, they had plenty of money. They did dine well, though, and, at his urging, she drank more than she ever had before, discovering a lovely licorice-tasting drink called Campari that she had with soda. She had a number of them, although Ronnie limited himself each night to just one glass of Irish whiskey, neat.

She braced herself for the sex, practically counting down the minutes until bedtime. But Ronnie was preoccupied with his book and made no move toward her the first two nights. Only on the third night, when she'd fallen asleep, sure—and somewhat relieved—that he'd lost all interest, did he slide his hands up underneath her night-gown to stroke the inside of her thigh. The way he touched her was surprisingly gentle, this time, and she tried to guide his hand, to show him what she liked, but he rolled onto her and, without a word, nestled himself in between her legs. He was rock hard. He pushed into her as he had before, but it hurt less this time, thank heavens. And as she lay under him, staring up at the ceiling, she thought that the sex might possibly be pleasurable one day.

Maddy returned with Ronnie to Boston and they settled in together in Milton, just to the south, in a big, early Victorian house, ringed by wide verandas, that had belonged to his aunt Jane. They had their activities, of course. He was busy getting a business degree from Harvard in a special program for returning GIs. And for her there were parties to attend. But as her old school friends slipped away, one by one, to raise children or travel or start a career of some sort, the new, younger ones who replaced them seemed cold to her. Ellen finally dumped George Loomis (she caught him embracing his second cousin) and then promptly fell in love with a ski instructor. She moved away to Vermont, leaving Maddy with only Molly Linden as anything close to a good friend, and Molly—high strung and fidgety—was no one to confide in.

With his windswept hair and thickening frame, Ronnie could look handsome in the English tweeds he favored. His eyes still carried the damage he'd suffered; his mournful gaze affected her when she caught him staring vacantly across the room, or out the window, thinking he was unobserved. His bad leg was a burden for him, obviously, but, as with most essential things between them, they never discussed it, although she did occasionally hear him curse when he had trouble with the belt as he strapped on his brace in the morning.

One time, though, after he'd had his bath, and he was dressing to go out to dinner, Ronnie actually bellowed with pain. It was a frightful, echoing sound that was quickly followed by an even more horrifying thud of some heavy object striking a wall. Afraid he'd hurt himself somehow, Maddy rushed to the bathroom door. She didn't dare go in; he was strict about his privacy. She did ask if he was all right, and if she could help. "Go away," he shouted at her.

But she went in anyway. She found him in his under things, slumped on the chair by the sink; the brace was lying on the floor across the room, where, evidently, he'd flung it. Seeing the contraption, Maddy briefly imagined that the brace was his leg itself, all mangled and hollowed out. She quickly rescued it, untangled the various straps, and took it back to him.

"I hate that damn thing," he told her, pushing it away. "I don't want it."

She was shocked by the language; he'd never sworn before. "But you need it, Ronnie," she replied. "You can't walk without it."

"You don't think I know that?"

"I'm sorry. Of course. But still—" She brought the brace down to fit it around his leg, and started to secure the various straps while he continued to fume. She had trouble with one of the buckles, though, and, in a fury, he swept her hands away and tried to work the buckle himself. But it would not unsnarl, and he heaved the whole contraption across the room once more. It bashed into the wall just under a small framed picture of a French chateau, and clattered to the floor.

"Ronnie!" Maddy shouted, appalled.

"Fucking thing." The language! Was he drunk? "I should never have gotten out of that goddamn plane. I'd have been better off burning to a crisp."

"Ronnie—please," Maddy begged. "Don't talk that way."

"It was my fault, the whole thing. I couldn't fly, couldn't land. I should've died sooner. Saved some lives, anyway."

"No, Ronnie."

He looked at her scornfully. "Oh, what the hell do you know? You weren't there. You were—" He stopped himself. "You have no idea. None."

"Well, *tell* me then," Maddy begged him. "I'm here. Speak to me. You never speak to me, Ronnie." She was near tears. "I feel so alone sometimes. I never know what you're feeling, whether you love me, whether you even *like* me."

He looked at her, touched her under the chin, as if he were seeing her for the very first time ever. He seemed sad, tender. She wanted to make love to him just then; she'd never had such a feeling for him. "Don't worry about any of that, Mads. It's me. It's just me."

She reached for his hand, grasping it awkwardly, and brought it to her face. "Oh, Ronnie. I worry. I worry all the time."

"Well, don't. I'll be fine." He straightened up. "Now, get me my brace, would you? Or we'll be late."

The anger had passed and, in her relief, Maddy didn't worry about that mysterious "just me" who'd been capable of such a fury. She was only glad that he was not enraged any longer. And if she had come to take up some of the rage he'd discarded, that was the way things would have to be. So it was with a feeling of gratitude, if not love, that she retrieved the brace for him again.

Ronnie calmly worked to strap the brace on once more, his lips tight with the effort. It buckled properly this time, and he was able to stand when he was done.

"There," he told Maddy.

In all their years together, he never again mentioned the war to her, nor did he ever again complain about his brace, nor, even, did he ever again get quite so enraged about anything. They went into Boston for a wonderful dinner that evening, but afterward, in bed, he did not reach for her to make love, much as she wished he would.

A few years later, he started using a cane to take some of the strain off the joint, which made him look ancient, especially in warm weather, when everyone else seemed to be dashing about on a tennis court or a beach. Ronnie took up golf, using one of the small motorized carts that were just starting to appear on courses in town to get around. Maddy had played as a teenager, but she preferred to spend her afternoons at home. She never felt comfortable at the country club he ultimately joined, in Brookline. The few times she had dinner with him there, or sat by the pool, she had the idea that people were talking about her.

Ronnie's work went well, happily. He got his degree at lightning speed, set up an office downtown trading institutional securities in partnership with a Harvard roommate. Soon he switched into commercial real estate with a small firm that featured the sons of several old-line families. It raised his spirits to acquire a building or, better, to actually construct one, later on, when the postwar boom was raging. One of them rose twelve stories, and impressed Maddy no end when he took her by to show her.

Maddy had counted on children to brighten their home life, and to fill up her days. But they tried for years, ever since that first, torturous wedding night. Despite her high hopes, the sex never did get to the blissful state she had achieved that one night with Gerald—a night that seemed all the more heavenly as the years passed. Ronnie invariably rushed her, never caressed her, never rhapsodized over her breasts, or tried anything the least venturesome, like bringing his tongue down between her legs—a practice that Ellen had told her about in hushed

tones, after several cups of brandy-laced eggnog one Christmastime
when she was back to visit her family. It was always unspoken between
Maddy and Ronnie as to what their intentions were.

It was also unspoken, inevitably, that those intentions were not
being satisfied. Maddy continued to receive her letter from Aunt
Suzie every twenty-eight days, and, as she'd done since menarche, to
note its arrival with a red dot in her date book. At the beginning, it
was a comfort to see that her body had returned to normal after the
ordeal she had put it through. But then, gradually, as the red dots
continued to punctuate her months, it began to strike her as a pun-
ishment—the latest of many—for her sins. Each time her period
came, her heart plunged. She'd enlarge the dots, scribbling with her
pen until she'd filled up virtually the entire page with a vast circle of
red.

Sometimes, when she thought back to the darling little boy
she'd given up in Golden, she'd retreat to the bathroom, lock the
door behind her, strip off her nightgown, and claw at her thighs and
belly with her fingernails, digging deep into the skin. If she pun-
ished herself enough, she reasoned, God might stop punishing her.
But He didn't.

Finally, six or seven years into the marriage, her mother-in-law took
her aside during a bridge party. They were in the pantry of the big
house in the Back Bay. Maddy was pouring coffee, when Grace—as
the more senior Mrs. Bemis let herself be called—asked her if everything was "all right."

"Fine, actually," Maddy replied. She'd gone for a walk in the
Blue Hills that afternoon, and Ronnie had seemed happier than
usual for a few weeks.

Grace was wearing glasses with a tiny jewel at each corner; the
jewels sparkled menacingly in the light. She bent closer to Maddy,
spoke more quietly, although no one else was about. "Isn't it time
you started a family?"

Grace might have nicked an artery; Maddy sensed herself losing blood, growing light-headed.

"George and I are getting on, you know." He'd recently turned sixty-five, with a big party in the ballroom at the Ritz; and Grace was only two years behind. "You are interested in children, aren't you?"

The pantry seemed to wheel about. "Why yes, of course."

"Well, that's a relief." The elder Mrs. Bemis placed a maternal hand on Maddy's forearm. "I was starting to wonder." She smiled. "I didn't mean to intrude. It is a private matter between you and Ronnie, of course." She set the coffeepot down and turned to Maddy, her mud-colored eyes magnified behind the lenses. "But, now, there isn't anything wrong with you, is there? You do still have the capacity?"

"Still?" Maddy managed to reply, afraid she might faint. "Whatever do you mean, still?"

Her mother-in-law paused, smiled. "After all this time, dear. That's all I meant."

"There's nothing wrong with me," Maddy insisted.

"I'm so glad!" The elder Mrs. Bemis allowed herself a smile, and she placed a hand on her chest as though, finally, she could breathe once more. "But here's a list of doctors anyway, just to put your mind at rest. I know *all* of them."

"But everything's fine," Maddy insisted, although perhaps too weakly.

The great lady set down the coffeepot, and dug in her skirt pocket for a piece of paper, which she handed Maddy. It was a list of names, all of which ended in M.D.

"Of course it is, dear," Grace said, and then carried the coffee tray through the swinging doors to the parlor, where the rest of the bridge players were waiting.

Several days later, when she was having coffee with her husband in the morning room by the garden, Maddy reported her conversation with his mother. He did not seem surprised. He scarcely looked up from the newspaper. That one word, "still," from her mother-in-law continued to echo. What had she meant by it? Grace often treated her as if she had weak health, although she had never once actually mentioned the word "tuberculosis." Had any rumors reached her? Did she know of the true purpose of Maddy's trip west? Did Ronnie? Maddy should have put such questions out of her mind, since they did her no good. But she could not; nor did she dare ask them, not after her affair—and certainly not after she had blamed the pregnancy on Ronnie. It was hideous. *She* was hideous.

She decided to see Dr. Cameron Wilder. Her own internist, Dr. Shattuck, had recommended him; the fact that his name was, in fact, on Grace's list, was merely coincidental, Maddy assured herself. Dr. Wilder's office was on Longwood Avenue, by all the hospitals. He was quite young for a doctor, early thirties it appeared, with a shock of black hair, and round-framed glasses that suggested eyebrows raised in wonderment. He sat her down in a university chair across from his desk so they could, as he said, "get to know each other a little better," before he delved into the medical aspects of her case. Getting to know each other, of course, actually meant getting to know her. He revealed almost nothing about himself, nor did Maddy ask. Still, it was his willingness to take time that struck her, to have a conversation, even if it was all centered on her. So different from that Dr. Eldridge, or even Dr. Shattuck himself, who was inclined to be gruff.

Dr. Wilder seemed kind, a characteristic she didn't associate with doctors, even handsome ones, and she liked the sound of his voice, which was not at all pushy.

They had been speaking for only about ten minutes. She was explaining about where she'd grown up, and how she was married now, for seven years, to her husband, who'd been an airman in the war, and how they'd been "trying" all that time. (She was beginning to hate that word.) Then he went to his desk, which was over by the window, beside a bookcase that was jammed with medical texts. He pressed down on the intercom. "I'm going to take a bit of time here, Gwen. Could you have Dr. Stevens cover for me with Mrs. Malacroyd at three?"

"Yes, Doctor," came a voice. "I'll ask him."

"Thank you."

Dr. Wilder took a seat at his desk again, leaned back, and crossed his legs at the ankles as if he didn't have much of a care that day.

They spoke at some length, Dr. Wilder listening intently to the long tale of her infertility. At one point, she'd slipped and used the word "infidelity" by accident. She flushed with alarm, but Dr. Wilder did not seem to notice. When she was finished, he took her into a blinding-white examining room and performed a pelvic examination, just as Dr. Eldridge had. Afterward, he looked over some of the test results that had already started to filter back, and then he looked up at Maddy. "So," he told her, "you want to tell me about it?"

By then, a tear had started to trickle down the side of Maddy's nose. She tried to wipe it away discreetly, as if it was just a bit of something on her face, but then another fell, and another, and her sinuses started to clog and then her head was throbbing and she couldn't find her voice. It was just an idiotic, helpless squeaking. And she was quaking, too, in the chair, and trying to hide from Dr. Wilder by putting her arm up over her face and then swinging her head wildly back and forth. And she pulled her legs up onto the chair, too, as though she needed to get tight, into a ball, to protect herself. He may have been saying something to her, she couldn't tell. She thought he might try to, he seemed like the type. But then she felt something on her shoulder, maybe it was his hand, but she flung it off. She couldn't bear to be touched, not in that state, and not by a man, who just did things to you, things you didn't necessarily want, just because he wanted to.

This was worse than anything could ever be. She couldn't speak, couldn't say anything. All she could do was cover her eyes with her arm, trying to hide from everyone, but especially from this nice man who, if he learned how awful she was, would cease to be nice to her anymore. He seemed to move away from her, but she was still crying so hard, she couldn't tell for sure. Her face was buried in the crook of her arm, her nose nestled there, and the rest of her arm pressed into her eye sockets to try to block, or at least blot, the tears that were still streaming.

"Here." The voice was close again, but she didn't look. She felt something smooth and cool on the outside of her hand, the one that was clinging to her left shoulder. A glass.

"Take a sip," he told her. "You'll feel better."

She sensed him crouching beside her. "It's never as bad as you think." The words came to her from her level, close by her ear, and they were fairly quiet. But she knew they weren't right, because this was bad, bad, bad, just as she was.

Gradually, she calmed herself and took the glass from him, sniffling, apologizing, wishing he wouldn't look at her. He ran a hand through her hair and smiled at her, although she must have looked absolutely wretched, her face all blotchy, her eyes smeared with tears and her nose running and—

Alice

⤐   thirty-one

M rs. Bemis," Alice was saying, "are you all right?"

The old woman had been staring off toward the far hills for a few minutes now, her hands in her lap. It was almost as if she'd fallen asleep. Except her eyes were open, the lids blinking occasionally, the breath passing smoothly in and out.

"What?" The woman turned back to Alice for a second, then glanced up at the sky, seemingly surprised to find it blue and radiant. "Am I what?"

"Are you all right?"

"Why—why yes. Of course I am."

"What were you thinking just now?"

Mrs. Bemis looked down at her hands. "Nothing in particular."

Alice sat down closer to Mrs. Bemis. "Really?" she teased. "You seemed sad."

"I'm just so tired," the old woman said. "I don't think I can answer any more questions just now."

Alice leaned in closer toward her, laid a hand on the old woman's shoulder. The air was cooling down, and Alice could feel the chill on her patient's skin through the thin cotton of her dress. "Please tell me."

"Oh, just something about when I was young," Mrs. Bemis said dismissively.

"How young?"

"Early twenties, somewhere in there. I was—" The old woman stopped again, startled by a sparrow darting by her, low to the ground. "Oh, you don't want to hear all this."

"Please."

Mrs. B took a breath and began again, this time with an air of resignation. "I was at the doctor's."

"What sort of doctor?"

"A specialist."

Alice tipped her head, eyeing her patient.

"A fertility doctor, if you must know. A Dr. Wilder." Mrs. Bemis looked away, her upper lip quivering. "Because I was afraid I was infertile." The way she said it, the word rhymed with infantile. "That is the term, isn't it? We used to say 'barren,' which is hideous."

"Were you?" Alice asked.

Mrs. Bemis nodded. Once, quickly.

It seemed that the old woman had something in her eye. She swiped at it with the back of her hand, furtively, hoping that Alice wouldn't notice, but of course she did. Peering at her from the side, Alice could see that the rim of Mrs. Bemis's right eye was red, and the eye itself was glassy with tears. Then a drop spilled down her cheek, then another, each one a pearl tumbling down her face.

Alice groped for a tissue, but found nothing in her pocket except a dry-cleaning receipt. Sniffling, Mrs. Bemis tried to blot the tears herself, awkwardly, with the shoulder of her dress. But it was no use. Alice stood up and pulled her own shirtsleeve down to her palms and told Mrs. Bemis to hold still for a second. Crouching, she dabbed her face with the fabric. It was an awkward, strained gesture, wiping

Mrs. Bemis's cheeks with her shirt's rough cotton. It reminded Alice of when she was a child, and having her own mother scrape at her face with a washcloth before allowing her to go off to school. Only she was the mother now, and she was trying to be gentler.

"Oh, this is awful," Mrs. Bemis declared, her head tipped back to make it easier for Alice. Her face was streaked with red from crying, and her eyes were bloodshot. "I was remembering how I cried with *him*." Mrs. Bemis breathed through her mouth, the way children do sometimes, since her nose was all stuffed up.

Alice sat down, but the tears didn't stop, and Alice again offered her sleeve. Mrs. Bemis shook her head, but Alice offered again, and this time, Mrs. Bemis took the loose fabric and blotted her tears herself, delicately, as if the material were a handkerchief. Then, sniffling, she glanced about the wide lawn, lined with its walkways where a few people now strolled in the distance. "I must be a sight," Mrs. Bemis said.

"A lovely sight," Alice assured her.

"Hardly," Mrs. Bemis said, sniffing.

Alice waited for Mrs. Bemis to gather herself.

"What did this fertility doctor tell you, exactly?" she asked finally. She held Mrs. Bemis's hand. It seemed natural now, to touch.

"He told me I seemed to have a problem with my fallopian tubes. An infection of some sort. He did a lot of tests, you see. Every kind of thing." She paused, gathered herself. "We'd been married, Ronnie and I, for seven years." Mrs. Bemis dropped her free hand down like a hammer on her thigh as she spoke. "We'd had—well, I suppose there's no reason not to say—we'd had—intercourse—any number of times. And his mother was starting to wonder, no, more than wonder, actually to ask about—about my 'capacity.' Charming way to put it. She could be very imposing. My 'capacity'? Can you imagine? I shook like a leaf." She withdrew her hand from Alice's grasp, turned to her. "And it was always me, of course. Never Ronnie."

"Might it have been him?"

"My dear, when his plane went down, he was smashed up within an inch of his life. One might think that possibly *he* had some . . . problem. But no, Grace—his mother—put the question to me."

Mrs. Bemis looked up at her. "Oh, Dr. Matthews, *Alice,* I've been—" And then, without saying more, she lunged toward her. It was as if she'd toppled over, the movement was so sudden and unexpected. But Mrs. Bemis brought her arms around Alice, grabbed on to her, and drew Alice to her, pressing the side of her face against Alice's ribs, just below her breasts. "I've been such a *fool!*"

The proper thing to do, Alice knew, was to pull gently away, to reassert a measure of professionalism. But Alice could feel the need, the desperate need, in the slender arms that now surrounded her, in the low, anguished moans. And Alice could feel the wetness of what could only be Mrs. Bemis's tears coming through the thin cotton of her blouse.

"All my *life,*" Mrs. Bemis cried softly. "From the very beginning."

Alice didn't know quite what to do; psychiatry made no allowance for touch. It was undignified, disreputable. Wrong. At first, Alice held her own hands away from Mrs. Bemis's back, which was curved and lean, quaking with her long, slow, tearful convulsions. Looking down, Alice could see white scalp, like a baby's, beneath the swirl of graying hair at the crown of her head, bobbing. She could not help herself. It seemed only right, for someone as stiff and unyielding as Mrs. Bemis to meet something soft at last. Slowly, uncertainly, Alice brought her own arms down around her patient, and she settled them there.

"It's okay," she whispered, bringing her own cheek down on the top of Mrs. Bemis's head. "My entire life!" Mrs. Bemis went on, sobbing now. "There is nothing I've done, nothing I've said that wasn't *all wrong.*"

Bent over on Alice's lap, she clung to her like a child. Alice had shut her eyes, the better to concentrate on the moment, but she could hear someone walk in front of them, slowing at first, then hurrying once they were past.

Alice paid no heed, dwelling instead on her own long, deep

breaths, which satisfied her as few breaths ever had. She could smell the faintly sweet scent of Mrs. Bemis's shampoo, the hint of the mothballs that her dress must have been packed away in.

Smelling her like this, Alice could enter a little into Mrs. Bemis's life, into her past. And as she did, a feeling rose inside her as she recalled her own youth, her own desperation. It was sharp and distinct, an ache, a longing, and it seemed to swell inside her temples and prick at the corners of her own eyes, and she sniffed a few times herself, to try to hold her own feelings back. But, soon enough, she needed to dab at her own eyes with the same now wet sleeve that she'd shared with Mrs. Bemis.

As she did, she had to smile and then, quietly, to laugh—this was all so ridiculous, the two of them bawling there in each other's arms.

With the sound, Mrs. Bemis straightened up. Her face was red from tears and there was a round mark by her temple where she must have been pressing against a button on Alice's front. "Oh, dear, I am sorry. I should never have—" Then she took in the tears on Alice's face, and looked startled for a second. "Oh, my heavens," she said. "Oh gracious. I didn't mean—"

Alice openly wiped her face with her sleeve this time. "I get a little sentimental sometimes." Alice tried to summon laughter again, but her face was all puffy, and no laughter came, just another sprinkling of tears.

"Oh, dear, now I'm going to start in all over again," Mrs. Bemis said. And it was true. The tears were starting to flow once more. "Would you mind if—" she began, then reached for Alice's other sleeve.

"It's fine, Mrs. B." Alice laughed, and cried, both.

Maddy

⤙   *thirty-two*

I may as well tell you," her father told her on the telephone. "She's at Montrose. That's a psychiatric hospital, Maddy, if you don't know."

She'd been working in the garden.

"Psychiatric? Why? What's the matter?" Maddy asked, a panic rising in her.

"She's been having . . . difficulties, that's all."

Maddy had had no idea how to dress for a psychiatric hospital, deciding finally on the slacks and sweater that she'd worn to visit her friend Molly in the maternity ward at the Boston Lying-In. Her mind was in such a swirl as she drove to the Dover house to meet her father for the trip to Concord that she lost her way. Her father was waiting in the driveway when she finally arrived. He'd been pacing; his shirt was stained under the arms. He kissed her hurriedly on the side of her face. She could still smell his aftershave. A pine scent.

On the trip out, her father explained that her mother had suffered a nervous breakdown. "You know how she's been," her father told her. "Ever since—" he stopped. "Well, you know perfectly well when."

The words echoed inside her as down a long, empty corridor.

"She blames herself, you know. She considers herself a failure as a mother. I've tried to reassure her. But—" Her father's hands were white on the steering wheel. "Well, let's just try to be as pleasant with her as we can." He reached over, slapped Maddy's thigh. "Okay?"

When her eyes adjusted to the dim light inside the Holmes building, Maddy found a nurse in a prim gray uniform waiting for them in the foyer. She greeted them, and then took Maddy's father aside for a whispered conversation. When she turned back to Maddy, the nurse's smile was exaggerated. "Well, welcome," the nurse told Maddy. "I'm *so* glad you could come."

The building was paneled with dark wood, and there were oriental carpets—threadbare in some places—on the floor. It was drafty in the big front hall where oil portraits of eminences hung, but the building was as quiet as a library. "Most of the residents are in the conservatory," the nurse explained as they strode along the wide hallway. "There's a recital." Another member of the professional staff came up the hall toward them. An elderly gentleman in a bespoke suit and metal spectacles. He nodded as he passed.

Mother was down on the right. The nurse knocked on the door. Maddy heard a feeble "Yes?" that she barely recognized. The nurse went in, leaving Maddy and her father outside in the hall for a moment. Maddy could hear her tell her mother she had visitors.

"Who is it this time?" her mother asked.

"Your husband and your daughter," the nurse replied. "Remember? I told you they'd be coming."

"But I never—"

"Please, Mrs. Adams."

There was a pause, with some whispers that Maddy could not

quite catch, and then the nurse opened the door for the visitors. "She'll be happy to see you," she declared.

Her mother was in the chair in the corner. She'd lost weight, her eyes were sunken and her face pale. She didn't fill out the simple, pale-blue housedress she was wearing, one that Maddy had never seen. She seemed to have aged ten years. She had been knitting, a new activity for her. A scarf, it appeared. A ball of yarn was in her lap.

She did not get up when Maddy entered.

Maddy said hello, and her mother nodded back, eyeing her as if she were a stranger. She reared back as Maddy approached to give her a kiss, and received her daughter's lips on her cheek, which was as cool as stone.

Maddy's father stood off to one side, his eyes moving from wife to daughter and back again.

"How are you feeling?" Maddy asked finally.

"Tired, thank you."

"She's here to get some rest," her father added hastily. "That's the whole idea. Isn't it, dear?"

"I suppose so," Mrs. Adams said halfheartedly. "I'm not sure I know what the idea is."

"Of course you do, dear."

The nurse offered chairs, placing the three in an awkward triangle, and then withdrew once the visitors were settled.

Alice

~ thirty-three

It was right there, the second window from the left," Mrs. Bemis said. She was sitting up now, pointing across with a shaky hand to Holmes, which was visible in the distance, to the left of the stables. An ancient building, really, clad in vines and boarded up with plywood. It was late in the afternoon; it seemed that the two had been there for hours, or for days. The way the light fell, Alice could still see the tracks of Mrs. Bemis's tears snaking down her sunken cheeks. But she'd told Alice the story of coming to see her mother without crying further. She'd been still, almost preternaturally so, as she'd spoken. And quiet. Alice had had to lean close to hear the words sometimes. It seemed as if they weren't spoken to her, necessarily, just spoken. As if it had been important to get them outside her; and once she had done that, she didn't care where they went.

"I wanted to tell my mother how surprised I was to learn that she was here," Mrs. Bemis told Alice. These words, too, came out in a reverie, as a memory that was floating loose. "It was a terrible shock to me. I didn't know anyone who'd had a nervous breakdown. I didn't know what it was, but Mother looked awful. Drawn. Exhausted. I wanted to tell her I'd been going through my own difficulties. Problems with my marriage. I needed a mother, I suppose. I'd always needed a mother, although I'd carried on as though I didn't. I wanted to apologize for any distress I might have caused her."

"What sort of distress?" Alice asked.

"The usual, I suppose," Mrs. Bemis said, her eyes still on Holmes. "I was a willful, difficult child."

"And what did you say instead?"

"I said, and these were my exact words, 'Weather has been terribly cool lately, hasn't it?' It *had* been actually—quite unseasonable. We'd put on the heat at Labor Day that year. And my mother said: 'Yes, terribly.' I'll always remember that, too. Then she reached for her knitting needles again, and nothing more was said until we bid her good-bye. I'll never get the sound of clicking needles out of my ears."

"What had caused the breakdown, do you suppose?" Alice asked. "You told me that your father started to tell you. 'Ever since—' he started to say. Ever since what?"

Mrs. Bemis shook her head.

Alice reached across to the old woman, gently stroked her shoulder. Moments ago, such a gesture had felt awkward, invasive. Now it seemed as natural as talking.

Mrs. Bemis laid her own hand on top of Alice's, smiled briefly.

"Was there something you feel you did?"

Mrs. Bemis looked back to Alice, a mournful look on her face. "I can't speak of this—not here. I can't!" She grasped Alice's hand, drew her closer. "I need to be home. I need quiet, I need my garden, my own bed. Please. Take me home, would you? We can speak of such things at home. I have something there to show you, something that might help you understand."

"What is it?"

"Just take me home, would you? Oh, could you? It will make more sense to you there."

Seeing Mrs. Bemis beside her, the wind in her hair, her eyes searching Alice's own, Alice saw again an image that she had woken up to in a sweat that very morning: graying hair that was swirling, but not in the wind. In water. Swirling slowly, billowing about. Under ice.

thirty-four

Frank LeBeau called that evening, shortly after Alice got home. Her thoughts on Mrs. Bemis, she assumed that he was going to report some development in the case, but his voice wasn't the brisk, professional cop voice, it was something warmer. "Just thought I'd say hi," he said.

"Oh." Alice settled into the chair by the phone in the living room, and put her feet up on the glass table in front of her. "Hi."

"I probably shouldn't be calling you like this."

"No, Frank, it's fine. Really. I'm glad." It was nice to hear from him, now that she had finally made such a gratifying breakthrough with Mrs. Bemis.

"I was thinking," he said tentatively. "Was there something you wanted to ask me? I know you don't know me too well."

The question surprised her. "Something like?"

"Hey, you're the psychiatrist." Another pause. "So you can get to know me better, that's all I meant."

"Frank—"

"Just ask, okay? Whatever it is."

Alice glanced nervously around her apartment, took in the photos, the view of the triple-decker next door. "All right," she began edgily. "Can you see the ocean from there?"

"If you get out binoculars."

"I assume you're home."

"That's not a question. But yes."

"How many questions do I get?"

"As many as you need."

"You still miss the mountains?"

"Every day. Especially in the morning. I don't like seeing the sun pop out of the ocean. Doesn't seem right. It should rise up behind hills."

"Your family's been there for a while, I take it."

"That's not a question."

"Frank!"

"Okay." He told her how his grandfather had come down from Quebec, bound for New York City, but had gotten off the train in Brattleboro for a smoke, liked the place, and never gotten back on. He worked in sanitation, only job he could get. His son, Frank's father, tried out for the police academy, but didn't make it, and had to settle for garage mechanic. "I guess I'm trying to make it up to him," Frank said. "Or at least that's how it started." He thought for a minute. "I'm also a Libra, not that you asked. I think that's a bunch of bullshit anyway. I like Chinese food, and I once drove two hours to see a James Bond double feature at the Springfield drive-in. I'm a nut about drive-ins." He paused. "I think that's about everything."

"Yeah, that just about covers it," Alice agreed.

"And you, Dr. Matthews?" he asked. "What should I know about you?"

"What do you want to know?"

"Where are you from? Let's start there."

"Pennsylvania," Alice replied. "Latrobe. That place where they brew Rolling Rock?"

"I've had a couple of those, maybe. How'd your family get there?"

Alice told about her great-grandmother, on her father's side, who was a full-blooded Cherokee Indian.

"That explains a few things," Frank said.

"Such as?"

"Go on with your story."

She told how the Cherokee's husband, Alice's great-grandfather, had worked in the mills in Pittsburgh; it was their daughter, the Grand, who'd moved out with her husband to settle in Latrobe. Her second daughter, Alice's mother, was the only one of the five children to stay. "I painted my bedroom aqua," Alice went on, getting into the spirit of the conversation. "It still has the tiny stars I stuck onto the ceiling to glow at night. I'm a Capricorn, and I agree, it's a total crock. I still think that deviled eggs are exotic, and my favorite board game is Sorry. That's about everything," Alice added with a laugh. "I don't think there's anything more you need to know."

They'd been talking for at least an hour, Alice coiling the telephone wire around her finger, gabbing like a schoolgirl. She'd kicked off her shoes, gotten comfortable. She could have talked all night.

"Just one last question," Frank said finally, then seemed to steel himself. "You free for dinner? I make a mean veal scallopini. I've got all the stuff for it."

"Well then," Alice said. "Okay."

On the way down to Marshfield, Alice gave herself a stern speech about how such impulsiveness had landed her Ethan before. But the traffic was light on Route 3, and, despite her reservations, the highway itself seemed to whisk her down the South Shore, past Braintree, to Marshfield in no time.

The directions were perfect, and Alice found Frank's house easily. It was a small Cape, unadorned with any of the tacky fishing trophies—buoys, netting—that decorated the cottages on either side. Alice caught the smell of the sea when she opened the car door, heard a low chuffing of waves against the shore as well. A few gulls glided by overhead, their undersides flashing in the streetlights.

The outside light flipped on, the door opened, and Frank filled the doorway with his towering frame. "You made it," he said.

Alice pulled her cardigan around her as she stepped from the car. Her heels clicked on the flagstone steps, and her jade necklace slid about her neck as she crossed the flagstones to his front porch. His eyes followed her as she approached.

If she was expecting a kiss, none came. No handshake either, which was good. He held the door open for her, and she got a breath of his aftershave, a musky scent that pleased her, as she stepped inside. She was impressed with how tidy everything was. The few magazines were squared on the wooden table under the window, and several jackets were hung up on pegs by the door. The man was organized. She poked her nose in the bedroom, saw the mountain scenes hanging on the pinstriped wallpaper, the neatly made bed, the spread as flat as a tabletop.

"You didn't actually clean up for me, did you?" Alice asked.

Frank laughed. "I like it neat. Drove Sheila nuts, the way I was always picking stuff up. She said I was anal."

"I think I'm qualified to decide that."

He laughed again. "And?"

"Definitely anal. But I like it."

He led her through to the kitchen, which was off the den, at the other end of the house. A small pot was bubbling on the stove, and the air was alive with spices and tomatoes. Big picture windows showed the sea beyond a couple of larger houses. When she cupped her hands to the glass to peer out, she could see the water gleaming dully in the twilight.

"Nice," Alice said, turning back around to him.

"Oh, here." Frank reached for a glass of red wine on the counter. "A chianti." He handed it to her. "It's an 'eighty-six. Guy in the wine store said it was a good year, but I think he was leading me on. Tell you the truth, I still expect the stuff to come in those straw holders." He handed her the glass, then went to get his own, which was over by the stove. He returned to her, and clinked her glass. "We should have a toast," he said.

"To Mrs. Bemis, how about?" Alice asked. The old woman was on her mind again. "She's the one who brought us together."

"Okay, to Mrs. Bemis," Frank said.

They were both smiling now.

He was stirring the sauce when he told her about Ethan. "He's been dealing, you know."

Alice must have gone pale, because Frank went on, "Or maybe you didn't know. Did a six-month hitch in the Concord penitentiary. Two years' probation afterward."

"How did you—?"

"Look, I'm a cop. I had to look into it." He took a breath. "I told my friend on the Cambridge PD and he went to talk to him. I don't think he'll bother you again. You nail him on an assault charge and he's back to Concord for some serious time." He set the stirring spoon down by the stove. "Okay, now you can yell at me if you want."

She did not.

A Marshfield cop had turned up a couple of fishermen who'd seen Brendan and Harry Brandt out in the Laser. "Sounded to them like our guys were arguing," Frank told Alice. "Couldn't tell about what. Seemed like a 'Fuck you,' 'No, fuck *you*' type of thing. And it wasn't that rough out there. No twenty-foot seas or anything."

"So you're thinking the drowning probably wasn't an accident." Alice pictured the two men in the water, arms thrashing, gasping for air, then Brendan going down, lungs heaving.

"I suppose that's the direction I'm heading in, yeah."

"Could Brandt have drowned him? Held him down with his hands?"

"Maybe. Or Brendan tried to drown Brandt and messed up. It's hard killing people out in the water. Anything can happen. Or they just got royally drunk and screwed up. There was a ton of alcohol in Brendan, don't forget."

"Still no sign of Brandt, I take it," Alice said.

"Nope. He was in real good shape, though. That's what his wife said. Always in the gym. Did lots of laps in the pool. They were four, five miles out in the bay. But he may have swum to shore someplace. We've had an APB out on him since we got the missing-person's report."

"And nothing."

"Nope. He could be lying low, hoping we'll forget about him." He paused. "Not a bad strategy. My boss *really* wants me to drop this whole thing. He was ragging me about it again just today."

"Despite the stuff about the argument."

"Boss doesn't give a goddamn about that. He says everybody yells, especially out in a boat when there's been some drinking. But I just want to know what happened."

"Well, thanks. I appreciate the work you've put in."

"It's had its rewards." He clinked her glass again.

The veal was a little tough, and the tomato sauce a touch too spicy. But Alice scarcely noticed, she was so intent on this tall detective who seemed to move so easily through the world of death and mystery, yet keep a gentle side, and some humor. He'd put on some light folk music, and the window was open to the sea sounds and the occasional gust of ocean air. She liked the quiet outside, and the darkness, the way it was only him and her. They went through the first bottle of chianti like nothing, and Frank pulled the cork on a second.

Maybe it was the wine, but Frank started telling stories. Funny ones, mostly: the kid who test-drove a Lincoln right through the dealer's window, the teenage girl who spray-painted the neighbor's cat, the geezer who planted a bug in his female neighbor's bedroom and it started an electrical fire. "It took us weeks to piece that one out," Frank said. Then Alice started telling him about some of her psychiatric cases, which weren't so different. Gradually, she moved over to the couch, and then she slipped off her shoes, and then she was cuddling some hot coffee she hoped would keep the room from spinning. And Frank was laughing at her—or was it with her?—for being a little out of it, and she was laughing, too. She couldn't remember when she'd felt this good, this loose, this safe. Everything was right except for the buzzing in her ears. The music, the talk, the air, the being-with-Frank. She slipped down into the couch while he cleaned up, refusing to let her lift a finger. And then he flipped off the lights by the kitchen, which were bright, and he came over to where she was and led her out onto the small deck behind the house. There were a few flower boxes around, the blossoms flapping in the light breeze. But the air had turned balmy, or was she simply too light-headed to notice the cold? He looked up, and her eyes followed to take in the night sky, so bright with stars. She was still looking up when she felt his lips on her hair. She turned, guided his face toward hers. He kissed her on one cheek, then on the other, and then on her nose, which made her smile. She was thirsting for him, and then she opened her mouth, and they drank each other in.

It was awkward, he was so tall, with Alice tipping her face up and Frank bending down over her, and so she was glad when he reached down, and hoisted her up into his arms. "Now I've got you," he whispered, pulling her tightly to his chest. She was nearly breathless, her heart was pounding so. He flicked the screen door open and carried her inside. Alice laughed as she watched the ceiling go by, the upper walls. Mostly, her gaze was filled with Frank, his strong chin all the more prominent from this angle. She thought he'd put her down on the couch, but he continued on through the living room, past the front hall and through the narrow doorway to his bedroom.

"This okay?" Frank asked, easing her down on the bed. "I thought it might go better here. I find it hard to screw standing up."

"You've done that?"

"No."

Alice laughed, brought her arms around him, pulled him down to her. She kissed him this time, first on the chin, then the cheeks, and then, just as he had, his nose, which was narrow and bony. And then she popped open a couple of the buttons on his shirt, and dipped her hands inside to feel his ribs, his beating heart. And he slid his hands under her sweater, and pulled up her shirttails, to slide his hands under her bra to cup her breasts. And then he loosened her clothes and was kissing her nipples, which sent her. She pushed her skirt down and she worked open his belt and ripped down his zipper, and she grabbed for him. He was already hard, and he told her to wait a second, just wait, and he rolled over to the side of the bed and pulled out a condom from the box by the bed. He ripped open the package with his teeth. She didn't care that he had them there, that he was ready. She was glad. She unrolled the condom onto him, down the whole length of him, and then guided him inside her as she lay back. He fit with her. And when he started to move in her, she rubbed the length of his back with her fingertips as if his back was the part that was in her. And gradually he drove in deeper, and the sound of him grew, his breath louder, just as her breath was. And soon she was writhing under him, writhing because her body could not take so much feeling. It filled her up, made her more than what she was. Finally he held himself over her, quivering, and she was pulled tight, just yanked by the string that was him, and then something released in her, and she gave a great sigh, like no sound she'd ever made, as he shoved himself into her one last time.

It wasn't until they were done that they took off their clothes, all of them, so that she could see the reddish hair across his chest, and curling about his plump genitals, the long, graceful limbs, the slender toes. And he could slide his hands over her bare breasts and pull at her nipples, his beard scratching her shoulder lightly where it touched. Only then did she feel that it was actually him she had made love with, and not some tall fantasy of the perfect man.

It was nearly eleven now. She had brought a few things, just in case, but she was too tired to go get them. He offered her a T-shirt to sleep in, but she thought she'd rather not wear anything, the better to feel him beside her all night long, feel that he was there. He didn't wear anything either. He was naked when he went back through the house turning off the lights and locking up, and naked as he slipped back in under the covers beside her. She ran a hand up his thigh once more and played with him a little, to see if he was interested, which he was. This time, she got the condom from the drawer. He lasted much longer, as she lay underneath him, hoping they could stay like this forever.

She woke early, before six, and showered, trying not to wake him. But he was gone from the bed when she emerged from the bathroom, a towel around her.

She dressed, and found him in the kitchen in his bathrobe, some scrambled eggs in the pan.

"I should be getting back," she told him. "I'm taking Mrs. Bemis for a visit home today."

"Hey, that's great."

"My boss has to give the okay, though."

"It's still great," Frank told her. He waited again. "You should have told me."

"I keep thinking I've told you too much as it is."

"I just mean that it's terrific she's ready to go home. That she's feeling better."

"Well, you know how it is with managed care. They try to move the patients out as soon as possible."

"Seems like you're doing a great job with her."

She looked at him, saw the caring on his face. "Yeah, well thanks."

"Don't you even want breakfast?"

"I've really gotta run." It was her early day at Montrose. She needed to be there by eight, and she had to stop in at her apartment to change first. "I can't exactly go in like this." She looked down at her rumpled skirt and sweater.

He spooned some of the eggs onto a plate, and handed it to her. "Come on, eat. You need something in you for your big day. I've got some coffee brewing."

She wolfed down the eggs and had a few gulps of coffee. Then hurried to the door. She turned back to him. "Look, you don't have to—"

"Hey, do I look like an asshole?" he interrupted. "I'll call you, okay?"

"Thanks, Frank," Alice told him, smiling. Then she was out the door and headed for her car—Frank watching her, she knew, every step.

Madeline

⤖ thirty-five

I t was late, well after ten. Ronald was downstairs in his study going over his papers from the office. Madeline was in her flannel nightgown, up in bed reading *The Forsyte Saga.* She was waiting, as it seemed she was always waiting. She was old now; she would be twenty-seven come September. She was Madeline. "Maddy" didn't seem sufficient anymore, especially once Ronnie started calling himself Ronald. She was old, yes, and would be getting older. When she peered at herself in the bathroom mirror, she could see slim worry lines beginning to radiate from the corners of her mouth, and squint wrinkles, as she'd always thought of them, starting to form about her eyes.

The house was quiet. She could hear Ronald's papers turn.

"Aren't you coming up?" Madeline called down to her husband. It was the exact midpoint in her cycle, which, as Dr. Wilder had explained, was the time of peak fertility. She tried to keep the pleading tone out of her voice, since he hated that.

Nothing.

"Ronald?" she called again.

She heard the click of his glasses, when he set them down to rub his eyes, an increasingly frequent gesture.

"Yes?" Impatience in his voice.

"I said, aren't you coming up?" Madeline repeated, with emphasis.

"In a minute."

"You know what Dr.—"

"Yes, of course," Ronald interrupted. He'd heard altogether too much about Dr. Wilder. "Very soon, dear. Very soon. No need to worry." From the sound of him, it was as if *she* were the cripple.

She returned to her book, but the words swam on the page.

It wasn't until nearly eleven that she heard the downstairs lights click off, first in the drawing room, then the living room, the library, and the dining room. Then an uneven tread on the broad stairs. Finally, the bedroom doorway darkened.

"Today's the day, I take it." Ronald set his cane—unbendable hickory—down in the corner and removed his suit jacket.

"I think so, yes." Madeline had kept careful track.

Ronald spent some time in the bathroom with the door closed. The tap ran once, twice, each time shutting off with a shriek from the pipes. Then he emerged in his wrapper, a scarlet, monogrammed one that his parents had given him for his last birthday. He was carrying his brace. Hobbling slightly, he set it down by the velvet wing chair.

Madeline closed her book and turned off the light by the bed, plunging the room into darkness. She knew he didn't like her to see him undressed. In almost a decade of marriage, she had done that only once, an accident that had shocked them both. He was toweling off after a shower when she'd come in, unthinking. He'd made a quick move to cover himself, but she'd seen the scars that ran down to his pelvis, several of them a dark purple.

Now, Madeline could hear him loosen his robe, and drape it over the high post at the head of the bed. He peeled back the covers, and he eased himself into the bed beside her, tipping the mattress away from her with a creak. She waited, scarcely breathing, for him to make some move toward her. He didn't like her to reach for him first.

He usually liked to slide his hands up underneath her nightgown, bunching the material up around her armpits, and then sidle between her legs. It was odd to feel him there: the damaged leg so slim, almost all bone. But normally it seemed to excite him, the forcing. Tonight, though, when he rolled onto her, his penis was still soft. That frustrated her after the long wait, but she said nothing. Neither did he. He clutched her, digging his fingers into her back, grinding himself against her pelvis, willing himself to harden. She could hear him gasp, and felt his muscles tense. "I can't—"

"What?" she whispered to him. "Is it something I did?" She assumed it had to be.

"It's not you," he assured her.

"Can I—?" She wanted to reach down to him, hold him in her hands. In all the years of their marriage, she had never done that. She'd tried once, years back, snaking a hand down his belly, but he'd pushed her hand away.

"Let me touch you," she urged him. "I'd like to."

But he'd rolled back onto his side of the bed. "Please—no. I'm very tired."

"Are you all right?" she asked. "Is your leg hurting you?"

He seemed to be moving more slowly these days, often with a grimace.

"Just tired," he assured her.

"You do care for me?"

"Of course," he assured her.

She was cupped around him now, whispering in his ear, her breasts pressed up against his back, her thighs against his rump. "Let me try something, then, would you?" Without waiting for an answer, she hooked a leg over him, straddled him, brought her pelvis down on the bone of his hip. She let the bedclothes slide back as she lifted herself up, baring herself. She pressed against him, thrilled to try something so shameless and wild. She'd craved that, almost as much as she craved a child. In all the years she had been with him, she'd never felt that wonderful burst between her legs she'd felt with Gerald. She wanted that—one time, with Ronnie, at least. Somehow.

He continued to lie on his side, while she rode him, her sex against his hip bone, her eyes closed, trying to concentrate on the small bubble of feeling between her legs. She wanted it to fill and grow—or perhaps inspire him to reach for her. To feel the happiness, either way. He did not move. And, under her, his body, the angled expanse of him, seemed not a body at all, just a shape. An inert one.

"I'm sorry," she said finally, slipping off him. "I should probably let you sleep."

"No, love," Ronnie said. "Go on. Do . . . that. If you'd like." He held her hand.

It was pathetic, in its way. And generous. But it was too late. The feeling had left her.

"Another time, perhaps," Ronnie said.

"Yes. Another time." And she pulled on her nightgown and retreated to her side of the bed once more.

She scarcely slept that night and rose well before dawn. She grabbed her wrapper and, tightening it about her, went downstairs to the kitchen. The knives, on their rack against the wall, sparkled in the light. She put on the kettle, and made a cup of chamomile for herself. Clutching the steaming teacup, she took a seat at the oak kitchen table and looked out the window. It was winter, February, and Madeline could see the snowflakes falling in clumps outside the window, lit up by the kitchen light. The beauty of the snowfall made her feel only more miserable, as if nature, too, were mocking her. She felt again the heartache she'd felt when Gerald left her, but it was worse this time. It was an ache that pushed outward from her heart to her whole body, thickening inside her.

For the next few days, she tried to enjoy the small pleasures of her life, the trip to the baker—a hearty, gloriously fat Italian—for the little cakes that Ronald would have discouraged, had he known, the glance through the society page of the *Transcript* for news of people she might know. But none of this amused her as it sometimes did. It was hard to tell if Ronald saw the change in her. They spoke so little, and he rarely inquired into how she was. Of course, she didn't ask him either. She knew too well the answer, so what was the point? Even on that wretched Tuesday morning after she'd been up half the night, he'd greeted her in the kitchen with his usual, "Good morning," and, once his driver, Edward, arrived, Ronald left for work with his usual good-bye.

And it was the same for the days that followed. The maid, Millie, must have sensed that something was amiss. A wan twenty-five-year-old, working days to put herself through community college at night, she seemed to look at her mistress more carefully than usual.

"Are you all right, Missus?" she asked finally.

"I'm very well, thanks," Madeline replied with a cool smile, and left it at that.

On Thursday afternoons, Madeline gathered for tea with some other young Milton wives at a neighborhood restaurant called Harween's. In theory, the group met to advance the cause of the Milton Historical Society. But few of the participants, Madeline included, had much interest in that. The gatherings were actually occasions for gossip and silliness that Madeline normally found pleasantly distracting. But on the Thursday of that bad week, the tea party didn't provide any of its usual lift. As Madeline surveyed the table—the mildly impertinent Annie Rogers, the nicely turned-out Myra

DuPree (wife of the son of one of Ronald's elderly business partners), the deliriously giddy Georgette Mays, and several others in their finery—Madeline felt nothing but gloom. Every one of them had children, several more than one.

On a good day, Madeline was reasonably talkative, but Annie's harping references to her "little Mikey" and the supposedly funny things that Myra's two-year-old, Evangeline, did in her bath pounded like a spike into Madeline's skull. She turned dead silent, and she must have looked ashen, because Georgette, who normally did not comment on such things, said, "Why Madeline, have some water. You look like I don't know *what.*" And then all the women, seven of them, were staring at her, and obviously wondering. Madeline saw nothing but eyes around her, each one boring a hole into her, and she felt something go off inside, an alarm of some kind, and her skin went clammy, and she wished she could disappear.

Fortunately, they left her alone after that, and continued on with their chatter about knitting yarn and boarding schools and summer places as if Madeline simply weren't there. It wasn't until afterward that Jordie Howe, a small, birdlike woman whom Madeline normally overlooked, came up to her and, after checking to make sure that she was not being overheard, said she'd been "seeing someone."

Madeline assumed she was having an affair and looked at her strangely.

"A doctor."

"I've seen plenty of doctors," Madeline replied, disappointed.

"Not that kind," Jordie whispered. "A doctor you talk to. About how you're feeling." She pulled Madeline further aside. "I think I know what you're going through, Madeline." She took a card out of her purse and scratched out a name on it. "Dr. Paul de Frieze," it said. And it included a phone number. She pushed the card into Madeline's palm.

"Call him, would you?"

Then Myra shouted for Jordie to hop to, since they were driving back together. And Jordie gave Madeline's hand a squeeze. "Good luck, okay?"

• • •

As the days passed, the ache seemed to settle into her bones. She found it hard not to retreat to bed, but once she was there, she couldn't sleep for more than an hour or two, and that sleep was so exhausting, it seemed to leave her worse off. She thought—hoped— that she was suffering a hormonal surge that might be a harbinger of pregnancy. They hadn't made love that month—or had they? She was losing track, each month folding into the next. Her nipples were slightly tender, and, when she examined them early one morning in the bathroom mirror, they seemed a bit larger. Was she pregnant? Finally? Was there hope for her after all?

She was alone in the kitchen sipping coffee when she felt the wetness between her legs. She dropped down onto the linoleum tiles right there, the blood pooling beneath her, and cried.

Millie helped her to bed. Madeline stayed there for a week, telling Ronald that she'd come down with the flu.

The blood that month seemed especially heavy and thick, as if she'd been wounded.

That spring, she tried to distract herself in the garden that Ronald's aunt had laid out years back, before the war. A wisteria-drenched pergola with Delphic columns extended out from the library, and rhododendrons clustered around a rectangular pool that was far too small for swimming (its waters were too brackish anyway), but was adorned with a sculpture of a naked Diana. Arranged beside it were low, brightly colored flowers—tulips in the spring, and then a variety of exotic species that Madeline couldn't then identify. Since Ronald and Madeline had moved in, a young French-Canadian with the fine name of Pierre-Francois St. Jacques had done all the gardening, but he'd married a Greek girl over the winter and left for the Midwest to work for her father's agricultural-supply business.

After consulting with Ronald, Madeline took over the task. "It might be good for you," Ronald told her. From a chest of drawers in a back room, he dug out several rolled-up diagrams that his aunt Jane had sketched to show how the gardens had once looked, the various beds all precisely outlined and then labeled with different flowering plants to bloom monthly between May and October. Madeline didn't even recognize the names: polyanthas, ageratum, coledestinum . . .

She took up the matter with her tea group, and Myra DuPree suggested she speak to her aging aunt Laura Randall, a famous green thumb who'd written several books on gardening. Madeline was hesitant, but, to her surprise, Mrs. Randall called *her* two days later and insisted on coming over that very afternoon. Mrs. Randall—as Madeline always called her—proved to be a big, bony woman in, Madeline guessed, her late sixties. She was born in England, but had been raised in India, where her parents were missionaries, and she retained the boundless energy that Madeline associated with foreigners. In her emphatic English accent, Mrs. Randall provided the most basic instructions about sunlight and fertilizers and certain plant varieties. Marsupia roses she said were "very friendly"; delphiniums, however, were "positively hateful." Mrs. Randall came two or three times a week, and Madeline soon found herself living from visit to visit. Together, they drained and cleaned out the pool, polished the sculpture of Diana to reveal a sparkling bronze, and added a flock of waterlilies. Around the sunny side of the pool they added sprays of gorgeous German iris to blossom in the spring, then tiger lilies, phlox, and some lovely rudbeckia that a cousin had brought Madeline from Vermont. For the shade, they put in masses of violets and foxglove, since Madeline loved the mix of purples.

Mrs. Randall's occasional smoking breaks soon persuaded Madeline to take up the secret pleasure; and as the two sat together puffing Turkish cigarettes, the older woman seemed to delight in astonishing her young charge with her own extravagant marital history. She'd buried two husbands, divorced a third, and had had numerous affairs as well. "Men never meant much to me," she told Madeline one afternoon as they paused over the wheelbarrow.

"*Hideous* creatures. *Most* disappointing. But I did enjoy a good go now and again."

The garden, and Mrs. Randall's company, carried Madeline through the warm weather, but gradually the dark came on earlier and the air cooled, and she felt the old distress returning. At first, she and Ronald continued their efforts to conceive, but only sporadically. He did apologize, once, but that wasn't enough to keep her from tears some nights. As the mercury in the big thermometer off the kitchen dropped, it seemed like the cold lodged inside her, chilled her soul, even, leaving her icebound, rubbing her arms to warm herself. She lit fires in the afternoon, tried to lose herself in the games of solitaire she'd learned in Golden, but it was little use. Gradually, though, a plan began to form, and she dreamed of building a greenhouse off the living room, a large one to grow the orchids that Mrs. Randall confided were her true passion in life. She had just the spot picked out, but Ronald told her she would have to wait. He needed the money for the business just then. A few months later, when Ronald declared that money had loosened up again, Madeline was in no mood for orchids. Mrs. Randall had just passed away, from a cancer she hadn't mentioned to anyone.

It was then that she remembered the knives in the kitchen, how they sparkled. It would be so easy. A slice here, and a slice there, and it would be done.

She'd gone to the kitchen, drawn down the longest one, tested its edge against her finger. She was mounting the stairs with it when Millie spoke to her. "Mrs. Bemis," she called out. "Are you all right?"

"I'm fine, thank you." Always polite, no matter what. She prided herself on it.

"But the knife—"

"It's for some string."

"You don't need that huge thing," Millie told her. "Let me get you some scissors." She eased the knife from her hand, helped her find the scissors in the desk by the front hall.

"Yes," Mrs. Bemis told her, once the scissors were in her hand. "Much better. Thank you."

Their eyes met.

"You need to be careful with a knife like this," said the girl, tapping the side of the long blade. "You could cut yourself."

"Yes, I know."

That afternoon, she called to make her first appointment with Dr. de Frieze.

Alice

⌇ thirty-six

There was a jam-up on the expressway returning to the city, and Alice didn't get back to Cambridge until well past seven-thirty. She jumped into fresh clothes and was nearly back out the door when she realized that she hadn't checked on Fido. It shocked her that she could forget. Sure enough, the water dispenser was dry, and he was all out of food, too. "Oh, sorry!" she told the mouse, lifting him out of his cage to her cheek. She could feel his nose poke into her as his little body squirmed. "Left you here all alone, you poor thing," she told him. She set him down inside a mixing bowl on the counter while she scooped a handful of high-protein pellets into his food dish and filled up his water dispenser, too. Then Alice brought his face up to hers and explained that she'd had a "sleep-over." For a moment, the mouse held still. "Suspicious, aren't you?" She set Fido back down inside his cage. "But it was fun." The mouse peered up at her through the glass. "Right," Alice said. "Whatever that means."

• • •

When she arrived at Nichols, Rita was watering the spider plant in the common room. The TV was blasting away as usual. Middle-aged twins, new arrivals, were staring up at the *Today Show,* the cheery morning voices offering ironic commentary on the grim surroundings of the ward.

"Dr. Maris left a note for you," Rita told her.

"Oh good. Thanks." Alice didn't always think to check her box. When she went to look, she found Marnie filling out a report over coffee. Alice wished her good morning, which Marnie acknowledged with a nod. She found the envelope in her box—from the Montrose director's office, no less, with her name typed on the front.

The note inside, however, was handwritten.

"Regarding Madeline Bemis, let's start slowly, shall we? Take her home for an afternoon, why don't you, if you can arrange it with your schedule. Helpful for you to be present, although not exactly according to Hoyle. A first trip back could be traumatic, and the development office has taken an interest—did I tell you? So keep me posted on your progress." Dr. Maris signed it with his initials then added a P.S. "Victor tells me you're doing very well. My congratulations."

"You know about this?" Alice asked Marnie, who was still busy with her paperwork.

"The field trip?" Marnie asked drily.

"So you discussed it." Alice was beginning to dislike Marnie.

"Only afterward. I don't have a lot of input with our leader these days. I'd have told him it was irregular, which is probably why he didn't ask." She returned to her work, adding offhandedly, "Somehow I imagine that psychiatry is something that should be practiced in a psychiatrist's office. Silly me."

Alice found Rita in the hall. "What's with Marnie?"

Rita shrugged. "Being so bitchy, you mean?"

Alice nodded.

She stepped closer to Alice, spoke in a gravelly whisper. "I don't think she likes being wrong."

"About?"

Rita glanced about, then took Alice down the hall with her. "About you, honey. She thought Madeline needed electroshock. She kept telling Dr. Maris that he was blowing it by letting you try therapy. She thought you were wasting everybody's time trying to get her to open up, to talk." Rita turned back to Alice. "And now she's pissed."

"And what about you?"

"Me? You asking me what *I* think?" Rita laughed. "Nobody's done that before. Sheesh! No, I don't think you're wasting anybody's time."

Mrs. Bemis was at her usual solitaire table, but this time she was sitting with Charles, the accountant who'd set his office on fire. They were close together over a tableau of cards, Charles hanging on her every word. Alice didn't want to interrupt, but she knew that Mrs. Bemis would want to hear Dr. Maris's verdict.

"Oh, hello," Mrs. Bemis called out to Alice. "I was just explaining a game to Mr. Packer here."

"Could I see you for a moment?" Alice asked.

Mrs. Bemis turned to her card partner. "Would you mind terribly?"

"Not at all," Charles told her, almost matching her formality.

Mrs. Bemis stood up, and suggested they speak in her room. Alice agreed, impressed to see her patient taking charge in this way. Mrs. Bemis led her down the hall.

Inside, Alice noticed some wildflowers in a paper cup on the windowsill. "Charles gave me those," Mrs. Bemis said. "Forget-me-nots. Charming, aren't they? He was out on the grounds yesterday, and he thought of me. Isn't that nice? He's quite a kind man, you know."

"He seems to have cheered you up."

"Oh?" Mrs. Bemis seemed surprised.

"I sense a certain spriteliness today."

"Spriteliness," Mrs. Bemis repeated. "Well, I never thought any-one would ever say *that* about me." Then, in a different voice, "Least of all a professional." Mrs. Bemis took a seat on the edge of the bed. "Must be the drugs," she added playfully.

"It can be a relief to speak of the past," Alice told her. "A relief and a release."

Always before, in revealing intimate details, Mrs. Bemis had turned away and dropped her voice. But this time, she faced Alice directly, and spoke right up. "I was thinking of Ronald last evening, after you left."

"Oh?" This was the first time Mrs. Bemis had offered such a rec-ollection.

"We were together, in bed. He couldn't . . . perform." With obvi-ous discomfort, she told Alice the story, leaving out only a few of the gamier details. Alice was impressed that she could bring herself to speak of such a thing. "I was remembering how awful I felt," Mrs. Bemis continued, haltingly. "After I had my menstrual period later that month, I wanted to—" She stopped, looked down at her hands. "Oh, this is difficult for me. I do try to be open with you, but—"

"There's no rush. I have time."

She told Alice about the knife, causing Alice to flash to Ethan and her scissors. The thought made her wince, but the distress went deeper, turned visceral, as Mrs. Bemis continued. "I wanted to hurt myself. I did. I wanted to *end* it all. I couldn't go on. I was no good, no good to anyone, least of all to myself."

"Oh, Mrs. Bemis, I'm so sorry." To have actually selected a knife, and to be climbing the stairs with it, bent on suicide—that was an entirely different realm of horror. "I am so glad your maid was there," Alice declared. "And that you stopped and called someone for help. That is a wonderful relief to me, I have to say. I'm proud of you, Mrs. Bemis. You saved your own life."

"Well, Dr. de Frieze was a kind man, very patient." She looked up. "As you have been, Alice." She looked troubled again. "It is all right to call you that?"

Alice felt so warmly toward Mrs. B just then. "It's fine."

Mrs. Bemis brightened. "I never expected to feel so close to you."

Alice looked at her, saw the directness, the clarity. "I'm glad you do," she said, smiling. "Really glad."

Mrs. Bemis was pleased to learn that Dr. Maris had permitted a visit to the Milton house, although she was sorry that it was just a visit. Alice tried to be gentle about it, saying that her boss "couldn't do without" Mrs. B just yet, but she was disappointed nonetheless. Still, she took it bravely. It was a job to assemble the necessary paperwork. Dr. Maris and Marnie, as the senior staff member, both had to sign off on it, which Marnie did reluctantly.

That evening, Alice spent a long time on the phone with Frank, speculating on how the visit would go. When she finally hung up, the telephone rang immediately. She thought at first that Frank had remembered something he wanted to add.

But, no, it was her mother. And her voice sounded flat, even for her.

"Who've *you* been talking to all this time? I've been trying to get through for hours."

"Just a friend," Alice said irritably.

"I've got some sad news." She paused. "It's your grandmother."

Alice squeezed the phone involuntarily.

"She passed away this morning."

"But she couldn't have!" Alice gasped.

"I'm sorry, Alice," her mother said.

Her mother wanted her to fly home that night. But Alice had promised to take Mrs. Bemis back to her house the next afternoon, and the funeral wouldn't be until the day after.

She told her mother she couldn't get away until the following morning at the earliest.

"But the funeral!" her mother protested.

"I'll be there, don't worry."

"It's that boyfriend, isn't it." She paused, letting the venom sink in. "I don't see how he can be more important than your own family."

"This has nothing to do with any boyfriend," Alice shot back. "This is about work." She stopped herself, took a breath, thought about how the Grand would have wanted her to stay to help Mrs. B. "Look, I'll be there for the service, all right?"

Alice scarcely slept that night. She found the remains of the quilt where she'd tucked it away in the chest at the foot of her bed, and pulled it out to nuzzle up against as she tried to sleep. Alice should have visited. She should have dropped everything and spent time with the Grand in the nursing home. Serious time, putting everything else aside. She tried to remember everything she could about her: the maple-shaded cottage she'd owned across town, her two stray calico cats, the winter hats she'd crocheted for her grandkids, the stories she'd told. But the memories left her with little beside longing.

In the morning, many of the patients were keyed up by the prospect of Mrs. Bemis's trip home, and several spoke to Alice about it, badgering her to take them home, too. Alice wished there could be some secrets on the ward.

When Alice came around to Mrs. Bemis's room a little after one o'clock, she was surprised to find the old woman in her best dress, with her hair freshly brushed and pinned back. And she was all packed, with her suitcase on the bed.

"But this is just a visit," Alice reminded her. "I thought I told you. A dry run. We wanted to make sure you fit back into your home setting before you're released."

"Oh, I know all that," Mrs. Bemis said unhappily. "But I'm just so tired of this place."

"Let's just see how this goes, all right? Nobody wants you to leave only to come right back."

Reluctantly, Mrs. Bemis opened up her bag again, and she got out a few things she needed for the trip—a pair of sunglasses, a floppy hat, a light sweater. "I would like to poke around my garden a little." Mrs. Bemis slipped the glasses and hat into a small canvas bag, and she draped the sweater over her shoulders, tying the arms around under her chin like a schoolgirl.

She recovered her good spirits as she headed down the hall, and called out brisk salutations to a few of the fellow residents she passed. When she spotted her friend Charles, she sang out to him, "Oh, Mr. Packer, false alarm. It seems I'll be back this evening after all. So we can save our good-byes, all right?"

"Sure thing, Mads," he told her.

The air was crisp, with a hint of fall in it, but the sun burned brightly high in the sky when Alice and Mrs. Bemis emerged from Nichols and made their way down the walk to the B lot where Alice had her car. Alice had made a point of cleaning it out that morning, but she was still embarrassed that the vehicle was so small.

Mrs. Bemis herself seemed to be pleased with it. "Isn't this nice," she said as she settled herself inside, clutching her bag on her lap. Alice reached across to roll down her window for some cross ventilation, and worried that the sun-warmed vinyl might be too hot for her passenger. But Mrs. Bemis didn't complain, and seemed to enjoy the view as they set out down the long winding drive to the main gate.

Out on the road, Mrs. Bemis kept a tight grip on the armrest, and placed her left hand on the dashboard to brace herself at virtually every stop.

"Don't trust my driving?" Alice asked finally.

"Of course I do." But she did not let go of the armrest.

Alice set the air conditioner going and, at a light, helped Mrs. Bemis crank the window back up so that the wind wouldn't muss her hair. They took Route 2 and then 128 around toward the South Shore. Alice knew the way to Milton, pretty much, but she had a map in case her patient blanked out on how to get to her house. As they drove along, they discussed the food at Montrose, which Mrs. Bemis declared "absolutely inedible." It was strange to have her patient right there in her car, with Alice herself at the wheel. And Mrs. Bemis in dark glasses, which gave her an aging movie-star look.

As quiet as she was, Mrs. Bemis remained alert, and she was quick to tell Alice where to turn off 128, and then directed her on a complicated shortcut through Milton. She pointed out the old-line prep school Milton Academy, which Mrs. Bemis termed "appalling" for the low standards of its dress code, and the high-steepled Congregational Church where, she allowed, she didn't "know a soul." Alice was struck by the general elegance of the town, considering that it shared a border with Dorchester, one of inner-city Boston's pockets of misery.

Two right turns and then a left and Alice saw the sign: "Deaver Way."

thirty-seven

Mrs. Bemis's house was a big, yellow place topped with a massive chimney. The driveway curled around past a carriage house and a shingled barn on its way to the front door, which was shaded by a wide porch and adorned with a few sprigs of holly. "Pete must have done that," Mrs. Bemis said, referring to her caretaker and sometime driver, Pete Needham, as she and Alice approached the door. She groped in her handbag for the keys, but found nothing. "I could have sworn—"

"That happens to me, too," Alice told her.

"Oh, does it?" Relief in her voice. She clutched Alice's arm. "I'm so glad."

Mrs. Bemis set her bag down and, declaring that Pete was sure to be about, pressed the bell, which rumbled inside. She rang repeatedly, though, and no one appeared, so Mrs. Bemis, her gray hair flashing in the midday sun, headed across the gravel driveway to the carriage house to look for him. She hadn't gone far before a slope-shouldered older man in mud-stained overalls appeared from around the far side of the house.

"You wanting me?" he asked. It was Pete. The words came from deep in his throat, an up-country sound that Alice remembered from her brief conversation with him. She hoped her own voice wasn't as distinctive.

"Why there you are," Mrs. Bemis called back. "Oh, it's the stupidest thing. I've locked myself out."

"I wasn't expecting you," Pete replied, clumping up the porch steps to the front door to let her in. Alice waited for something more, about how he was glad to see her again after all these weeks, or where had she been all this time. But obviously that was not their way. They were like a pair of old rocking chairs by the fire.

"Just here for the afternoon, actually." Mrs. Bemis paused. "I'll be back before too long. This is a friend of mine, Alice Matthews," she told the caretaker. Then she added, for Alice's benefit, "Pete Needham. He takes care of the place for me."

"Hello then." Pete nodded at Alice, said he was pleased to meet her. Alice tried to tell if there was some uncertainty in his tone, as if he were trying to place her. He offered Alice a dusty hand to shake; he'd obviously been working in the garden. He pulled a key chain out of his pocket, and opened the door. "There you go, missus," he told Mrs. Bemis.

Dim light in the wide, front hall—until Mrs. B flipped a switch, and a leaf-patterned chandelier blazed up, making all the woodwork sparkle.

Mrs. Bemis asked Pete to come in for a moment to keep Alice company while she went into the kitchen to get some tea started. Alice offered to help, but Mrs. Bemis would hear none of it. "I can do this. I'd like to do something for you after all this time."

"But I can help," Alice protested.

"Please, Alice."

Once Mrs. Bemis was out of sight down the hall, Pete turned to Alice. "The missus doesn't normally give a person much."

"Yes, I know."

As Alice glanced about the high front hall, she caught a glimpse of herself in the mirror. With her hair pulled back today, she looked, just for a moment, a bit "swish," as Mrs. B might say, as if she belonged here. A grand staircase rose up to her right, but she kept on toward the big living room that opened off some pocket doors to her left. There was a Steinway piano off in a far corner, draped by a cloth that ended in gold tassels. The grasscloth-covered walls were lined with shelves full of leather-bound books and hung with oils in gilt frames, each one with its own light. It might have been a museum, a library, or perhaps one of those exclusive clubs that Alice herself had heard about but never entered. The windows were wide but closed, accounting for the late summer mustiness to the air, and the shades were lowered halfway, casting a greenish light across the orientals and to the mahogany wainscotting on the far wall. Pete busied himself raising the shades and throwing open the sashes, which lurched upward with a squeal, to let in a breeze. "I wasn't expecting her back today, or I'd have opened the place up." He pushed up another window, admitting a view of a great copper beech. "I'm sorry I didn't cut some flowers from the garden." He gestured out another window through the back porch, toward a mass of greenery that was dabbed with color. "The missus loves her flowers."

Pete was beside her, but Alice sensed a greater presence over her shoulder. She turned; an oil portrait hung on the wall, full-length, of a stern gentleman with a slender mustache, his pained eyes peering down at her. "That's her husband," Pete explained, seeing Alice's interest. "Before my time here. A pilot in the war. Plane went down. He wore a brace on one leg, but you don't see that in the picture, now do you? Walked with a cane, too." He looked up at the imposing man in the portrait. "Or so I heard. Missus never mentions him." He turned back to Alice. "You're from that place where she is, aren't you?"

"What makes you think that?"

"You don't say much."

Mrs. Bemis returned from the kitchen. "Well, I think we're all set now." She turned to the caretaker. "You care to join us, Peter? Take a break from your labors?"

"I should get back to it." He shook Alice's hand, said it was good to meet her, and withdrew out the back door to the garden, carefully closing the door behind him.

"I don't know what I would do without that man," Mrs. Bemis said once Pete was gone. "Sell the place, I expect." Mrs. Bemis glanced around the living room.

"Your husband, I gather," Alice said, looking up at the oil portrait.

"*Late* husband," Mrs. Bemis corrected her. "Ghastly, isn't it? His mother had it done, insisted we put it there. It would leave an awful gap if we took it down, although I must say I have been tempted." She turned away, taking in the rest of the room, the books and the oils. "I spent thirty years here with him," she said. "And twenty more by myself. He was a good man—in many respects, anyway. Conscientious, upstanding, quite accomplished in his field. He had a bit of a sense of humor after a drink or two. He'd have been a good father. But that blasted war—it broke him. Broke his spirit. I don't know which period of my life was more lonely, with him or without."

"But those parties?"

"Oh, hang the parties," Mrs. Bemis told her. "Drunken stockbrokers. Great ladies squealing in my ear. Self-important dignitaries. A big bore, all of it. I was better off alone." She moved toward the window, where she could see Pete digging by the arbor. "That was the only fun I had, down on my knees there. But I'm too old for it now. Arthritis, you know."

Mrs. Bemis ran a finger along the lip of one bookcase, then examined it. "Could use some dusting," she said.

They had tea on the veranda, around the back of the house, overlooking the rose garden. Mrs. Bemis had brought out a full tea service, right down to the sugar tongs, and she seemed to take pleasure in every portion of the extravagance that had been denied to her at Montrose. "Sorry we don't have any cake to go with it," Mrs. Bemis said. "I do love a slice of cake with my tea, don't you?"

"This is fine," Alice assured her.

Mrs. Bemis seemed to breathe in the view around her—the long, sloping lawn that angled down to a rectangular pool that was edged with violets, even now at the very end of summer; the spreading copper beech off the corner of the house; and, nearer at hand, the wisteria-draped pergola and the roses about the fountain. Blush pink, cinnamon, orange, and all still in luscious bloom. "It takes strength to come back here," she told Alice.

"And why's that?"

"The memories."

"Of?"

"Of my solitude, I suppose. I mean, look at this place."

"It's beautiful."

"Yes—but it mocks a person sometimes. Many nights I wished I could burn it to the ground. Douse it with gasoline and light a match." She stopped. "That was always my big fear as a child—that our house would burn. But I longed for it some nights as an adult, have the whole place go up in a great roar."

There was the occasional twittering of birds, and the click of Pete's clippers as he pruned the climbing roses. "Still, it is nice sometimes to have the quiet," she added.

Mrs. Bemis had two cups of tea, each with several lumps of sugar. When she was done, she said she had something to show Alice. "It's the thing I care about most in this house. If there *were* a fire—" She stopped. "It's upstairs." Mrs. Bemis stood up. "In my bedroom. Let me take you."

Alice followed Mrs. Bemis up the wide stairs from the front hall. The upstairs opened onto a long corridor, with high doorways leading into antiques-filled rooms. There was a grand bedroom in the corner, with a double bed and splendid views of the gardens below. She led Alice to the door, but did not go inside. "I shared this with

Ronald for thirty years. Imagine." After his death, she'd moved into the small bedroom, done in pale blue, beside it. It was very narrow, with just an iron-framed bed, like something out of an orphanage.

"It's a good size for me," she told Alice. "I don't need much." There was a black album beside the bed, and Mrs. Bemis handed it to Alice.

"The book," she said.

It weighed heavily in her hand, and some of the leather binding flaked off. She sat down on the bed and looked again at the cover. "BRENDAN HURLEY," it said in block letters.

Alice could not cover her surprise. "Brendan Hurley?" she gasped. "Isn't that—?"

"Yes. The body they found."

"But what—"

"He was my son."

Alice looked up at her, stunned.

"Surely you knew."

"No, I didn't. How could I?"

"How curious. You seemed to know everything."

Mrs. Bemis stood up, went to the window, looked out to the garden again. It was while she was looking out that she began to speak. At first, it was as if she were talking to the view, or, more than that, to the great expanse that lay outside her, beyond her. To God, perhaps. Haltingly, wistfully, she told Alice about Gerald.

It was so sad to hear it, this tale of lost love. Their affair was so brief, and yet so meaningful. And so lasting, as the emotional reper- cussions rolled on and on—the misery of her banishment to Colorado, the anguish of giving up her child, and the long frustra- tion of her marriage. Mrs. Bemis spoke quietly, at times her voice barely a whisper; Alice sometimes had to fight the urge to ask Mrs. Bemis to speak up, to repeat that, because she didn't quite hear. But Alice sensed sometimes that her patient did not necessarily direct her words to her at all. Instead, she merely intended to put them out-side her, where they could no longer bring her harm. She punctuated her story several times with deep sighs that made Alice fear tem-porarily that Mrs. Bemis would not be able to continue, that she would instead be convulsed by tears. But, each time, she gathered herself, and continued on once more with a "Well, *then* I . . ."

It was only at the point where she returned once more to how Millie had kept her from carrying the kitchen knife upstairs that she herself seemed to register the agony that she was describing. Mrs. Bemis dropped her head down onto her forearm, which rested on the sill, and seemed to slump against the window.

Afraid, suddenly, Alice rose from her chair to drape an arm over the old woman's shoulder. "I'm so sorry," she told her. "It sounds unbearable."

Mrs. Bemis reached back to touch her hand. "It was torture for me. Absolute torture. I truly didn't think I could take a minute more. But Millie took the knife from me, bless her heart. So gently, saying nothing about her suspicions. That was a monumental kind-ness."

"Did you ever feel that way again?" Alice asked.

"Suicidal, you mean?"

"Hm-mmm," Alice murmured gently from behind her.

Mrs. Bemis shook her head. "No, thankfully. The pain subsided. So I could go on. As I told you, I spoke to Dr. de Frieze. A wonder-ful man in many ways. Not particularly insightful, but immensely kind and reassuring. And he gave me some perspective, I guess you'd say." She turned back to Alice. "All lives are difficult, though, aren't they?"

"They can be," Alice said. She drew Mrs. Bemis away from the window, toward a small chair in the corner of the room.

"You know, I sometimes wonder if Gerald ever existed," Mrs. Bemis continued, settling in the chair. She spoke more lightly now, as if she were merely musing over her history. "Oh, I know he must have. But I never saw him again after that night. I didn't know his last name. So odd. After all that's happened, I've never ever found out who he was! I didn't know how to find him again. I'm not sure I did want to. To find out the truth of him, you know."

She glanced over at Alice, who was careful not to react, but to open herself to whatever Mrs. Bemis might choose to say.

"I believe my husband must have known of Gerald," Mrs. Bemis went on, anticipating the question that had formed in Alice's mind. "I think he knew from the very beginning. He was a changed man after the war. So much of his spirit went out of him, he was so bitter about his wounds. He once wrote me that we were two broken people. I'm not sure he could bear my wounds on top of his own. If he hadn't suffered so, he might have had the energy to win me back, to make me want to forget the man who had come between us. But he didn't, and he couldn't. He had little to offer me except his own disappointment. And I had plenty of that myself."

"How did he know?"

"From Ellen, I expect. She admitted as much to me several years ago, shortly before she died. We were on the porch of her summer place in Maine, the last summer she spent there. She asked me if I could ever forgive her. She must have sensed I suspected. Death casts a shadow, you know, when it's circling overhead. She had a cancer, abdominal cancer, and it was torture for her. I did forgive her, of course I did. I doubt she said anything direct, but she was a terrible gossip. Ronald was no fool. He could put the pieces together."

Mrs. Bemis stood up, returned to the window, ran her hand along the top of the sash, prying up the little flecks of paint that had peeled away. "Golden, Colorado," she declared with new energy. "Pretty name, isn't it? For such a wretched place. But it did advance my education. It was my college, my graduate school. I earned a Ph.D. in misery. Saw it, felt it, ate it, slept it. A useful thing to know about this world, I suppose. All the suffering in it."

She filled Alice in on the rest of the story, of her return east to Milton—her friends at the Milton Historical Society, the "dear Mrs. Randall," her infertility, and her turning finally to Dr. de Frieze.

She'd been speaking for well over an hour. The sun was dropping in the west, where this window faced, lighting up Mrs. Bemis's hair. She turned back to Alice, finally, and tapped a finger on the album beside her. "But Brendan, I always thought he would be my salvation."

She returned to her small chair, settled herself, and told Alice how they'd met.

Madeline

> ✒ thirty-eight

Shortly after her mother returned home from Montrose, sometime in early March, Madeline received a written invitation from her to attend a small going-away party for the maid, Bridget, who had stayed on with Madeline's parents, at that point, for six years after Madeline's marriage to Ronald. Madeline was ambivalent about attending, needless to say. She'd come to loathe Bridget after her time in Golden. Many nights, Madeline closed her eyes for sleep, only to see Bridget tramping through the snow, coming for her. But this was her mother's first attempt to reinitiate a social life for herself. When Madeline rang her mother to tell her, of course, she would be happy to come, her mother explained that Bridget was moving to Chicago. "Her cousin's ailing, poor thing," Mother explained. "She'll be taking care of her. She has another position lined up out there." Madeline reiterated that she would be "delighted" to attend; her mother said she was "so glad"; and that was that. They had become so formal with each other.

The party was set for a Tuesday afternoon, making it impossible for Ronald to attend, since he chained himself to his desk during the week, as Madeline's mother must have known. All she could think was that her mother had selected the time with that eventuality in mind.

As they sat in the living room of the Dover house, their backs to the windows, Madeline realized that she had never seen Bridget wear anything other than her uniform in that house, so it was almost alarming to see her there in the living room: she was wearing a fashionable dress with diagonal stripes. The dress didn't fit her quite right—Bridget had an indefinite shape that would be hard to clothe—but it did give her a touch of superficial elegance, as though the maid were attempting to elevate herself. More striking, Mother positively fussed over Bridget, insisting that she stay seated in the big, comfortable chair while she herself tended to the tea biscuits that were warming in the oven. Madeline always tried to hold democratic beliefs—this might have been her husband's influence; Ronald was surprisingly liberal on some points—but she felt uncomfortable making small talk with Bridget while her mother, fresh out of a psychiatric institution, attended to the food. She wondered about Bridget's new standing in the family. Madeline had scarcely been back to the house since her own wedding. In her absence, had Bridget somehow become one of them? Had she taken Madeline's own place? A galling idea, and one that distressed her no end when she was left with her father to chat with Bridget about how things would certainly be different around here without her. And then the telephone rang with a business call for Father, and he took it in the library, leaving Madeline alone with Bridget.

Madeline wished acutely that she had not come, was not with this overdressed hag who had stolen her baby from her. She was pleased to see a bit of discomfort in the maid, as well. She noticed a film of perspiration glistening in the folds under Bridget's thick chin, just above her dress's drooping bow.

Madeline had not planned to speak of her son. She hadn't thought she could bring herself to form the words and then send them floating toward this particular human being. But the emotion surged up in her, and she couldn't hold it back.

"What did you do with my baby?" Madeline blurted out.

Bridget's face was like iron, as she said nothing for a moment, eyeing Madeline. "Now, what would you be wanting to know something like that for?"

Madeline wanted to dig her hands into Bridget's fat cheeks, to push the truth, the pain, inside. "He's my child, Bridget. My *son!*"

"I haven't any idea."

"Tell me right now," Madeline insisted.

"And I'd keep my voice down if I was you."

"Where is he?"

"How should I know?" She said it lightly, her plump chin wobbling.

"You know where you took him."

"Perhaps." She paused. "Perhaps not."

Madeline settled herself back into her chair and took a moment to straighten out the skirts of her dress, which had gotten terribly ruffled. Then she returned her eyes to the maid and spoke more calmly. "My mother was asking me about a going-away present for you, you know."

That captured Bridget's attention.

"She was thinking of giving you some money."

The maid's gaze was locked on Madeline.

"She thought a few hundred dollars would be sufficient."

Bridget's face hardened.

"But I was thinking you'd been with the family *such* a long time, and done *so* many things for us, I thought you deserved at least a thousand. Don't you agree? I know how expensive it can be to move." Madeline smiled, artificially. "I'm sure they'll come around to my position, if I ask them to. But perhaps I shouldn't bother."

This time, Bridget was the one to smile. "A thousand, did you say?"

That night, on the telephone, Madeline arranged her end of the bargain, and in a few weeks, a letter arrived for her from "B.S." with no address, but a Chicago postmark. "St. Anne's Church, Boston. Name of Hurley. This is all I know."

It took Madeline several telephone calls to determine which St. Anne's it was, since there were several in the city. But the only one that involved itself with adoptions was the Catholic church on Albemarle Street in Boston's South End.

The church proved to be an imposing stone structure with a high steeple and a parish building in back. Madeline took a moment to compose herself after she stepped out of her Opal. It was a bitterly cold day, well below twenty degrees, with a threat of snow in the grayness all around. Madeline pulled her coat about her, tucked in her scarf, under her chin. She made her way to the door, and rapped twice with her gloved hands. When she received no answer, she tried the heavy metal knob. It turned, and the door opened onto a broad hall with a stone floor. Diagonally across was a small, brightly lit office, and Madeline could see a head leaning forward into the glow of the lamp at the desk. It was a frail woman bent over some papers. She didn't look up as Madeline approached.

Madeline summoned the courage to knock against the door frame. A slender, benign face peered out at her.

Madeline had spent much of the night plotting what she would say. But now that the moment had arrived, she couldn't remember any of it.

"Is this St. Anne's?" Madeline asked stupidly.

"Yes, dear." The woman sounded kind, which was a relief. "But this is the adoption agency. If you're looking for the parish office, it's over there through those doors." She pointed down the hall.

"Oh good," Madeline said, relieved. "It's the adoption agency I want."

"Well then." The woman stood and cleared off a seat for Madeline on a bench by her desk. Madeline settled herself, hugging her purse to her side.

She was a Miss O'Brien, the agency's assistant director. "Sorry we're so understaffed," she said. Her secretary was out sick today, and the receptionist had recently had a baby. She smiled at the irony. "Now, how can I help you?"

"I'm here for a child," Madeline said.

"Oh, well, yes. That." Another smile. "That is the business we're in." She turned back to her desk and drew out a form from the upper-right-hand drawer. "Well, perhaps we might begin by your filling this out for me." She handed the lengthy form to Madeline. "You're married, I assume," she added, fumbling in her desk for a pencil.

"Yes, but—" Madeline glanced down at the paper. "But—" This was harder than she'd thought. "I don't want to adopt a— I *meant*—" She paused, her resolve weakening. What *did* she mean? "I meant that I—"

The woman looked at Madeline as if she couldn't imagine what could possibly be troubling her.

"I want to find *my* child. My *baby*."

The woman's face fell. "Oh dear."

"It was—he was—*taken* from me, you see." Haltingly, she told Miss O'Brien the story, enough of it anyway, all the while staring at her chilled hands, her wool skirt, anywhere but in the woman's eyes, which were filled with disapproval. She'd never told anyone what had happened. Not even that nice Dr. Wilder, although he had pressed her. It was a secret buried so deeply inside, it might have become part of herself, like bone. And it hurt now, to extract it, to deliver it to this stranger.

"So, you just want to see him?" Miss O'Brien asked. "Is that what you're saying?"

Madeline nodded. She tried not to cry. The urge was coming over her, as it so often did in those bleak days.

"And then what? You'd leave him alone afterward?" Her skeptical, opinionated tone frightened Madeline. Surely she should be sympathetic.

"Yes, I would. Of course! I *promise.* I just want to see him once. I need to see that he's okay. I haven't been able to have another child, you see, although my husband and I, we've been—"

Miss O'Brien shook her head. "We get this all the time, you know. Woman puts her baby up for adoption, then changes her mind. It's a problem, don't you see?" She pulled away from her. "We cannot permit it. I'm sorry."

"But I didn't give him up!" Madeline exclaimed. "I tell you, he was *taken* from me."

"But you signed a form, surely."

Madeline had forgotten all about the form. Had she signed such a thing? Several months before the hospital, Miss Morely had presented her with a long paper. She supposed she had signed it. This was before she'd felt the kick, before the baby was a baby. The form was just words. "In recognition whereof." "Henceforth." Words like that. Yes, she'd signed it. She couldn't *not* sign it, not the way Miss Morely stood over her, waiting.

"And all this was years ago, my dear. Gracious me, the boy has another life now. He has parents of his own, a home of his own. You can't interfere with that."

"Not even once?" Madeline was pleading now. If she weren't so bundled up, in such fine clothes (not that they'd done her any good), she would have gotten down on her knees to beg, to cling to this woman, anything to get her to understand. "But I just want to see him. Just once. Please!" She reached for Miss O'Brien then, imploring her. She felt herself growing faint, desperate.

"It's never just once—believe me." Miss O'Brien stood up. She did not extend a hand, offered no further assistance. "Good day to you." The life taken out of her, Madeline grabbed her handbag, rose.

The woman stepped toward the doorway. "This way now." Miss O'Brien led her across the hall to the front door, then opened the door for her. As Madeline passed in front of her, stricken, she thought she might make a last try. "So who are the Hurleys?" she asked.

The woman stiffened for a moment, her face frozen in an awkward look. "The who?" But she seemed to Madeline to tighten down again as, glaring at her, she declared, "Never heard of them."

According to the telephone book, there were thirty-eight Hurley families in Boston, but a good number of them, thirteen altogether, were in South Boston. To Madeline, South Boston might have been in another part of the country. She'd never been there, and knew no one who had. But it was just a neighborhood away from St. Anne's there in the South End, so she passed over the narrow, rickety bridge that separates Southie from the rest of Boston, and kept on until she reached the cluster of low, forlorn buildings that marked the center of town. Madeline parked the Opal by a tobacconist and, finding that shop too forbidding after peering in the window, stepped next door into a cheerier stationer's that didn't look too busy. She waited until two elderly customers had been served, and then tried to strike up a conversation with the young salesclerk. But she proved to live in the West End, across town, and had only been working there in Southie for a few months.

Madeline got little help from the harried greengrocer two doors down, and the men working in the garage spoke in such a thick brogue she could scarcely understand them. But one of them pointed a greased finger to the bar on the corner, the Tam-o-Shanter, one of several in the square. It was a dark, narrow, smoky place of the sort that, normally, she would never consider entering. It was like a cave to her, even in midafternoon, and there were shamrocks by the many liquor bottles up front. No other women were in evidence, only tough-looking men wearing Irish caps, and heavy jackets with the collars flipped up. The bar quieted when she came in, and she felt dozens of eyes peering out at her like rats from the shadows.

"What can I do for you this afternoon, darlin'?" the aproned bartender asked.

"Here for a poke?" someone else asked, an unshaven man with heavy eyebrows, to general guffaws.

"None of that now," the bartender admonished him with a wag of a finger.

Madeline wanted to leave. Everything about the room told her it was not a place she should have entered, and certainly not remained. But the thought of her baby froze her to the spot. "I'm looking for the Hurleys," she declared, in a voice that she hoped would sound steadier than she felt.

"Any Hurleys here?" someone shouted.

Madeline realized that the entire bar had gone dead silent; everyone was paying attention only to her.

"Guess not," the bartender said with a shrug.

"I'm looking for the son, actually. He's only six."

"That's a little young for the Tam, isn't it Dickie?" someone shouted to the barkeep. That brought another explosion of laughter, bigger than the first.

"I'll help ya, miss," came a voice, closer by, and a hand grabbed her buttock, forcing her to wheel, desperate to swat it away. But the man hung on to her, bringing himself around to face her, close up, chortling madly, as if her distress were the most amusing thing.

She whacked at his forearm with her fist. "Let go of me!"

"We don't take kindly to women here," another man shouted to her over the din.

"Unless you want to be nice, that is," added a third voice.

Madeline finally managed to push her attacker away. "I'm just trying to find a boy. I've got a package for him."

"I'll bet you do!" said another man to her left, setting off another round of laughter.

"Show us yer tits, why dontcha!"

"Oh, you men are horrid!" Madeline shouted, thinking that would shame them into some semblance of decency, but it just made them laugh all the louder and repeat that last word among themselves with great amusement. She twirled around, and hurried past the hands that were reaching for her, tearing at her. "Let me go!" she cried. She staggered outside, grateful for the rush of frigid air on her.

She gathered her skirts, straightened her coat, and trudged back to her car. She vowed that she would not cry, would not cry. Those foul men were not worth her tears. Not! She was about to turn the key when there was a tapping on her window. A face loomed up in the glass. It frightened her at first, and she reared back.

"Excuse me? Ma'am?" More tapping.

It was a young man. Not much more than a boy. His face had hardly any beard. She rolled down the window.

"Sorry about that in there," he said, tipping his head back toward the bar. "They shouldn't be like that. I can see you're a lady."

"Why, thank you," Madeline replied. "That's very kind of you to say. I appreciate that." She thought of offering him a coin. She assumed that's what he wanted, what they all wanted. But instead she just smiled politely, and was about to roll the window back up and continue on when the boy placed his gloved hand on the top of the glass.

"I know the family you mean," he told her, bending down. "The Hurleys? They're up there on C Street, by the projects. Number 112. Got a little boy there, Brendan. He's six. He's in first grade. He plays with my little brother, that's how I know. I'm sure he'd be happy to get your package or whatever it is you've got for him."

"Why, thank you." Madeline was startled by the boy's kindness. He deserved a coin, possibly even a dollar or two, and she reached into her purse for her wallet.

"No, thanks, ma'am. I don't need your money. It was just because of, you know, in there." He cocked his head toward the bar again.

"Well, thank you."

He came a little closer. "My name's Stephen, by the way." He smiled nervously.

"Thank you, Stephen."

She shook his hand, through the window. She did not tell him her name.

C Street was just three streets over, but Madeline sat in the car awhile, running the engine, wishing that the heater would do more to warm her. Finally, she composed herself and put the car into gear. She followed Stephen's directions and drove up two streets, past a pawnshop, a locksmith, and a Bible shop, and turned left on Second Street, where a stubby apartment building stood. Three streets down, the numbers reached into the hundreds. The Opal was a black, nicely rounded car, with white sidewalls. Ronald always preferred English imports to the Detroit models. He made sure it was kept spotless, even through the winter with all the slush. His fastidiousness was a virtue, she'd always thought; it represented his industry, his attention to detail. Now, seeing the rusted cars parked beside these spare, crabbed houses, she realized how conspicuous it must be. And herself in her coat, with its fur collar, and her marvelous cashmere scarf that Ronald had given her for Christmas. She was comforted by the softness, the warmth. But no wonder the men in the bar had dug their hands into her. What had she been thinking?

Madeline slowed, pulled over, let a small truck pass, trailing a black cloud of exhaust. There were three row houses here, and then a freestanding brick house, quite small, just past it, with a tiny yard blanketed by soggy snow. Was that her son's house? She parked by the first of the row houses, number 108, stepped out onto the pavement. There was a film of wetness on the road, all that was left of the snowfall two days previously; her shoes felt unsure on the pavement.

The cold air was like water; it seemed to have substance to it, heaviness that she had actively to push through. She continued along, clutching her purse. She passed a gap, not wide, before number 112. Was that her son's house? It was small and drab, with just one window on either side of the front door. A low trellis rising up on one side. For roses, possibly, although there were no branches in evidence. But that was a nice touch, a good thought. It made her feel better. The yard was protected from the street by a chain-link fence, with a swinging gate. And a metal mailbox, with "Hurley" on it.

Madeline looked at it for a long time. Was the name really Brendan? Not a name she would have chosen. Would Gerald have liked it? She breathed heavily, as she recalled her nights with Gerald. Not the hayloft, but the walk through Jamaica Plain, and the dancing. Where was he now? Was he alive, even? Was he married, with a family of his own? Did he ever get his business degree, make something of himself? How she longed to be in his arms again, dancing slow.

She retreated to her car, slid behind the wheel, waited. It was chilly, even with the windows rolled up, and her coat buttoned all the way up. A few people went by, many cars. Gradually, the light started to fade. A few kids came running with a clatter, their voices shrill, nagging. But none turned into the gate at 112. Madeline watched. She watched in the mirror, she watched through the windshield. No one turned into the gate. Until—

A little boy came along, kicking his books ahead of him in a green pouch that hung down off a long strap. He was by himself, his head down. Brendan. It had to be. *Her* Brendan. Only six, but his face was rough. She tried so hard to see Gerald in it! He wore a cap, and his pants were patched at one knee. He had no mittens, no gloves. Madeline could see his breath as he scuffed along. Brendan stopped by 112, opened the gate, and, still kicking the books, headed up the walk.

Alice

thirty-nine

"And that was my son," Mrs. Bemis said.

She was sitting by the window in that small, wooden chair, like something designed for a schoolchild. She slid a hand down behind her to soothe her stiffened back. "He was all I had. I guess I kept expecting he would rescue me somehow."

Alice's mind was swirling. It was as if a wind were blowing through it, like the one she sometimes saw tossing branches on the Concord hills, and fluttering the vines on Danzinger and Holmes. It was unsettling, these gusts, but they brought a clarity. She could see, finally, what she'd been searching for all this time—the dark, powerful truth that had propelled Mrs. Bemis to her. She'd hunted for it at the pier in Duxbury, dug for it during those frustrating sessions at Montrose. Now, here it was: the form, the colors, the movement. The truth. The pulsing heart of Mrs. Bemis's past, the place from which all her sorrows had come.

"Oh, Madeline, I'm so sorry," Alice exclaimed. "This must be so hard." She rose up from the bed where she'd been sitting. She hadn't dared interrupt before, but now she couldn't bear the thought of her alone in that tiny, stiff chair, so far from her. "Please, sit here?" She turned to gather up the pillows on the bed and mount them up for her, to make her comfortable, but there was only the one, and a meager one at that, lying at the head of the bed. "Wait a moment," Alice said, and stepped into the hall and made for the big bedroom, the one Mrs. Bemis had shared with her husband. She yanked a couple of the pillows off the bed, tucked them under her arm, and brought them back into Mrs. Bemis's bedroom. She piled them up by the headboard of Mrs. Bemis's narrow bed, and plumped them up for her with a few whacks of her hand.

"Please," Alice said, patting the spot where she wanted Mrs. Bemis to lie down.

Mrs. Bemis witnessed Alice's efforts with some amusement. "Heavens, I don't need all that," she told her.

"But I want you to be comfortable," Alice insisted. "I don't like to see you sitting there in that hard chair. Your back must be breaking!"

She came toward Mrs. Bemis to help her up. But the old woman rose on her own, her arms raised in mock surrender. "All right, my dear. If it makes you feel better." As she crossed to the bed, Alice was surprised by how easily she moved; it was as if some great burden had been lifted from her. She eased herself back amid the pillows that Alice had arranged. "There. You see? I'm reclining."

"Wonderful," Alice said.

Mrs. B sat there a moment, seeming to enjoy her perch. Then she turned and looked over at Alice. "Now, perhaps you would do *me* a favor."

"Sure. Anything."

"Sit by me here, would you?" Mrs. Bemis patted the bed beside her. "I'd like you to be comfortable, too."

Alice felt reluctance, and must have shown it. This was about Mrs. Bemis, not herself. She wasn't the patient here.

"You deserve a little something, too, don't you?" Mrs. Bemis asked. "After all this time? I know I haven't been the easiest person."

"You've been fine, Mrs. B. Really."

"Then sit with me."

There was no point in trying to resist. Alice came over, settled herself on the edge of the bed.

"No, I mean here, by me."

The bed was narrow. Alice wasn't sure there would be room. But Mrs. Bemis moved over and patted the bed beside her. Alice slipped off her tan pumps, and swung her feet around to lie back against the pillows herself, close by Mrs. B. She felt a certain peace—a joy, even— as if she were floating. And she somehow wasn't surprised when an arm came down around her.

"There," Mrs. Bemis said, giving Alice a pat. "That's better."

They sat there together for a while without speaking. Alice stared up at the ceiling, thinking about how Mrs. Bemis must have stared up there, night after night, as she waited for sleep. And that made her think of solitude, and need, and sorrow. That brought her to the Grand.

"You remind me of my grandmother sometimes," Alice began. She told her how she'd thought of the Grand that first time she'd seen Mrs. Bemis at Filene's.

"Another aging beauty?"

"She died yesterday."

"Oh, I *am* sorry," Mrs. Bemis said, with great conviction. "You should have said something. Oh, that's awful." She shifted around to address Alice directly. "You shouldn't have let me go on and on. I'm surprised you paid any attention to me at all."

"She had Alzheimer's," Alice told her. "She'd been in a 'unit' for three years. If you think Montrose is horrible, you should have seen it. The Monhegan Center for the Aged. Talk about dreary."

Alice described the Grand's voice, which had always had a wonderful lift to it, the bright dresses she wore, the elaborate costumes she helped make for Halloween. Talking this way to Mrs. B had the quality of a dream, the lightness, the floating. And the room there, where Alice had never been before, and smaller than she would have expected. With blue walls that reminded her of the color of her own bedroom, growing up.

"It's never easy," Mrs. Bemis said.

"The funeral's tomorrow. I'll be leaving early in the morning."

"Well, it's good of you to make time for me," Mrs. Bemis said. "I've enjoyed my visit here."

"You still want to burn the place down?"

"No." She gave a wry smile. "At least, not at the moment."

Quietness all around, except for the click of Pete's shears.

"We both have our secrets, don't we?" Mrs. Bemis said finally.

"Everyone does."

"I've never told anyone about Brendan, you know. Not even Dr. de Frieze. And I told him absolutely everything else." She took a breath. "For a while, a long while, I lived through Brendan. I told you how I watched him wrestle one time. But I did more than that. I used to drive by his house. I went several times to his church. I needed him so much."

"There's nothing wrong with that," Alice assured her.

"But I've failed him!"

"You did what you could. Please, Mrs. B, don't talk that way."

"No?" Mrs. Bemis pulled her arm back and climbed off the bed to pick up the large black album off its small table. "Take a look. It's what I've been meaning to show you." She handed the book to Alice.

It reminded her of a family Bible, it was so large and imposing, with its black-leather cover.

"It's all I have of him," Mrs. Bemis said.

Alice ran her hands over the leather. "You sure you want me to—?"

"Go on, open it. He's *our* secret now."

The album seemed so solid. It lent a certain heft to the image of Brendan as a little boy scuffling along the sidewalk. Alice opened the cover, the edge scraping across her shirt.

The first page was blank—just black paper, with filmy tissue paper over it.

"I didn't know how to start," Mrs. Bemis said, sitting down beside Alice as she leafed through. "I didn't have much, you see. There were so few . . . things."

Alice turned the next page. Still nothing. Alice looked up at Mrs. Bemis.

"It starts further on."

Alice turned a couple more pages, then another, and here, when she pulled back the tissue paper, she discovered a gum wrapper. Somewhat scuffed and crumpled, with a few bits of the corner missing. Alice looked up at her patient.

"He dropped it that day, when I first saw him," Mrs. Bemis said. "It wasn't much, I know. But I thought I'd keep it. I kept it in my dresser for a long time, toward the back. I liked to think of him chewing that gum. Blowing bubbles. I liked to think of him happy."

Alice turned the page. A yellowed snapshot of a small house, somewhat blurred, with icicles dripping from the doorway. "That's Brendan's house. I took the picture from my car, since I didn't want anyone to see. Didn't turn out too well, but it's the only one I have." Another blank page, then a newspaper clipping, almost brown with age, mentioning the name of Brendan Hurley in a Little League game. "I'd come around the neighborhood to see if I could catch a glimpse of him. Actually, I missed him that day. But I was thumbing through the neighborhood paper, and I found that. He played for a team called the Bombers. I saw him play once, a year or two later. I took a photograph." She flipped to the next page for Alice. The photo was taken from behind a chain-link fence, and it showed several boys, their faces shaded by their oversize caps, out in the field. "That's Brendan there." She touched a finger down on the disheveled right fielder, his shirttail out. Then a pressed dandelion, dried and whitened with age. "That was from their lawn. I could just reach it through the chain-link fence. I'd been waiting for a couple of hours, hoping to see him. I wanted to have *something*." A sheet from the *South Boston High School News* detailing how "B. Hurley," which was underlined in pen, had gotten a single in Tuesday's game against Boston English. Then a small, boxed account of the prospects for the wrestlers' coming season, saying that Brendan Hurley "will not, unfortunately, be wrestling for us this winter." Alice looked up at Mrs. Bemis, who shrugged. "I never found out why. His grades, I suspect."

Alice flipped through the next few pages, but the rest were all blank. "That's all?"

Mrs. Bemis nodded. "Pathetic, isn't it? That's what I mean. I have almost nothing of him."

Alice reached out to her, held her hand. "You have your love," she said.

"But nothing came of it," Mrs. Bemis replied, shaking her head. "I hardly ever saw him."

"He never came to your house?"

"Only once." Mrs. Bemis's face started to fall. "Oh, Alice, this is so difficult for me."

Alice stroked her hand, drew it to her lap. "It will be all right."

"Brendan was terribly needy. I was so eager to give that it took me a while to recognize it. But he was. I suppose he was unstable. Now they'd call it ADD or one of those. He never did well in school, was always getting into trouble. I heard . . . things. I blamed myself. Any problems he must have suffered were my fault. I felt obliged to make it up to him."

Sitting by her, Alice held Mrs. Bemis's hand tightly, and looked into her eyes. "I need to ask you something. Now, you don't have to answer, but—did he know who you were?"

She shook her head slowly. "He never asked. Maybe because he was so young when I started. Only six. He started to think of me as someone who had always been there. A guardian angel." She smiled. "That's what he called me once, in one of the few times we actually conversed. He didn't say it very nicely, either. Brendan was always inclined to be gruff. But that was the phrase he used."

"So you never explained who you were?"

Mrs. Bemis sighed. "Who I was," she said softly. "Who I was."

"I only meant—"

"I *know* what you meant." Mrs. Bemis withdrew her hand to smooth out the last tissue, which was somewhat crumpled on the album's page, and then gently shut the album. "I was his mother, but I wasn't. I was no one to him."

"But you gave him life."

"Some life." She stood up, put the album back on the table where it had been.

Alice thought of her own mother, always so preoccupied with her own worries, scarcely a mother to her, leaving the Grand to fill that role, with her amusements, her cheer.

"But —tell me, would you?—did he ever suspect, do you think?"

Mrs. Bemis shook her head. "No." She took a breath. "I should be grateful for that, I suppose."

"Why?"

"So that he never knew how I'd failed him." Mrs. Bemis moved on to the window. "But the number of times I thought about him. Here in this house, or out in the garden. But I had to keep him to myself. There was Ronald to consider, of course." She turned back to Alice, resting her hand against the sill. "Brendan became a drinker, you know. Never could hold a job. He fought with people. With his fists! I saw it once. He was in a bad phase. I was trying to keep an eye on him—from a distance, you see. He was down at the piers, and he slugged someone in the face. There was blood. It was horrible. He'd drunk himself silly. He staggered off and passed out in an alley. It was a cold night. Winter. A snowstorm was coming. I couldn't just leave him. So I had Pete bring him to me here. This was four or five years ago. He slept over there, across the hall." She pointed through the doorway. "He wet the bed. Absolutely soaked the mattress with his urine. But I gave him breakfast in the morning. He had a prodigious appetite, I'll say that much. I took him for a walk in the garden. He loved it. He was very impressed with what he called my swimming pool." She smiled.

Alice tried to picture the man she'd seen in the photographs stretched out on the narrow bed across the hall. She thought of the clothes he must have been wearing, the greasy hair. "And he never asked why you brought him here?"

Mrs. Bemis shook her head. "I was his guardian angel. That was enough for him."

"And when he died—"

"Pete told me. Terrible."

"That's when you ended up at Filene's."

Mrs. Bemis looked up in surprise. "Yes, of course. You were there." She sighed again. "I must have been wandering. My mother used to go there, you know. Every August, for her linens." Her face hardened again. "Oh, I don't know, Alice! All I remember feeling is the emptiness. A great, windy emptiness inside me, as if everything I was had been removed and there was just nothing left."

"I'm glad I found you."

Finally a smile. "So am I."

The evening had come on by now, and Alice knew that she needed to drive Mrs. Bemis back to Montrose for the night. Mrs. Bemis stood up with a sigh, closed the black album, and returned it to its place beside her bed. On their way to the stairs, Mrs. Bemis pointed out the little-used sewing room, and two other small bedrooms beside it. "These were always meant to be for children," she told Alice. She led Alice down the front stairs to the living room again where Mrs. Bemis took a moment to show Alice the piano that had always been in her parents' house. It had photographs of the Adamses on top of it, standing beside the family Studebaker. Mrs. Bemis's father wore a hat that darkened his eyes, his wife was in a pale dress beside him, her face a blank. "That was just before her own visit to Montrose," Mrs. Bemis said.

There was a small case on the piano, too. Alice thought it might be a music box. "That was Ronnie's," Mrs. Bemis told Alice. "Go ahead. Open it."

The box was light, and quite ornate. She tipped up the lid and found blue velvet inside, with a lock of brown hair lying upon it.

"That's the bit of my hair he took with him to England," Mrs. Bemis explained. "He kept it with him in the hospital, said it helped him get well." She took the box from Alice, set it back down on the piano. "He'd always had it in a little envelope, but he put it in this box for my fiftieth birthday."

"Sweet," Alice said.

"Ronnie had his sentimental side." Mrs. Bemis looked at Alice. "But it was not often in view."

Evening had fallen. It was well past the time that Alice had assured Dr. Maris that she would bring Mrs. Bemis back to the hospital. Still, before they left, Mrs. Bemis insisted on taking Alice for a quick walk about the grounds that meant so much to her. Pete had retired to the carriage house by now. So they were alone as Mrs. Bemis led Alice down past the grape arbor, under the pergola, by the lapping fountain, and out toward the stone bench under the copper beech where she and Mrs. Randall had often stopped for a smoke. In the darkness, Alice could barely make out the flowers that were clustered all about them. She had the feeling that she was wading through a sea of plants, some of them lying in low pools, others cresting into waves, but Mrs. Bemis seemed to be able to see each blossom in a bright light and she pointed out the ageratum, the Madonna lilies, the peonies, as if they were family members, although to Alice these few blooms were merely shades of gray. "There's a bit of heliotrope over there," Mrs. B said with a gesture toward a low, hooded plant, its head drooping. "They're done now, of course. But the roses are still doing well. I just love them, don't you? They're like suns—and so persistent." She bent down to a rosebud, cupped a hand about it as if being reunited with an old friend. "It was always the saddest thing when fall rolled around, and the frost came, and the last of the chrysanthemums started to fade. I had to beg Ronnie for my greenhouse. I told him my life depended on it. He finally relented. He wasn't a bad man. There, you see?" Mrs.

Bemis pointed to the greenhouse off the back of the kitchen. "That got me through many a winter. I grew my orchids in there. Do you want to see?"

It was very late, but Alice couldn't refuse. The door was unlocked, and it opened with a squeal of hinges. Alice at first noticed only the humid warmth. But then Mrs. Bemis pulled the chain to blink on the fluorescent lights overhead, and Alice could see before her a flock of brightly colored heads poking up out of clay pots. A long, giddy array, dozens and dozens of orchids, all different: some spiky, others nearly cloudlike wisps of white, and still others fat gobs of color. And such a range of hues—chocolate browns, radiant yellows, gaudy purples. Stripes, dots, swatches. Alice nearly laughed, there were so many.

"There are rather a lot, I suppose," Mrs. Bemis said sheepishly. "But once I got started, I found it very difficult to stop. Orchids are seductive, that's their secret. Mrs. Randall was a genius with them. I saw hers, and I wanted my own. I'm so sorry she didn't live to see this. A few of these are hers—the one over there, *Dendrobium unicum.*" She pronounced the Latin with a bit of flare as she gestured toward a plant with five blades the color of orange sherbet and a veiny head. "From Laos, of all places. Very rare. Devil of a thing to keep alive." She turned back to her left. "And that yellow delight. Just like a pansy, isn't it? But look at the subtlety of that yellow." Mrs. Bemis took Alice by the hand. "Now, come along. This one here is the real prize." She led Alice down the aisle, past rows of dabbed color, to an orchid that seemed to be a pair of fairy slippers, tiny pink ones, trailing a long, twisted strand of the same color. "*Phragmipedium caudatum,*" Mrs. Bemis said proudly. "I've never seen another, except in photographs. Lovely, isn't it?"

At first, Alice was too stunned to speak, there was so much to take in. "They're glorious," she said finally. "Absolutely glorious. I've never seen anything like them."

"Pollinating insects creep up that long shoot there," Mrs. Bemis explained, pointing out the long, twisted petals that dangled clear to the soil below. "And slip into that tiny pouch there," she added, nearly touching one of the pink slippers. "Oh, the furtiveness of love," she quietly told Alice. "The way it sneaks into your heart, when you're least expecting it."

"That night of yours in the hay barn?" Alice asked. "Is that what you're thinking of?"

"Heavens no." She turned to Alice. "I was thinking of you."

"Me?"

"Yes, I want you to take it, would you?"

"Oh, I couldn't."

"Of course you can. You have a bathroom, don't you?"

Alice nodded.

"Well, leave it there. It will get plenty of moisture. Water it once a week. And keep it away from the light. Things that are beautiful can never bear the light."

At Montrose, they returned well after dinner had been served, but Mrs. Bemis said she wasn't hungry. Marnie acted a little huffy to see Mrs. Bemis return so late, but Dr. Maris, who was working late in his office, was not concerned. For her part, Mrs. Bemis herself was tired after their long "excursion," as she termed it, and asked if she could skip the usual evening meetings and go straight to bed. Alice told her that would be fine, and she helped Mrs. Bemis down the corridor to her room. She stepped inside with her for a moment. Mrs. B's big suitcase was still there in the corner, all packed, just as she'd left it. As Mrs. Bemis settled herself for a moment on the bed, Alice took her hand, and then leaned down to her patient. After a quick glance back into the doorway, to make sure no one was about, she planted a quick kiss on the side of Mrs. Bemis's face. "Good night," she told her.

"Good night, dear," Mrs. Bemis replied, her eyes alight. "It was a wonderful trip, wasn't it?"

forty

Back in her apartment, Alice set the orchid down on a
small table away from the window in the bathroom, just as Mrs.
Bemis had recommended. The plant looked magical there, a bit of
Pre-Raphaelite whimsy, with its delicate pinks. She was still keyed
up after her day with Mrs. Bemis, and Fido seemed antsy, too.
While she tried to set down the results of this long, remarkable day
for her files, Fido kept racing on his treadmill, which finally
annoyed her so much she parked him in the closet. She tore through
page after page of her yellow pad as she wrote about Mrs. Bemis's
secret lover (whom she carefully identified only as "G"), the home
for "unweds," the loveless marriage, the discovery of Brendan.
When she was done, she released Fido from his jail and perched
him on her shoulder while she looked in at the orchid in the bathroom one last time.

Still, she went to bed very uneasily, and tossed about under the
covers for an hour or two until she finally nodded off—only to dream

of Brendan lobbing rocks through Mrs. Bemis's greenhouse windows. She awoke with a start, and called LeBeau.

He sounded groggy when he finally picked up. "Yeah?" he said.

"It's me."

"What time is it?"

"Late. Listen, I want you to meet me at the Howard Johnson's on the expressway tomorrow morning at nine, all right?"

"Wait—*what?*"

"Just be there, nine o'clock, Howard Johnson's on the expressway."

At first light, Alice was in her car, heading for Milton. It was well before eight when she arrived. The morning light gave a shine to the copper beech out front, and made the house itself glow like something out of a dream. Pete Needham must have been working in the garden, because he came around to her car from the far side of the house. "Oh, it's you again," he said. "Thought it'd be the missus."

Alice might have offered some words of explanation, but Pete never even asked. "Go on in if you want, door's unlocked."

The big front door felt heavy and stiff when she pulled it open. The hall was open and airy; its sparkling woodwork entranced her, pulled her in. She smelled the freshness of the house as she climbed the stairs, each step creaking underneath her. She stepped past the other doorways, each of which seemed to invite her in, and returned to Mrs. Bemis's little blue bedroom. The spread was mussed where they'd lay down on it together; the extra pillows remained out, against the headboard. The book was on the table, just where they'd left it. She moved to it, ran her hands over its cover, then opened it up and scanned its pages, searching, again, for pictures of the boy. There were only two good, clear ones, and the better of the two was the scene from Little League. What was he—eleven, twelve? She searched the face, the wide mouth, firm brow, plump nose. There was so little of Mrs. Bemis in him. Absolutely none of her refinement, her precision, her clarity. Was he——? She almost couldn't even think the words. So little connected them. Just Bridget saying the Hurleys, then that boy Stephen pointing to Brendan.

Was he hers?

There was light, brightness, as Alice rose, left the room, and descended the stairs once more.

In the living room, the morning light was streaming in from the garden. A dappled light, coming through the trees. And it fell on the tapestry covering the lacquered finish of the baby grand piano, where the little, inlaid box was still out from the evening before. She stepped toward it, her heels silenced by the wide oriental rug. She laid her hands lightly upon the box, opened it. This time, she noticed a slim bit of paper tucked into one edge, beside the lock of hair. Alice teased it out. It was a tiny envelope, much crumpled, and smudged from dirty hands. How often Ronald must have opened it to slide the hundreds of tiny hairs onto his palm, shift them this way and that with his finger, and then slip them back inside again.

She looked again at the hairs themselves on their velvet tuft. They were darling, with their reddish highlights. Mrs. Bemis must have been so pretty, so radiant, when she was young.

Alice scooped a few of the hairs into a sandwich bag she'd brought along, and carefully folded down the lip.

Frank was standing beside his car when she pulled into the Howard Johnson lot. He was looking a bit put out.

"Thanks, Frank, for coming."

"No problem."

Alice stroked his chest for a moment, absentmindedly. Then she reached into her handbag and pulled out the sandwich bag for him.

His eyes did all the asking.

"It's some of Mrs. Bemis's hair. From when she was a teenager. But the DNA's still the same."

He looked at it, then at her.

"Run it, would you please?" She handed him the plastic bag.
"Compare it with Brendan Hurley's."

"Alice—"

"I need to know, okay?"

"Alice—"

"I just do!"

On the flight down, Alice's plane veered wide over Massachusetts
Bay, the blue water on this nearly cloudless afternoon rippling like
fish scales. She saw again how immense it was, a sparkling ocean all
of its own, stretching from Boston, with its stubby high-rises, out to
the tip of the Cape, barely visible in the shimmering light. And
somewhere down there, two men had gone for a sail in a Laser . . .

The service would be at the grave site at three. She'd planned to
go straight there. The Grand was so much on her mind, she couldn't
think of seeing her family until she'd gotten through the service.
Even in the best of times, she had to settle herself before she saw
everyone. Maybe it was being the youngest, but it was important for
her to seem strong, in charge, on top of things. Anything but fretful
and distracted, which was how she'd be if she saw them now.

It was normally an hour's drive to Latrobe, but construction on
Route 30 slowed her down, and it was past three by the time she
pulled her rental car into the Forest Lawn cemetery, off Meadow
Avenue on the far side of Latrobe. She was frustrated with herself for
being late, for not planning things better. Still, it settled her to see
the all-concrete Willard Elementary, where she'd gone as a child.
The jungle gym—banned from most playgrounds—was still there,
by the picket fence where her friend Debbie had nearly impaled herself after slipping one rainy recess. The cemetery was tightly
bounded by a wrought-iron fence, shaded by a few scraggly spruces,
and backed up against several of the weathered houses that made up
the bulk of Latrobe real estate.

The Grand had brought Alice here a few times to picnic by her husband's grave site, and they'd once played Frisbee until the groundskeeper had shooed them off. Now, a hearse was parked along the narrow drive by the family plot, and a young minister whom Alice did not recognize was intoning by the open grave, with the Grand's glossy casket up on a catafalque beside it. The Grand had been a loyal member of the First Presbyterian Church until she'd moved to the Alzheimer's unit, but that was several years ago. Alice's mother stood by the casket. She was veiled, with a broad black hat, which tipped up as if the wind had caught it when Alice came along. Below the flapping veil, Alice could see the corners of her mouth curved down in sadness as she glanced up at her daughter, but she said nothing, and then tipped her head down once more. Her father, in a dark, rumpled suit, managed a grim smile at Alice. She grasped his arm and took her place beside him, squeezing in beside her sister, whose eyes were as lively as ever, but Alice noticed that her hair was flecked with gray. Alice's two brothers were bunched to Carla's left, along with their children. The younger of her brothers, Danny, the tae kwon do instructor, had dyed his hair orange, which was a shock. Other relatives stood behind them, along with several friends of her grandmother's whom Alice recognized, like George Ebbitt, who ran the local playhouse, and Chrissie Baker from the library.

The minister read several prayers from the prayer book, and he gave what seemed to Alice to be an all-purpose eulogy, praising the Grand as a bedrock of the community. Her father spoke on behalf of the family. Since when had he been so old? After clearing his throat several times, he told the story of meeting the Grand for the first time after he'd started dating her daughter. "I was a little intimi-dated by her, of course," Alice's dad said, his hands in his pockets, his gaze down. "You all remember how she could be. But she put me right at home. Offered me a beer, actually. Seemed to think I might need it." That got a chuckle out of the small assemblage. "I know that we're all really going to miss her." When he was finished, the minister asked if anyone else would like to say a few words.

Alice had not planned on speaking, but she didn't think that the

Grand's life should be left at that. She thought surely that the Grand's younger brother, Alice's great-uncle Timothy, would speak up for her. But he was there with his walker, and may not have felt he had the strength. Her mother stared down at the casket, lost in thought. She caught the eye of her own siblings, all of them older, but it was clear they had no intention of speaking. Heart pounding, Alice asked if she could add a few words.

"Please," the minister said, opening a hand to her.

Alice stepped forward, went to the casket and laid her hand down on the varnished wood. It was instinctive to touch it, just as Alice would have touched the Grand herself when they'd greeted each other. With a kiss, usually, and a hug, and then, often, the Grand would run her hand along Alice's shoulder and down her arm, saying how wonderful she looked. The joy on the Grand's face when she said that! She hadn't thought that a simple gesture like touching the Grand's casket would affect her, but the coldness of the wood got to her, and she could feel the tears well up. She dug in her handbag for her Kleenex pack, managed to fish out a tissue to swipe across her eyes while she tried to calm herself. It was impossible to speak, almost impossible to breathe. The young minister came over to her, asked if she'd like him to take over. Annoyed, she waved him away. Still, her heart was thumping so loudly she could scarcely think.

"I just wanted to say—" Alice began, finally. "I'm sorry." She blew her nose. "I'm not used to doing this." A bit of humor rose up through the gloom. "If you can't tell." She tapped gently on the casket. "*She* always knew just what to say." Alice looked out at the faces of the mourners, softened now. "She could size up just about any situation, and know exactly what to say, or what to do. Like when she got me to stop sucking my thumb. You remember this, Carla?" She looked out at her sister, who shook her head. "I must have been nine or ten. I'd sucked my thumb forever, and I didn't think I could ever stop. I didn't want to, to tell you the truth. The Grand came into our house for dinner one night, and I was sucking my thumb—and she started sucking hers. I was so embarrassed! For *her!* I never sucked my thumb again. She had a touch, that's all I'm saying." Alice paused, tried to think. "If it weren't for her, I'd never have thought that the old and the young could understand each other. Their ways are too different. But the Grand showed me that age doesn't matter. Nothing matters. Except, well, except for love. Only love matters." She looked around, felt the silence, balled up the Kleenex in her hand.

When she returned to the others, her sister reached over to give her arm a squeeze.

After the burial service, Alice told her father she wanted to be alone with the Grand one last time, and he trudged on with the rest of the family to their cars. The minister stood beside Alice for a few minutes. She could smell his cologne as he spoke to her about the mystery of death. But then he finally realized that she simply wanted to be left alone, and he strode back to his car, too.

The cemetery was small, but it seemed large once it was only Alice there. The Grand's casket had been settled down into its hollow grave, but it was covered only by the few handfuls of dirt that the mourners had thrown in. Alice got down on her knees on the grass beside it.

She wished, as she closed her eyes, that she believed in God. As a child, she had thought there had to be a Big Someone up in the clouds, arms extended, a brilliant light in His eyes. But that conviction had faded with age, and the only feelings of any Almighty lay in Alice's respect for the vastness of time, the endless stretching out of it. And it was into that infinite ocean that death had plunged the Grand.

Or was it, Alice wondered, really that bleak? Perhaps something of the Grand did remain here with her. After her long life, the Grand had left ripples. No, more than that. Waves. Alice felt them moving through her. A certain spark, an instinct, a feeling. A touch, perhaps?

Alice squeezed her eyes shut so tightly that she saw, not black, but pink.

"You were always her favorite, you know," her mother told Alice. They were in the kitchen together, her mother up on a stepladder to reach for some more wineglasses from the top shelf of the pantry cabinet. The other family members and friends from town had been drinking for an hour now, and the stories were getting louder in the other room. But Alice's eyes were on her mother, the pinched mouth, the sadness she carried.

"I sometimes thought that you loved her more than me," her mother said.

"Oh, Mom," Alice said. She reached out, slid her hand across her mother's back.

Her mother twisted away from her. "It's true, though. I have thought that." The way she looked at Alice, Alice could tell that her mother still thought it. "I don't think you have any idea what it's like, either."

"It's not like that," Alice said. "It's not a competition."

"Well, that's what it felt like. I kept feeling that I came in second, or third—or last. And I was always trying so hard!"

"I know you were, Mom."

She dropped her voice. "Your father's started on the pills again. The antidepressants? They've made a big difference."

"I'm glad."

A look of disgust. "Oh, you say that, but I feel like it's a professional talking."

"Mom, what do you want from me?"

Her mother got down from the stepladder, reached for a tray under the countertop. "Just—just take this, would you please?" She pushed the tray into Alice's hands while she loaded the glasses onto it, two at a time. "There, that's helping me. That's what I want from you. Just a little help occasionally."

"I've always tried to."

"Have you?" her mother asked. Then, turning her back to her daughter, she climbed up onto the stepladder again to get some other things down.

Alice spotted her old friend Debbie in the living room. She still lived in Latrobe, although she'd long since moved from the house next door. Debbie gave Alice a big hug, quickly filled her in on the essentials. She was married, with sixteen-month-old triplets. "I don't know quite how it happened, either," she told Alice with a shrug. She told Alice how sorry she was about her grandmother, and then said that she hadn't been at all surprised that she'd gone into psychiatry. "You always seemed to be able to see into people," Debbie told her.

"I wish," Alice replied, then confided about her conversation with her mother.

"Maybe that's just her way of being sad about her mother," Debbie reassured her.

"Or being mad at me."

"Oh stop," Debbie said, and she flicked out a hand onto Alice's shoulder, just as she had when they were best friends.

There was a dinner that night at a local hotel, the Wildemott. By this time, people were speaking less of the Grand and more of their own lives, and those of their children, and troubles at the high school, and the big mess in Washington. And Alice had started to think of Mrs. Bemis, back at Montrose. She nearly called to see how she was doing before she realized that that was silly. It had been only a few hours.

Alice sat with one of the Grand's nurses at the unit, who told Alice how, even in the advanced stages of her disease, her grandmother had always lit up whenever Alice's name was mentioned.

Afterward, Carla came up to her and grabbed her by the arm. "Come over here," she insisted, hustling her into a small, quiet sitting room off the front hall. "I've hardly seen you all day."

Alice started to explain that she'd been caught up with other guests, but she could tell that her sister had had too much to drink, and there wasn't much point in going into it.

"You all right?" Alice asked.

Carla nodded toward their mother, back in the dining room. "I'd be better if it weren't for her."

"I know what you mean," Alice told her.

"This whole family is really fucked up," Carla said.

Alice nodded. "Yeah."

"You always knew that, didn't you?"

"I don't know what I knew."

Carla laughed, a boozy sort of laugh. "Danny and Jeff are scared of you, you know."

"Oh?"

"Being a headshrinker. They think you're on to them."

"But they're family."

"All the more reason." A new, shrewd look came over Carla. "Besides, it seems like your family's up in Concord, at that place."

"It's called Montrose."

"Maybe we should *all* go there. Whaddya say, sis?" And then she started to laugh.

Alice checked her watch before she finally went to bed in her old bedroom back at her family's house. Past two. She'd thought Frank would have called by now. She nearly called him, but figured it was too late. She climbed into bed and, exhausted, dropped quickly off to sleep—only to be awakened by a loud knock on the door maybe an hour later. It was her sister, who had a glass in her hand. "Telephone."

Alice sat up in bed, her heart pounding.

"Guy named Frank. Boyfriend?"

"You sound like Mom," Alice said hurriedly as she pulled her robe around her and went downstairs to the kitchen phone.

"Sorry to wake you," Frank told her. "But I thought you'd want to know."

"What is it, Frank? Tell me."

"The lab just finished its work. Guy there, Joey, stayed late for me. Super nice of him."

"And?"

"No match." He paused. "No, check that. Joey said there was a .00001 chance that Madeline Bemis was related to Brendan."

"He's not her son, you mean."

"That's about the size of it."

"Oh, God."

"You were right to question it, that's for sure."

Alice settled herself down on the long bench her parents had by the wall phone, and tried to think where that left them.

"Confused," Frank said. "At least I am." He tried to work it backward, to figure out what made Madeline think that Brendan was her son.

Alice told him Mrs. Bemis's long story from yesterday about Bridget and the adoption agency.

"And she's remembering this right?"

"Considering she's a lunatic, you mean?"

"Hey, easy there. Just asking. Under the circumstances, it's a reasonable question."

"Well, the answer is yes. I believe she's been telling me the truth."

He paused for a second. "Okay, here's what I'd do. I'd start by making a list of all the people in her life who might know."

While Frank stayed on the line, Alice jotted down names on a sheet of paper by the phone. There was Bridget, of course. But there were others Mrs. Bemis had mentioned: her in-laws; Gerald; that old friend of hers, Ellen; the girls from the home in Colorado; the women in her kaffeeklatsch at Milton. "Mrs. Bemis didn't mention many people," Alice said. "She's never had a lot of close friends."

"Keep thinking."

Alice tried, but she kept circling back to Bridget. She'd written the name in capital letters right at the top of the list, and now she underlined it with a couple of bold lines as she realized how central Bridget had been to Mrs. Bemis's story. Bridget had taken the baby from the birthing room, had placed him up for adoption, had directed Mrs. Bemis to the Hurleys. "Bridget was in the middle of everything," Alice said.

"That's the maid?"

"Hm-mmm."

"Look, what are you trying to accomplish here?" Frank asked.

"I told you, I need to know what happened."

Frank exhaled into the receiver, said nothing for a moment. "All right, then maybe you should have a talk with her. That's what I'd do."

"But I'm not even sure if she's alive."

"You got a last name?

"Shaughnessy, I think she said. Mrs. Bemis told me she'd moved to Chicago after leaving their place in Dover when Mrs. Bemis was in her twenties. And she's seventy-six now. So—"

"Bridget Shaughnessy from Chicago. Okay. Well, that's a start."

Frank called back an hour later. Alice had dozed off by the phone, and it rang twice before she was able to think to pick it up. In her dream, it was a burglar alarm.

"There's a Bridget Shaughnessy in a Chicago suburb called Oak Park. A low-income place there for the elderly. Date of birth May 16, 1918, which would make her—what?—eighty-four? I ran her Social Security number, and that kicked out her employment history. She worked in Dover, Massachusetts, for thirteen years, until 1952. She returned to Massachusetts for a few years in the eighties, but she's been back in Chicago ever since. "I think you just got lucky."

• • •

Alice had planned to take the two o'clock back to Boston, but she called the airline to rework her return by way of Chicago. She'd have to fly standby, which meant getting to the airport no later than six. At five-fifteen she came into the kitchen to grab some cereal before the flight back. It was dark out still, but the light was on in the kitchen. She found her mother at the kitchen table, coffee cup in hand.

"You're up early," her mother said. Puffy-eyed, she looked as if she hadn't slept at all.

"I've got to get back."

"Now?" Her mother looked up in alarm.

"Something's come up."

"Oh, all those phone calls last night?"

Alice nodded.

"Something's come up here," her mother replied irritably. "If you didn't notice."

Alice wished she didn't have to have this conversation, wished she could just slip away. "I'm sorry, but this is something I've just got to do right now." She'd set her bag down by the door, and she went over to it now.

Her mother pushed her fingers into her closed eyes.

"The Grand would want me to."

"Abandon us?"

"That's *not* what I'm doing. Look, I can't explain it. But I'm doing this for her."

"By leaving?"

"No. By helping. I am helping, Mother. It's my job."

Alice gave her mother a hug, told her she'd come back soon for a longer visit, full of explanations of everything she was doing. She *promised*. She asked her to say good-bye to everyone. But her mother wasn't looking at her when she went out the door.

forty-one

*O*n the plane, Alice tried to lose herself in the in-flight magazine, but the wheezy profiles of fading celebrities didn't grab her. She downed two cups of black coffee to shake her sleepiness, then turned to the clouds outside the window. Around her, everyone else was bent over their paperbacks, or tuned out, listening to their headsets, but Alice stared out at the great puffs of white, trying to let her mind go blank.

She should not be here, should not be doing this, flying to Chicago. As groggy as she was, every time she returned to this fact, she felt a chill on her shoulders and the back of her neck. A trip like this, on the spur of the moment, was, well, it was crazy. She couldn't afford it, for one—$1,324, including airport taxes; it was nearly a month's rent, and that did not include the rental car. And even if she could find her way to Oak Park, who knew if Bridget Shaughnessy would be there?

She'd left her own family for this?

• • •

The heavy-jowled lady at the rental-car desk gave Alice instructions to Oak Park and highlighted the route on a map. The car proved to be a tiny Chevrolet without the power steering she was used to, and the buttons on the radio were tuned to religious stations. As she followed the signs to the interstate, she was conscious of the wide sky overhead. But the traffic thinned once she turned onto 147 north, and on the still narrower 302, with its regular traffic lights, she was feeling proud to be way out there in the Midwest on her own. She pulled in to a Mobil station for directions to 111 Sparks Street, where Bridget Shaughnessy's Manor House was, and a few minutes later she was turning in by a wooden sign on a chain-link fence, bearing the words "Manor House" in large blue letters.

The building was a giant block of mud-colored brick, studded with rattling air-conditioning units. The parking lot was half full, and it bristled with towering security stansions that, in the early afternoon, sent shadows over the surrounding cars. Alice felt the sun on her head, and through the padded shoulders of her jacket when she stepped out of her rental. Even with her sunglasses, she had to shade her eyes to find the main entrance: it was off to the right, by a flagpole from which no flag flew. Her handbag hanging off her shoulder, Alice sidled between the cars to the walkway leading to the glass door. Inside, in the cool foyer, there were a few older people checking their mail, and a massive, bald-headed man glided by in a motorized wheelchair. Alice approached the receptionist behind the counter.

"I'm looking for Bridget Shaughnessy," Alice declared.

The woman's face was all glasses. "Who'd you say, hon?"

Alice repeated the name, afraid her quest was hopeless after all.

"Oh, she's up on three." She gave Alice a hard look. "She expecting you?"

"Not right now, no. I'm a family friend. From Massachusetts. I'm out here on business, you see, and I thought I'd say hello." She hoped she didn't sound duplicitous.

"Your name?"

"It's Madeline Bemis." Her heart banged in her chest. "B-E-M-I-S."

"Hold on a second, there, please, and let me call up."

After consulting a sheet, the receptionist pressed a few buttons on the phone while Alice waited, trying to slow her heartbeat.

"Bridget, dear," the receptionist said. "We have a Madeline Bemis down here at the desk." Pause.

"Friend of yours from Massachusetts, she says."

Pause.

"Well, she's here. Can I send her up?"

A longer pause. Alice felt pulled, as she had on the highway when the big trucks passed.

Finally, the woman set down the receiver and turned her eyes to Alice. "Well, Madeline, you surprised *her* pretty good. You can go on up. Elevator's there on your right. Third floor, like I said. Room 312."

Alice thanked the woman and proceeded to the waiting elevator. The mirror inside it was cracked, splitting the image of herself as she peered at it to straighten her hair and smooth out the front of her jacket. Two flights up, the doors lurched open. The narrow hallway was poorly lit, and had soiled carpeting and artificial air. It reminded Alice of the cheap motels her family had stayed in on their rare vacations. Room 312 bore the initials B.S. in kelly green, along with a postcard view of Ireland's Dingle Bay. Alice knocked. The door swung open, and a stout, ash-gray woman in a wrinkled dress stood facing her. The face sagged with age, but the pupils were hard as she stared at Alice, obviously trying to square her with the image of the elderly woman she was expecting. Or did she actually see something of the younger Mrs. Bemis in her? Of Maddy, as she was then called? Alice tried to think how old Mrs. Bemis had been when Bridget left. Twenty-five, maybe twenty-six? Almost exactly Alice's age now.

"Wait a moment," the old Irish woman said. "You're not—"

"No, but Madeline sent me," Alice interrupted, reaching out a hand to the door before Bridget could shut it on her. "I should have said so downstairs. It's—well, it's a little complicated."

"Then who are you, exactly?" Bridget's eyes were locked on Alice's face.

"I'd rather not discuss this in the hall."

More aggressive now: "What, she sick?"

"Please, Miss Shaughnessy. May I come inside?" Alice pushed the door open slightly. She expected resistance, but Bridget yielded, curious, perhaps, or simply weak.

"Just for a moment," Bridget said reluctantly, and with some irritation. Unused, perhaps, to losing arguments.

The hallway led past a spare kitchen, then a narrow dining area, and a sitting room with just a few sticks of ill-padded furniture that were oriented toward a TV. The walls were heavy with photographs that underscored the room's eerie stillness. Snapshots, mostly. But a few formal portraits, freeze-framed. Through the slivers of light admitted by the venetian blinds, Alice picked up a view of the balcony of an adjoining building, blazing in the bright light.

"Well, isn't this nice," Alice said, trying to change the tone of the conversation.

Bridget's eyes had not left her. "Who are you?"

"I'm Alice Matthews." She reached out a hand toward Bridget, but the woman did not take it. "I'm a friend of Madeline Bemis's."

Bridget continued to eye her, head to foot. "A little young for her, aren't you?"

Deep into the apartment now, Alice had become conscious of an acrid odor that was not entirely covered by some flowery disinfectant. And just then, a plump Persian cat crossed the rug, its tail swishing, and, with a cry, sprang up onto a chair whose arms had already been well worked by its claws.

"So Madeline sent you?" Bridget asked, drawing Alice's eyes back to her.

The roots of her hair, Alice could see, were white, but the ends were curled into ringlets meant for a woman half her age. The breath passed through Bridget's nostrils with an angry sound.

"Perhaps we should sit?" Alice replied.

"Go ahead." Bridget pointed to a seat at the small table in the dining nook off the kitchen. There was a photo of a more youthful Bridget standing with a middle-aged couple on one side and a teenaged boy on the other. In the companion shot, the boy was alone, in a cap and gown.

"Nice," Alice said again. The uneasy sound of her own voice made her scrunch up her toes.

Bridget settled herself down into the chair across from Alice with a groan. "My knees. They're killing me. I've had surgery, but that just made them worse." She eyed Alice again. "So, how is dear old Madeline?" There was an edge to the question that could nick.

"She's had some difficulties."

"Has she." Only mild interest.

"Yes, that's why I'm here."

"Well, there's nothing I can do for her."

"Perhaps you can," Alice continued. "It's her son."

Bridget's eyes flared. "Son? She had no son."

"Miss Shaughnessy, please. Let's not pretend. You know all about her son."

"Do I now."

Alice sensed some of the bluster leaving her.

"You handled the adoption."

"I haven't any idea what you are talking about." She drummed her fingers on the ends of the armrest, and turned her head away, revealing a rocklike profile.

"You know perfectly well, Miss Shaughnessy." Alice's voice rose, and she could feel her pulse quicken. "Through St. Anne's, remember? The Hurleys?"

Bridget turned back to her, a flicker of interest on her harsh features.

"Brendan Hurley died last month," Alice told her.

"I'm sorry to hear that." The tone was indifferent.

"It sent Mrs. Bemis into a tailspin." Alice bit into her words, trying to make Bridget feel something of her patient's suffering. "She never had any other children, you know. Thanks to you, she believed Brendan was her son, not that she ever dared tell him that. She didn't want to disturb his own home life."

"Well, wasn't that good of her." The old woman's mouth was pinched, as if to scale down the praise to fit the tiny goodness Mrs. Bemis had showed.

"But you don't understand. Brendan was all she had."

"She had plenty," Bridget fired back, all bile. "Living in the lap of luxury, she was. That house of hers, it was like three normal houses. Married that rich fella. A bit of a stuck-up, I always thought, but rich as Croesus."

"He died twenty years ago."

"As if I ever cared," Bridget spat out. She glared at Alice, her eyes burning.

"What did she ever do to you?" Alice asked.

"Nothing. I didn't exist for her. No one did. She could spend her days nibbling bon-bons as far as I was concerned. But I wasn't going to like it. And she sent her mother to the nuthouse! Nothing and no one ever mattered to Maddy Bemis. Fooling around with an Irish boy. Who's to notice? Well, *I* noticed. And now she can rot, for all I care."

"Was that your plan? For her to rot?"

A new look came over Bridget's face. "What do you mean?"

"When the police investigated Brendan's death, they discovered something unexpected."

Bridget's eyes tightened, but she said nothing.

"The DNA didn't match." Alice looked at Bridget coldly. "Mrs. Bemis and Brendan are no more related than you and me." Seeing her now, Alice knew what it must have been like to have been young Maddy. The coldness of the woman before her was the chill of the household. With Maddy's mother so preoccupied, and her father off at work, Maddy might have looked to Bridget as a surrogate mother. But Bridget's disdain could only have deepened Maddy's isolation.

"This has nothing to do with me," Bridget insisted.

"It has everything to do with you." Alice fixed her eyes on the former maid. "You misled her. I think intentionally."

"But I—"

"You wanted to hurt her, didn't you?"

"The girl was spoiled, I'll be honest with you. Her with her fancy ways. And there I was, doing her dishes, her laundry. And then an Irish boy comes along, and she thinks she can have him, too, along with everybody and everything else she ever wanted. But that was none of my concern. It didn't bother me any."

"It sounds like it did."

Bridget glared back at her. "Well, it didn't."

"Even when she offered you money?"

"She told you about that?"

Alice nodded. "A thousand dollars."

Bridget stirred in her chair, signaling that she'd had enough and it was time for Alice to leave. "She brought it on herself, that's all I can say."

But Alice was not about to go, not now. "So you lied to her."

"What was the difference? One Irish boy was as good as another. To her."

"Except, Brendan wasn't her son."

"So *you* say."

"And he was nothing but trouble."

A bit of merriment in the old woman's eyes. "Oh, really? What a shame."

The frustration was building up on her patient's behalf. The coldness of the woman. "Mrs. Bemis spent most of her life feeling responsible for him."

"Well, perhaps she should've. She *was* guilty, you know. I knew all about them two. I saw them sneaking around. I said nothing. Even when Mrs. Adams came to me asking if I knew anything about that business, I said nothing. You talk to me about grief. The grief that that lady suffered because of her!"

Fed up, Alice stood up and, without asking, went to the sink to pour a glass of water for herself. She took a long drink, then poured another for Bridget. She handed it to her and returned to her chair and asked a few less charged questions about her moving to Chicago. "What is this, an inquisition?" Bridget asked.

"No, Bridget, think of this as a chance to talk," Alice replied. "To unburden yourself. It can't have been easy all these years, keeping such a secret."

Bridget harrumphed at that, but she began to answer Alice's questions all the same. The replies were grudging at first, but gradually Bridget loosened up and responded with answers that were at least as long as the questions that had provoked them. Alice learned that Bridget had come a half century before, in 1950, invited by Mary Mears, the cousin—the daughter of her mother's sister—whom Bridget had come to help out. "She came down with a palsy a few years after her son was born," Bridget told her. "She needed some help, you see." She stayed with the Mearses for thirty years, became one of the family.

"The family in the photographs?" Alice asked, gesturing to the photograph on the wall beside them.

Bridget nodded.

As Alice glanced around, she noticed that all the other photographs on the walls were of the same family. She took a closer look at some of the pictures. A few were of the parents, but most were of the boy. Graduating from high school, from college. His wedding. "Nice wife," Bridget said tepidly, pointing to the small, grinning woman with her hair up, beside him in the formal photograph taken in a garden. "They met in college."

"You're fond of the boy, I take it," Alice said.

"I took care of him long enough."

"What's his name?"

"Now, what would you want to know that for?" Bridget asked, her jaw out.

"Why does it bother you?" Alice shot back.

"Toby. His name is Toby."

"Well. There." Alice smiled. She looked at the photograph again, especially the full-color shot of Toby that must have been taken at the beach. He was in a swimsuit, smiling broadly at the camera, all slim and vigorous looking.

"An only child, I gather."

Bridget nodded.

"How old is he now?"

"Who can remember a thing like that? Ages, dates."

"Well, I'll bet we can figure it out," Alice said. She stood up, went to the wall, and started to peek at the underside of the photographs. That's where her mother had always recorded the vital data; and that's where she wrote her own captions on her portraits of her friends.

"What are you doing?" Bridget demanded, reaching up toward her. "Leave those alone." She stood up, started toward Alice. "You shouldn't be doing that. What makes you think—" With a clink, Bridget tipped over the glass of water at her feet, sending a pool of water across the carpet and causing the cat to scramble to the far side of the room with a shriek. "Oh, now look—" They both watched the water darkening the carpet, but neither moved to scoop up the glass.

Alice continued to take the photos down off the wall and check behind them. They left smudged rectangles on the painted wall behind, they'd been there so long.

"Wait a moment, I tell you," Bridget exclaimed, nearly upon her.

Alice looked at one after another. Nothing on the family shot at the beach, nothing at the wedding, nothing of the group portrait under an elm. But the graduation photo bore a typed inscription that had been carefully affixed with Scotch tape: "Toby's graduation from Mark Twain High—17th in his class!" And it included a date: June 11, 1962.

"Give me that, would you please," Bridget told her, barely controlling her fury.

Alice handed her the photograph, and Bridget quickly restored it to its hook and straightened the other pictures.

Alice did the math. "So he was born in 1944."

"I don't want you here," Bridget told her. "I'm calling the front desk." She dropped down on the sofa by the telephone, reached for the receiver. "This is outrageous. Coming in here, pretending to be someone else, saying these things."

"Where does Toby live now, Bridget?"

"Don't you worry about that."

"I bet you've got a letter from him somewhere."

Bridget slammed down the receiver, and tried to scramble out of the sofa again, but it was a struggle for her, with her bad knees. "You won't be going through my things," she shouted.

"What's his name?" Alice demanded.

"I'm not having you bother him with any of this." Bridget picked up the phone again.

"I think that's up to him." Alice noticed a small black book beside the phone. Her address book. Alice moved toward it and snapped it up before Bridget could stop her. "This should have it." She flipped the book open.

"Now stop that, would you please?" Bridget tried to yank the book away from Alice, but Alice stepped away from the old woman, flipping through the pages to the *As*.

Alice's heart fluttered: Mears, Toby, was listed just below Mears, Mary and Ed, which had been scratched out. It showed an address in Belmont, Massachusetts, a Boston suburb that was perhaps ten miles from Milton.

"Belmont?" Alice asked Bridget, who had slumped back onto the couch, defeated. The coldness had left her, replaced only by— what? Frustration? Mourning? The cat came mewing for her, sidled under her elbow. Bridget gave it a few reluctant strokes. Past her, Alice could see through the venetian blinds to the line of trees that bounded the parking lot, and beyond it, to the highway in the distance, the cars and trucks moving silently.

"I supposed that someone would come here eventually," Bridget said with a sigh. "Didn't think it would be anyone like you." She leaned back wearily. "I wish this day hadn't come. I'm old, and I'm not well."

"I'm sorry," Alice said.

Bridget ignored her. "I shouldn't have done it. I shouldn't ever have done it. But Mary—that's my cousin Mary—was so desperate for a baby. She'd been praying for it for years. Her health wasn't good. It didn't seem that she could bear a pregnancy. I'd hinted about Maddy's problem, and they leapt at it, begging me to do what I could. They took me in the bargain. I was so sick of the Adamses, with their ways. And I did love Toby, not that I ever expected to."

"He never knew?"

"He knew he was adopted, but nobody talked about it. That wasn't something you discussed. Not like now. But he didn't know any of the details. Jesus, Joseph, and Mary. I don't think he wants to know, if you want the truth. He's settled where he is, has his own family. Both his parents are dead. At this point, I'm the only one who knows." She turned to Alice. "And I thought I'd go to my grave with this."

"So he's in Belmont?"

"Yes, he moved there a while ago. Broke my heart, seeing him leave. But I couldn't follow him there. He writes, sends the photos. He's got a nice house there. Put two kids through school. He's set to retire soon."

"From?"

The cat dropped to the floor with a thump and skittered over to slide its back against Bridget's leg. "The high school there. He taught history, then got into administration a few years ago and made it to principal." She pointed to another photograph on the wall. "That's Toby with the award he got two years ago. Principal of the year for the whole state."

Alice told Bridget a bit more about Mrs. Bemis's frustrations with infertility, her break with her family, and her mother's institutionalization. She was trying to develop the old woman's sympathy, but Bridget scarcely listened. The light was angling in deeper through the blinds, illuminating a length of the gray carpet in the sitting room. The cat's back was up against the old woman's thigh, and she was petting him lightly.

Bridget said that Mrs. Bemis had actually met Toby once. Bridget had been traveling east with Toby to look at colleges at the time when the Adamses had a garden party. So they had come over to the Dover house, the two of them. Bridget had shown him around. "Even pointed out that barn they had," she told Alice.

"But why?"

"Oh, revenge, I suppose," Bridget said airily. "Toby was impressed. Madeline was there, acting so superior. I introduced her to Toby, just in passing. They had the same build, those two. Wiry, like. And deep blue eyes that go right through a person. Maddy was a beautiful girl, I'll give her that much. But she didn't know who he was. Couldn't have cared less. She was lost in her own little world, just like always."

It was nearly six, and Alice had the eight-thirty plane to catch at O'Hare. She told Bridget that she needed to be going. Bridget did not stand up to see her out, but called out to her instead: "So what'll you be doing now? With all this?"

Alice had expected to be liberated by the truth, but she felt only a heavier burden. "I haven't any idea," she said.

forty-two

Alice slept on the plane the whole way back. It was nearly midnight when she descended the sky ramp to the terminal at Logan. She was so weary, trudging along, her mind filled with events from so long ago, that she almost didn't recognize the tall, ruddy man in the leather jacket waiting for her at the gate.

"Hey," Frank told her.

"Hey," she replied, smiling.

He reached for her and gave her a kiss. "Harry Brandt turned up," he told her.

"Alive?"

Frank shook his head. "Body washed up in Long Island Sound." He took a few more paces. "Not much left—but enough to know it's him. His wife did the ID. She's pretty wiped out. The whole thing, Jesus. But at least it's over."

"So there's no way to tell what happened."

"Nope. Could have been a fight. Could have been an accident.

Could have been a lot of things. They'll do an autopsy, so we'll find out about blood alcohol and all that stuff. But no, I'm betting there's no way we'll ever know what happened out there."

"Well, I don't think it will matter so much to Mrs. Bemis anymore."

"Because he's not her son."

Alice nodded.

"Isn't that a bitch," Frank said. He took her overnight bag, hoisted it over his shoulder.

"You could say that."

She told him the story as they walked back through the terminal, and then went through it all again over beer in the one airport bar they could find that was still open at that hour. He'd slid his coat over the back of the chair, revealing a light, tropical shirt that seemed to invite her hands on him. Frank just shook his head in amazement once Alice was done. "So the maid screwed her over."

"Something like that." Alice nodded sullenly. "Wish I knew what to do about it." She sipped her beer and longed for a cigarette. Just something to do with her hands, to work out the worry.

"You going to tell Madeline?" Frank asked.

"God, I don't know." Alice absently swished a swizzle stick around her beer, heaping up its froth.

Frank hunched forward, drawing her eyes up toward his. "Why'd you go out there, then?"

"*I* had to know, Frank. That's all I can think." She felt confined in the smoky bar, with the Red Sox game going on four TVs. She glanced past Frank to the runway where massive planes shuttled toward their gates.

"You are in this deep," Frank said.

Alice nodded. "Yeah."

"But what about her, Alice? This is going to throw her. Shit, it throws *me*. For fifty years, she thinks her son is this pain in the ass from South Boston, and then he dies, sending her into the psycho ward. But now it turns out the guy's not her son. Her son is this other guy, who—"

"I *know,* Frank." This was irritating. He wasn't saying anything that she hadn't thought a thousand times already.

Frank picked at the pretzels in a bowl on the table, waiting. She appreciated that, glad that he knew to back off. Ethan would have pushed this right into the next room.

"I assume you checked to make sure the woman isn't screwing around with you all over again."

"There is a Toby Mears in Belmont, if that's what you're asking." Alice nodded. She'd called information from O'Hare.

"You checked with the school?"

"Yeah. They were open late. Some play going on."

Frank shook his head again. "So what are you gonna do?"

Alice shook her head, crossed her arms in front of her, and pushed back a bit from the table to give herself some room. "I just don't know."

Frank drove her back to Cambridge in his cruiser. "Can I come in?" he asked her when they pulled up by her apartment building.

Alice looked up at the building again. All the lights were out on her floor. She was frightened by the blackness within. "Sure."

He placed his hand on hers and led her up the stairs.

Once inside her apartment, she took him into her bedroom, closed the door behind them, and popped open the buttons of his shirt, which she'd been aching to do, and slid a hand underneath to the firm skin that was starting to feel familiar. He pulled her shirt up over her head, then smiled at the mess it made of her hair. They made love quickly, urgently, Alice grateful to have Frank, the full, wonderful expanse of him, close to her, right up against her skin.

Afterward, Frank leaned up against the headboard, the sheets around his waist, and put his arm around her while she lay against him, idly running a hand across his chest. He was familiar—the slight give to his abdomen, the patch of hair on his belly, the dry sound to his voice after they made love.

"I think I've got to tell her," Alice said, rolling a coil of his chest hair around her index finger. Then, uncertain, she asked, "Don't you?"

He leaned over to kiss her on the top of her head. "It's up to you, sweetheart. You're the one who knows."

They slept in each other's arms, Frank's long legs sticking out off the end of the bed. Alice woke up several times in the night, tempted to wake him, to ask again for advice. It was such a responsibility to discover a new truth, to change someone's life. Beside her, Frank seemed so peaceful, she didn't have the heart to wake him, anyway. She finally dozed off, and woke with a start when she felt the bed quake. Frank was getting out of bed. "I gotta get back by seven." He kissed his finger, then placed it on her nose.

She watched him dress, the light on his flanks, his shoulders.

She offered to get up to make coffee for him, as he had done for her, but he told her to get her sleep. She'd need her rest.

"But what should I do?" Alice asked him.

"Sleep," he told her.

"No, about Mrs. Bemis."

" 'Bye, Alice," he told her.

forty-three

*M*rs. Bemis was sitting with Charles, from Alice's anger-management class, outside on the bench across from Holmes. The wind was up, and Alice had to sweep the hair out of her face as she stood in front of Mrs. Bemis. "Good morning," Alice told the two of them.

Mrs. Bemis's face had lit up at the sight of Alice. "How nice to see you," she said. "Isn't it, Mr. Packer?"

"Of course it is," Charles said. "Always." He turned to Mrs. Bemis. "Such a pretty girl."

"Oh now, Mr. Packer, really."

Mrs. Bemis turned back to Alice. "I was just telling Mr. Packer about my mother. We thought we might actually go for a closer look down there, see what's left of the old place."

"Perhaps later," Alice said.

"Oh?" Mrs. Bemis seemed to notice the seriousness in Alice's eyes.

"There's something I need to talk to you about." She turned to Charles. "Privately, if that's all right."

"Absolutely fine," Charles said. "Absolutely fine." He picked himself off the seat, and dusted off some of the pollen that had fallen from the trees onto his trousers. "I should probably be getting back anyway. Meeting coming up."

Alice and Mrs. Bemis watched him go. "He's a very kind man, you know," Mrs. Bemis said. "I know he's troubled. Feels more pressure than anyone should. But basically a very kind man."

"I'm glad you can see that."

"So am I."

Alice took a seat beside her.

Mrs. Bemis found Alice's hand and squeezed it. Alice turned to her.

"The funeral, dear," Mrs. Bemis said. "How was it? Was it all right?"

"It was difficult," Alice told her.

"They always are. You had a chance to cry?"

"Oh yes," Alice said. "I did do that."

Mrs. Bemis looked into Alice's eyes. "You want to speak to me about Brendan, don't you?"

Alice nodded. "How did you know?"

"Because you seem so serious. You always look serious when Brendan is the topic." Mrs. Bemis surveyed Alice more closely. "What, have you found out how he died?" More searching. "Please don't tell me he was murdered. I'm not sure I can bear that."

"No, it's not that. The police don't know, and frankly, it's not clear they ever will. The other body turned up yesterday. The friend of Brendan, Harry Brandt. He drowned, too."

"Oh, I am sorry." Mrs. Bemis shook her head. "What a sad thing."

"But that's not it either," Alice said.

Alarm now: "What is it, then? You are starting to worry me."

Alice looked over at Holmes, its vines rustling uneasily in the light breeze. "I flew to Chicago yesterday," she began.

"I thought your grandmother's funeral was in Pennsylvania."

"It was. I flew to Chicago afterward."

Mrs. Bemis furled her eyebrows.

"I think you know why I went."

"I'm not sure I do." The old woman looked back toward where Charles had gone. "I hope Mr. Packer found his way safely to Nichols. I wonder if I should check."

Alice reached out for her hand. "Don't be frightened, Mrs. Bemis. It's all right. I'm sure he's fine. Listen to me, would you?" She held Mrs. Bemis's hand in both of hers, like a lover. "In all those years with Brendan, were there ever times when you wondered about him?"

"Well, of course. I told you. He could be very difficult."

"No, I mean wondered about his connection to you, about his being your son."

Mrs. Bemis went still, staring at Alice. "I'm not sure I follow."

"Several times, you told me how different he seemed."

"Why, yes, I suppose I did. But I always assumed that was because of the way he was raised, and that neighborhood of his, and some of the, well, some of the things he did—"

"Did you wonder about that?"

"Why, of course! So many times I wished I could save him from—oh, I don't know what. That place, I suppose. South Boston. But I decided that I couldn't. I shouldn't. He was there. He was the Hurleys' boy, not mine." She paused, fiddling with the material of her dress. "Of course, I have wondered if I would have made a difference. If I could have given him a better chance at life. That's why I watched over him, gave him money, don't you see? Because otherwise . . ." Her voice trailed off.

"What?" Alice prompted.

"Well, otherwise, it was just him. No, more than just him. It was *me*. *I* was the horrid one. *I* was that way. Vicious, impetuous, and so utterly stupid. Oh, I shouldn't have thought of him in those terms, but I had to. For that's what he was. That's what I was, don't you see? That's why I've wanted to know how he died. To know if he died the way he lived."

"We don't know that yet," Alice reminded her. "I'm not sure that we ever will."

"Yes, well—" Her eyes turned back toward the building again. "I do hope that Mr. Packer has made it back safely. He's not entirely reliable, you know."

"Mrs. Bemis, please, look at me. I went to Chicago to see Bridget Shaughnessy."

"Who?"

"Your maid, Mrs. Bemis. In Dover. Remember?"

"Oh my heavens yes. I'm not used to her full name. She was always just Bridget." She turned serious again. "Goodness, she's still alive?"

"She's in a Chicago suburb called Oak Park. In a geriatric center." Alice held Mrs. Bemis's hand more tightly. "She told me something that I think you should know."

Mrs. Bemis continued to stare at Alice, but her look softened, as if, on some level, she knew what was coming and she was preparing herself to take it in, to make it part of her.

"Brendan is not your son, Mrs. Bemis. Bridget misled you. She did not give the baby up for adoption at St. Anne's, as she'd told you. She delivered your son to a cousin of hers in Chicago, who was childless. Bridget thought this was the perfect solution. She went to live with that family, and help raise the boy."

Mrs. Bemis said nothing, just gazed into Alice's eyes, a vacant look on her face. It was like the look she had given Alice back at Filene's when she'd talked of moths.

"I'm sorry. I know this must be a shock."

"But all this time—?"

Alice nodded.

"But my scrapbook."

"He wasn't your son." She lowered her voice. "But he was a boy you loved."

Mrs. Bemis's head was down now, tapping at her thigh with her fingertip. "All that time!" she said at last. "I feel so . . . foolish. Another stupid mistake in a life full of stupid mistakes. I married the wrong man, and now I've cared about the wrong child."

"No, Mrs. B. He was the right child."

She glanced up, irritation on her face. "What do you mean? You just said—"

"He taught you things. About caring. About love."

"But it was all folly!"

"Love isn't folly, Mrs. Bemis. It's what keeps us alive."

Mrs. Bemis's eyes turned toward Holmes, and she reclaimed her hand from Alice.

"I know this must be hard," Alice told her.

"*Hard!* I'm an old woman, Alice."

"That's why I wanted to tell you here, at Montrose, so that—"

"So you can strap me down if you have to?" Mrs. Bemis asked.

"Please—"

"Oh, I know. I'm being melodramatic again."

"I understand this is a shock."

"What am I supposed to do now?"

"What would you *like* to do?"

"I would like to leave this place."

"And—"

"Go home."

"And—"

"Oh, I don't know. Work in my garden, tend my orchids. That's when I do my best thinking. I need to be more settled, that's what I feel more than anything. This has all been so distressing for me." She turned back to Alice. "Who did you say he was, that other boy?"

"Toby Mears."

"Toby, you say?"

"That's right. Toby."

Silence while Mrs. Bemis studied the trees.

Madeline

> forty-four

It was chilly that day, even though it was the first week of May. A light drizzle that evening had frozen overnight, encasing the whole backyard—the lawn, the bushes, the flowers—in a glaze of ice. No day for a garden party, but her parents had insisted on going ahead with theirs, even though they'd had to move the whole affair inside. The house was filled with guests from all over. Lots of people from the club, and many of her father's business friends. Ronald had invited his parents, who'd come with houseguests. It was all so overwhelming, Madeline positioned herself in the corner by the vegetable dip, speaking mostly to a couple of cousins who'd flown up from Philadelphia.

Even though it took place indoors, the whole event still seemed, at least in memory, gray and indistinct, as if the fog that rose off the ice outside had somehow penetrated the interior of the house as well. The only moment of clarity, of brightness, came toward the end when the party was at last drawing to a close. Madeline was standing by the piano, that Steinway on which she had struggled with her mazurkas years before, when she saw Bridget, of all people, approach. She hadn't laid eyes on her maid in a decade, when Madeline had attended her going-away party. Now, Madeline's instinct was to search out escape routes, but there were none. Bridget was coming for her, just as she had in Golden. The woman had put on weight, and harsh lines dug into either side of her mouth. But her face was like the head of a hammer, as always.

She had a young man beside her, though. To see him was to feel the sun break through the clouds. Not to see the sun, since that would be blinding. But to feel its warmth on her. No one else seemed affected by his presence, however. The few other remaining guests milled about, oblivious, drinks in hand, her own husband somewhere among them. Madeline could not take her eyes off the boy. Lean, with sly, hawklike eyes, he seemed familiar in a way she couldn't figure. Did she know him somehow? He couldn't have been more than sixteen or seventeen. He stood so upright, so confident, casting Bridget into shadow. But he was a most attractive boy. Bridget explained that she'd brought him east to look at colleges; she'd called Madeline's parents to see if it was all right if she came around to say hello. They'd told her about the party and insisted she bring him. She hoped that was all right; Madeline assured her it was. Bridget went on about colleges or something. Madeline's attention was focused on the boy. Toby, was that his name? She had to fight an urge to embrace him, to take him into her arms. Finally, Bridget paused long enough to let the boy speak.

"I'm sorry we didn't get a chance to talk more," the boy told her, very maturely. "Perhaps I'll see you another time?"

That was all he said. But—so odd!—those were the only words she distinctly remembered from that entire day.

Epilogue

forty-five

Mrs. Bemis was released from Montrose a few days later, but nearly two months passed before Alice saw her again. She would have tried to see her sooner, but Victor had already accused her of being, as he said, "grossly overinvolved" with Mrs. Bemis, and Alice hadn't dared. She should have told Victor that he was simply jealous that she should have succeeded with such an obviously difficult patient—and been singled out for praise by Dr. Maris at a staff meeting, in front of everyone. And Marnie wasn't being very nice to her, either. So she thought it better to bide her time.

Still, Alice did think of Mrs. Bemis every time she passed her old room at Montrose, or walked by the bench with the view of Holmes, or even felt a hankering for chocolate. So she was delighted to receive a letter from Mrs. Bemis in the mail. It contained a nicely monogrammed card inviting Alice to come around to the house in Milton. "There is something I want to show you," Mrs. Bemis wrote in her round cursive, then added a P.S., asking how her orchid was doing. When Alice called back that evening to accept, she was happy to be able to report that the plant was doing fine. Frank LeBeau, whom Alice had continued to see, had proved to have just the right touch with *Phragmipedium caudatum.*

The Milton house was a little gayer now that its owner was back in residence. There were fresh flowers in the front rooms and signs of her habitation here and there—a small pile of mail on the table in the front hall, some music out on the piano. And Mrs. Bemis herself seemed more spritely, too. She'd appeared in an elegant dress and gold earrings just moments after Alice rang the bell. Exclaiming what a joy it was to see Alice, she'd hooked an arm about her guest and sat her down for tea in the dining room. With cake, this time.

Alice was thrilled to see Mrs. Bemis so full of zest. It was like a kind of blossoming. And she listened happily as Mrs. Bemis told her about several horticultural projects, including plans for a vegetable garden at the local elementary school. "I'd love to work with the children on that," she declared.

When they'd finished off the last of the cake, Mrs. Bemis took Alice into the garden. Once again, Alice was nearly swallowed up by all the elaborate planting, even though much of it had faded now in mid-November. But Mrs. Bemis led her to the rectangular pool where the statue of Diana stood at one end. This time, Alice noticed a brightly polished stone bench on the pool's lip at the other end; she hadn't remembered it from before. Mrs. Bemis drew her closer to it. "This is what I wanted to show you."

As Alice approached, she could see that the bench was made of black marble. "Very handsome," she told her hostess.

"Yes, yes, but look." Mrs. Bemis beckoned Alice closer.

The surface bore an inscription, Alice could see: "In Happy Memory of a Good Friend, Brendan Hurley."

"I'd have liked to call him my son," Mrs. Bemis confided, gazing down at the bold letters. "But 'good friend' is right." She looked back toward the pool. "His body is buried with his parents', in South

Boston. But I'm glad to think of him here, safe on shore, with a view of my garden."

Mrs. Bemis's eyes misted over, and Alice nearly offered her sleeve to the old woman, but this time, Mrs. Bemis recovered on her own.

"I do have a favor to ask, though," she said.

"Anything."

Mrs. Bemis took Alice's arm, drew her closer. "Now, I'm not asking this lightly. I've thought about it a good deal."

Alice waited, unsure as to what would come next.

Mrs. Bemis lifted her eyes to Alice's. "I've rewritten my will, and I'd like you to have this place when I'm gone. To look after it."

Alice felt a buzz of electricity go through her. "Mrs. Bemis, please, I can't—"

"Of course you can," Mrs. Bemis told her. "I have no one else. Besides, you would enjoy it here. I know you would. I've seen it in your eyes. And I'd feel so much better knowing you would be here after me."

"I really don't think—"

"I'm not your patient anymore, you know. There is nothing improper. We're friends, you see. And it would . . . complete things between us."

"But what about your son?" Alice asked. She'd been wondering about him for weeks now.

"Oh, Toby?"

"You could give it to him," Alice pleaded. "I shouldn't inherit a place like this."

"He knows nothing of me," Mrs. Bemis replied.

Alice's jaw slipped open. "You never got in touch with him?"

"I just couldn't." The old lady shook her head resolutely. "It's too late for all that, dear. He has his life now, just as I have mine."

"But—"

"But nothing," Mrs. Bemis interrupted. "It's fine. Really. I have Brendan. I don't think I have space in my heart for Toby. A woman my age can take only so many jolts, you see. It was enough for me to tell you about Gerald, and about my son. I never thought I would. I'm an old clam, and you pried me open. And I'm grateful, Alice. It hurts to hold a secret for that long." She fell silent for a moment, eyeing Alice. "Then at least you'll think about my offer?"

"Sure," Alice said. "I'll think about it." She glanced back at the house, saw the shadows the great copper beech threw across the yellow clapboards, and the many windows, with their extraordinary views. Could she actually live in a place like this? It was inconceivable. Almost.

"I just have a small request."

Alice turned back to her.

"That when I'm gone you add my name here beside his, with my dates."

Alice glanced down again at Brendan's inscription, picturing the name "Madeline Bemis" beside it. It would seem right.

"Well, then." Mrs. Bemis smiled. "Good."

Nothing had been settled between them, not really. But everything had. Mrs. Bemis took a seat on the marble bench, and Alice joined her, sitting close enough that their shoulders touched as they looked out together across the rippling waters of the long, narrow pool.

A Note on Psychiatry

In constructing my portrait of a young psychiatrist, I have relied heavily on the therapeutic approach of Irvin D. Yalom, especially as it is expressed in his memoir *Love's Executioner and Other Tales of Psychotherapy,* which awakened in me the realization that psychiatrists are not, and should not be, the opaque surfaces that they are conventionally portrayed as being. As Yalom makes clear, the psychiatric effort is not solely the patient's journey, but the psychiatrist's as well. While I recognize that ours is an era when psychiatrists are under particular constraints not to cross the boundaries of propriety, I continue to share Yalom's conviction that psychiatrists should attend at least as much to their human instincts as to their professional training in responding to the patients under their care. It was in this spirit that I constructed my heroine, Alice Matthews, M.D., and crafted her actions.

To better grasp the dimensions of a lifelong depression, I have turned to *Trauma and Recovery,* the seminal work of Judith Herman, M.D., on post-traumatic stress syndrome; to the collection of essays *Trauma: Explorations in Memory* edited by Cathy Caruth; and to *Unchained Memories: True Stories of Traumatic Memories, Lost and Found* by Lenore Terr, M.D. William Styron's *Darkness Visible* remains, for me, the classic text of the experience of depression, although I found *A Mood Apart* by Peter C. Whybrow, M.D., and *Black Sun: Depression and Melancholia* by Julia Kristeva to be especially helpful as well.

For guidance in understanding the ways of psychiatrists and psychiatric hospitals, I am indebted to my old friends Robert Stern, M.D., and Fran Arnold, Ph.D. But this novel, of course, is a work of the imagination, and, if I have strayed from standard psychiatric procedures, I can only plead that I did so to reveal a larger truth stemming from my own convictions.

Other Acknowledgments

For considerable assistance in giving me the basics of how a Marshfield detective might operate, I am indebted to Detective Lieutenant Robert Wright of the Marshfield Police Department. To get some sense of life as a pilot in the Eighth Air Force in World War Two, I have relied principally on a colorful memoir, *The Wrong Stuff: The Adventures and Mis-Adventures of an 8th Air Force Aviator,* by Truman Smith. The gardening passages were aided by my friend Alan Emmet's terrific *So Fine A Prospect: Historic New England Gardens.* My friends Steve and Linda Weld kindly showed me around their house in Milton, Massachusetts, to provide a bit of domestic atmosphere for my Mrs. Bemis. And whatever understanding I have of her orchids comes from the book *Rare Orchids,* a gorgeous volume of photographs taken by Béla Kalman, with text by Rosalie H. Davis and Mariko Kawaguchi. I am indebted, also, to many early readers, especially Mary Sullivan, Ted Delaney, Christopher Tilghman, Caroline Preston, and Sally Brady. Once again, my editor at HarperCollins, Dan Conaway, has been a writer's dream for the patience, insight, dedication, and friendship he has provided. Many thanks also to his ever helpful assistant, Nikola Scott. My agent, Kris Dahl at ICM, has been her usual steady hand. Finally, I cannot let this book go by without giving my daughters, Josie and Sara, a hug of gratitude for inspiring me with their zest for living and a million other things. And, for her love, reassurance, and guidance through the sometimes tumultuous writing of this book, I am more deeply grateful to my wife Megan Marshall than I can possibly say.

ML

5/0